16.00

Thunder Road

THUNDER ROAD

By Chadwick Ginther

RaveN
STONE

Thunder Road
copyright © Chadwick Ginther 2012

Published by Ravenstone
an imprint of Turnstone Press
Artspace Building
206-100 Arthur Street
Winnipeg, MB
R3B 1H3 Canada
www.TurnstonePress.com

All rights reserved. No part of this book may be reproduced or
transmitted in any form or by any means—graphic, electronic
or mechanical—without the prior written permission of the
publisher. Any request to photocopy any part of this book shall
be directed in writing to Access Copyright, Toronto.

Turnstone Press gratefully acknowledges the assistance of the
Canada Council for the Arts, the Manitoba Arts Council, the
Government of Canada through the Canada Book Fund, and
the Province of Manitoba through the Book Publishing Tax
Credit and the Book Publisher Marketing Assistance Program.

This novel is a work of fiction. Names, characters, places and
incidents are either the product of the author's imagination or
are used fictitiously, and any resemblance to actual persons living or dead, events or locales, is entirely coincidental.

Printed and bound in Canada by Friesens for Turnstone Press.
Second printing: March 2013

Library and Archives Canada Cataloguing in Publication

Ginther, Chadwick, 1975-
    Thunder road / Chadwick Ginther.

ISBN 978-0-88801-400-9

    I. Title. II. Series: Ginther, Chadwick, 1975- . Thunder
road trilogy.

PS8613.I54T48 2012   C813'.6   C2012-904932-8

For Wendy,
who has done so many things,
little and big, to help me do this.

Thunder Road

Prologue
When the Levee Breaks

There was no warning. But then, there never is.

His world exploded.

The site was a spiderweb of pipes and steel, sprawling over the earth like the screensaver on his computer. There had been a pinprick of light, maybe a welder's torch, maybe a cigarette lighter had flashed, and then everything had gone white.

An acrid cloud rushed past Ted, carrying gravel and bits of shale that stung like hornets. Within the cordon of string surrounding the bench where employees were allowed to smoke, the ground trembled beneath his feet. Ted didn't fall. If you were close enough to get knocked down, you weren't ever getting up again. The site was designed to funnel explosions upward; to keep destruction of company property to a minimum. Small comfort to those who might be stuck in the flames.

Men he'd known for years; shared beers or fistfights with—sometimes both. Friends

A high-pitched whine filled his ears, but Ted had to imagine the sirens and screams shooting through the crackle of flames and the smaller, secondary blasts. He squinted, trying to get a better look.

Fire.

It was all he saw. Hell, they'd see the flames from Edmonton. His cigarette fell from his lip. He'd promised Susanna he'd quit. *We promised each other a lot of things when we got married.* Ted fumbled for his cell, his fingers numb. The emergency response numbers were programmed into the phone, and he scrolled down, frantically looking for the water-bomber team. Site fire response wouldn't be able to handle this—*if they were even still alive.*

The metal left standing in the wake of the blast started to twist and crumble inward. Greasy black clouds flared and plumed, filling the air with the stink of burning oil and melting PVC. He could see more explosions. One following another like footsteps marching in time.

And then something stepped from the fire.

It was too big to be real. Shaped like a man, but the height of a building, it stepped out of the inferno grinning like the devil himself. Ted dropped his phone as the creature tore a length of metal from the ground and held it aloft, brandishing it like a club. The challenge the creature bellowed at the sky somehow cut through Ted's deafness, reaching some primal part of him. Louder and more terrifying than anything he'd ever experienced. He wanted to scream, but no human cry could scare away what towered over the wreckage.

The creature's hair and beard were made of the same flames it had stepped from. Smaller tendrils danced along its bare arms and chest, where a man's body hair would be. Its every breath came out in gouts of smoke, quickly welcomed by the burning work site. Its coal-black skin cracked and broke, the molten lines leaking lava. Its eyes were the blue of an acetylene torch, and it grinned with broken teeth of white metal.

Smaller forms followed the thing out of the fire. They could have been man-shaped, but they were oddly hunched, dragging themselves over the rough ground like wounded dogs. They screeched and pawed at the earth, rubbing up against the legs of the giant. It patted their heads with rough familiarity, before allowing them to retreat into the flames.

Rattling its rough sabre in the air, the giant opened its mouth to roar the deep belly-laugh of a Bond villain. Through the screaming in his ears, Ted heard a sound like *lock, lock, lock*. The creature turned to join its servants in the blaze, but as it strode away, explosions flaring with each step, it paused and looked back over its shoulder.

At Ted.

Their eyes locked. In the intensity of the creature's gaze, Ted felt he could've caught fire. He looked away as the creature spoke in no language heard on Earth. And yet deep in the core of his being Ted understood what the words meant.

"I will burn the world."

Ted sank to his knees and stared at the fire.

It was over an hour before a rescue worker found him. His phone remained on the ground, unused. He hadn't even called Susanna to tell her he was alive. That he still loved her.

That it was the end of the world.

1. Riders on the Storm

Ted let the steady sound of the windshield wipers distract him from the rain spattering against the glass. One of the wipers squealed as it brushed the rain aside. He'd grown accustomed to it, but knew he should get it fixed. The car—a 1968 GTO that his Uncle Chuck had dubbed "The Goat" when he'd bought it new—and the meagre contents of its backseat and trunk, were all the possessions he had left in the world. She'd gotten everything else in the divorce. The house, the dog. Ted told himself yet again that their split was for the best. But he did miss the dog.

Working the oil sands hadn't really been what he'd wanted to do with his geology degree, but if you lived in Alberta you had two choices with geology. Dig up dinosaurs in the badlands—and good fucking luck getting a job doing that—or work the patch. When he'd quit, Ted had turned his back on over 100K a year, but he couldn't go back there, even though company counsellors kept assuring him it was all in his head. Post-traumatic stress.

Bullshit. He'd seen PTSD in the faces of the veterans his dad drank with at the Legion. No one had believed him. Not friends. Not family. Certainly not the hippie reporter with the dreadlocks and axe to grind. But Ted knew what he'd seen.

Chadwick Ginther

Anyone who asked how he could give up the money had never worked the patch. Or seen what he'd seen. The patch was a kind of hell Dante should've written about—with its metal frames and pipes choking the ground, enveloping the rock, and pulling black blood out of the earth. It was a place where they tested your piss constantly to make sure you were working safely, cleanly. But working there was so horrible, you needed the booze, the weed, or the coke to stand it. Often all three. Booze and weed in the p.m. to knock you out when you were too exhausted to sleep. Coke and speed in the a.m. to get you up and ready to do it all over again. Buying and supplying clean piss had quickly become a deeply entrenched, and profitable, enterprise.

Regulations prohibited smoking on the actual site, but everyone there smoked. Inhaling what that place shat out all day, why wouldn't you? Of course, for safety's sake—everything was for safety's sake there, not profit—they had put the smoke pit at the furthest edge of the work site. Looking back, Ted had to admit, those regulations had saved his life.

They'd blamed the accident on a guy who couldn't wait. Some poor bastard who'd just finished the last bit of welding he needed to do on a hydrogen tower. Yes, hydrogen, like Hindenburg hydrogen. Job well done, and ahead of schedule no less. And so he lit up. And the site lit up. Or so the official story went.

The official story didn't explain why, after months, the fire was still burning. Still growing despite every effort to stop it.

Ted felt the tension creeping into his knuckles as they tightened over the steering wheel. He still had nightmares about that day. When he closed his eyes at night he saw that demonic face. With a sigh and more effort than he would care to admit, Ted took one hand off the wheel to turn up the volume on the stereo.

The stereo and speakers were the only features in the car that weren't original. He'd had a modern deck installed because his musical tastes were too eclectic to be satisfied by any one radio station. And the fourteen-hour drive to Winnipeg along the Yellowhead—he'd done it in under twelve before, but the weather wasn't cooperating this time—didn't lend itself to sifting through his CD collection. Easier to just plug his iPod into the deck's port, hit *shuffle*, and let it sift through a few decades of his musical tastes.

He skipped past Leonard Cohen—not the best for night driving—and settled in with Zeppelin, tapping his fingers to Bonham's drums, nodding his head to Page's guitar, and waiting for Plant to start wailing so he could sing along, badly. Ted eased off the accelerator. His car didn't have cruise control, and any time the right song hit, he'd start to speed. He couldn't really afford the ticket right now; his lawyer was already building a cottage with his savings. And it wasn't like he had anywhere to be.

Or anyone to meet him there.

Ted banished the thought, looking down the road towards his future. He'd received a call out of the blue from someplace called Svarta Mining and Smelting, offering a job in Winnipeg, of all places. They didn't seem to care his background was in petroleum. Ted was running out of money and had long ago exhausted the good will of friends and family. Winnipeg—or, The Heart of the Continent, as they were calling it now (it had still been One Great City the last time he'd been through)—offered a fresh start. Susanna had no family or friends in Manitoba, that Ted knew of. Even if the divorce had been surprisingly easy to cope with, Ted didn't want any reminders of what had been.

He wanted a clean break and a fresh start.

A new life.

He tapped the as-yet-unwrapped package of cigarettes on the bucket seat next to him; he'd vowed to quit when he'd left the rigs, and he had succeeded off and on in stopping—if not quitting. But it was hard not to smoke while he was driving; it had always been one of his triggers. He shouldn't have bought that pack of Canadian Classic when he'd topped up in Saskatoon; Ted had never smoked in The Goat and didn't want to start now.

He glanced down: a moose head grinned at him from the blue packaging. A moment's silence as Zeppelin ended and the iPod chose the next song.

Fuck it.

He reached for the pack and tore into the plastic with his teeth, thumbing the bottom of the packaging upwards. He flicked the foil away and, with a practiced motion, eased one tube of tobacco above its fellows. At the same time, Ted brought the pack to his mouth and caught the raised cigarette in his lips. As he slid the smoke free, he flicked the pack onto the seat beside him and groaned.

He didn't have his Zippo. In a fit of optimism, Ted had packed the lighter away. He pushed in the lighter on the dash and hoped for the best. It'd never been used. His uncle had actually thrown the original one away, figuring he'd never use the thing. When Ted had inherited the car, he'd wanted it to be as "factory" as possible, and so he had hunted down a replacement.

There was no putting the cigarette back in the pack. Now that it was free, and between his lips, it *had* to be smoked. And so Ted waited. And watched, keeping an eye on the lighter as often as the road.

With the stereo on, he doubted he'd hear the click of the lighter popping up. But he did; maybe he heard the noise because he was listening for it, maybe because Howling Wolf had just started to fade out. *What do you know? The fucking thing works.* He pulled the lighter free and turned it towards him. The sight of the rings of hot, orange wire and the lighter's heated metal scent were too close to the patch, to the explosion, to… it. He pressed the cigarette tip into the lighter.

Air was replaced with the doubly sweet and acrid cloud of burning tobacco as Ted took a drag. He put the lighter back as he exhaled through his nostrils; then he rolled the driver's side window down a crack. The smoke curled about him briefly, then was pulled away and out into the night.

The open window was facing north, the same direction the wind was pushing the falling rain. Droplets ran down the glass and dribbled over The Goat's vinyl interior.

Ted's coffee had gone cold and what remained in the bottom of the paper Tim Hortons cup would serve as an adequate ashtray. He tapped the cigarette over the cup, letting the ash fall, and exposing the hot ember at its tip.

A semi in the oncoming lane flashed its high beams at him,

blinding him for a moment and bringing him back to himself. Ted tapped the button on the floor by the clutch and darkness folded in from the tree-lined sides of the road. *Stupid.* He shook his head. He usually paid closer attention to the opposite lane at night, priding himself on remembering to cut his brights before he got flashed. And swearing bitterly at those who didn't show him the same courtesy. He knew why truckers got so pissed about it; the average vehicle's lights hit them directly in the cab. Nobody wants a blind trucker on the road.

The semi rumbled past The Goat, its running lights glimmering like fireflies in the darkness. Ted flicked the high beams back on. In the momentary shift in brightness, a figure appeared in the middle of the road.

A human figure.

His mind did the mental calculations as his foot pumped the breaks with just enough pressure not to lock them up. He slammed the car into neutral, feeling the weight of the vehicle drop, slowing him further. Ted's eyes darted to the speedometer. *Fuck.* A hundred and twenty klicks. Distance was hard to judge at night, but he already knew he wouldn't be able to stop in time.

The road was shit and his car started to hydroplane, skimming over the slight ruts worn into the asphalt by constant travel. Still braking, Ted eased the wheel to the left and slid into the oncoming lane. When the wheels caught the road again The Goat tried to shoot straight into the ditch. Ted ground his teeth and fought for control. He'd driven just wide of the idiot in the road, sliding past as he skidded to a stop in the soft gravel on the shoulder.

Ted's fingers were crushed tightly against the steering wheel.

His short, hard breaths fogged the windshield. A trickle of sweat ran down one cheek.

Stupid motherfucker could've killed me.

He put the car in reverse and backed up slowly, ready to give the stranger a piece of his mind. Gravel skittered across the wheel wells as the tires fought for traction. In the dim illumination of the reverse lights, he could just make out the person—a woman—still standing in the centre of the lane. Motionless.

His words died on his lips. Ted turned The Goat's motor off and stepped out into the rain.

"Hey!" he yelled. "Are you okay?"

She was soaked to the skin. Her three-quarter T-shirt clung tightly to her chest, and her baggy multi-pocketed cargo pants hung low on her hips. The woman shook her head and turned to face him.

"Thanks for stopping," she said. There was something odd about the way she spoke. The shadow of an accent, unfamiliar, foreign—attractive—that lay hidden around the edges of her speech. "I've been hitching in the rain for hours."

"You always wait for a ride in the middle of the highway?"

She looked around, puzzled as if noticing where she stood for the first time. "How the hell'd I end up here?"

"I dunno," Ted said. "But you're damn lucky I didn't run you over."

As she walked closer she still seemed distracted. She attempted a smile, but it didn't quite reach her eyes. Her eyeshadow and mascara had run in the rain, giving her an Alice Cooper makeover. Ted judged her to be in her early twenties, but also knew he was shit at estimating things like that. And girls looked like women a lot sooner now than they had in his day.

She asked, "Mind if I push my luck a little further and ask for a ride?"

"I'd better say yes, since you don't seem to have the sense to stay off the road, let alone out of the rain."

Squeezing the rain from her soaked black hair, she pulled it into a tail, fastening it with an elastic she'd had around her wrist. She had several small gold hoops in her left ear, none in the right.

"Wait, I don't have my shit," she said, running back across the road and into the darkness. Out here at night, with no moon, the other side of the road might as well have been a mile away. She came back with a small, sodden bag slung over her shoulder.

"You travel light," Ted noted.

He opened her door for her, as she ran her hand over the curves of the car.

"Cherry ride," she said appreciatively.

"Thanks. I'm Ted."

"Tilda."

She slid into the car, dropping her bag on the passenger side floor mat and settled in like she owned The Goat.

Ted climbed into the car and closed the door behind him. The Goat's ignition was on the dash to the left of the stereo, not on the steering column. He turned the key and gave the car some gas. The engine rumbled and the back wheels spun up mud and gravel as he pulled back onto the highway.

"So," Tilda began. "What's with the locks? You know, kids today don't use coat hangers when they're boosting cars."

She was observant enough now. Ted's uncle had sawed the tops of the locks off, so you'd never be able to open them with a wire hanger. His sisters, Ted's aunts, had stolen The Goat for a joyride once, and almost rolled it. Afterwards, steps had been taken.

"Speaking from experience?" he asked, rather than offering the story.

She smiled.

"We'll stop at the next town or rest stop so you can get out of those wet clothes," Ted said.

"Don't bother." Tilda rummaged in her pack; Ted flicked on the interior light so she could see. She drew out a towel in a bulging Ziploc bag. "Thanks."

Ted cut the lights as Tilda slipped the wet T-shirt over her head. She wasn't wearing a bra. When she started patting her torso dry, Ted cocked his head to the side and tried to watch the road without gawking at her. *She might be fucking nuts, but she's hot.* He wanted to look.

She kicked her sneakers from her feet and pulled the cargo pants off, letting them drop onto her discarded shirt.

Ted could feel an erection tightening his jeans. Tilda glanced down at his lap and said nothing, but her lips held the ghost of a smile.

"You can peek, you know. I don't mind. It's just skin."

"I should… probably keep my eyes on the road. Who knows who else is standing in the middle of it waiting for a lift?"

She laughed and pulled something else from her bag. "Suit yourself."

Ted heard some rustling that he carefully ignored. Tilda's elbow bumped into his arm on more than one occasion, so Ted slid his hand from the gearshift to the steering wheel.

"It's safe to look now," she said finally.

She wore cut-off jeans and a roughly cropped black T-shirt. Tilda raised her arms above her head, stretching like a cat and raking her nails over the upholstered ceiling of the car. She reached down and pulled the lever to recline her seat, then kicked a leg up to rest her bare foot on the dash of the car.

She reached for the pack of cigarettes and tapped one out. "You mind?" she asked.

"Help yourself," Ted said, as she put the cigarette between her lips.

"Light?"

Ted pushed the dashboard lighter in as Tilda waited, bobbing her head to the music—a synth-heavy industrial cover of the Stones's "Gimme Shelter"—with the unlit cigarette dangling from her mouth.

"Never would have pegged you for a Sisters of Mercy fan."

Ted shrugged. "I like what I like." Then, "So what would you've pegged me for?"

"Judging from those Alberta Wild Rose Country plates, I would've said Dwight Yoakam or some shit like that."

Ted laughed, but was glad she hadn't been in the car when Willie Nelson was playing. "Why do you think I'm heading east?"

"Your divorce," Tilda whispered.

"What?"

The lighter popped out, and Tilda snatched it from the dash, pressing it to the cigarette.

"Psychic," she said quickly, as she exhaled the first drag.

Definitely fucking nuts.

"Plus the car is filled with all your shit."

"Oh. Good eye." He should've known she'd fuck with him. He glanced at the finger that had borne his wedding ring for fifteen years. It still felt light. "Mind lighting one for me?"

Tilda nodded and tapped another cigarette free of its package, and put it to her lips. She lit the fresh cigarette with the hot cherry of her smoke, then passed it back to Ted. The filter was moist from her mouth.

"Thanks," Ted said. "You know, you seem awfully... trusting."

"About what?"

"Christ, you got changed right in front of me. You don't know me from Adam."

She shrugged. "I've always been a good read of strangers. You're a decent guy."

"You can't know that," Ted said, shaking his head and wondering why he was pressing the subject, why he was trying to make her not trust him.

"But I can," Tilda said, putting a hand to her chest. "I've been hitching the continent for the better part of a decade. I trust my feelings."

Ten years?

"How old are you?" Ted asked.

"I thought a gentleman didn't ask questions like that."

"Well, a decent guy I may be, but I'm no fucking gentleman."

She snorted a quick laugh before answering: "Twenty-three."

"You ever been wrong in those years?"

Tilda didn't answer.

"Well? Have you?"

She nodded. "Once," she said, but didn't elaborate.

Ted wondered what had happened. *Nothing good, I'll bet.* Tilda had turned her head away from him and was watching the rain. *And now I feel like an ass.*

"Sorry," he said.

She smiled a brittle smile. "You didn't do anything."

Ted tried to change the subject. "So where you headed? Winnipeg?"

"To start," she answered. "Then north to Gimli."

"Gimli? Like the dwarf?"

"No," she said, rolling her eyes. Ted got the impression she had tired of the joke a few years ago. "Like the town. Time's come for me to join the family business."

"And what business is that?"

"Fortune-telling," she said, making a face.

"You're shitting me."

"'Fraid not."

Ted snorted. "Shit, so how's someone get into that gig? Community college? Near-death experience? Alien abduction?"

She made a playful stab at his hand with her lit cigarette. Ted jerked his hand away with a laugh.

"Ha, ha, fucking ha. I told you." She was serious now. "I'm psychic."

Ted drove in silence for a while, trying to keep the smirk off his face. Then she started laughing.

"I'll have you know," she said, giving him a poke in the side, "that I received a letter from my grandmother informing me that forces were aligning quite nicely, and it was time to get my truant ass home, so I can accept my doom."

"Doom?" Ted asked, the word feeling thick on his tongue. "What the fuck does that mean?"

"In this case, same as fate or destiny. It's an Old Norse thing. Amma came over from Iceland with her mom before there was electricity, or the wheel, or some damn thing. She's pretty hard-core. And pissed about being behind schedule."

"What kind of schedule can a group of fortune tellers be on?"

"You'd be surprised. Mom took a long time to get knocked up—too long, Amma always says—and if business is to go on, I have to get home and get my ass knocked up too. Then Amma will finally be able to go to her retirement in peace."

"Are you even married?" Ted asked incredulously.

"Aren't we old-fashioned?" she said with a delighted laugh. "Nope, no room for husbands in our family. Just a long tradition of single moms. You know, the whole maiden, mother, crone thing."

"Jesus Christ, wasn't expecting this story when you got in the car."

"What were you expecting? Teen runaway? Roadside killer? Hand job?"

"A hand job is never expected, sweetheart. But it's always appreciated." Ted winced as soon as the words left his mouth. He couldn't believe he'd just said that. *You're not on the patch anymore, Callan.* "I don't know," he hastened to add. "I just think it's sad, you've your whole life ahead of you and—"

"I don't need your pity," she said. "I've lived a life, believe me. I knew what was in store for me, and I've enjoyed what freedom I've had. Trust me, I'm ready to face my doom."

Ted was quiet as he considered her words. "Well, if you ever change your mind, let me know. I'll drive you where you want or need to go." And he meant the pledge. It surprised him that he did, but he knew if she ever called, he'd go running.

"Why, Ted Callan." She smiled coyly and stretched her arms back. "Are you making a pass at me?"

Ted felt his face flush. He'd always liked small-breasted women. Always joked with the guys at the bar that more'n a handful was wasted anyway. He forced his eyes back on to the road before he became too damn curious about this particular handful. Tilda had thrown him off-balance and he forgot to wonder how she knew his last name.

"Nah, I just don't want to see a smart kid barefoot and pregnant before her time."

"*Aw*, aren't we progressive? That's just the thing you're not getting: I'm no kid, and this is my time."

"So, fortune teller," Ted asked. "What does Winnipeg hold for me?"

"You're serious?" Her voice said she felt he was anything but.

"Sure, why not? If you're going to do this for a living, you may as well get some fucking practice."

"It can be a dangerous thing to know too much about your future, Ted."

"And yet, you're going into the family business."

Tilda stuck her tongue out at him and leaned forward to root around in her bag. She pulled out a sheet of paper and a pen.

"I'll have to do a rough read without my stones," she said, scribbling on the page.

"Stones?"

"Runes."

Ted gave her a blank look.

"You're on a first name basis with a dwarf and you've never heard of runes?"

"Were they in the movie? Anyway, they didn't come up on the patch too often, sorry."

"They're stones, tiles, really. I toss them and read the patterns in how they fall and which rune is face up or face down. If you're asking something specific, I can lay out a spread suited to answering that question. Kinda like tarot. Amma wouldn't let me take the stones when I left home. Didn't try and stop me from leaving, but she kept the damn stones. I can still see shit without them, but only flashes mostly. Amma says if I'd practised harder, I could control the power better. Practise. *Pfff*. Like I always wanna know what's in store for me. If you come visit me in Gimli, we'll do this properly."

Tilda took another cigarette, without asking. She lit it and rolled down her window enough for the rain to trickle into the car.

"Fire, water, earth, and air," she said and turned off the stereo. "Natural elements. They'll help with the read."

Ted tried to suppress another smirk. "Whatever you say."

She tore the page into many small squares, and gripped them tightly. Ted's hand had fallen back to rest atop the gearshift. Tilda closed her hand over his, her nails digging into his skin. He chanced a look at her face, and saw that her eyes had rolled back into their sockets, showing only white behind flickering lashes. The air rushed in through the open window. The discarded cellophane from the cigarette packaging fluttered and crinkled as it was blown about. The interior light flickered on, and the stereo suddenly cut back in, though neither one of them had touched it. Tilda tightened her grip on Ted and thrust her other hand out the window. The lights and stereo went out again.

She released Ted's hand and slumped in her seat.

Ted looked down. Blood oozed from crescents of puckered flesh where she'd held him.

"What the fuck was that?" Ted demanded, his voice sounding strange even to his ears.

Tilda stared at her hand, not answering. There were three wet squares of paper plastered to her palm.

"Well? What did you see?"

"Ted," she said with a quaver in her voice. "Could you turn on a light?"

He did, and he could see now that the scraps of paper had strange symbols drawn on them in blue ink.

He asked again, "Well?"

Tilda avoided his gaze. "I don't know."

"And you're going into the family business?" He forced a chuckle, hoping to break the tension. "You may want to rethink your career options."

"This isn't funny," she said darkly. "The read could be interpreted in two ways. It shows two destinies."

"So?"

"A reading never shows two."

"I don't follow."

"Your basic thread of fate. You will either have a good, bad, or exceptional life. No matter what you do, there is no escaping that. One lot is drawn for every man, woman, and child on the planet."

"I don't buy that."

Tilda glared at him, and Ted flinched. He was old enough to be her father, if only by a biscuit or so; but right now, he couldn't even look her in the eye.

"Your belief has nothing to do with it." He could hear the certainty in her voice. "In Winnipeg, you will live the life of a hero or prince—"

"Not fucking likely," Ted said.

"Or you will come to an abrupt and ugly end."

"Oh."

"Yeah," Tilda said, frowning. "Oh."

Flashing amber lights on a sign over the road told Ted to prepare to stop, and he slowly braked the car, stopping at the junction of the Yellowhead and the Trans-Canada highways. He made the left turn towards Winnipeg and turned on the stereo, masking the heavy silence that had settled between them. Tilda didn't respond to his jokes, or questions. She sat in silent contemplation and smoked his cigarettes.

After the better part of an hour, they were in Winnipeg. The rain either hadn't reached the city yet, or had left long enough ago for most of the runoff to have dried up. At her request, Ted dropped Tilda off at the University of Winnipeg, a big, castle-looking structure. He'd scrawled his cell number on a torn portion of his cigarette pack, and encouraged her to call him if she changed her mind about Gimli. She nodded, but Ted doubted he'd ever see her again.

Before she left, Tilda leaned over and kissed him on the forehead. She pressed the paper scraps into his hand. Her skin was clammy and the ink from one of the squares was still damp, leaving an "x" in blue that transferred on to Ted's palm.

Tilda's fingers lingered over Ted's scabbed knuckles. "You're a fighter. I hope that's enough. Don't lose them," she added solemnly, tapping the paper scraps. "Maybe they'll keep you safe."

"I thought you said fate couldn't be changed."

"It can't, but... I don't know, I've spent the last eight years ignoring this shit. Maybe yours hasn't been set yet. Either good or ill can still choose you. Be careful," she said, and stepped out of the car.

2. A Town Called Malice

There were no seats to be found in the packed pub.

"Try downstairs," the old man behind the bar said over the noise of the crowd and the blaring music. His brogue was just thick enough that Ted would have had trouble understanding him even had the pub been empty. He had a balding pate, and what grey hair remained was long at the back and pulled into a tail. Walleyes looked out from behind Coke-bottle glasses, waiting pointedly for Ted to leave. As he stepped back outside Ted shook his head at the sound of The Pogues behind him. He actually liked the band, but he found pubs in Canada always tried too hard, playing Celtic music that few of their patrons really wanted to listen to. He'd been overseas for his honeymoon and they drank at some pubs outside of Dublin that all played pop contemporary stuff. Of course, pop music in the UK often sounded like a college radio station here.

It seemed so long ago, now; that trip.

He could have taken the spiral steps down to the basement level bar, but he decided to go outside instead. Smokers were perched upon the stairs like gargoyles. Ted pulled his cigarette pack from his jacket pocket, and joined his fellow pariahs.

It took a couple of tries to get his shitty, small Bic lighter to ignite. He'd searched through his things, looking for his Zippo, but eventually had given up in frustration.

The woman standing next to Ted was young and despite (or perhaps because of) her outfit Ted suspected she was underage. She regarded him with a look that was half boredom, half malice and then turned her back to him.

The province's licence plate slogan came back to Ted at that moment. *Friendly Manitoba, indeed.*

She took a last drag, and ground her spent butt into the pavement with a black boot. Turning back, she softened her look.

"Bum a smoke?"

Ted nodded and handed one over, despite her having just finished one. Unless he was down to his last cigarette—or he flat-out hated the fucker asking—he always gave up a smoke.

"Thanks," she said, holding up a loonie.

Ted waved the coin away. "No problem."

She slumped against the steel handrail. "Sorry, I assumed you were another creepy old damaged fuck trying to get in my pants."

Ted winced slightly at her use of the word "old" but given that his skin showed off a lifetime of working outdoors, and with how early his reddish-blond hair had started to grey, he couldn't really blame her. At least he still had his hair. Another thing for his brother Mike to envy.

"Well, you're partly right," he said finally.

"Which part?" she asked, putting the cigarette between her lips and struggling to light a match.

"Old and damaged, kid," Ted said as he lit the cigarette for her. He took a last pull from his own before flicking it away.

Then he tipped a non-existent hat, and walked to the door. "Old and damaged."

The glass had muffled the sound of the music downstairs, but when he opened the door, The Jam welcomed him into the bar. Making his way down a few more steps, he realized this shithole was aptly named. The floor was bare cement, and the tables were plain and black with few patrons sitting at them. It was a stark contrast to the pub upstairs. At the back of the joint was a slightly raised stage, with instruments on stands. The bar was about ten feet ahead and to his left.

Behind the bar and paying far more attention to a bored-looking waitress than to the drinkers, was a college kid. That didn't instil confidence in Ted about ordering anything that needed mixing. This must be strictly a what-kind-of-beer-d'ya-want-rye-and-coke kind of establishment. Ted stepped up to order, and with a relieved smile, the waitress slid from the bartender's presence and out to graze for tips. The kid watched her walk away while Ted tapped his fingers against the bar.

Ted waited a few breaths, and wasn't acknowledged. He waited a few more. He slapped his hand down loudly and yelled over the music, "Jim Beam. Neat."

"Uh..." the bartender murmured. *At least he isn't deaf.*

"Bourbon."

"Uh... Sindy?" the bartender yelled towards the waitress. "We have bourbon?"

Jesus Christ.

Ted scanned the bottles behind the clueless kid. He couldn't see any of his preferred liquor.

"Just give me a JD then."

"Uh…." The bartender half-turned, and Ted could see him squinting at the bottles.

"Jack. Daniels. Black label, brown liquor. Behind you."

He'd have pointed out the bottle of Jack if he thought trying to listen and look at the same time wouldn't have hurt the kid.

Finally the shot found its way into a highball glass. When the bartender's hand reached for the ice scoop Ted snatched the glass away.

"Neat," he said, putting a five on the bar, "means no ice." Ted waited for his change; it wasn't forthcoming. The bartender didn't deserve a tip—*Christ, he couldn't even ID a bottle of Jack. What do they teach kids out here?* Ted let it go. He took a sip, and savoured the warmth as the liquor slid down his throat.

He found a booth in the furthest corner of the bar from the stage and eased himself into the black vinyl cushion. Before long, his glass was empty, and he didn't relish the idea of getting up to ask Numbnuts behind the bar for another. Fortunately, the waitress—Sindy—had a keen eye for an empty glass. Ted figured she did well for tips. Sweeping in, she plucked his glass from the table, giving it a little shake and flashing Ted a 100-watt smile.

"Another?" she asked.

Ted nodded."JD neat, in case Numbnuts over there forgot already."

She smiled knowingly.

"How the hell did he even get a job?"

"He didn't," she explained. "Regular guy called in sick, Vin's just filling in."

Ted shrugged, "Well it looks like you picked the right night to call him up from the minors, but I still say his momma must've dropped him on the head if he doesn't know what bourbon is."

Sindy laughed and headed back towards the bar. She returned promptly with his order, leaning over the table as she deposited the drink.

"Four dollars."

Ted peeled off another five and handed it to her. "Keep it," he said as she reached into her apron for his change. "And don't be a stranger."

Settling into his seat, calmer now, he took a sip of his drink. The bars he was used to had a habit of fights breaking out in them, and Ted found himself automatically scanning the patrons to see who might decide to give him trouble. Ted, being six-foot-four, usually warned off most potential assailants, and he kept to himself well enough not to give anyone else an excuse. Of course, every bar had someone looking to start some shit. And six-four didn't mean now what it did when Ted was younger. *Someone's always gotta prove how big a set they have.*

A group of kids sat at the two tables closest to the stage. They were either fans of the band, or the band itself. Most likely the latter. Ted doubted this place sported a green room for its performers. They clinked a round of shot glasses together before downing the clear liquor and returning to their beers.

A couple of smokers wandered back in and ordered beers—an order the bartender seemed able to handle—and took seats near the stage.

Coming out of the washroom was a small, wiry guy who looked to be about Ted's age, give or take a decade. His thick, dark hair was buzzed to the same short length as the beard that followed his jawline. With the man's coppery skin colour and hatchet-shaped nose, Ted would have guessed he was Native, if not for the beard. He wore glasses and seemed to be smirking to himself.

Across from the Smiler, sitting in line on a bench, with their backs against the wall, were three men Ted figured for either tradesmen or refugees from some sort of ZZ Top convention. He found it was hard to tell how tall they were while they were sitting down, though they seemed short. But while their feet barely touched the floor, each man was very broad. Two wore heavy beards that started just below their eyes and disappeared below the plane of the table, the other sported a pretty elaborate moustache. Each had a pitcher of beer in front of him, and the pint glasses left for them to drink out of appeared to have gone unused. Moustache held up three thick sausage-like fingers as the waitress walked by, and Ted looked away. They didn't seem the type to be in this kind of bar, and that might be trouble. Ted decided there was no point drawing their attention by staring.

ZZ Top, however, had no such compunctions. Before long Ted felt the weight of their looks. Moustache's in particular. The bearded men had eyes like coal embers, smouldering in their dark corner of the bar. They stared harder and meaner than an ex seeing you out on a first date. Ted began to feel decidedly uncomfortable and was about to walk out, when Sindy—lovely Sindy—had noticed his empty glass and set another one down in front of him. Ted sighed and fished for some coins. He didn't feel like breaking a twenty—hell, he barely had a twenty. If he did that, he'd stay here till he drank the whole bill, and in five more drinks—four with tip—he had a feeling a fight would have found him.

Turning around to walk away, Sindy nearly dropped her tray of empty glasses. The Smiler had slipped in right behind her. Ted wasn't sure how the guy had crossed the bar without being seen, but there he was. Five-seven or five-eight, he stood on tip-toes, his arms clasped behind his back, sporting a broad Hollywood grin that didn't quite reach his eyes. The laugh-lines at the corners of his mouth twitched, as if holding the smile was harder than lifting weights.

Sindy stomped away, muttering, and the Smiler sat down next to Ted without waiting for an invitation. The suit he wore was rumpled, and ill-fitting, like he'd pulled it from a larger man. Maybe he had. Jabbed through the lapel was an odd bouton-niere: a sprig of mistletoe.

"I have a proposition for you," the Smiler offered, his voice as oily and false as the smile.

Ted eyed the mistletoe. "No offence, stranger, but it's not Christmas, I'm not in the mood for a kiss, and we're not in that kind of bar. So you can fuck right off."

When he didn't answer, Ted made a point of ignoring him, hoping he'd leave. The group of kids had taken the stage. Heavy bass notes hit him like a punch, while a shrill woman's voice said "check, check." He hoped she wasn't the singer. The DJ gave a thumbs-up from the sound booth, and the drummer clacked his sticks together four times before attacking his snare.

Ted glanced to his side. The man was still there, still smiling. Still saying nothing.

Ted turned his head back to the stage. The guitarist had his instrument slung low, strutting across the stage with the confidence of a Wild West gunslinger. He was good. Ted played a bit, enough to recognize that were he given a million years, he'd never be able to play like this kid. Here was someone who wanted to be Jimmy, Eddie, Angus—maybe even Jimi—and might just get there. What the hell he was doing with the rest of those clowns, Ted couldn't say. He did, however, wish the kid were a gunslinger, if only so the guitar could silence the singer. Her yowling made it seem like she was singing in Japanese, a language she probably knew about as well as she understood things like tone or melody.

The Smiler was still there.

Ted had had enough. He stood up, towering over the smaller seated man. The way the suit hung off the guy, Ted pegged him for a buck-forty, buck-fifty, tops. With nine inches in height, and damn near a hundred pounds on the guy, he couldn't believe how intent the man was on pissing him off.

Maybe he was one of those karate experts, trying to make up for every lick of shit he'd been forced to eat in school.

Maybe. Maybe not.

Either way, Ted was sick of looking at him. A real martial artist didn't go out of his way to pick fights, so he was probably an amateur—*or one of those* MMA *fucks.* Even a trained fighter's odds aren't great against someone with as much of a size advantage as Ted enjoyed here, whatever Hollywood wants you to believe. While he wasn't in the habit of starting shit, Ted knew he could take a hit and he knew how to throw a punch. His dad had seen to that in the ring. His days on the gridiron had conditioned him, and a hard life of manual labour had kept him tough. He was pretty sure he could take whatever this jerk threw at him—at least long enough to get in a few shots of his own. A few shots was all he'd ever needed.

"You can stand up and walk away," Ted said, making a fist, "or I can kick your ass right now, and Numbnuts behind the bar can have you carried out. Your choice."

The man spoke—*finally*—as he slid across the vinyl seat to stand, and straighten his tie.

"By all means," he said, sounding unconcerned by Ted's clenched fist. "I intend to walk away. No need for… physical violence."

He was still smiling that shit-eating grin of his.

"You remind me of someone I knew once. An old friend. He was impulsive and quick to anger too. He died."

Ted bristled. "Is that a threat?"

"No, merely a fact. Most of my family—such as it was—are dead. I have no one, I am alone. Like yourself."

Scowling, Ted said, "You don't know me, asshole."

"I know you better than you think," the man said. "You played organized sports at a high level, but weren't good enough to make a profession of it. You've made an effort to stay in shape since your 'glory days,' but silently, you regret the loss of what no exercise can keep, the speed and power of youth. You've worked a hard job, one that has seen you spend most of your adult life out of doors, exposed to the elements."

Ted shrugged, determined not to let the stranger know how right he was. "Not bad, Kojak, but you're wrong. I could have played at a higher level. I chose to pursue something else."

The words sounded empty even to Ted.

"A choice that still bothers you."

There was no arguing with that, so Ted stayed silent.

"Everyone is wistful for the path not taken. In your case, heroism and fame. Would she have stayed with you, your beautiful wife? Would she have stayed had your life taken that other road?"

Ted opened his fist and brushed his palm down over his jeans. Spending his first night in Winnipeg in jail wasn't really how he wanted to start his new life. And, he knew, as angry as he was right now, he wouldn't stop hitting this irritant after one punch.

"Self-control," the man said, pursing his lips and nodding as if impressed. "How unexpected. My family never did learn that trick. Let me give you some advice: don't long too hard for a return to the glory of youth. Youth is fleeting, and despite what my family believed, so is glory. Leave here. Live your life, and make the most of it. Forget about me and the drunks with the beards."

"What... why?"

"I overheard their plans for you. They believe tonight holds your doom and they intend to make it so, for good or ill."

"You're insane," Ted said, though Tilda's warnings bubbled up from his memory. She'd used that same word. Doom. "What am I to them?"

34

"What indeed?" The man's smile slipped off for a moment before he plastered it back on. He pulled the sprig of mistletoe from his lapel and, reaching across the table, pressed the boutonniere into Ted's hand.

The branch was sharp where it had been cut, and Ted felt the wood bite into his palm. He gave an involuntary little shiver.

"Take this, for good luck if nothing else, or if you have any intention of leading a mortal life."

"Mortal life? What the shit is that?" Ted snarled. "We're all mortal. And all I have is your word that three complete strangers…." Ted looked over to the table. zz Top had left at some point during his argument with the Smiler. "Three strangers, who aren't even here, want to kill me. I'm afraid you're a few dwarves short of a set, Snow White."

Ted threw back the last of his drink, and slammed the glass down hard on the table. He turned to walk away and then stopped and looked at the sprig in his hand. With no expression, he tore the leaves from the wood, then snapped it in two, and let it fall to the floor.

"I don't need your luck, your warnings, or you."

The man's smile grew even wider. Ted turned and left the bar. He walked through a cloud of cigarette smoke as he climbed the steps back to street level.

Several tries were needed to get the cheap, fucking Bic to light. Several more attempts were made before Ted thought to cup his hands over the guttering flame to keep the wind from blowing it out. He wanted to get into his car and just keep driving, but he'd put his three drinks back quickly. Ted reckoned he'd blow over if he drove now. He didn't like the idea of leaving The Goat out on the side street where he'd parked. But he liked the idea of losing his licence even less.

Back in Alberta, Manitoba had a rep among its many expats for being tough on drunk drivers. And as Tilda had pointed out, the sawed-off locks in his car were no deterrent to a real thief, which was something else Winnipeg had in spades. He decided to split the difference between worry and caution.

Ted got into his GTO and took the side streets around to the parking lot for the motor inn just down the street from the bar. Judging from the looks of it, the place would be in his price range. And, he noted, any place that also had a bar attached— which every motor inn did—was likely to have at least a few bouncers around the lot at closing time. As he drew closer, he noticed a long line of Harley-Davidsons on the south end of the lot. From the look of the guys looming over them, they didn't belong to Bikers for Christ. Ted doubted anyone would fuck with them and he hoped The Goat would gain some protection by proximity.

Even with a few drinks in him, the smell of mould and piss and a variety of other unpleasantness rankled his nose as he opened the door to the lobby. The woman behind the counter was a mean-eyed old broad whose sour face reminded him of his French teacher in school. She passed a set of keys to a young drunk couple with her thumb and forefinger like she was handing them a bag of dog shit, and they practically ran up the stairs.

Ted hoped his room wasn't next to theirs. All he needed was another reminder of what he wouldn't be getting. He'd grown pretty used to the idea of not having sex—he'd had plenty of practice in his marriage after all. But meeting Tilda, them hitting it off, her smile, her teasing, had got his juices flowing again.

The woman took his credit card, and she handed him the keys with same disdain she'd shown the previous guests. Ted waited for her to give him back his card, and then followed the happy drunks up the stairs with much less enthusiasm than they had shown. His room was on the third floor, the penthouse of this shithole.

He let the door to Room 306 swing shut behind him. His room wasn't as bad as he'd expected, and far worse than he'd hoped for. Ted turned into the washroom to have a shower and take a piss—not necessarily in that order. The lemon scent of some kind of cleaning product wafted out in a brief miasma. He flicked the switch for the bathroom fan; light spread out and across the room's drab grey carpet. He sloughed off his clothes. After starting the hot water, he stepped up to the toilet, lifted the seat, and stretched his arms above his head with his fingers locked. An evening's worth of urine splashed into the bowl below. Two quick shakes, and then Ted flushed the toilet. He couldn't help but notice he'd dropped the seat down on reflex as he turned towards the shower. He wondered how long it would take before he lost that habit.

Running his hands across the shower tile, he could feel that most of the grime had been cleaned away, at least. He pulled the knob to engage the shower and hopped back a step as the first burst of cold water hit his body. It quickly heated up to the temperature he had chosen, and he stepped into the tub to wash the day's drive and the smell of cigarettes from his body.

When he had dried off, he stepped out of the washroom without bothering to wrap his towel around his waist, instead letting it fall to the floor amid his damp footprints. It was his habit to sleep in the nude and he hoped the bed was free of parasites.

Ted rounded the corner that hid the bed. There was a flash, a glint of something golden. Something tightened around his throat. He tried to get his fingers underneath the binding, but it was so slender that it had already begun digging into his flesh. He couldn't breathe. Whatever was around his neck was metal, and tightening. As he gasped for air, his head was jerked roughly backwards, and he saw the top of a short man's head.

"Take him," said a voice behind Ted. It was gravelly and croaking, and sounded the English words with care, like a foreign language. Two short, bearded men in army jackets stood up from their hiding place behind the bed.

The men from the bar.

The first one around the bed easily captured Ted's flailing legs, holding them together in his oversized, meaty hands. The other man grabbed Ted's hands, pulling them away from his throat. He looped more of the thin golden chain around Ted's wrists. It looked so frail, so slender. Ted couldn't believe it wouldn't break. He gritted his teeth and strained against both attackers. He may as well have been a kitten they were drowning.

"Who the fuck are you?" he choked out between gasping breaths.

A whisper came from behind Ted. The lights flickered and Ted felt an electric jolt. Spasms rippled through his muscles, but he was still unable to move his body.

"This chain was made of a cat's footfalls and the roots of a mountain; from the breath of fish and the beards of women. You cannot break Gleipnir." Moustache came around to face Ted, giving the chain a little shake. "Gleipnir held the wolf until Ragnarök. It will hold you."

"I'll. Fucking. Kill. You!" Ted knew the threat was hollow, knew he was powerless. But it had to be said.

Moustache looked up. "Silence him," he said and then went back to whispering to the chain.

Beard One looped the chain between Ted's legs, wrapping it three times around each ankle. Beard Two pulled what looked like a metal bit from his jacket and pressed it against Ted's teeth.

He wanted to swear. To spit. But he clenched his jaw as tightly as he could. Beard Two closed a hand over Ted's face and squeezed like a vice. It felt like those thick fingers were going to rip through the flesh of his cheek. A cry of pain was muffled by his attacker's rough hand as his mouth was forced open. Ted tried biting down on the fingers, but only cut the inside of his cheeks. Blood trickled past his teeth. Beard Two pressed the bit to Ted's mouth. The bit was black, and judging from the rust flaking off of it, old, and pure iron.

The metal scraped past Ted's teeth, forcing his mouth open wider, and he winced at the sound. His tongue flattened against the bit, and he couldn't tell if he tasted his own blood, or the iron. The pressure of Beard Two's grip slackened slightly, but not enough for Ted to take advantage of. Beard Two began a whispered chant of his own.

Ted tried to scream through the obstruction, but there was

no sound, only pain. It felt like he'd already screamed his voice raw. Like they'd torn every scream, every yell, he had ever—or could ever—cry. His voice was all that had remained under his own power. But they took that away too.

He wished he could weep, though his dad would've called him out on it. But the men had made him so powerless even tears wouldn't come. Moustache released the chain, and Beard One took up the chant. The three of them dragged Ted towards the bed and shoved him face down upon it. He was suddenly aware of his nakedness. They forced his legs and arms wide. He lay spread-eagled, expecting horrors to come.

He couldn't cry. Couldn't scream. But he could feel pain. They'd proven that.

Ted had been no stranger to pain in his life. Pain, he understood. But this was different. This was so far beyond his knowing that terror magnified the minor hurts he'd already received. His heart pounded hard in his chest; Ted thought it would break free from his rib cage. Adrenaline surged through his body, but the energy had no outlet. No release.

Sssssk. Sssssk.

From behind him he heard the scrape of metal on stone, followed by Moustache's low chanting.

"Shave him," said Beard One.

"Shave him," said Beard Two.

Ted nearly voided himself when the sharp edge of a knife pressed lightly against his skin. The knife scraped down his back. Pain exploded in his mind, which was anticipating the blade to dig deep at any moment. Ted felt the knife edge rest again on his back. Again it slid down, and again he heard the rasp of metal over stone. *Sssssk, sssssk.*

The ordeal went on for a seeming eternity. Moustache would drag the knife over Ted's body twice, sharpen the blade, and make two more passes. They'd done his back, his arms, his legs, and for a moment, Ted allowed himself to hope. Maybe they would let him live. Fingers hooked under Ted's chin, raising his head up and exposing his throat.

Or, maybe not.

"The World was made from Ymir's blood, and you must bleed to join the World," Moustache intoned.

Now Ted could see the blade. It was more of a dagger than a knife, close to a foot long and edged on both sides. His eyes pleaded in the mirror-bright shine of the metal. They were watering from being held open so long. Blood vessels had burst—Ted couldn't see any colour in his eyes but red. The blade rasped over his scalp once, twice.

"And you will bleed, Theodore Callan, or your world will bleed."

Moustache showed Ted the dagger in between every stroke. Ted wished he could just pass out. He should have hyperventilated and slumped into unconsciousness, but whatever they were doing to hold him still was keeping him awake as well.

"Flip him," Moustache said, and they did. Ted was staring up at the ceiling now, but still immobile. By peering downward he could make out what they were doing. Moustache ran the dagger over a whetstone. *Oh, God.* They weren't done with him. Beards One and Two had shrugged off their army coats. Sturdy leather aprons were underneath. He smelled a stink like burning coal, and felt the heat of white metal wafting from them. Something in the scents, in Ted's fear, brought back the explosion and fire at the patch.

Their pattern continued. It was no less terrifying now that Ted could see what they were doing. They shaved his chest. Moustache grinned as he dragged the knife lower. Ted's heart pounded and he thought he'd grind his teeth to powder on the bit. His assailants barked a laugh, and then spoke a few words to each other in a guttural tongue that Ted didn't understand. They spoke so fast he could hardly make out the separation of their words.

Finally, Moustache put the dagger down. Ted wanted to cry with relief. But the Beards hadn't stopped chanting as they held the opposite ends of the braided golden chain. Ted tried to spit the bit free of his mouth. It remained stuck fast. Moustache drew out what looked like a thin metal stylus. Its tip was narrowed to a sharp point. Moustache pressed it to Ted's chest.

And that's when they started cutting.

3. Welcome to My Nightmare

Ted woke up to shrieking. Surprisingly it wasn't his own. The cleaning lady stood in the hall, her scream trailing off as the heavy motel door slowly closed itself. His head pounded, and his stomach roiled, like he had the mother of all hangovers. And then he felt the real pain. *How can I hurt this much and still be alive?* Ted looked down; the effort nearly made him throw up. He lay on the bed, naked, and covered in blood. The bed looked like a scene from *A Nightmare on Elm Street.* The tang of copper wafted up his nostrils, and his fingers were tacky with half-dried blood. He clawed at his arms. Metallic blue tracings glittered through half-formed scabs.

It really happened.

Ted leaned over the side of the bed and threw up. He'd always hated vomiting; hated the smell, the sound, the taste. But now he welcomed it, as if he could erase what had happened to him if he retched hard enough. He hadn't eaten much the day before, and all that came up was bile and blood. The pungent taste of the bile cut briefly through the coppery blood scent, before being choked back down. Ted could feel the tears beading in the corners of his eyes, the snot running from his nose as he shook and sobbed.

It really happened.

He pulled himself from the bed. The drying blood had fused the cheap motel bedspread to his body. Ted peeled it free and left it on the floor. Staggering over to the chest of drawers with the mirror attached, Ted kept his head down for a moment. He wasn't ready to see what they had done to him.

He had to look.

Slowly, he lifted his head. His eyes were still bloodshot from struggling. Hardly the most disturbing sight. Blood coated his entire body. The blood had been hot, scalding hot. They had poured it over him before they'd left, the blood hissing as it ran over his flesh. Even now it was still a brilliant red, not the dull rusty brown he expected. Eerily, it still felt warm to the touch. On his arms—across his whole body—metallic blue lines were visible wherever they had cut him, which seemed to be everywhere. Stylized birds climbed his neck; their heads coiled over his temples so their beaks were pointed at each ear. There was a soft hissing, like Ted could almost hear them whispering. He shook his head, disoriented. He'd been humiliated. Disfigured. For what? No answer came.

Ted thought the cleaning lady must have told her boss and someone would have called the cops by now. *What do I do?* When he and the guys from the patch were in town and tying one on, the blue had gotten involved more often than Ted would care to admit. He had a pretty good idea of response times in Edmonton, but he had no idea what they were in Winnipeg. The difference here was that he hadn't done anything wrong. He was the victim. Looking at the room, though, he was going to have a hard time convincing the cops of that.

What to do? Run? There wouldn't be time to clean up before the cops got here. *Sure as shit, I'm not getting anywhere looking like Hannibal Lecter.*

Ted didn't hear the rattle of keys in the lock, but he turned as the door opened. It wasn't the cops. Two big, biker-looking fucks with shaved heads and wispy Vandykes squeezed into the room. One was big, over six-foot, and paunchy, but the kind of big you still don't want to fuck with if you don't have to. He carried a baseball bat in his left hand. The other was the kind of big you never want to fuck with. Closer to seven-foot than six, and three hundred pounds if he weighed an ounce, he had no visible weapon other than himself. That was enough. He cracked the knuckles of his right hand as he closed it into a fist. Both men were wearing black T-shirts that read ZOOKEEPER.

"You're not going anywhere, sicko," Big said, slapping the bat into his open palm.

"That's right," said Bigger. "Just sit down, cover your cock, and wait for the pigs." He smiled. "It would be a shame to have to subdue you."

"I didn't do anything," Ted said, gripping the chest of drawers and looking at his bloody hands. "I was attacked in my room last night."

"Don't give a shit," Bigger said. "Sit the fuck down."

"Listen to me, you dumb fucks—" Ted couldn't help but feel he would have been better off if the cops had found him. They at least had procedures to follow, and probably wouldn't beat on him just for jollies.

"Look Les, he's coming at us," Bigger said, turning to Big—Les—and smiling.

"So he is, Ernie, so he is."

Ernie slid the door chain into place. It wouldn't stop anyone who really wanted in, but it would slow Ted down enough that he wouldn't be able to get around them and out the door.

Trapped. Again. He didn't like the feeling. His odds hadn't improved much over last night, but at least these two jokers hadn't stolen Wonder Woman's magical lariat. He may get his ass beat, but this time he was going to get a few shots in. He'd be damned if he'd go twice in one day without a fight.

Les, who was holding the bat like a southpaw, came towards Ted's right, and Ernie circled left. They were going to work his sides. They'd done this before. Ted figured they didn't view him as much of a threat, as they were leaving their middle open to him lunging forward. Les would swing the bat and however Ted moved to dodge or cover, Ernie would be waiting to land a punch.

It was the bat that would end up dropping him. He had to get it out of the bouncer's hands. Ted shot towards Les, so fast they didn't have time to move, faster than he knew he could move. Les stepped back. He didn't have room for a proper swing and jabbed the bat at Ted's chest. This time, Ted's adrenaline had an outlet, and he hardly felt the aluminum bat tap against his chest.

Or the punch that Ernie delivered to his kidney.

He should have felt the strike. But instead he heard the soft slap of knuckles hitting his skin. Then a cry of pain. The cry came from Ernie.

Les had the space for a proper swing of his bat, and he was going headhunting. Ted was too surprised by the sight of Ernie cradling his hand and swearing to dodge. Ted put up his forearm, figuring the bat would break the bone, but that beat taking a shot to his skull.

The aluminum squealed as it bent against Ted's arm. Les's eyes went wide as Ted gripped the remains of the bat and tore it from the bouncer's hands. Ted brought his fist back down and punched Les square in the chest. The impact sounded like a hammer hitting cement, and he heard a sick crack that was somehow audible from inside the bouncer's body. Les crumpled to the floor.

"Fucker!" Ernie yelled, closing again.

Ernie's long, muscled arms reached out faster than Ted had expected. He enveloped Ted and started to squeeze.

Ted couldn't feel it.

By the look on Ernie's face, Ted's ribs should have broken by now. But they didn't. Ernie's bear hug didn't hurt any more than Grandma's embrace. Easily, Ted broke the hold, grabbed the bouncer by the shirt and shoved. He'd expected the man to pinwheel backwards and fall over the bed, not sail over the bed and out the window.

Fuck! I've killed him!

Ted ran to the window. Fortunately there was an overhang just beneath where taxis parked to wait for drunken night fares and hungover morning fares. It wasn't too bad a fall. Ernie was on the overhang, scraped up and moaning.

But alive.

As Ted looked out the window, people on the street looked up and pointed. He could hear sirens getting closer. He looked down at his hands. Enough of the blood had come off them in the struggle to see the designs engraved in his flesh. There was a stylized hammerhead on his right palm, and a sun upon his left.

What the fuck did they do to me last night?

Ted thought about running. But where would he go? The motel had his credit card number, they had his name. *And only guilty men run, right?* His head still swam with the events of the last night and this morning.

No, he didn't have the energy to play Richard Kimble. He sat down on the bed and waited for the police. He could hear the ruckus, the preparations of the cops in the hall as they approached the door to his room. Ted sat still, and raised his hands. He was about to lock his fingers behind his head, but the touch of his shorn scalp made his gorge rise.

They'll be coming in with their pieces out, better they can see my hands anyway.

The door opened.

Ted saw the Glocks enter before the cops who carried them. A man and a woman shouted in unison, "Police, freeze!"

Ted didn't move.

"Jesus Christ!" the man cursed, "Look at this place."

The woman kept her gun trained on Ted, while the man did a quick survey of the room, and checked the bathroom.

"Are you all right, sir?" she asked. Ted was surprised. She was speaking to him.

"Yeah, I guess," he answered.

She leaned her head to the radio on her shoulder. "We need an EMT up here."

"Bathroom's clean," the male cop said. "Looks like whoever did this didn't have time to clean up."

"We have a report of a dead body. Where is it?"

"They probably meant me," Ted said slowly. He wasn't sure how much of last night he believed, let alone what the cops would think.

"You?" the woman said, keeping her gun level.

"This is my room. I was attacked last night. I was out on the bed when the cleaning lady opened the door. Her screams woke me up. Must've thought I was dead."

"Were these men the ones who attacked you?" the female cop asked. Her partner checked on the bouncer on the floor.

"He's alive," he said quickly.

"Not last night," Ted tried to explain. "They came in after the cleaner left. Tried to rough me up."

"Big men. Are you on something?"

"No. Adrenaline, I guess."

"Are you going to be trouble?"

He shook his head.

"Let's see those hands in front of you," the woman said, unconvinced. "Slowly, now."

The male cop snapped handcuffs around Ted's wrists. The woman kept her gun trained him.

"What's your name?" the male cop asked.

Ted told them.

"You're under arrest for suspicion of murder, Mr. Callan," the male cop said and then kept talking. Ted drifted off while the man spoke, he'd heard the spiel before. Only the charge was new. "Do you understand the rights as I have read them to you?"

"Yes," Ted said.

They wouldn't let him clean up or even throw on his pants. Evidence, they said. The EMTs did provide a hospital-style dressing gown to cover him, after a cursory examination.

"The blood stinks," the EMT said. "But I don't think any of it's his."

As Ted was led from the motel, a crowd had gathered around some news trucks. EMTs and more cops had blocked the entrance to the building. Out in the crisp morning air his nose wrinkled at the stink coming off of his body. Normal morning BO was masked by the oily, iron scent of the dried blood that coated his body. Ted shivered as the lady cop grabbed his head to ease him into the back of the cruiser. Her skin was rough on his tortured scalp.

It struck him that there was nothing they could really do to hold him. He'd broken a metal bat. Punched a man out a window. Maybe he could snap these cuffs. Kick the door from the frame of the cop car. They might shoot him. The bat hadn't hurt. Would he feel a bullet?

Ted didn't feel like finding out.

He rode in the back of the car in silence, wondering about the previous night. Maybe that smiling fucker had slipped him something. Would that explain the night away? The nightmarish events, the superhuman strength. He held his eyes tightly shut. When he opened them the tattoos were still there.

At the station, they processed him. Fingerprints, mug shot, and then the crime scene techies got involved. Ted hoped for at least one to resemble Marg Helgenberger from *CSI*, and was disappointed. They prodded Ted's body—swabbed samples of the blood that covered him and saliva from his mouth; they scraped under his fingernails and looked for stray hairs that had been preserved in the dried blood. When they were done he was led away.

The room they put him in reeked of bad coffee and old fear. They made him sit and sweat for a while before the detectives came in. One had the standard seventies cop moustache, the other a shaved head and florid baby face. Ted answered their questions as best he could without mentioning the odder parts of his evening. Odder? What about last night wasn't odd? But the truth would put him in the loony bin. They kept mentioning a lawyer. He didn't care. He kept repeating over and over, "I got the room. I took a shower. Three guys jumped me. They tied me up. Shaved me. Tattooed me. I passed out. Woke up to the cleaning lady screaming."

They wanted more details, of course.

"What did they look like?"

"What were you tied up with?"

"How'd you take down the two bouncers?"

Ted grimaced, clutching the table, trying to relax. He felt it deform under his grip. Opening his palms, he eased his hands to his lap. The table hardly looked new, he hoped they wouldn't notice.

A lawyer—dressed too sharply to be public-appointed—was finally led into the room. The detectives who had been interrogating Ted smiled and said he'd never asked to have a lawyer present. The lawyer's anger was evident in the warning look he gave the cops. A look that asked how far they were willing to take this. Baby-Face shrugged. Neither made a move to get a chair for the lawyer.

Ted listened dully as the lawyer—he'd already forgotten the man's name—began orating on how the Winnipeg Police Service had treated his client. The lawyer cut the interrogation short, ostensibly to confer with his client, but also so that Ted had the opportunity to clean up and get dressed.

He wasn't given enough time in the shower to feel clean, but he did feel better. The heat and steam gave him back at least a measure of himself. Guards watched him through the whole procedure. Ted didn't care. More designs were visible now. A stylized horn—in golden ink, no less. The horn made Ted think of his father, the Sergeant blasting reveille to wake up the house in the morning. Thoughts of his father often turned to the grandfather Ted had never met, who'd survived the Great War only to die in the next. Two markings on either side of both Ted's legs, making eight in total, were what looked like horse legs. Black and grey storm clouds covered his chest and lightning arcing within their rolling depths spread out over his body to touch the hammerhead that marked his right forearm. And there were more. Brilliant green interlocking scales, like a lizard's, filled the spaces in between the images. They'd carved up his back too, Moustache and the

Beards. Ted wondered what he wasn't able to see. What else had they done to him.

He was given an orange jumpsuit to wear and sent to the holding cell. The lawyer hadn't waited for him. Ted wondered who was footing the bill. He sure as shit didn't have the money.

Heads turned as he was let in. The guys in the cell—likely some hardened criminals, some kids, some wide-eyed johns worrying about being the date for some prison bull-queer— they all knew, on some primal, instinctual level that Ted didn't belong with them. He knew it was a matter of when, not if, a hard man would make a move. Ted bided his time.

The bouncers hadn't been able to hurt him. And neither did the first prisoner to try. After that, no one else made a move.

It was still an uneasy night.

The suspicion of murder charge quickly evaporated without a body. Misdemeanour assault. That was all Ted ended up being charged with. The bouncers had evidently filed the charges. They'd wanted to try for assault with a deadly weapon, but couldn't find any evidence of him using one other than his fists. He was still on the hook for the damages to the room too, and that was going to eat up what little remained on his credit card. One nice thing about getting arrested, he hadn't needed to sort out a place to stay.

The fancy lawyer, whose name Ted still didn't know, had paid for an independent lab to DNA test overnight the blood they'd found on him, rather than waiting for it to be sent to the RCMP lab in Ontario.

Lizard blood.

That's what had soaked the bed—that and traces of Ted's own blood. Statements from the old boot at the counter confirmed that Ted had had hair and no visible tattoos when he asked for the room.

He was set free with his effects after being held for twenty-four hours, but was told to stick around. That he was still a person of interest. *Whatever the fuck that meant.* The cops didn't apologize for the misunderstanding, but did say they'd do their best to find the three men who'd attacked him.

Ted wasn't holding his breath.

He checked his cellphone as he walked down the station steps towards the street. His mailbox was full. He could also tell the messages had been viewed.

Damn snooping cops.

Ted sighed and started to listen to his missed calls. He doubted there would be anything too important there.

"T-Bag, buddy... you in Winterpeg yet? Heh, heh. Give me a call when you're set up, fucker. Rye and Coke out."

Ted was surprised and touched that his friend from work had actually made the effort to stay in touch. Ryan came from a Mennonite family, all in Alberta now for the money, though their roots were in rural Manitoba. He was a pretty conservative guy—if you didn't look too hard at the whoring and drinking—and he hated ink. Ted wondered how welcome he'd be at the family barbecues with his new look.

"Uh... it's Tilda. You said to call, if... well, I don't need rescuing, white knight. But... I'm worried about you. I've seen some things. I know you don't believe in… just… just call me, okay? I'm staying at a friend's in the city."

A rapid recitation of the friend's number followed. Ted didn't have a pen, he'd call her later. It was sweet she was worried. He shook his head. What would he tell her anyway? He went to the next message.

"Ted, it's Susanna." His wife, like he needed her to introduce herself. He surprised himself by thinking of her in those terms—the papers had been signed, after all. *Ex-wife, I have to get used to saying that. Thinking that.* Her voice sounded raw, like she'd been crying. It was too much to hope that it was over him. "Loki died. She was running around fine, and then just stood still and fell over. It was too late to get her to a vet. Ted, I'm sorry." She meant about the dog, of course, not their marriage. "I know you loved her. I'm going to bury her under the apple tree on the yard." Loki had loved apples. She didn't eat them, but she'd run with them in her mouth, throw them up into the air, or bat them with her paws and chase them. On hot days, she'd relax, panting in the shade of that tree. It was as good a spot as any to bury the family dog. *Not like they were a family anymore anyway. Fuck, the hits just keep on coming.* Ted hadn't realized the call wasn't done. There had been a long pause. What words was Susanna reaching for? "I… I just thought you should know. Goodbye, Ted."

"Ted…." It was Tilda again. "I thought you would have called by now… call me when you get this."

"Mr. Callan, Conrad here." His lawyer in Edmonton. Conrad was fat and loud, and sounded even more so over the phone.

"I've been informed your last payment was unable to be pro-cessed." *Nice way to say your cheque bounced, you deadbeat fuck.* Ted would've had enough money if Conrad hadn't dragged the settlement out fighting for things Ted hadn't even wanted. "If you could address this ASAP that would be fantastic. Take care, and stay in touch." *What kind of fucking divorce attorney says stay in touch?*

There was a call from Svarta Mining. "I'm sorry, Mr. Callan, the position has been filled. But thank you for your interest."

"Motherfucker… how's it hangin'?" Ryan, and he sounded drunk. "You must be back in the saddle or you woulda answered by now? How was she? Look, can you do me a favour since you're in Winnipeg? My sister's havin' a bit of trouble. Nothing serious… uh… could you look in on her? Thanks, dude. Much appreciated." Ted had forgotten Rye's sister Jenny had married her way back into Manitoba. There was a pause as if Ryan were getting ready to hang up. "And no you still can't fuck her, T-Bag. Rye and Coke out."

It had been an ongoing thing between them. They'd get drunk and Ted would offer to *take care of Ryan's sister's needs.* Ryan would offer to keep Susanna satisfied, *if things didn't work out.*

At least you'll like the guy puttin' the dick to her, he'd say.

Let me know how my dick tastes, had been Ted's standard comeback. The joke just wasn't as funny anymore.

He missed the camaraderie that had come from drinking with the guys on the patch. But most of them had disappeared from his life when Ted had left. Ryan included. There was no room for monsters in their world. Two messages in twenty-four hours. Well, one message and one favour, but at least the guy was trying to stay in touch. Ted doubted he'd ever see Ryan again, unless his friend made his way east—an unlikely prospect. And Ted was never going back to Alberta.

He hadn't realized he'd scrolled to the next message. He heard just the last breathy words before Tilda hung up the phone. There was no electronic beep. She'd been using an old phone, a street corner pay phone, maybe. He looked at his display. The next ten messages were all from the same number.

"What the hell?" he muttered, holding the phone to his ear and letting them play. Each call was some variation of "why haven't you called?" "are you okay?" and "what happened?" By her final call Tilda was sobbing. "I don't know if you'll get this now, but I'm sorry I got you into this."

What did she mean? Did she know those bearded fucks? Were they what she had seen during the ride?

The cawing of crows squabbling with each other for food echoed for a moment in his ears, aggravating the headache he hadn't been able to shake since the night at the motel. As he left the Winnipeg Remand Centre a few pedestrians and some drivers turned to stare at him. Ted gave the finger to a couple that went out of their way to cross the street to get away from him.

Next message.

"Why the hell are the Winnipeg police calling me at work to ask about you?" Susanna sounded pissed. Ted winced. She had a set of lungs on her when she wanted to be heard. "What did you do? I don't need this shit, Ted. I really don't. Don't you even think about calling me for bail."

So much for heading home to pay respects to the dog, with a mercy fuck to follow.

For the next call, it took Ted a moment to place the voice. "Mr. Callan, right now, you are likely wondering how I knew to call you—that, or how your life took such an unexpected turn. I won't say I have answers. But I do have the questions that you should ask. And more importantly, I know who you should ask them of." It was the Smiler from the bar. *How the fuck did he get this number?* "And just so you believe me, check a pocket—any pocket—" There was a pause. "I'm waiting." Ted put a hand in a jacket pocket, not sure why, and closed it on something rectangular and metal. He knew the shape. His Zippo. "A peace offering. You will see me again. You need only start to look. Goodbye, Mr. Callan, and I am sorry about your dog."

4. Gimme Shelter

The police had towed The Goat to their impound lot. Ted stared at the ticket they'd given him to reclaim his car and wondered how he was going to get there. He had no money for a cab and didn't know the city well enough to want to try the bus. And he hated the bus. He was a driver, dammit. With a sigh, he realized Rye was going to get his wish. Ted called Jenny.

Her phone rang twice before she answered.

"Hello?"

"Jenny? It's Ted—"

"Hey, how are you? Ryan said you were moving to Winnipeg. You here yet?"

"Yeah, I'm in town now. Look, I got this call from him the other night—"

"Oh, for shit sakes." Ted had only seen Jenny a handful of times in the last decade—mostly at family dos, but for the life of him, he couldn't remember her ever swearing. It sounded odd coming from her. "He wants you to take care of me, doesn't he?"

There was a definite edge to her voice.

"He said you'd had a spot of trouble, but wouldn't elaborate. Said it wasn't a big deal. He just asked me to stop by. Look, I hate to bother you, but my car was impounded. I need a lift to pick it up and—"

"Christ, you're up to your old tricks in a hurry." Ted flushed, feeling embarrassed. He hoped she hadn't been following the news. "And I'm the only one you know in the city?"

"Yeah."

"No worries." Jenny laughed. "Of course I'll come get you. So, was that all he said? Ryan? To check up on me?"

"Uh," Ted paused, remembering his friend's "hands-off" warning. "Yeah."

He thought he heard a chuckle on the other end of the line. Jenny didn't seem to believe him. "Okay, where are you?"

Ted had walked a couple of blocks while they talked and gave her the address where he was now. He didn't want her to know of his arrest.

"Down by Remand," Jenny said. "See you in fifteen, give or take."

Ted debated calling Tilda, just to let her know he was fine. He shook his head. *Fine.* What had happened to him was too weird to bring a self-professed psychic into the mix. Besides, if she had half the foresight she claimed, she should know by now what had happened.

True to her word, Jenny rolled up in twelve minutes. She was still driving the same car, a black mid-nineties Accord. He could see her through the windows, scanning the streets, looking for him. She'd looked past him twice already. Ted swallowed and walked up to the car and rapped on the window. He heard the power locks engage as Jenny squinted to get a better look at him. Then recognition dawned. The passenger door lock clicked again. Ted opened the door and slid into the seat.

"My God," she said, reaching a trembling hand to brush his cheek. Ted flinched and Jenny drew back her hand. "What happened to you? I barely recognized you."

"I got jumped, they did this to me."

"I… see." She stared at him for a moment.

There was an awkward silence as Ted buckled his seatbelt. Then Jenny signalled and pulled into traffic.

"Sorry," she said, not looking at him.

"For what?"

"Bringing it up."

"You didn't do anything wrong."

Jenny smiled. It was forced. "Well, I'm not a size two anymore, so I guess we both look different."

She had changed. Ted remembered her with wild edges of girlishness about her. She didn't look anything like her brother, which was definitely a point in her favour. Something in the way she carried herself had changed, even if her beauty hadn't. Her arms weren't the spindly little things they'd been when she'd tried to play basketball with him and Rye. Her face wasn't a beacon of energy or optimism, either. She still kept her hair tied back in a ponytail; that hadn't changed, even if it might have been for reasons of expediency—she'd arrived awfully quickly. He looked away and watched the buildings and pedestrians zip by; it was bad form to run your eyes over your buddy's sister. There were two coffee cups sitting in the drink holders by the gearshift, filling the car with the rich scent of dark roast coffee.

Ted picked up the one with no lipstick on the rim.

"For me?"

Jenny nodded.

"Thanks." He took a sip. Black. Excellent.

"I should have just left you there," she said quickly. "Payback." She laughed then, finally seeming at ease. "Don't think I didn't hear the way you two talked about me back in school."

"Oh, it couldn't have been that bad."

"Between Rye's insults and you constantly threatening him that you were going to... what was it?"

Ted remembered, but he wasn't about to repeat the words to her.

Jenny changed lanes quickly, slipping through traffic to avoid a car backing up to parallel park. The lurch cracked Ted's head against the window.

Sheepish, Ted offered up an apology. "Look, guys are assholes, especially in high school. I'm sorry."

"You should be sorry," she said sternly. Then she started to laugh and jabbed at his ribs. "You never followed through."

He cleared his throat, shifted in his seat and tried to change the subject. "So... this trouble Rye was talking about?"

"Oh, it's nothing, really. Kind of embarrassing."

"After this conversation, I'm used to embarrassing. What's up?"

"Did you hear that Jim and I split?"

He hadn't, but it wasn't the sort of thing her family would

talk about. She didn't sound too broken up about the divorce. So it was either old news or her decision. He wondered how her Mennonite parents were handling it.

"No."

"Well we did. It's no big thing, but I didn't want to sell the house. So I've got a too-big house, and a too-big mortgage. I was going to put some suites in, rent out a couple of rooms to help with the payments and such, but—"

"That costs money too."

She cocked a finger at him, mock fired.

"Maybe I can help you out."

"I don't want your money."

"That's a fucking relief," Ted laughed. "I don't have any."

"What happened? You were pretty well set up in Edmonton, if I remember."

They rolled to a stop at a red light.

"Susanna and I split, too."

"Oh. Sorry to hear that," Jenny said. She gave his knee a quick squeeze and offered a sympathetic smile. "Aren't we the pair? Our folks must be thrilled to death. If my dad saw us, he'd marry us on the spot for his own peace of mind."

Ted laughed. "Good thing he's not here, then."

"Good thing," said Jenny. "What happened?"

"There was a big accident at work—"

"I heard. My folks were freaking out about Ryan. I'm glad you're okay."

"Thanks. Let's just say my marriage couldn't survive me being home more than a week at a time."

Ted had been working three weeks on, one week off. And they'd hardly seen one another during that week off. Over time, their interactions had eased from furious lovemaking to obligatory lovemaking, to… awkward silence.

"I thought she was fooling around."

"Was she?"

"*Nah*." His reaction shamed him now, that instinct urging him to believe that if she wouldn't be with him, she must have given herself to someone else. *Though if she had, my lawyer would have been a lot happier.* In those last few months the only stranger in their bed had been him.

Ted was quiet for a while. "I could probably help you with your renos, if you're willing to let me crash on a couch or something," he offered.

"I could live with that." Jenny pulled the car over and parked. "Here we are."

Ted took a sip of coffee and caught sight of the tattoo on his hand. He sighed.

"You're sure you're okay with having someone who looks like me around? What'll the neighbours think?"

"Screw 'em. If you can swing a hammer and hang drywall, I don't care if you've turned purple. When can you stop by?"

"I have a few things to look into, but soon. Where's your place?"

She rattled off the address; it didn't mean anything to him as he typed it into his phone.

"Thanks, Jenny. For everything. Talk to you soon."

"No worries. It was nice to see you again." She cocked her index finger at him like it was a pistol. "Catch ya later."

Ted returned the gesture, but he wondered whether she'd regret that statement when later rolled around.

Ted settled into The Goat's driver's seat and lit a cigarette. He exhaled with a deep sigh and closed the door behind him. He set his coffee on the dash while he turned the engine over. The label caught his eye. Second Cup.

There had been a Second Cup by the shithole bar where Ted had first seen ZZ Top and the Smiler. In fact, the bar was right beside a tattoo shop. He'd passed it as he left the bar to make his way back to his car. It must have been one of the college or hipster districts, because he'd seen more tattoo and piercing shops than banks. Maybe someone there could tell him what he'd been inked with.

Traffic was a bitch. As Ted drew closer to the tattoo shop, his anxiety grew at every red light. He'd sit impatiently, as The Goat idled, tapping at the steering wheel. He must have skipped through forty songs before he crossed the bridge over the Assiniboine River. The hotel was in sight now, only a couple traffic lights away. Ted peeled off the road at the first side street after the bridge to look for a parking spot. He had to wind his way up and down a couple of residential streets before he found a free space. With the sun out, the area looked decidedly different than the shadow in his memory. The green canopies of large trees peeked over top of the old brick buildings that lined

Osborne Street. A couple of scraggly-looking buskers played guitar in front of a restaurant. Ted ignored them and crossed the street, keeping his head down, not wanting to look at the bar or the hotel.

Ted started to sweat as he took the steps down to the shop. Looking left he could see the bar, and to the right, about half a block away, the motor hotel where he'd been assaulted. He took a deep breath, steadied himself with a long exhale, and pulled the door open. A loud chime sounded as he stepped into the shop. He had to admit it wasn't what he was expecting.

It was clean.

He hadn't been in a tattoo parlour—did they even call them that anymore?—since he and the rest of the football team had got the ink to commemorate an undefeated season. *That shop hadn't looked like this, that was for sure.*

Behind the counter was a chubby bulldog-faced man, Winston Churchill with tattoos. He wore a hat, one of those button-down on the front affairs, like Sean Connery had in *The Untouchables*. He was reading a paper, and looked up from it long enough to nod at Ted. His arms were inked right to his fingers and if he wasn't an artist himself, the amount of work he'd had done pretty much ensured the only place that would hire him would be a tattoo shop.

Tattoo art covered the walls—koi fish, flowers, and pin-up girls—and there was a bookcase full of binders, presumably full of more of the same. Three girls who were sprawled on the leather couches chattered and laughed as they flipped through a photo album of tattoo images. They looked a little younger than Tilda, and entirely too thin. The shortest girl was Indian, the tallest a freckled redhead; in between them, like they'd been arranged by height, was a black girl with her hair cropped tightly to her scalp. Ted looked away; it was time to get some answers about his ink.

He rapped his fingers on the counter, and the guy in the hat looked up.

"How can I help you?" He was very soft-spoken. Ted was surprised. He was expecting… well, the place had already broken his expectations, but a quiet and polite tattoo shop-keep?

"Yeah," said Ted, "I need…." He struggled for the right word, glancing around until he saw a sign that said FREE CONSULTS, "a consult, I guess."

"Awesome. Getting more ink?"

"No," Ted shook his head.

The guy behind the counter looked confused.

"Look, this'll sound weird… and… hard to explain. I just want to get some advice on what these tattoos mean."

"You don't know?" the clerk asked, his nose wrinkled with what was possibly disdain. "You chose them didn't you? What, did you just get some pretty pictures and now—?"

"I didn't choose them!"

The girls on the couch stopped their conversation as Ted raised his voice. He could feel their stares boring into his back. Ted unclenched his hands. He sighed. "Look, I know I sound crazy, and I don't expect you to believe me—the cops sure didn't—but I was attacked in my hotel room. The guys who jumped me gave me these tattoos. I want to know if there's any meaning behind them. I want to understand what's happening."

Silence.

It was quiet behind him too; Ted craned his head around, and the girls, caught listening in, made an exaggerated display of going back to their conversation and flipping through the sample photo album.

The clerk nodded and set down his paper. It was a tabloid, with the headline: "Bloody night on Osborne," across the top. Beneath the header was a picture of Ted being led out of the motel. Fortunately, between a combination of dried blood and bad photography, it would be difficult for the average citizen to recognize him. At least he hoped it would be.

"That was you?"

Ted nodded.

Getting off of his stool, the clerk took Ted's right hand in his and turned it over. His eyes scrolled up the arm, following the metallic blue lines, and then he did the same with the gold lines on Ted's left hand and arm.

As Ted watched, slightly uncomfortable with the contact, he noted the work was beautifully done. But it would have been easier to appreciate if it wasn't on his body.

"These weren't done yesterday," the clerk said.

"They were."

The clerk raised an eyebrow and shrugged. "Well, they're definitely Norse."

Ted asked, "What, like vikings?"

"Yeah," the clerk said. "Like vikings. We have a guy here,

Robin, he specializes in Celtic and Norse stuff. He could probably tell you more."

"Is he here?"

"He will be," the clerk said, frowning. He flipped open an
appointment book on the counter. "He's got a back piece to do
today. It's scheduled for an eight-hour sitting."

"Jesus," Ted said. "Eight hours?"

"How long did yours take? If you don't mind me asking." Ted
could sense the eagerness in the man's voice, barely contained
by good manners.

Or good sense. Ted wanted to slug him. "I don't know," he
said, raising his voice, "I wasn't able to look at my watch while I
was tied down."

The girls behind him snickered, but the man behind the
counter held up his hands in a mollifying gesture. "Look, I'll try
Robin's cell, maybe he'll come in early."

Ted nodded and took a seat on the couch opposite the girls.
He crossed his arms and knew he wasn't keeping the scowl from
his face.

"Rob... Don... yeah... I know.... Look, can you come
in a bit early?" There was a loud squawk that sounded a lot
like "fuck." The clerk, Don, bobbed his head back and forth.
"Yeah, yeah, I know you're doing a back piece today. It's just
a consult. Trust me, you're gonna wanna see the work this
guy's had done."

Ted closed his eyes and tried to tune out Don's loud cellphone
conversation. He felt a tap on his knee.

It was one of the girls. The Indian one.

"Hey, mister," she said, a tremor in her voice. "Did… did your tattoos hurt?"

"Yes," Ted said simply, hoping she'd leave him alone.

"A lot?" she pressed.

"Yes," he told her, "a lot. It felt like I was being burned alive and smothered at the same time. Happy?"

"No," she said, her face growing ashen.

Ted opened his eyes as hard-soled footsteps approached him. It was Don.

"You're in luck. Robin'll see you when he gets here."

"When will that be?" Ted asked.

Don bit at his bottom lip and bobbed his head slightly. "His appointment is at two. He'll see you… maybe one thirty? That okay?"

Ted looked at his watch. Twelve fifteen.

"Guess I better get some lunch."

Don went back to the counter, and his paper.

A heavy-set woman with a shaved head came out from the back of the shop; she, too, was a walking billboard for the tattooing art. She scowled at the girls on the couches, but nodded appreciatively towards Ted.

It was small comfort to know he'd always be accepted at tattoo shops, biker bars, and probably the circus.

"All right," the woman said loudly, "who's Nika?"

"Me," squeaked the girl who'd talked to Ted.

"Get your ass in here, princess."

The girl, Nika, cast a nervous glance at her friends as she followed the artist into the back of the shop.

"Can… can my friends come too?" Nika asked.

"If you need to hold someone's hand," the woman shrugged without looking back.

"Guys?" Nika pleaded, turning towards the couches and motioning with her hands.

Her friends didn't look up from the photo albums.

"Who would get a tattoo on her butt?" One asked the other. "Let alone take a picture of the fat, ugly thing."

Ted rolled his eyes and went to get some lunch.

He sat in the Second Cup playing with his Zippo. A small newspaper called the Northern Miner had been stuffed into his effects. It wasn't his, but he read it. Maybe Moustache or one of the Beards had left it in the room. There was mention of a blood drive sponsored by Svarta Mining, an article about the sharp decline of northern caribou herds, and a puff piece about the mine's record profits last quarter. His bowl of soup came and he set the paper down with a sigh, ate, and tried to relax while he waited for Robin, the Norse Tattoo Guy.

He had those goofy plugs in his earlobes, the kind that stretched them out to a ridiculous extent. Ted figured if he popped them out, he'd be able to fit his whole hand through the flap of hanging skin on the guy's ear. He was youngish, of course. A communist army hat tilted back revealed the stubble of a shaved head. He tossed his jacket behind the counter and the wife-beater he wore revealed the brightly coloured tattoos on his arms. So many, Ted had to stare to find a spot of skin not covered. A paper coffee cup was in his hand and Ted could smell the stale cigarette smoke coming off of him.

Ted stood up from the couch and walked over. "You Robin?"

"Yeah," he said.

"Ted."

"Hey. You the guy who needed the consult?"

Ted nodded. Robin clapped a hand on Ted's shoulder and took a sip of his coffee.

"Look man, I have a bitch of a day ahead of me, so we'll have to make this quick. What do you want done?"

Ted shook his head. "It's not what I want done. I need you tell me about what's already been done."

"Right, right," Robin said slowly, nodding. "I generally don't like working over another man's ink. Well, let's head in the back and take a look."

Again, Ted was surprised by the room that he was led into. He could have believed the cleanliness of the shop's front was to put customers at ease, but even the tattoo rooms were immaculate. It felt more like he was in a doctor's office. White walls, a raised table to lie down on. Supplies all individually packaged and marked "sterile." Of course, these white walls had sketches of dragons and intricate knots all over them instead of block-mounted Monet prints. Over the table was a large mirror. Ted watched Robin's reflection drop an iPod into a speaker port and hit the shuffle button.

"You mind?" he asked.

"Nope."

The tattoo artist nodded as Black Sabbath's "War Pigs" came over the speakers. "Cool. Well, don't be shy, let's see the ink."

Ted pulled the knit cap off of his head, tossing it onto the bench and then pulled the long-sleeved shirt up and over his head. He felt weird, undressing in front of this complete stranger. *What part of the last few days haven't been weird?*

Robin whistled, and Ted could hear it over the music. He had his eyes closed, he'd been avoiding his reflection since he'd taken the first long, clean look while he'd been in custody.

Get used to it. You'll be looking at it for the rest of your life.

"Shit, man, who did this?"

"It's that bad?" Ted winced.

"I've been tattooing ten years and never seen anything like this. Did they do it with a machine or traditional?"

Ted wasn't sure what was traditional about getting carved up with a knife in a motel bed, but he remembered his first tattoo, back in his football days. ZZ Top hadn't used a tattoo gun. "Traditional."

"Nice," Robin muttered, more to himself than Ted. "Always wanted to learn to do that. Do you have the guy's card?"

Ted shook his head.

"Damn, where'd you get it done? I might know the shop."

"The motor inn down the street."

"No way!" Robin said, incredulous. "Quit shitting me."

"I shit you not. I can't help you find the guys who did this, cause if I find them, they're dead. They tied me up, and inked me for some twisted reason. I'm just trying to figure out why."

"What, you're saying they did this, without a machine, with you tied up, in one night?"

"Yeah, evidently it was front-page news."

Robin shrugged; he obviously believed Ted was fucking with him. "Don't read the paper enough I guess."

"So why isn't it possible?"

"It takes longer to tattoo the old way, and they did your entire back, arms, and chest. Outline, shading, colour. It's not possible. No one could sit long enough to get the work done, and no artist would work that long. You said there was more than one artist? Even then… this is the kind of work you'd get done over months, years even."

"Years?"

"More for the cost, man. I charge two hundred an hour, and I'm reasonable. Someone this good…." Robin whistled again. "Shit, you've got tens of thousands of dollars of ink on you."

"Great, wish I could use them to pay off my lawyer."

Robin laughed. "If you want to get these removed, I'd start with this shitty football though, doesn't fit the rest of your theme."

"It's still there?" Ted felt his heart pounding. He was worried it had been covered over. That he'd lost that part of himself.

"Yeah," Robin said.

"I got it when I was eighteen, our football team went undefeated. Coach paid for all of the starters to get the tattoo with their number, the date and undefeated."

"Nice of him."

"Got him in some hot water," Ted said. "Not all of us were eighteen. A few parents raised a stink about it, but—"

"No one fires the coach after an undefeated season."

"Exactly," Ted agreed. "Christ, my mother still brings up that tattoo over Thanksgiving turkey. What the fuck will she say now?"

The tattoo artist laughed. "Aren't you a little old to worry about what your mother has to say?"

Ted shook his head. "You've never met my mother."

"Well, at least these don't look like shit." Ted felt a light touch trail over his back, and he knew instinctively it was following one of the designs on his flesh. "No scabbing... these couldn't have been done recently."

"That's what Don said."

"He was right." Robin pointed at the football tattoo. "You remember how long it took that to heal?"

Ted didn't. It had been over twenty years ago.

"Whatever, man," Robin said noncommittally. "So what do you wanna know?"

"What do they mean?"

"Tattoo's gotta mean something?" Robin asked.

"They usually do," Ted said, suddenly unsure of himself. "Don't they?"

Robin nodded. "Usually they do. If only to the guy paying. These though, you're right, they do have some deep mythology behind them."

"And?"

"Look, I can tell you the basics. I'm no folklorist."

"I thought you were the Norse tattoo guy."

"I am," Robin said. "That means I'm good at inking them, not that I know Thor personally. I just look at the pictures, I don't read the books."

"Fuck," Ted muttered.

Ted could hear Robin looking in a drawer for something. "But I pick up shit. Everyone yammers on and fuckin' on about what their tattoo means to them, and the history behind it. Mostly I just tune them out and pay attention to Sabbath, but every now and then, something sticks. Okay man, seriously, open your eyes, you need to see what I'm pointing at."

Ted complied. Robin was wearing a pair of magnifying goggles, the long plastic kind that model painters used for really fine detail work. He'd also pulled a small circular mirror on an accordion mount from the wall.

"Okay, turn around. Your back has some pretty interesting shit going on, that's where I want to start."

Ted did so, and leaned on the table for support. Robin played with the mirror's position.

He asked, "Can you see your whole back now?"

Ted nodded.

"'Kay. Here goes." Robin traced the lines on Ted's back with a pointer that looked like a broken-off car antenna. "The tree here, going up your spine?"

"Yeah." The tree topped out across Ted's shoulder blades, the leaves spreading to envelop much of his back. The trunk ran the length of his spine, its roots disappearing below his belt line.

"It looks solid, but if you look close enough, its trunk is made up of different symbols, all tightly packed together. Give it a few years and some sun and they'll likely bleed together and you'd never know it, but for now they're really crisp. The symbols are the Elder Runes. I've tattooed enough of them to know that. Each leaf has a rune engraved too. It looks like all twenty-four are represented. The tree is Yggdrasill." As the artist spoke the word, its odd spelling came to Ted, as if he'd dredged it up from some half-remembered childhood story. "The vikings called it the World Tree or World Ash. I've done a few of them in my time, but nothing like this."

Robin paused, then said: "Hey, do you mind if I take some photos of this? It's not my work, but shit, now that I see what he did? Gives me all kinds of ideas."

Ted wasn't keen on letting the guy photograph him, but after a moment decided it didn't really matter.

"Whatever."

"Cool, man. Cool."

Robin pulled a digital camera from one of the drawers nearby, and set it down on his workstation.

Ted clenched and unclenched his right fist, where the hammerhead was. On both the top and bottom of his forearm, identical images had been inked. When Ted closed his hand into a fist, the hammerhead that ended across his knuckles lined up perfectly with the one on his palm. Where the handle should have ended was a stylized man's face with a conical helmet atop his head.

"Thor's hammer," Robin said. "Mjölnir. Each of the Nordic nations has their own version of it. This one is Icelandic. Piss off anyone from Gimli?"

"Doubtful, never been there."

"Oh. Lot of Icelanders up north of the city." Ted couldn't help but notice that everyone in Manitoba referred to Winnipeg as the city, *but where else would they be talking about? Portage la Prairie?*

"They even have a festival up in Gimli every August, Ingledingle or something like that. Prime Minister or President—whatever the fuck they have in Iceland—comes out for it."

Gimli, again.

He had to track down Tilda. Ted wondered if she'd left Winnipeg already. It shouldn't be too hard to find her in a small town. She didn't strike him as the type who could blend. Not that he could either. Not anymore.

"What about the sun?" Ted said holding out his left hand.

"Every culture has some kind of sun god or myth. I don't know anything about it in relation to the Norse. Mustn't have been too important." Robin shrugged. "Or maybe it is, I don't know. I've tattooed hundreds of suns, man, they all kinda blend together. The horn though, that I know."

It coiled around Ted's arm like creeping ivy. The bell of the horn opened on the back of his left hand.

"One of the gods, I forget his name…." Robin was talking faster, almost excited, "he blew this horn to warn the other gods when their home was attacked, or the end of the world was coming, one or the other, maybe both. It summoned all the dead warriors to fight for the gods." He tapped one of the raven tattoos. "And the ravens, I know these ravens.

"Odin, he was the head god. You know like God of the gods. He had this pair of ravens, Thought and Memory—he called them something else—this is only what I remember. Every morning they went into the world to get information for him, and then they'd perch on his shoulders, whispering what they'd learned."

"So I can expect to start hearing voices?" Ted said harshly.

Robin screwed his face into a grimace. "It's just a story, man, nothing more. Look, I don't know why this happened to you, but look on the bright side. There are people who would kill to have this kind of work done on them. Me included."

A knock at the door cut Ted off before he could tell Robin where to shove his tattoo gun.

Don opened the door a crack. "Rob, your appointment's here."

"Shit, man," Robin said to Ted, "I gotta do this. He booked, like, a year ago. Let me snap those photos, and leave your number with Don, I'll see if I can dig anything up."

Ted nodded and ground his teeth while the tattoo artist fiddled with camera settings. Robotically he followed Robin's directions, so the man could capture an image of each of Ted's tattoos.

Robin gave him a thumbs-up. "Thanks man. You're good to go."

Ted pulled his shirt back on, settled his cap over his ears and walked out of the room. He nodded to Don, still sitting at the front counter as he walked out the door. He'd given Don his number for the consult earlier, and didn't feel like hanging around any longer. Not when they viewed what had been done to him like some kind of fucking gift.

The sky was overcast; white lines of cloud stood out against the grey in a line along the western horizon. He'd never made much of a habit of playing weatherman, but when you work outdoors most of your life, you learn to pay attention to the signs nature gives you.

And a storm was coming.

He could feel it in his bones; the tattoos that covered his chest itched in agreement. Ted unlocked his phone and entered the number Tilda had left him.

It rang four times. Ted was getting ready to end the call, before voicemail kicked in and he had just started to leave an awkward message, when a breathless but young-sounding woman came on the line.

"*Bonjour?*"

French. Why did she have to speak French? Ted had picked up enough German from Ryan's family to be able to get his point across, but the French he remembered was pretty much limited to Sesame Street. He hoped he'd been left the right number.

"Hi… Tilda left me this—"

"Hi Ted!" She sounded far too excited to be talking to a stranger. Her English held only the faintest hint of an accent. "I'm Melody. Til will be so happy you called. She was really starting to worry."

"Was?"

"Yeah, she caught the Greyhound home this morning."

Shit.

"Do you have a number for her?"

There was silence on the line. But Melody spoke after a few

moments. "You know, this is kinda embarrassing. I'm sure I have it written down somewhere, but I've never called her there. Every time I get it in my head that I want to talk to Tilda, she calls before I can find the number." She laughed. "Like she's psychic, or something."

Or something, indeed.

"Well, if she dials you up on the Psychic Hotline, you want to let her know I want to talk to her?"

"Sure thing." Melody hadn't hung up, like she was waiting for something. "Hey—"

"Yeah?"

"Have fun in Gimli."

"Unlikely," Ted said, "but thanks for the good thought."

"Cheers, Ted." There was an electronic beep as Melody ended the call.

Gimli.

Ted looked up at the ominous sky and said the thought aloud. "Gimli."

He rubbed at his itching chest and, in the distance, heard the peal of thunder.

5. THE UGLY TRUTH

Ted ran to where The Goat was parked as the first fat drops of rain began to fall. Fuck sakes, the first time he'd had the GTO out of storage in years and it would get hail damage. He sure as hell wasn't going to hit the highway until the brewing storm blew over. Fortunately, downtowns are always filled with parkades.

The storm was already doing an admirable job of sending buskers and bums for shelter, and it was still growing. Sheets of lightning charged through the clouds and gave the sky a strange yellowish cast he'd rarely seen in Alberta. His imagination was playing tricks on him. In the afterimages of the lightning flashes, the clouds took on monstrous shapes.

He rounded the corner by the Second Cup and kept going past a large gothic-styled church. The Goat was parked on a narrow residential street, the kind that only allowed parking on one side, and Ted could tell immediately that someone had fucked him. A car had snuck in behind him and somebody's piece of shit Beemer was sitting flush with the stop sign to the front of the GTO.

The sedan was small enough that if he'd had a buddy with him, they could have bounce-moved it forward enough so that he could have rocked The Goat out of the tight spot. Hell, with a couple guys they could have just flipped the Beemer on its side to teach the fucker a lesson in parking etiquette. When the guys from the patch hit Edmonton for their week off a lot of such lessons happened.

He clenched his fist to slam it into the offending car, but stopped short, remembering what he'd done to the bouncers in the hotel. Water slid down his face as raindrops slapped into him with more frequency. There was no telling what would happen if he punched the car, but he had a feeling it would leave more than a dent. He'd either flip it on its side—or knowing his luck—into the house it was parked in front of. Ted didn't need much room. Maybe a foot, though two would be better.

It was time to see how strong the bearded freaks had made him.

Ted didn't know much about European cars. He couldn't remember if BMWs were front- or rear-wheel drive. It shouldn't matter, for how little he'd be moving the car. The worst-case scenario was he'd wear down the tire treads. *Like I give a shit.* There was a bright red tow hook lying flush to the right side of the car's bumper. Ted glanced around to see if there was anyone on the streets, but the rain had sent any potential witnesses running. Flipping up the hook, he gripped it with his hammer hand and centred his body over the point.

Here goes.

He lifted, expecting some resistance. He knew he was stronger than he had been, but the Beemer may as well have been made by Hot Wheels. The car's alarm sounded as soon as the tires left the ground. Ted ignored the noise and took a few steps backward and let the car drop.

He'd lifted a car. A fucking car. *What did those freaks do to me?*

There was enough room to get The Goat out now, and if the parking patrol happened by, the BMW might even get towed. The thought made Ted smile as he hustled back to open the GTO's driver's side door.

He drove away, the screeching alarm of the Beemer following him accusingly. Ted flicked on the wipers, hearing them squeal across the windshield, and sank into the bucket seat. He soaked up the rumble of the engine as he idled at a stoplight. The driver in front of him hadn't left enough room for Ted to sneak past and make his turn.

"Fuck, buddy!" Ted yelled to himself.

The light changed, and the car in front darted across the intersection. Ted pointed The Goat north, and headed downtown for the shelter of a parkade to wait out the weather.

There was a multi-story parking facility attached to the Hudson's Bay Company. He had driven past it after dropping Tilda off. The wipers were having a hard time keeping up with the rain, and the patter against the windshield was sharp now, like rice hitting a metal bowl. Ted rolled down the window, pressed the button to release his ticket and raise the arm blocking the drive into the parkade. His coat was soaked through in the moment the action took, the arm rose and he drove into the skeletal concrete and headed up.

Ted wanted to be able to watch the sky while he enjoyed the

safety provided by Impark. He stopped one level short of the open-air top. He parked The Goat and got out of the car, pulling his coat off and wringing out the wet sleeve. The sounds of the rain and hail were deafening—like being at a Motörhead concert. His jacket he left on the passenger seat and he closed the door, locking it. From the western edge of the parkade Ted had a good view of the storm. He looked out over the city, watching the lightning and rain.

There was a NO SMOKING sign posted just a metre or so from where Ted was standing. He tipped an imaginary cap to it before tapping a cigarette free from its pack and into his mouth. Ted flicked the lid open on his Zippo and ignited it with a snap of his thumb and middle finger. He savoured the scent of the butane for a moment before holding the flame to the cigarette and taking a deep drag.

Ted couldn't wait for the tattoo guy to get back to him—assuming he ever would. Instead, he opened the web browser on his phone, and Googled Norse mythology. The Wikipedia entry was the first link to pop up, and he tapped the screen to take him to the webpage.

There were paintings of Thor and Odin along the right of the screen, too small on his phone to make out any details, or artistic merit. Like he was any fucking judge of art. *That had always been her thing.* Ted shook his head, and tried to knock his ex from his thoughts. As always, it was easier said than done. The painting of Thor, hammer raised and doing battle with monsters, was above a sombre grey image of his father, Odin, who stared ahead with his one eye, alternately sad or accusing, depending on how Ted tilted the phone.

Was Odin sad his creation had come to an end? Or that he had, in the mouth of a giant wolf?

Troubled, Ted looked up from the phone. Why had he thought that? He didn't know shit about mythology. Raven calls were echoing throughout the structure. Sharp and piercing, like they were right next to him. He dug his fingers into his ears, trying to block their cries, but they did not diminish. The tattoo on his chest was tingling in time with the rolling thunder, and the wind rushing through the parkade was both loud as a scream and soft as a whisper. He scratched at his neck and forced his attention back to his phone.

The page talked of gods and heroes, of books called *Eddas* and rune stones. Many words displayed blue, a link to another page solely about that subject. Sigurd the Volsung, invincible hero and dragonslayer, and other, stranger words that should have neither meaning nor place in Ted's life.

But they did.

He squinted his eyes shut, trying to ignore the echoes of the birds' squawking. With each raven call another image flashed. He knew the creatures, the people and gods as if he had lived among them. And the time as if it had occurred yesterday. His heart thundered and his head throbbed. Somehow this invasion of his mind hurt every bit as much as what Moustache and the Beards had done to Ted's body. The harder he fought the flashes the faster they came. This shouldn't be happening. It was impossible.

But lately, impossible was making reality its bitch.

Ted locked the screen on the phone and slid it into his pocket.

The images stopped flashing, the immediacy of the knowledge they'd brought faded. He still felt every rush of blood to his head like a ringing hammer blow.

Doom.

Ted closed his mind to the wind and whispers.

Tilda. She knew more than she'd told him in The Goat. He wasn't sure what to think of her fortune-telling, but he was certain of one thing—what was happening to him belonged more in her world than his. He was going to Gimli, and no fucking storm was going to stop him. A hailstone, blown into the parkade, shattered a car's rear window.

But it might delay him.

"I wouldn't do that if I were you," said a voice from behind Ted.

He spun around to see a man leaning against The Goat, rubbing a hand appreciatively over the trunk of the car.

The Smiler.

Ted could feel his nostrils flaring as he took a few short, angry breaths. "*You.*"

"Hey, Ted."

The Smiler made a point of ignoring Ted as he closed the distance between them, only looking up when Ted grasped a handful of the man's ill-fitting suit that looked like it had been slept in.

"I see that violence remains your first option," the Smiler noted. He had shaved his beard and moustache since the first time they'd spoken. He'd also lost the glasses. Pinprick white scars decorated the skin above and below his lips.

Ted spun the man away from The Goat and gave him a shove. The Smiler was nimble on his feet and didn't fall over.

"Keep flapping your jaws and I'll sew your fucking mouth shut for you again." Ted stopped short, surprised. Why had he said that? He wasn't sure, but he tried to keep the confusion from his face. The ravens called loudly in a mocking staccato.

The man just smiled back at him. "So you are starting to listen," he said cryptically. "And to remember."

"Remember what, exactly?" Ted asked.

"Who I am."

"And just who the fuck are you?" Ted said, exasperated.

"Loki."

"Loki? Loki?" Ted rolled his eyes. "My fucking dog was named Loki."

"A role, I think, I played to some acclaim." The Smiler nodded, then bowed theatrically and spread his arms wide. "You don't believe me?"

"Of course I don't."

Shrugging, the Smiler continued. "I certainly enjoyed watching Susanna in the shower. And those rare occasions when you were home from work and rutting like fools. Who was there and wagging his tail? Friendly old Loki."

"Our dog was female, you stupid fuck."

Ted felt ridiculous, latching on *that* as the point that didn't make sense.

The Smiler nodded. "Another role circumstance saw me in from time to time."

"And dead," Ted added.

"Ah yes, now that was the greatest part that I have ever played. How better to escape my enemies than to let them think they'd won?"

Ted shook his head. "You're crazy as a shithouse rat."

"And you're still alive thanks to me."

"Yeah, that mistletoe you gave me worked like a fucking charm all right."

"Maybe you shouldn't have ruined it. It was a lovely boutonniere, after all."

Ted stepped closer, practically resting his forehead on the crown of the Smiler's head. "Look what they did to me." He held up his palms.

"The *dvergar*? They gave you power." He drifted off for a moment, frowning, his eyes not focusing on Ted. "They always gave us power, why they never used it against us, I'll never know. I certainly would have." The smile was back in an instant. "I didn't lie when I said they meant to kill you. They did. Had I not spoken to you, had I not provoked you, they still would have come for you. But instead of each thrice gifting you, you'd be dead. Want to know how?"

He must have suspected what Ted's answer would be, as he didn't wait to hear it.

"Let me tell you. You would never have reached that room. They'd have slit you here. And here." He turned and drew two lines on his back with a finger. "Then pulled your lungs through your back and left you to bleed out in an alley while you died gasping your last tortured breaths amongst the city filth. It's been a while since anyone has been given a blood eagle." He turned back and jabbed at Ted. "So, you're bloody welcome."

Ted grimaced. That was an unsettling image. "So why didn't they?"

"They believed that you'd angered me, and they were right. That pleased them." Loki ran his fingers over his scars. "We have, in their minds, an unpaid debt and they must have loved the idea of again handing out power, but not to me. No, never to me. It was me who had the walls of Asgard built. Me, who earned Odin his spear. Me, who won the thunder god his hammer. What did I ever get? What was left for Loki? Nothing!"

"Focus, Loki." Ted put sarcastic emphasis on the name.

"You don't believe me; but you've called me by my name, it's a start. What were we talking about again?" Loki asked, his smile feigning innocence.

"Me," Ted said. "And those bearded fucks."

"Ah yes, of course, *you*. How foolish of me. The dwarves have had enough of this age of man, and your 'science.'" Loki actually made the quotation marks with his fingers. "They long for a return to their old ways. A return to doing what they have always done. They want the magic to rule Midgard—that's Earth, Teddy—and they had to start somewhere. They must have decided to start with you."

"Why me?"

"Ah, a question I often asked myself during my eternity of punishment."

"And?"

"Oh, I suppose that I deserved it. At least in their eyes."

Ted made a strangled sound and clutched at his head.

"You were asking about yourself, of course," the Smiler noted.

"You're as quick as the myths say," Ted said tightly.

"Why thank you, Theodore. Do you prefer Ted or Theodore? I think I'll call you Ted."

"I'd prefer you answer me."

Loki cocked his head to the side quizzically. "About what?"

"Why? Me." Ted said, tapping violently at his breastbone.

"It's simple, really," Loki said, and Ted caught a glint of flame in his eyes. "You'd already been touched by a remnant of one of the Nine Worlds."

"The rig fire." The words were barely a whisper. Much louder, ringing in his memory, Ted heard the giant's laugh. *Lock, lock, lock.*

"Yes, when your people woke Surtur—well done, by the way, he plans to start up where he left off."

"I knew that giant was real. No one believed me."

"Why should they? What in their puny, boring lives would allow them to believe that a nihilistic fire giant was planning to destroy the Earth? If you hadn't seen that, would you accept that you were talking to a god? Or that some tight-assed little hitch-hiker wanted you?" Loki pursed his lips and made a kneading motion with his hands.

"She… what?"

"Ted, foolish, naïve Ted." Loki chuckled as he spoke. "Free spirit or no, no girl shows her tits to a complete stranger like that without good reason—or liquor—especially for an out-of-work, homeless, divorcee twice her age. Your tie to the Nine

Worlds, tenuous though it was then, must have pulled at her. I can't believe you didn't take the ride when offered."

"I can't believe you fucked a horse and an ogre."

Loki grinned wide as if reliving the moment. "Not at the same time, Ted. Not at the same time. Horses are jealous brutes. I'm glad those meddlesome ravens are starting to do their work. It would be a long drive if I had to fill you in on everything."

Ted touched the sides of his neck, and each of the raven tattoos in turn. Thought and Memory. *Huginn* and *Muninn*. The cawing whispers weren't coming from birds in the parkade. They were coming from his tattoos.

And he understood them.

Finally, Huginn said.

This is what should have been, Muninn added.

On a field of bright colours, the Smiler and a larger, bearded viking man lay bleeding and broken. The horn tattooed upon Ted's left arm lay cloven beside them.

Heimdall should have killed you, Muninn hissed.

The raven's words left Ted's lips before he realized he was speaking. Loki rolled his eyes and picked at a fingernail with his teeth. "The day I couldn't outwit that old bore…." He waved off whatever Ted was going to utter next. "The world was ending. It was easy enough to slip away in the chaos."

"You betrayed your family, why should I trust you?"

Loki's face blazed, red as a lobster, and Ted smelled smoke. "They were never my family. You should know that much if you know anything. They killed my family. Cast out my children as monsters. The Aesir reaped what they had sown."

Like after a summer storm on the prairie his demeanour quickly shifted, the clouds thinned, the sun returned to his eyes and he smiled warmly.

"I will not betray you, Ted. I was a friend to the Aesir once, despite what they had done to me and mine. I would like to be yours."

Lies, Huginn said.

He always betrays. Loki knows nothing else. See how he caused the best of Odin's sons to be struck down. See how Baldur died.

Another scene flickered across Ted's mind. A glowing man, bright as the sun, and in the prime of youth, was laughing as mugs of beer, arrows, and knives were hurled at him. All bounced away, leaving the man untouched. Ted looked down at the sun that had been tattooed on his palm; the ink had the same golden hue as the man. The glow faded from Baldur as an arrow fletched with leaves, not unlike the boutonniere that Loki had worn in the bar, struck him. A drop of blood blossomed against his chest and he fell to the ground.

Dead.

"So I can look over my shoulder for the rest of my life waiting for a mistletoe dart?"

"Just never turn your back on a blind man." Loki clapped his hands happily. "Besides, it will take a lot more than mistletoe to kill you now."

"What will?"

"That girl you've been trying to go a-viking with, more likely than not."

"Tilda?"

Loki tapped his nose and pointed at Ted.

"I find that hard to believe."

"Would you find it harder to believe that a Norse god is living in Winnipeg? That you have been gifted with the power of the Aesir? Those things have happened, and yet, you refuse to believe a woman can betray you."

"*Your wife didn't.*" Ted grimaced. Again, one of the ravens had spoken through his lips.

"She was my jailer," Loki said, gnashing his teeth. "And it was in the form of a woman that I refused to weep for slain Baldur, trapping him in my daughter's grey kingdom of the dead. It was meant to be a prank, to show them their foolishness. But… there are too many hormones in the human female. Clouds the judgement. Every mistake I ever made was as a woman."

"Yeah," Ted said with exaggerated understanding. "I'm sure that's just what your problem was. You tried to end the world because of PMS." Ted sighed. "So where do I go from here?"

"I can't take too heavy a hand in this, Ted, the Norns will be looking for me. They have opposed me since I found a way around the doom they'd spun for me."

There was that word again. Doom.

"What the fuck are Norns?" Ted asked.

Loki shook his head, presumably at Ted's lack of reaction. "You know of my wife, you know of Baldur, and you don't know the Norns?"

"Haven't come across them on Wikipedia yet."

"Watch what you read, then, a lot of lies on there. And you've already met one of the Norns."

"I have?"

"How many other seers have you met in Winnipeg, anyway? Are you that thick?"

Tilda.

Ted said nothing while Loki rubbed at his shaven cheeks. "You could speak to my son, instead," he offered. "He sees more than you'd expect."

No.

Do not.

The trickster's children are even more monstrous than he, Huginn and Muninn warned.

They showed Loki standing, smiling behind three figures. A pretty—if somewhat thin—girl sat with her right side towards Ted. On one side of the girl was a towering black wolf. White froth dripped from its hungry mouth. To the girl's other side was the head of a coiled serpent. Every breath the thing belched was poison. Its tail stretched past the horizon. The girl didn't seem to belong between the two beasts. And then she turned. Ted shuddered. Half of her body was a fire-blackened skeleton.

Sarcastically, Ted asked, "Wolf or dragon?"

"Dragon," Loki said, nodding. "Definitely the dragon. Though technically, Jormungandur is a sea serpent, dragons have limbs. He's easier to find. Jorry's big enough to circle the world after all. Fenrir's get will likely find you, sooner or later. Even I have no sway with them anymore."

"So how am I supposed to find this 'Jorry' of yours then?" Ted asked, exaggerating the "Y" sound of the name. It's a bit of a hike to the ocean."

"Find a lake, preferably one with a history of monster sightings or strange occurrences. He will feel the touch of the Old Power and the scent of the Nine Worlds on you. It should be enough to make him appear, if not help you."

"So how the hell am I going to get to Scotland? I'm broke."

"No need to go so far afield Ted. Ever heard of Manipogo?"

Ted shook his head.

"Ogopogo?"

"Sure." It was the Loch Ness Monster of the Okanagan Lake in British Columbia.

"Same idea, but in Lake Manitoba. Every sea serpent or lake monster sighting is just someone spotting my boy."

"Right," Ted said.

"Or a drunk."

Now that, Ted believed.

"So where is Lake Manitoba?" It had been a while since Ted had looked at a provincial map. "Is that the big one? The one Gimli is on?"

"No," Loki said. "It's the other one. But if you're dead set on seeing your prospective rutting partner again, Jorry will be in Lake Winnipeg too. He usually avoids it. Too many people in Gimli know his name, and even that small belief… it's like a lakeside buffet that's just out of reach. He also fears the Norns. He should be dead too, after all. Let's get an ox head. We'll go fishing. It'll be just like the good old days."

"I'm not taking The Goat out in a hailstorm," Ted said. "Not on some ridiculous errand to see your bastard dragon son."

"If you don't like the weather," Loki said, grinning wide, "do something about it."

Ted turned his back on the deranged wannabe god, and immediately regretted it. He stood looking out over the rain-drenched city, its trees bending in the wind, and tensed. Waiting for a blade to slide between his ribs.

He clenched and unclenched his fist, watching the tattoo of Thor's hammer. He tried to ignore the whispering of Thought and Memory, their rasping voices suddenly louder than the storm.

It is yours. The sky power, Huginn said. **Call to it.**

Shafts of sunlight pierced the heavy clouds like spears, extending from heaven to stab the earth, while pins and needles prickled at his chest, spreading and dulling to a mild tingle as the sensation reached his extremities. Despite the sun, rain still fell and the storm hung over most of Winnipeg, and Ted couldn't help but think of the Creedence song.

"Have you ever seen the rain?" Ted whispered to himself.

"That's it," Loki's voice took on a croaky Muppet-like quality. "Let go of your anger."

Ted hated *Star Wars*. That had been his brother Mike's thing. The sun disappeared behind the clouds and the rain returned.

Loki sighed. "I cannot teach him, there is too much anger in him."

Ted made a fist and took a large step towards Loki. "Mention *Star Wars* one more goddamn time…."

He smiled as the smaller man shrank from him and moved to cover his face. He had him. No god should be worried by a smack to the jaw. Something slammed into his hand, striking the tattoo. The flash was so bright that Ted went blind. He stumbled over his own feet and fell to the cement. The sharp bite of ozone filled his nostrils. Thunder crashed, shaking the parkade.

"Christ!" Ted yelled. "That one was right on top of us."

"On top of you, actually." Loki said. "I warned you about your anger."

Ted's nose felt burned, like he'd gotten a whiff of sulphur, but beneath that stink, he could smell something else. Something burning. Wisps of smoke passed his slowly clearing vision and he realized what was burning. Him.

"Christ!" he swatted at his clothes frantically, but he felt no heat from the flames.

"You're on fire," Loki said calmly.

Since the rig explosion, fire had haunted Ted's dreams— nightmares—and his moans became higher pitched as he clumsily tried to extinguish the source of the fire.

"Don't worry, you won't burn, you can't burn. Not anymore. The *dvergar* have seen to that."

Spots drifted across the plane of Ted's vision. He blinked tears from his eyes, but everything was slightly soft focus, like some art school film. His clothes were in tatters. Scorched holes pockmarked his pants and shirt. He was suddenly glad he'd left his jacket in the car.

"Your clothes *will* burn, though, for future reference."

Ted ignored Loki's lecturing tone. The thunderclap was

still ringing in his ears, and he felt a tingling in his fingertips. *Struck by lightning.* He'd always wondered what that would feel like, how someone could survive it. He was glad he hadn't shit himself.

Clouds of black ink rolled over his hand just beneath the skin. White electricity arced, dancing over the tattoo of Mjölnir. Ted reached out hesitantly to touch the hammer's image. His finger brushed his palm. There was no shock, just the same tingle he'd felt in his chest. The power was beneath the skin, mingling with whatever the dwarves had used to mark him.

Behind him, the sky was clearing. Sunlight cast long shadows across the parkade. The constant hammering of the rain had slowed to an uneven patter as it dripped from the edges of the ceiling. Ted ignored the sights and sounds. He couldn't stop staring at the thunderstorm playing out in miniature within his palm. He only looked up when he felt a finger poke repeatedly into his chest.

"I said, do you want me to get you some new clothes?"

Ted nodded dumbly. Loki reached out and heaved Ted to his feet with a grunt. The ravens' whispers started to fill his ears again.

Don't trust him. You don't know everything.

He betrayed us before.

Strike.

Strike.

No better than Surtur.

Pressing his hands over the heads of the raven tattoos did nothing to silence them.

Who to trust? A lunatic claiming to be a Norse god? Or talking tattoos some freaks had carved into his head? Hearing voices was never a good sign. Had the explosion broken him? Had there even been any dwarves?

"Shut up." Ted forced the words past a clenched jaw as the cawing voices continued trying to sow mistrust. "I said shut up! You'll give me advice when I ask for it."

If hearing voices was bad, answering them must be *worse*. They did stop, however.

At least they listen.

"Here you go," Loki said, tossing a bag at Ted.

Ted caught the parcel, feeling the lump of fabric within.

"That was fast," he said, pulling the clothing out. Tags dangled from the lightly washed blue jeans and three-quarter T with black sleeves and a grey torso.

Loki smiled. "I find retail transactions go much faster when one avoids the checkout counter."

"Stolen?"

"Do you have the money to pay me back?"

"No," Ted said with a sigh. "I don't."

"Then yes, they're stolen. Is that a problem?"

Ted stared down at the ravaged pants he was wearing. If he walked down to the street, he'd be picked up for public indecency. He wasn't too keen on seeing the inside of the police station for a while.

"No, I guess it isn't." When Ted was satisfied there was no one else around, he peeled himself out of his charred clothes. The shirt had Maiden Manitoba across the chest, written in the Iron

Maiden font. As he pulled it over his head, Ted was glad for the longer sleeves; they helped hide his tattoos. He'd better get used to people looking at them, though. This was how he looked now, and Ted doubted very much that laser removal was an option.

The clothes were a good fit. Loki obviously had an eye for men's sizes, despite his own ill-fitting suit.

A prolonged bleat from The Goat's horn shook Ted from his reverie.

"Move your ass," Loki said. "We're losing the light."

Ted stared at the car for a long moment. He still didn't trust his unwanted advisor. But what else did he have planned for today?

6. MISERY LOVES COMPANY

Following Loki's directions, Ted made it out of the city with only a small amount of profanity. The traffic on Highway 9 eased once Winnipeg started to diminish behind The Goat. Loki fiddled with Ted's iPod, skipping from track to track, letting a song play just long enough for Ted to start feeling the music before he moved to the next.

"Do you fucking mind?" Ted finally asked through ground teeth.

"No, I don't," Loki said as he skipped to the next track.

"Just fucking leave it."

"But I need to find the right song," Loki said, skipping past Soundgarden's "Fell on Black Days." "We want a perfect start to our road trip, don't we?"

The previous song had perfectly fit the start of this foolish enterprise. "That is already impossible," Ted said tightly.

"Oh, ye doubters shall be proven wrong." Loki let the opening notes play for a few moments before the upbeat guitar of the Eels started. When the singer, E, started in, the lyrics were a black cloud hanging over the sunny music; a melancholy hiding in plain sight, perfectly blending with the otherwise cheery melody.

Loki had been right, damn him. The perfect song.

When he looked over, the trickster was inhaling deeply from a cigarette, no doubt pilfered from Ted's jacket. "Want one?" Loki asked.

"Seeing as how they're mine, yeah, I do."

"Need me to light it for you?" Loki said, playing with Ted's Zippo, flicking the lid open and lighting it with a snap of his fingers before jerking it shut to snuff the flame.

"No thanks," Ted said, snatching the lighter from Loki's hand.

Birch and spruce trees lined the highway and separated the properties of people who'd tried to escape city life. To the east, after numerous Canadian Heritage signs, were stone walls surrounding some place called Lower Fort Garry. Further along, three rail cars sat, abandoned and covered in graffiti, on the tracks that wound their way along the road, emerging from and then disappearing into the treeline by turns.

They entered a town called Selkirk, passing a giant statue of a catfish. It smiled stupidly in front of a Smitty's restaurant.

"You read comics, Loki?"

The trickster had tilted his bucket seat back and had a soft-soled shoe resting on The Goat's dash. He reached behind the seat and his hand came back with an open beer. Beads of condensation ran down the neck of the bottle.

"'Course I do," he said, holding the drink, almost delicately, with his thumb and first two fingers, like he was having high tea with the fucking Queen of England. Loki tilted the beer up and took a long pull.

"I enjoy seeing them portray a drunken, stupid lout as a

bucket-wearing, baby-faced blond paragon of virtue. Always good for a laugh, how much they got wrong."

Ted remembered reading *Thor* comics—he'd been thirteen, fourteen, something like that, when he'd given them up. Football, music and girls, not necessarily in that order, taking up the slack.

Loki took another sip and then added, "But they had their moments."

"I didn't bring them up to discuss their fucking literary merit."

"So why did you, then?"

"It's starting to feel like I'm living one."

Loki took another long drink. The beer was half gone.

"I didn't ask for this power, and I don't want it. But if I'm the one riding the crazy train, maybe I should use them to do some good?"

"Easy there," Loki said, draining the bottle. He tossed the empty out the window, but it disappeared before it hit the ground. He glanced sideways at Ted. "You don't quite have the six-pack for spandex."

"That's not what I meant."

Reaching behind the seat again, this time Loki pulled out two beers. He put one in Ted's hand—it was as cold and wet as if it had come out of a backyard barbecue cooler. Ted hesitated briefly; it was a bad idea, but he could really use the drink. He took a quick swallow, draining the neck.

"I'm not talking about running around in my underpants and red pirate boots. I'm talking about doing something real.

Joining the cops or fire department. Fuck, I could end droughts, bring water to deserts."

"Not a good idea, Ted."

"Why not? I can't be burned. I'm stronger than I have any fucking right to be. I can control the weather—"

"Barely," Loki added.

Ted ignored him. "Why shouldn't I try to help people?"

"If you use your powers to interfere in the lives of mortals— try to push back the darkness, as it were—things will start to shove back. All who dwelt among the Nine Worlds are jealous and spiteful, like the Aesir were. Petty gods and monsters, that's us."

They drove on, and then Loki gave Ted a punch in the shoulder. "Look."

He did. Above the door of a two-storey, brown shop, a large sign read: THOR'S MEATS & GROCERIES.

"Ha!" Loki laughed. "That's all you get, bastard."

"I don't see any stores named after *you*." Ted looked back to the road. "What happens when I find those dwarves and fuck them up?"

"Vengeance is fine," Loki said, tossing his second empty out the window. This bottle, too, disappeared. His eyes twinkled as he looked at Ted. "It's encouraged. Be a champion if you want, but for every crop you irrigate, a dragon will wake to burn it. Take out a crack house and a troll will move in and start eating children. Maybe if the Greek powers had survived. They did a lot more fucking than fighting. That's where I always thought Odin got Valhalla wrong. Die in battle to wake up to endless feasting and fighting? Fuck. That."

"I don't believe you," Ted said.

"Why would I lie? The Valkyries were as frigid as a high-school girlfriend—they're worse now." Loki considered his words for a moment. "Maybe not like your girlfriend, Mr. Football Player, but there was precious little play."

"I wasn't talking about the fucking."

Loki shrugged. "You could use a good roll. You're awfully tense."

"That is beside the point."

"I think it is exactly the point." Loki's voice had changed in pitch and timbre. Surprised, Ted looked over to see a lanky blonde suddenly sitting next to him in ill-fitting clothes, and unbuttoning her top. She—he—reached over to walk fingers up Ted's leg. "We have time to rub out a quick one if it'll help."

"Christ!"

"What? Fine, but I figured we'd have to work our way up to head."

Ted kept his eyes on the road. "I'm not gay, Loki."

"I know. That's why I'm a woman."

"You're not a woman," Ted said through clenched teeth and slapped Loki's hand from his lap.

"I thought you'd prefer a blonde, given your track record. If not, I can be whatever you want. Whoever you want." His features changed in between eye blinks, displaying a dizzying array of hair, eye and skin colours. But each time the grin was pure Loki. Mischievous, mocking, and malicious all at once.

A grim, brick rectangular building was coming up just after where they would turn towards Gimli—the Selkirk Mental

Health Centre. Ted wondered what his odds were for getting Loki admitted.

More likely, they'd take me.

"Yeah," Ted said, snorting. "I really look forward to you turning back to yourself, or a horse, in the middle of it."

The voice had changed back to Loki's familiar tone; Ted glanced over, but the trickster still wore a borrowed face. She was pretty, whoever she was. Ted wondered if she was real or just a figment of the trickster's imagination.

"You *wound* me, sir."

"I notice you're not saying you wouldn't have done it."

Loki chuckled. "It would have been pretty funny, Ted."

"For you, maybe."

"Well, that is the point of a practical joke."

Loki grinned back at him, as a man now. Ted hadn't seen the change—one moment Loki was one thing, then another.

"That just doesn't seem right."

"Right and wrong. Good and evil. Abstractions. They differ from person to person. There is no universal good to be served, only what matters to you. Now take that *jötunn* who wants to kill you—"

"What?" Ted asked.

"Giant," Loki said casually.

"Like...." Ted thought of the thing from the patch.

"I'm speaking metaphorically. Not specifically."

"Then why does it want to kill me?"

"Every giant wants to kill you. The sight of that hammer on your arm'll bring 'em running like pigs to a trough."

"Jesus. They actually eat people?" Ted shuddered. "Fuckers."

Loki feigned hurt and insult. "Again, you wound me."

"How does that wound you?"

"I'm a *jötunn*."

"So you're saying you want to kill me?"

"Touché," Loki laughed. "Of course not, but then, I am a special case."

You've got that right. "Just finish telling me about your giant."

"No."

"No?"

"Say please."

"Oh, for fuck's sake." Ted ground his teeth. "Fine… please finish telling me about the giant."

Loki smiled and patted Ted's shoulder.

"There's hope for you yet, Teddy."

Ted grimaced and shook Loki's hand free.

"That giant that wants to kill you, at home in his cave or barrow—wherever the poor, damned thing is forced to live now—probably has a mate, and squalling little giant children, waiting for papa to come home with the meat. When you kill that giant, do you think of them? No, you think, *I'm glad to be alive.* Or *the monster deserved what it got.* After all, you're not a bad guy, so if it tried to hurt you, it was the bad one right?"

Ted had to ask, "Are you high?"

"No, but I could be in short order," Loki reached behind the seat again. Ted expected to see him pull a bag of grass out, but it was just another beer. "Whereas the giant needs to eat, needs to feed his spawn, and wants you dead. So if he succeeds, it's all good to him, y'know."

"So what are you saying?" Ted asked.

"Damn, I don't know, I guess, do what you're going to do, Ted. I won't stop you. Use your power for whatever you want. But like everything else in life, actions have consequences."

Music filled the space between them as Ted drove on. Winnipeg Beach ran into Sandy Hook. To the east, Lake Winnipeg spread out behind the homes and the trees like a hidden ocean. Many of the dwellings were built about a foot off the ground, clearly without basements. Ted wondered if they were just cabins, and not meant for year-round living. They were an odd mix of run down and flash.

Loki had affected a serious look, one of contemplation. It seemed out place on the trickster's face. Ted wondered if the whole scenario was just another example of Loki trying to play him. Huginn and Muninn hissed their opinions over the music, but Ted ignored them, the way Loki was ignoring him. Finally, after taking the last swallow of his beer, Ted opened his mouth to speak.

"So," he asked. "Where did you get the beer?"

The malicious grin cut across Loki's face again. "Susanna's," he said, offering another beer to Ted. "She has her family over to meet her new guy. Snagged them right off your old deck. Enjoy a taste of home, brother."

A blue-and-yellow road sign welcomed them to Gimli. At Loki's direction, Ted turned right at the lights across from the Viking Inn and headed towards Gimli Harbour. The town's stop signs were too damned low. Even with the flags that'd been tacked to the top of them, he blew through one, drawing honks, and no doubt curses.

"What are you doing?" Loki asked.

"I'm looking for Tilda."

"I thought I told you that was a bad idea," Loki said. The trickster grabbed his arm and waved to the right excitedly. "Oooh, mini golf!"

Ted ignored him. "You did, but maybe I'm not so certain I want to meet a dragon just yet."

Loki sighed as they passed the Astroturf and windmills. "Serpent," he corrected.

"What?"

"Remember? Jorry's a serpent."

"Right," Ted said. "Dragons have limbs."

"And wings."

"What the fuck difference does it really make?"

"You really don't want to find out."

Ted noted the seriousness, rare on Loki's face since they'd met, shrugged, and stayed silent.

Loki was almost pleading now. "Ted, this is a bad idea. Forget the Norns. Turn around and head for Lake Manitoba. Let's just go fishing."

"I hate fish, Loki, but I like answers."

"You won't find them here." Loki shook his head. "And what

you do find, you won't like. The All-Father hanged himself on the World Ash for a fraction of the knowledge locked within your flesh. You already have more answers in you than I or the Norns can provide."

"But how do I find them?" Ted wanted to pound the dash in frustration, but that would just total his car. The ravens had gone mostly silent since Ted had taken up with Loki, *don't trust the little fucker* being their only advice. "Goddammit!"

"I wouldn't trust the Norns either. Their arrival ended the early days of bliss for the Aesir. Before they came, Odin's golden halls were filled with those whose sole concerns were drinking and fighting. Suddenly we were confronted with the end of days."

Ragnarök.

Ted whispered it too. "Ragnarök." Even ignorant of the word's meaning, it held weight, inevitability.

"Yes, Ragnarök," Loki said quietly. "The fate of the gods. Where my life was to have been spent upon Heimdall's blade. Where my seed spent their lives against the All-Father and his army of sons. The Norns meant the end to us, but they promised a new day for Odin's favoured creations. A new day for humankind. A golden day without gods and war."

"That didn't work out so well."

"No, well, no one counted on Christians hijacking our end of the world."

"Uh, wasn't Jesus born *before* the viking heyday?"

Loki waved Ted's question away. "Details. It was one of the ways missionaries peddled their faith to our old followers. Your gods are gone, this is that new day they've been telling you about, blah blah blah, it made it a little more palatable, I suppose, reimagining Baldur as their Christ and turning all myth and magic into the tools of their 'Adversary.' I mean, the Thunderer's hammer was melded into the Christian cross by people who wanted to go both ways. And they did pray to Jesus, at least until they needed rain for the crops or wind for the sails. Then it was time for old Hammertoes to come out of the closet.

"Anyway, there used to be many norns, before Ragnarök, at least. Any witch, elf ,or giant with a touch of the sight called themselves a norn in those days. But there were only three Norns who mattered. And these three wanted to end the cycle. They still do. I want to stop them. You should, too. To save the world, a mortal man succeeding where the gods did not—well, with my help at least, I like that. They want the last vestiges of magic to fly into the darkness and be gone." Loki looked over at Ted, his face eerily serious. "And now that includes you, Teddy Bear."

Ted stopped the car and they both stepped out. An overwhelming scent of water greeted Ted. It was different than the times he'd been to the coasts. There was no hint of salt in the air, just… water. The sun beat down on him and caused beads of sweat to pool at his brow, but a breeze from the lake chilled the trickle as it ran down his face. Ted felt uncomfortable in his own skin and tugged at his cap, wishing it had a brim, as if avoiding their gaze would stop the townies' stares.

Except no one was staring.

An old man in a Chevy hat and sporting a bushy, white beard

ambled past them without looking up, his hands crammed into the pockets of his green work pants. One old woman with a cane did flash him the stink-eye, but when Ted stepped aside for her, she bobbed her Q-tip puff of curly hair and smiled. Despite their indifference, Ted still expected to get the bum's rush out of town. He didn't hear a police siren, only the loud calls of birds, happily chattering to, and over, each other.

Loki stepped onto the street, and slammed the passenger door of The Goat.

"Mind doing me a favour? Don't slam my fucking car doors. It's not a Geo. It's a vintage 1968 GT-fucking-O. Greatest Of All Time. Try treating The Goat with some respect."

Loki shook his head sadly. "Do or do not, there is no try."

Again with the fucking Yoda voice. Ted was shaking so hard, he was surprised he hadn't cracked the pavement.

They crossed the street in silence and walked along what must pass for the town's Main Street. A tall pole, damn near covered in birdhouses was in front of the local art gallery. Attached to it was a sign reading MANITOBA PURPLE MARTIN CLUB. Above that, a wise man had written "Birds Suck" in blue marker.

"So what's the plan, *kemosabe*?"

"I figure I'll start at the harbour and walk around until I find Tilda, or her family's shop."

"Great plan, walk around." Loki stooped to fish something out of one of his shoes. "Could you narrow it down a bit? I'm not exactly wearing my Bo Jackson cross-trainers here."

"My heart bleeds," Ted said without stopping. Loki quickened his pace to catch up. "Gimli's a small town, it shouldn't take that long."

Ted peered into windows and read the signs above the shops. They passed a large corner building with beaten tin siding. Rust flaked at the edges of the panels. There was a plaque beside the store, detailing its history in English, Icelandic, and French. It seemed everywhere Ted looked there was another unwelcome reminder of what had happened to him. Even the Gimli Credit Union had a fucking longship on its sign.

"Do you even know what their shop is called? Why don't we ask around?" Loki gestured at a young woman in grey on the veranda of a large two-storey house. She had her back to them and was sweeping away broken glass amid many wrought-iron tables and chairs. The house was honey-coloured with green trim. It was either recently restored or very well maintained. A waist-high white picket fence separated it from the sidewalk. "Why don't you ask her?"

"I doubt she'll answer me."

"I could do the asking," Loki said, grinning. "I can be pretty persuasive. Look at how I changed your outlook."

Ted scowled.

"Here we are looking for some mythical Norns, in Gimli, Manitoba, on our way to talk to my dragon son—"

"Serpent," Ted interrupted. "You said he was a serpent, not a dragon."

"So I did," Loki said, laughing. "So I did. And it seems you believed me."

Ted clenched and unclenched his right hand. "It's kind of

hard not to when I've already been attacked by dwarves… and I have a fucking thunderstorm living in my hand."

"That's why I love you, Teddy Bear, absolutely nothing gets past you."

Ted ignored Loki and turned to the woman on the veranda. She'd stopped sweeping and was reaching up to adjust the sign hanging from the porch that read GREY LADIES TEA HOUSE. Dressed all in grey, her skirt was snug, hanging to her ankles.

She turned and he was staring at Tilda. Ted almost didn't recognize her, dressed as she was. Hints of blonde—he couldn't imagine her blonde—had started creeping out from her scalp. The sun emphasized a smattering of freckles on her pale skin, flushed pink from her chore. There was no jewellery in her ear. He meant to start up the walk, but hesitated. Now that he'd found her, he wasn't sure how he felt about seeing her. What part had she really played in all the shit the dwarves had put him through?

"You're right," Loki said, too loudly, as he clapped Ted on the shoulder. "She does have a great ass."

Tilda raised a middle finger at them without making eye contact.

"Loki," Ted said with a low growl.

He had been walking closer without realizing it. She was even prettier without makeup, as if she used it to dull, rather than accentuate, her beauty. A chill wind off Lake Winnipeg let him know she still wasn't wearing a bra.

"You."

Ted started at the loathing in the word. He assumed she

had to be talking to Loki. But no, her gaze smoldered as she looked at him; she took a step back, tightening her grip on her broom.

"Finally." She mouthed another word, a name, an imprecation, under her breath.

"Til—?" What the fuck was with her?

"Ted?" Tilda said his name like he'd only now come into view. "Ted!" She reached towards him like he was an apparition. As if only touch would prove that he was there. When her fingers brushed his cheek, she pulled him, stunned, against her. "Sorry, I thought you were someone else. You're alive. The reading—I thought you'd died. I tried calling but you didn't answer. You never called back."

What was there to say? "I had a bad night. Then a bad morning. And then I was in jail."

"Jail?"

Ted shrugged. "Long story."

He patted her back, feeling awkward.

"How are you?" she asked.

"I feel like death warmed over, but I'm still here."

Tilda tilted her head up to look into his eyes. He could see her surprise at the dwarves' handiwork. She cocked her head from side to side, taking in his visible tattoos. And her expression changed; happiness and surprise shifted to wary suspicion. She stepped back, as if he'd threatened her.

"You shouldn't be here, Ted. It's dangerous."

Ted didn't know what to make of her hot-and-cold attitude. She'd come on so strong in his car. But now, she seemed to regard him with the same disgust that had twisted Ted when he saw his new reflection. "Dangerous for who?"

"Everyone." She looked past him then, stiffening as she noticed Loki. "And you definitely shouldn't have brought him."

"Hey," Loki said, lighting a cigarette. "I told him not to come."

"Keep your mouth shut, trickster. I don't know what part you're playing in these events, but you'd better get the hell out of here before my Amma sees you." Ted was surprised Loki didn't interrupt her—and somewhat worried she recognized the annoying god. But he had to admit, it was pretty cool to see her tell Loki off.

"Can't do that, Grey Lady," Loki said, shaking his head. "Ted wants some answers."

"You promised me a proper reading," Ted said, gently thumbing Tilda's chin up so their eyes met. "In the car."

"So I did." She ran her fingers over one of the raven tattoos. "Don't take this the wrong way, but I'm starting to wish I'd never met you. Maybe things would have turned out better for you."

Ted flashed a grin. "You don't know that," he said. "Meeting you is the best thing that's happened to me in this fucking province."

"Hey…" Loki whined, but Ted ignored him.

Tilda pressed a smooth, warm hand against Ted's face. "You are my guest, my fire is yours."

Muninn whispered in his ear, **"And my sword is yours."**

Without knowing why he did so, Ted repeated the raven's words. Tilda smiled.

"Goody gumdrops," Loki grinned at Ted, who was wondering

what exactly was going on. "The forms have been observed. Where's my invitation?"

"Not forthcoming," Tilda said. "I suggest you make yourself scarce before Amma comes down the stairs."

"Too late, Skuld," rasped a voice like knives over gravel.

7. In the Houses of the Holy

A tall, big-boned woman stepped out onto the walk. Her grey hair hung in two thick braids that ended around her waist, one in the front, the other down her back. Like Tilda, she wore a long skirt, also grey. She looked as if she was shaped from the angry clouds of a thunderstorm. Ted never thought he'd see someone and say they looked too old to be a grandmother. Her face had wrinkles so deep they could have been cut with a hatchet. He judged her age at somewhere between sixty and six hundred.

"So, we have a guest. I've been waiting for you," she said, holding the door open; wind chimes jangled as the breeze caught them. She smiled in welcome. It was the grin of a cat playing with a mouse. "For both of you."

"Have you now?" Loki said, lighting another cigarette.

"You can't smoke in here,"

"You going to stop me, Urd?" Loki exhaled the smoke through his nose.

"It's a bylaw," Tilda's grandmother said casually. "Suit yourself, though. I'll be happy to let the constabulary give you the ticket. Maybe arrest you for being a scofflaw. The RCMP are just down the road."

"But we're guests," Loki said.

"No, you're not." Urd gestured towards the inside of the shop.

A homey-looking café greeted them as they walked through the door. A hearth crackled with fire, despite the warmth outside. Ted, while no carpenter, knew enough about woodworking to tell that every piece of furniture in the place was handmade. And well-made. Every chair looked solid, if not particularly comfortable, and the tables were of such heavy construction, it must be a struggle to slide them around the floor. The floor itself was tiled in stones, all carefully chosen to make a mostly level surface. Ted could tell they hadn't been shaped at all; at least, the faces that were showing hadn't been shaped. None of the stones appeared at a glance to be common to the Canadian Shield, and all had symbols carved upon them. Something stirred within him as he looked upon the rocks. They were volcanic. He wondered if Tilda's ancestors had brought them over from Iceland. And why.

There was a stand that held books to Ted's left, the authors had names like Sigurðardóttir, Indriðason, and Arnason. Not all of them appeared to be in English. A set of open stairs was at the back of the shop against the wall—perhaps where the real business of Grey Ladies took place.

A blonde woman with a stern expression stood behind the till—Tilda's mother, by the look of her. Her hair was pulled back from a friendly, heart-shaped face. Like her daughter, a dusting of freckles was spattered over her nose and cheeks. Whereas Tilda's eyes were the pale blue of early morning, her mother's were the rich colour of a cloudless noon sky. And she, too, was tall. Tall enough to look Ted in the eye. She had aged well—better than the wrinkled piece of leather that had let them in the door—and, Ted had to admit, better than he had. If what Tilda had said was true, her mother was probably younger than him anyway.

She stepped out from behind the register and crossed her arms under her breasts.

"So, this is the instrument of the *dvergar*. Welcome. I am Verdandi." A smile softened her face as she spoke to Ted. "But I usually just go by Vera."

"If you say so."

Urd took Ted's hand and rubbed a thumb over his fingers. Ted wanted to protest, but a smart man never mouths off to a hot girl's grandmother.

"He is strong, their creation. They have bested their work even from the days of old." She drew a knife from her apron and slashed it hard over Ted's palm.

"What the fuck?" Ted yelled.

"Amma!" Tilda protested.

"*Hmph*." Urd held up the blade. There was no blood. "I thought I smelled a dragon's reek upon you."

Loki smiled. Ted did not.

"Pretend I'm not here again—" Ted let his words hang in silence—"and I'll have to make myself known. Somehow."

Urd's face revealed no sign of worry at the implied threat. Wind whistled through a broken window, intensifying as Ted scowled.

"You are strong, Theodore." She slapped him then, hard. "And arrogant. Do you think because you cannot be wounded, you cannot be hurt? Tender the touch of the *dvergar* is not, but you went to them easily. Like you wanted them hurt you."

Rain fell outside as Ted yelled, "I'll show you hurt!"

"You would threaten an old woman? Were you not raised better than this?"

"Maybe, but maybe a Norn isn't a woman at all. Just a myth with tits."

Urd barked a harsh, quick laugh and turned to Tilda.

"You see, Skuld? You see what he thinks of you?"

"I know what he thinks of me." Tilda's hard façade faded, for just a moment.

"And yet you still have no child in your belly, and your poor old Amma still has the weight of the Nine Worlds on her shoulders."

Loki sniffed. "The Nine Worlds are gone, old woman, and they aren't coming back. Despite what the *dvergar* and *jötnar* want. Only Midgard is left, and the games you are playing may tear her asunder."

"I did not give you leave to speak, trickster," the old woman said as she tossed a braid over her shoulder so they both ran parallel down her back. "There was a time when even old One-Eye himself stepped carefully around the Norns. Fate is fate, and we are the last who can make it."

"No matter how highly you think of yourself, or your sisters, squatting in that hovel at the roots of the World Ash, Odin didn't step carefully around anyone but Frigg," Loki said through gleaming teeth. "And that was only when he had his spear out, if you get me."

Ted's eyes followed each speaker. The dim light in the café seemed to be growing brighter. Light seeped up from the floor, from the scratches in the uneven stones. A faint blue glowed along the edges of the carvings in the floor.

Runes.

"Loki…" Ted warned.

"Be quiet Ted, I'm enjoying this—" the trickster was cut off as glowing blue thread snaked up from the floor, winding itself through the scars along his lips. They'd sewn his mouth shut.

"This is *my* place of power, little *jötunn*." Urd smiled then, showing off a row of teeth like grey, worn tombstones. "And you should not have come back."

Panic lit up the trickster's eyes. Ted still wasn't sure if he believed Loki was… well, Loki. He wasn't sure what he believed, but if the cocky little shit was terrified…. Fear began to seep into Ted also.

You shouldn't be here.

You should never have come.

Doom.

Doom.

Huginn and Muninn were chattering over each other so fast Ted couldn't separate the birds' voices.

He clamped his hands over his ears, as if it could silence their cawing.

"Shut up, shut up," he mouthed.

Loki clawed at his bindings while Urd smirked. Verdandi came to Ted's side, gently touching his temples. Tilda took a step towards her mother—and Ted—but stopped short of joining her.

"We can make this go away Theodore," said Vera—it was easier to think of her as Vera. Her voice was soothing. The wind softened. "We can take their marks from you. It is too much responsibility for a mortal man. Let us take your burden. Let us punish and cage those responsible. You can go home. Go to your wife. Start the family she wanted. Lose yourself in her. You need not think on us ever again." Her words undulated into one another with almost no beginning or end, like the hint of waves on a calm day.

Loki's muffled sobs were barely audible as Ted bobbed along on a sea of sugared words. Words so sweet they silenced the whispers. Ted wanted to listen, to spend forever floating in that moment. But the Norns were mistaken.

He hadn't been happy in his old life, even before mythological figures had invaded it. An athlete gone to seed. A job he'd hated. Shitty day blending into shitty fucking day. He didn't want to go back. And even the most potent spell couldn't bring Susanna back to him, or give them what they'd lost.

As for Loki, Ted didn't know what to think. But the dwarves… he owed them. And Ted had never stood back to let someone else do his fighting for him. If he gave up his new power, that's exactly what he'd be doing. *If anyone's going to beat down those twisted freaks, it's going to be me.*

"No," Ted practically growled.

Vera stopped speaking; her jaw dropped in surprise. Loki's cheeks puffed out as he tried to exhale a sigh of relief.

"You dare—"

"I came here for answers," Ted cut her off. There was a peal of thunder outside. "And I'm gonna have them. Stop this. Now."

"You—"

"I offered my sword in defence of your home," Ted said. His voice hollow, as if it came from deep in the earth. "And I will choose how and when to use it."

One by one, the glowing stones winked out as the runes gave up their power. The threads sewing Loki's lips shut disappeared as well. Ted could feel every one of the runes upon his back where the dwarves had marked him with the World Tree.

"Go… to … Hel," the trickster said, drawing out his daughter's name as he pointed at each of the Norns.

Urd levelled a stare at Ted; her eyes bored into him. He couldn't feel any malice in the look, just an intense scrutiny.

"You would pair your *wyrd* with this rogue?"

"No," Ted answered.

Tilda exhaled a loud sigh.

"Hey," Loki protested.

"My *wyrd*, fate, doom—whatever—belongs to me. It is mine alone."

Loki looked ready to bolt at any moment. The two elder Norns grinned broadly.

"But for now"—Ted said and jerked a thumb at the trickster—"he's with me."

Loki let a short whistle past his lips and waggled his finger smugly at the Norns. Immediately their scowls returned.

"So be it," Urd said. "If you would play the Thunderer, I offer you his seat."

She gestured to the hearth corner of the room, at one of two over-large wooden chairs. They appeared more suited to a throne room than a café. Inscribed into the headrest of one was a hammer to match the one inked on Ted's arm. Two ravens—Huginn and Muninn, Ted presumed—could be seen on the other.

Stepping towards the offered seat, he eased himself down onto the chair. It had no cushion and felt hard as slate. The heat of the fire caused trickles of sweat to run freely down his back. Ted's knuckles tightened over the armrests, carved to resemble snarling goats. He shifted uncomfortably.

"Those with power must never rest easily," Urd said.

As the two older women set themselves down on wooden footstools, he felt odd. Self-absorbed, arrogant, even; a pretender on a throne that didn't belong to him.

"You," Urd said to the trickster, "may stand."

Loki rolled his eyes at her. "As if I care," he said. "Do you really think I still desire that dead old murderer's throne?"

"Yes," Vera said. "We do, or you would not have come before us. Your fate will catch you, son of Laufey." Ted caught her glance in his direction. "As it finds everyone. Huginn and Muninn are not the only ravens set against you, are they?"

Urd grunted. "And I have not forgotten your role in the Greenland Affair."

He blanched at that, but quickly recovered, shrugged, and sat down next to Ted. Urd's jaw could've cracked rocks. Loki's eyes grew wistful and distant.

"So this is what it would have felt like to rule," he murmured. "Strangely anticlimactic."

"Skuld," said Urd. "Refresh our guest. And, if you must, Loki as well."

"But—"

"Now."

Tilda scampered behind the counter and disappeared through a door into a back room.

"Why do you call her that?" Ted asked.

"It's her name," Vera said, as if speaking to a child. "For now."

"A good girl, too good for the likes of us," Urd said. "Or for you. Remember that, Thunderer."

"I don't know what you're getting at," Ted said quietly.

"She doesn't want you to fuck her granddaughter," Loki whispered in Ted's ear, but loud enough to be heard by the Norns.

"Thanks," Ted said dryly. "I appreciate the insight."

"I live to serve."

The Norns ignored the exchange; they remained focused on Ted until Tilda came out of the back with a tray of steaming drinks.

"So," Urd stated. "You have come seeking wisdom. Ask your questions and we will answer. But there will be a price."

"There is always a price," said Vera.

Ted nodded, expecting no less. "Name it."

"The Head of Mimir," the three Norns spoke together. Their tones differed though, and Ted could pluck out Tilda's fear, Vera's awe, and Urd's avarice.

The Head of Mimir.

It shouldn't have meant anything to Ted. But it did. Muninn wouldn't let it not.

Odin traded an eye to drink from Mimir's Well and gain the jötunn's wisdom.

Ted winced. *Ouch.*

His sacrifice was worth it, Huginn added. It allowed him to learn the magic of the Runes when he hanged himself from the World Tree.

Wisdom would tell me not to fucking hang myself.

Sacrifice has power. Between Odin's twin sacrifices, the All-Father had learned to beat death.

Just not his own, Muninn said, sadly. Mimir counselled the Aesir long after his head was taken from his shoulders.

Mimir lives on still.

"Jesus," Ted muttered.

"Let the poor thing rest," Loki said.

"Did you let the poor thing rest, Loki?" Urd demanded. "When you coaxed secrets from him? Promised him oblivion? Do you not owe your survival to luckless Mimir? Do you ever intend to keep your promise?"

"Yes," Loki said. "I do."

"Where is he?" Ted asked.

"North," Vera said. "In the hands of the *jötnar.*"

"Giants? There're fucking giants here too? I thought Loki was just shitting me."

The Norns smiled. "Much of the north is wilderness. When the Rainbow Bridge shattered, many who trod upon it landed here."

Ted shook his head. "Well, I've been attacked by dwarves. I've talked to fortune tellers and I'm on my way to talk to a dragon—"

Loki interrupted, "Serpent."

"Serpent. With its divine father. I can stretch my disbelief to include really tall people, I suppose."

"Ask your questions, Theodore," Loki said. "The Norns always answer true, don't you ladies?"

"Yes, unlike some," Urd answered. "We speak the truth of what was, will be, and what is."

The truth. Could he believe their word any more than Loki's? But he knew what he wanted. Payback. If they were willing to give it to him.... "I want the fucking dwarves. Where are they?"

"Flin Flon," Vera said. "They own the mining company up there."

"Good luck getting to them," Loki said.

"Shut up," Ted barked.

"I'm just saying—"

"Not now."

"Two questions remain, Theodore," Urd said. "One of the past, one of the future."

"That's it?"

"That's it, Ted." Tilda said. "Choose carefully."

"What about my reading?"

"You'll get no such thing from me."

"Not from you." Ted pointed to Tilda. "Her."

Urd spun on her granddaughter. "You promised him a reading?"

"I did," Tilda said. She looked about to drop her gaze, but instead held her grandmother's stare, defiant. "Before—"

"And what did you ask in return?"

"I didn't—"

Urd waved away Tilda's answer. "It matters not. Ask, Theodore."

"Can this," Ted gestured at his tattoos. "Be undone?"

"There is a way," Tilda said, her eyes moistening; she looked back and forth at her mother and grandmother. She rubbed the tears away with her knuckles. "But it requires the Head of Mimir."

"Convenient," Loki said.

Ted shot the trickster a glare.

"One question remains," Urd said, tapping her fingers on her knee. "What will you ask of me?"

"Why do you want the Head?"

"Isn't that a question for Verdandi?"

"Has the reason changed?" Ted asked.

"Another question for my daughter."

"This isn't *Jeopardy*. Does how I phrase things matter so much?"

Urd's lips parted in a thin, dangerous smile and Ted felt suddenly that yes, how he asked was as important as what he'd asked. He was starting to wish he'd thought a bit more carefully about the answers he really sought. The Norn sighed finally, and spoke.

"Within Mimir's Head was the knowledge to end Ragnarök, or to escape it, had Odin been brave enough to seek that answer. Your... friend here," she waved at Loki, "evidently made use of it. But there is more. Surtur is awake. You have seen him. He set fire to Asgard. He will not be satisfied until he burns this world as well. Would you stand against him, Theodore? Truly?"

Ted started to sweat. The firelight was reflected in Urd's pale eyes. Surtur's laughing face grinned back at Ted. He felt the heat, flames no fireplace could contain. Tremors ran through the earth. He started to shake.

"Even the thought of that day on the oil sands makes you quail. With Mimir's aid, we can end it all: the giants, the dragons, the sight, what was done to you."

Ted asked, "Can you, now?"

The Norns nodded together.

"So where's the Head?"

"I'm afraid you're out of questions." Vera said. "We told you to choose carefully."

"And to think before you spoke," Urd added.

For fuck's sake. "You want me risk my life for you? And you play at fucking words?"

"Come on," Loki said. "Bros before hos. Let's roll. Jorry'll know more."

"Go then," Urd said, nodding. "Speak to the Midgard Serpent, speak to Jormungandur. It may help you. Perhaps Skuld's promised reading"—the elder Norn shot Tilda a look and continued—"will bear more fruit. And perhaps not." Tilda flushed. "She has not been practising."

"I wish we could help you further," Vera said. "But even we have rules that must be followed."

"We have a boat," Tilda offered.

Loki smiled, stood and bowed with a flourish. "I accept the

Grey Ladies' generous offer to continue their hospitality on water as it was on land."

Urd shot Tilda a warning look.

"But first," Vera said. "We eat."

Loki rubbed his hands together. "What's on the menu?"

"I hope you like fish," Urd said with a sly smile. "I just netted a slippery one this morning."

"I will take any delicious opportunity that presents itself," the trickster said, mirroring the Norn's grin.

"And you, Theodore?" Vera asked. "How does battered gold-eye sound to you?"

"If it's some kind of beef, it sounds fantastic."

The Norns shook their heads dismissively.

"Hey, I'm from cattle country. Anything less than Triple-A Angus is for the dogs."

"You will have to look beyond your upbringing if you want to live through the next days and weeks." Urd said simply. "Can you?"

"If I couldn't do that, I wouldn't be here talking to you right now." Ted hitched a thumb at Loki, "And that son of a bitch would be in whatever Asgard uses for a hospital."

"I love it when he acts butch," Loki said to Tilda with a laugh. "Don't you?" The trickster nodded as if she'd agreed. "She does."

Tilda ignored him and Ted tried his best to do likewise. He figured he'd better get used to doing so, as Loki showed no signs of leaving him alone.

"So where are the customers?" Ted wondered aloud. "Will it be safe for us to talk business here?"

"Customers." Vera rolled her eyes towards her mother. "We haven't had a customer in years."

Urd crossed her arms over her breasts. "You know my mind on this, daughter."

"Yes, I do." Vera smiled, Ted caught a sly wink. "They irritate you."

"They ask to know their futures, and refuse to pay when I tell them."

"They don't come to you for the truth of their destiny, Amma," Tilda said. "They come to pay for some comfort. To believe that everything will be okay. They come for the lie."

Urd snorted. "Well, they won't get that from me."

"You still don't have to tell everyone they're going to die."

"But they will, eventually," Urd said.

Vera sighed. "Which is why I haven't sold a scone in ages."

"So how the hell do you keep this place open if you have no customers?" said Ted.

The three women looked at him as if he were from Mars. Loki joined them.

"What?" he asked.

Vera shook her head and laughed. "I forget how new all of this is to you, Theodore. Let's just say we have made some excellent investments over the years. Much simpler and more profitable than burying coins under the hearth."

"Could you throw me a tip?" Ted added bitterly, "My portfolio is in the shitter."

"Ted," Tilda said, almost pleading, "don't ask that."

"There would be a price..." Urd answered, licking at her lips. "A heavy one."

"The Head of Mimir isn't worth tossing me a stock tip?"

"We have already negotiated the payment for that service. Would you like me to alter our arrangement?"

"Pray she doesn't alter it any further," Loki said in a deep deliberate baritone.

"What did I tell you?" Ted said, jabbing a finger at Loki. "No more *Star Wars*. Can't you be serious for one fucking minute?"

"Oh, I am," Loki said, not taking his eyes from the Norns. "I am."

"It will be nice to have company for a change," Vera said lightly, ignoring the tension that lay heavily between her guests and family. "Til, be a dear and set the table, would you?"

"Sure, Mom."

"I'll help," Loki said.

"But—"

The trickster cut off Ted's protest before it went any further, waving a hand in the air between them.

"I wouldn't hear of anything else. Have to earn my hospitality, don't I? You stay, entertain the in-laws."

Ted waited with the Norns in silence while Loki followed Tilda into the kitchen. He shifted his posture uncomfortably. *Damn Loki.* This could go very poorly. It had been a long time since Ted had needed to play meet-the-family. He didn't know what to say, so he said nothing, instead listening to the sound of rain falling in fits and starts.

Just before the awkward silence between them forced Ted to speak up, Vera asked, "How did you meet my daughter?"

"You don't know?"

"Indulge us." Coming from Urd, it was not a request. "I would hear the tale from you."

Ted shrugged, briefly considering, then discarding, a demand for something from them in return for his answer. "I was on my way to Winnipeg, she was hitching her way home. I gave her a lift. We talked. She trusted me enough to tell me a bit about herself."

"And that is all?"

"More or less."

"So when did she offer you this reading, free from consequence, or payment?" Urd asked. "I would like to hear more, rather than less."

"On the way, after we'd talked a bit."

"Details lie at the heart of things, Theodore. And right now, you seem as evasive as Loki."

"I don't really know what else you want to know. What she did was weird, and it kind of ended our conversation, I'll tell you that."

Urd's eyes narrowed. She asked, "She read your fortune in the car as well?"

Ted nodded. "I think she blames herself for… this." He spread his arms wide, and his sleeves crept up slightly, revealing more of his tattoos.

"What did she see?" Vera asked.

Ted shuddered. He didn't like to think of the fear and unease that had been in Tilda's speech when they pulled into Winnipeg.

"That… that I would either live the life of a prince or hero, or die a quick, dirty death. Said it was odd that I had the option."

"It is," Urd said. "For a mortal man. But then this wasn't your first foray into the Nine Worlds, was it?"

Flames danced in the fireplace, reflecting queerly in the glass doors of the cabinets behind the counter. Ted stared into the reflected flames and again wondered why the Norns would have lit a fire on a sunny September day. He knelt by the hearth and reached tentatively forward. The flames licked at his hand, but did not harm him. He heard Surtur's laugh in the pop and crackle of the burning logs.

"No," Ted said, removing his hand from the fire and standing up. "It wasn't."

"So, Skuld was waiting for you on the roadside when you resolved to pull over?" Urd asked. "Do you normally stop for hitchhikers?"

"No, I don't."

"But she was young, lovely, and stranded in the rain. You had no choice but to help her. How romantic."

"There was no choice," Ted said angrily. "She was standing in the middle of the goddamned road. I almost hit the ditch trying to avoid her."

"Yes, you tried to avoid her," Urd nodded. "Tried to avoid Loki. And yet, here we are, with you here for dinner, admitted under my granddaughter's hospitality."

"What's with the third degree?"

"I would like to know your intentions towards my daughter," Vera said.

"What is this, the 18th century?" Ted said. "My intentions? I don't have any intentions."

"Oh, I think that you do."

"Look, I know I'm a lot older—"

"Oh, hell," Vera cursed, laughing. "I don't care about that. Tilda has never shown any particular interest in men. So why you?"

"She did," Urd countered. "Before she decided to endlessly delay my retirement."

Ted was surprised to hear Vera say Tilda was interested. She'd been so hard to read since he'd arrived in Gimli. "I gotta say, I think your little family business is fucked up." Ted shook his head. "I don't get it."

"Our business is as it has been, is, and will be. We cannot change who we are. Skuld has an old soul. Older, I think, than yours, Theodore Callan. She is more than your match. But I doubt very much whether you will be good for each other. Or for us."

"Now, Langamma—" Vera said.

"No," Urd said firmly. "No good will come to us if Skuld stays with this one. I have foreseen it."

"If it is her will to be with him, it will be. She is that which shall be, after all."

"Yes," Urd agreed with a sigh and tapping at her lips. "She is. Ever has she been the fire burning in the darkness."

Vera gave Ted's arm a squeeze and led him to a table, pulled out one of the heavy chairs, and gestured for him to take a seat.

"Relax, Ted."

"You know, nothing tenses me up faster than someone saying, 'relax.'"

"And what might put you at ease?"

There was so much more he wanted to know. Instead, Ted narrowed his eyes and asked, "What'll it cost me?"

"I think there will be a saga written about the two of you," Vera said. "Perhaps I'll play the skald. I've always wanted to write." She ran a finger over the raven tattoo of Muninn. "Remember to be kind to her. In some ways this is as new to her as it is to you."

"Verdandi…." Urd let Vera's proper name hang in the air.

"Fine." Tilda's mother sighed. "I'd better see if the trickster has emptied our larder. Play nice."

The look on Urd's face convinced Ted she had no such intention. She took the chair directly across from Ted and sat in silence until Vera disappeared into the kitchen.

"She is a good woman, Verdandi," Urd said finally. "Not truly meant for this life, but she has done well just the same. She would not be swayed. Skuld was to experience something of Midgard, was to have a life outside of this—as if such a thing were truly possible. I thought I had beaten all the wilfulness out of her when she was younger, but still she tries to irritate and provoke me."

"Tilda seems to have done okay for herself."

"She is wholly unprepared for what is about to come. Her mother… she has never truly wanted this life. But it was the only one I could give to her, and to her daughter. But you may change that."

"By getting you the Head of Mimir?"

"Yes."

"And that will be the end of magic?" Ted asked skeptically.

"Why do you think that's a good thing? What makes it your fucking decision?"

"There is no one else who has seen what we have. Who else has the perspective of our knowledge? Magic, our powers, your trickster friend… and your unwanted gifts, none of these have a place in today's world. Perhaps, if you survive the journey, there would be a life waiting for you with Skuld."

"I just *left* that kind of life. I don't know that I'm ready to leap back into another one, with someone I just met, no less."

"She is not your wife. Will never be. Even without her visions, that much would not change. You think she would be your maid? Your cook?"

Ted snorted. "If you think I expect that, you don't know my ex."

8. Little Miss Fortune

They ate in a small nook that overlooked the treed back-yard. Ted wrinkled his nose at the scent of the fish at first, but tried it so as not to appear a total dick in front of Tilda. It was better than he'd expected. The conversation was surprisingly mundane, and unsurprisingly awkward. Despite the mystical quest, the day had gone better than Ted's first meeting with Susanna's parents.

Vera dragged Loki away to do the dishes.

Urd pointed to the stairs. "Do your reading, Skuld," she said. "And may it bear more fruit than we have plucked thus far."

"Yes, Amma." Tilda rose from her seat.

Swallowing the last bitter mouthful of tea in his cup, Ted followed Tilda to the stairs leading to the second floor.

"Your Amma seems a little…" *withered, mean, terrifying…* "older than I'd expected."

"Oh," Tilda said. "She's not my grandmother. Not really. I call her that. It's easier. Simpler."

"Do I rate the truth?"

"Whether you want it or not." Tilda smiled, but still hesitated. "My real Amma and Langamma died right after my mom was born. It was a pretty bad time for us. Amma raised Mom, and then me after that."

"So she's really your great-great-grandmother."

"Great she is, and you'd best not forget it. Amma's forgotten more than I'll ever know. C'mon." With an impish grin, she crooked a finger, inviting Ted to follow her. She led him to another set of stairs. These were steep, open wooden steps, but Tilda scampered up without the handrail. Ominous creaks met each of Ted's footfalls, and he missed the slight duck of her head as she cleared the landing to the second floor. There was a sudden jolt as he cracked his head against the angled ceiling above the stairs. It didn't hurt, but the unexpected resistance cost him his balance. Ted took an awkward step backwards, and his flailing arm caught the handrail.

"You okay?" Tilda asked.

"Did you know that was going to happen?"

Tilda smiled. "Sorry, I should have warned you about the ceiling."

"I'm old enough that I should have learned to walk long past now anyway. Though Loki did say you'd be the death of me."

"Did he now?"

She offered him her hand. It felt small. Clammy. She was nervous, despite her outward demeanour. Ted ducked under the angle of the ceiling until he could straighten up. They were standing in a pantry of sorts. Supplies were piled on shelves. A broom with a cracked handle lay angled between the shelves, and across a closed and padlocked door. The lock was big—old, too—and not likely to be found in a hardware store.

Tilda reached above the door frame and fished down a key. She opened the lock, moved the broken broom, and beckoned for Ted to follow her as she stepped into the room.

There was a sense of vertigo as he crossed the threshold of the door. The attic was immense. Far larger than the main floor of the tea house. There was a round table in the centre of the room—heavily built, like all the furniture here—with a stool facing the entrance. Bookshelves lined the walls, filled with an odd mixture of musty-smelling leather tomes and modern coil-bound notebooks. They were jumbled together in no order that Ted could discern.

Walking over, he reached out to hook a finger into the wire coil of one of the modern journals. It was sitting on a shelf next to a book whose cover was made of thinly beaten metal. The journal had three brightly-coloured cartoon girls on its front cover and an angry-looking monkey sporting a turban on the back. Tilda wrenched the journal from Ted's hand and smacked him with it before she returned book to its place on the shelf.

"I'd really rather you didn't try to read anything up here." The flush in her face quickly faded from anger to embarrassment. "Especially that."

"Sure," Ted said, shrugging. "What is all of this stuff?"

Tilda hesitated before answering.

"Our records. Every vision a Norn has received going back until… the fifteenth century, I think. There are some earlier entries, but they were recorded after the fact. It was all oral history and story then. Used to be we'd have had to memorize every other Norn's visions. Amma still believes in it; Mom and I had a hell of a time trying to get her to record anything. And when she does, she only writes in runic script. She says the words lose

some of their power otherwise." Tilda rolled her eyes. "I sometimes think she's still holding out on us."

"I take it from your blushing that this notebook isn't Urd's?"
Ted joked. But he was still curious as to its contents. "Is there
anything about me in here?"

"Ted, please," she warned. "You're in a different world now.
Your actions can have very real and deadly consequences. We
are bound by certain rules here. Everything has a price. I promised you a reading—and you'll get it—but no one may know of
our visions."

"Okay, fine. I guess I have to trust you on this."

"You can trust me, Ted. Always."

He wanted to believe her, and was surprised by how much
he did. Still, he felt she didn't trust him. But she had warmed up
to him a bit.

Ted decided not to push his luck, and changed the subject.
"So what's up with this place? It's just too big."

"Is that really the question you want me to answer for you? I
thought you'd have learned better by now." She winked. "I can't
give everything away for free you know."

"I guess not."

Ted reached up and ran his fingertips over the grain of one
of the rafters.

"What kind of wood is this?" he asked.

Tilda answered, "Ash."

"Just like the World Tree, then?"

"Stop fishing, or I'll ask Amma to do your reading." Judging
from Tilda's face, it wasn't an idle threat. And not a scenario Ted

wanted to endure. "You'd be better off. No one knows the stones better than Amma."

"You were the one to promise me the reading," he reminded her. "It's your responsibility."

Instead of being irritated with him, she smiled. "Then you'll learn what I can tell you. As much as I can. It won't be all you want to know, but it will have to do."

"Fine," he said, trying to sound positive. "Fine."

These are remnants of the walls of Asgard, Muninn said. **And the ash was salvaged from the fallen World Tree.**

That is how the room can defy its space, Huginn added.

"Could you get a fire started?" Tilda asked.

There was a hearth at the opposite end of the room. Like the floor of the Norns' tea house it was made of large natural stones, though these didn't appear to have been shaped at all. Cut wood was piled in a corner nearby. Ted shuddered. Open fires still made him twitchy, but he doubted this room was connected to a natural gas account.

"It isn't that cold up here."

"It will be. Trust me."

"You know, I'm getting a little tired of hearing those words."

"I'm not Loki."

"You're not just another woman, either. Not really."

She smiled queerly. Ted hoped she'd taken it for a compliment. "When we begin, we will be opening ourselves up to the void between worlds. The fire will serve to warm us, anchor us and show us the way back. Satisfied?"

Clear as fucking mud. "At least it's an answer. Sorry. Since I first saw Surtur…."

Tilda nodded, as if understanding. "That's a good instinct, but you're safe from him here. He won't find you. Start the fire."

Ted nodded and walked to the hearth. He tossed a few logs in and knelt down to build a fire.

"Matches?" he asked.

Enigmatically, Tilda answered, "You won't need them." There was a quiet hiss, and then a loud pop. Flames leapt up over the logs. Ted scrambled backward, his heart pounding. But the fire remained bound to the hearth. The logs burned heartily—normally—as if the fire had been started long before.

"Jesus, you could warn a guy that you've got an automatic fireplace." He squinted closer at the stones and saw the same rune scratched into the surface of every rock that made up the hearth.

Tilda answered his unspoken question. "*Kenaz*, the flame of the torch, power harnessed by the will of man. It represents knowledge. It's a rune of spirit and mind. A powerful part of seidur—sex magic—taught to Odin by Freyja."

The goddess's name got Muninn squawking again. **A goddess of the Vanir, sister to Freyr, daughter of Njord. First enemies and then allies of Odin's Aesir.**

At the raven's prodding, Ted saw a woman, both pale and golden, wearing nothing but a feathered cloak and a necklace of heavy gold encrusted in gems. She lounged in between two great cats.

Tilda asked suddenly, "May I see your tattoos?"

Ted lowered his eyes. "I… I don't even want to look at them."

"I don't want to belittle what the *dvergar* did to you Ted. It must have been awful. But these—" she turned his hand over and traced a finger around the outline of Mjölnir. "These are beautiful."

"I'm not quite there with you yet."

"Even if you get the Head of Mimir, and magic is stripped from the world, only the power locked within these images will disappear. The tattoos themselves are very, very real. You'd still need to have them all removed by mundane means."

"Oh." Ted dropped his head away from her gaze. "I'd hoped—"

"—they'd disappear more painlessly than they appeared?"

"Yeah."

"Sorry to disappoint."

"Ah, fuck it. Should have known better than to hope for the easy way out." Ted shook his head and forced a grin. "Man, the Sergeant would be laughing at me now."

Tilda cocked her head quizzically.

"My dad," Ted answered. "My little brother and I call him the Sergeant, even though it wasn't his actual rank. Chief Warrant Officer Benjamin Callan, Regimental Sergeant Major at the Wainwright barracks in Alberta, drilled the parade square until he retired. Even captains and colonels walked light around my dad."

"You were raised by a drill sergeant? And I thought I got yelled at."

Drill sergeant was an oversimplification, but it wasn't worth correcting. "Not sure who had it worse, me or my brother. Mikey actually enlisted. Dad never quite got over me not wanting to serve. Took it out on Mike. Wanted to make sure he didn't get any 'special treatment'."

Tilda winced. "How'd that go?"

Ted laughed. "Poorly. Dad rode him until he finally agreed to get in the ring." He could sense her rising confusion. "That's how we solved disputes. If you wanted your way, and it wasn't the Sergeant's, you'd better be prepared to fight for it. Open your yap, put on your gloves and put up your dukes."

"He beat you up?"

"It sounds worse than it was. Neither Mike or I were dumb enough to get in the ring with him until we were teenagers. Fucking full of ourselves, and thinking, hey, he's getting older, greyer, slower. We could take him. He's from a different era. I used to resent it, I guess. But now… he's a pretty good guy."

"As long as you agree with him."

"Who isn't?"

"So how'd the fight go?" Tilda asked.

Ted smirked. "About how I'd expected. Mikey was pissed. Dad was overconfident. He was pushing sixty then, and as much as he wouldn't admit it, had slowed down some."

"So your brother won?"

"Shit no." Ted laughed. "Dad faked a heart attack. When Mike tried to get his gloves off to help him, Dad punched him in the balls."

Tilda tried to stifle a laugh of her own. "That must have hurt."

"Hell, yeah. Mike should have seen it coming, though. The

147

Sergeant pulled the same trick on me the first time I really tagged him."

"One of these days that trick's going to backfire on him."

"Already did. Mom had the ring torn down. Showed us all who the real boss was that day, let me tell you."

"Since you're used to a woman being the boss, get that shirt off. I'm going to look at those tats."

"Sir, yes, sir." Ted saluted crisply. Tilda laughed; it was a light-hearted little trill that made Ted feel better about the idea of exposing the dwarves' handiwork. He pulled his shirt up over his head and then reached for his belt.

"Patience, Ted." She put her hand on his to stop him. "No need to rush to the good stuff." She ran a finger over the storm cloud on his chest. He exhaled deeply. It had been a long time since a woman had touched him with any tenderness. Closing his eyes, he could feel the clouds, far out on the lake.

"Sit on the stool," Tilda said.

The stool wasn't a stool at all, but a large section of a tree trunk about two feet high, sanded and level on the top, but with the bark left on.

Tilda walked to what Ted thought was the south wall and pulled open the thick curtains that hid almost all traces of light from the room. Sunlight broke through the darkness, illuminating motes of dust in its rays. The warmth of the sun added to the stuffiness of the room. Ted felt some of his vertigo returning. He knew there was no corresponding window to the attic visible from outside the house. The sun reached the table, but stopped just at the far edge where Ted was sitting, leaving him in darkness.

"It's better for a reading to take place under the light of the sun, where Odin sees all."

"I thought Odin was dead."

She nodded and dragged a similar stool from beneath the table. "Best to assume nothing where the High One is concerned. Alive or dead, it doesn't matter; there are rules and observances that must be made." She smiled wanly. "I know it sounds hokey, but I want you to clear your mind and try to relax."

"You know it's impossible to clear your mind entirely? Unless you're dead, I guess," Ted said, trying to joke.

Tilda wasn't having any of it. "Or brain dead," she muttered. "If you want this to work, you need to *believe* it will. You have to be receptive to the runes. Your previous encounters with the Nine Worlds will help bridge that gap of belief, but if you're fighting me it'll skew the results."

"So… empty my mind…."

"Forget that, you're close enough."

Ted was pretty sure he'd just been insulted.

Tilda tore a page from a notebook and walked around the table to give him the paper. She said, "Think about what you want to know. Concentrate on that."

He wanted to know what the fuck was happening. The Norn pressed a pen into his hand.

"Now," she said, turning away from him. "Write it down."

In block letters, Ted printed *WHAT THE FUCK IS HAPPENING?*

"Fold the page so I won't be able to read what you've written, please."

Ted folded the paper three times, smoothing and picking at the ragged edges where it had been torn free of the notebook.

"Done," he said.

Tilda held out her hand, and Ted placed the folded paper upon it. She crushed his question in her fist and held it tight to her body.

"You're certain this is what you wish to know?"

"Yes."

She nodded, "Good. We can begin."

Tilda set a leather pouch on the table. It was obviously old, though the leather had been oiled and well cared for over the years. Its contents clattered against each other. She opened the drawstrings of the pouch and pulled out a white cloth. The stones were wrapped within it. She poured the rune stones into a heaping pile on her hand. Ted was surprised they didn't tumble from her spread fingers. He leaned in closer to see what she was doing.

"The runes know it isn't time for the reading yet," she said as if that explained anything, and slowly slid them back into their pouch. Ted's written question followed the runes into the bag. "There are twenty-four Elder Runes, sorted into three groups of eights. These groups of three eights are more common than you'd think. The best reference for you would probably be…." She paused, and thought about it. "Shift work. Days, swings, and graveyards."

Between them she spread the cloth; it was silk and roughly the size of a man's pocket square. Symbols were embroidered upon the fabric in a circle. The Elder Runes. The same symbols that Robin had told him were tattooed on his back. The same ones cut into the stones downstairs. The same symbols upon Tilda's stones.

She sat in her chair with her back to the south window. She tied a veil over her eyes and smoothed the sheer fabric down to cover her face.

"The future is unknown to you," she said, her voice taking on a measured, ritual tone. "And so must I be."

Her breathing had changed, becoming slower and deeper. She picked up the pouch of runes and began tumbling the stones within it. Reaching inside, the Norn drew out a rune. The stone was irregularly shaped, but polished smooth. She set it face-down atop the cloth. In the drawing of that first stone, the room turned winter-cold—despite the magic fireplace. Gooseflesh peppered Ted's body. If he still had hair on his arms it would have been standing on end.

We are in Ginnunqaqap, Huginn noted. The space between worlds.

As Tilda drew another stone and set it down to the first rune's left, her slow breathing was visible, like clouds of mist on a cold winter day. She built two rows above the first, both times laying the stones right to left. It took some time before she settled on the seventh and final stone. This, she set at the top of the spread positioned between the fifth and sixth runes.

"This spread is best used for questions with many unknowns. And right now, there is so much you don't know. The first two runes represent your question, and the problem at hand," she said as she turned the first stone. "You struggle against your power."

Some psychic. I haven't been exactly quiet about coming her to get rid of the dwarves' damned "gifts."

Ignoring the snort Ted hadn't intended to be heard, Tilda turned the second rune, and said simply, "Creation and destruction. Fire."

"Fire." Ted repeated. He saw the flames rising over the rig, and for a second, his nose was filled with the thick, choking smoke that followed the explosion. "Surtur."

"Yes," Tilda nodded. "Good, your belief is growing. It will help you make the connections you need. The next two runes will tell us of reasons that underlie your question."

Tilda reached out and flipped the third stone. She stiffened as she saw the symbol. It was an "н" with a slightly diagonal cross line. Despite his skepticism, somehow her reaction filled him with much the same dread as hearing his doctor say, "Oops."

"What is it?" he demanded.

Tilda gave herself a little steadying shake. Her lips were pursed beneath her veil. "*Hagalaz.* The first rune of the second *aett.* It is the mysterious. Transformation. Evolution. It is also symbolic of the journey into the underworld to seek wisdom from the Norns."

"You're saying you're the reason—"

Tilda held up a hand to silence Ted and he let his protest die. "The rune is linked to the past, to my Amma. It could mean anything. Someone who came to her for answers long ago could be misusing that knowledge. You drove here with one such likely candidate. These can't always be interpreted literally. This rune is as closely linked to Hel, Loki's daughter, and Ymir, the father of the *jötnar*, as it is to my Amma."

"That's some company she keeps."

"Not anymore, she doesn't."

Tilda traced the outline of *Hagalaz* once more before flipping over the next stone. It matched the symbols on the hearth, *Kenaz*, Ted remembered. Another fire rune. Ted shuddered a bit at that. *So much fire*. Why couldn't he escape the flames?

Though from Tilda's earlier description, Ted gathered this rune was controlled fire. A tool, not a disaster.

Ted was starting to see the pattern. If the first pair of stones were his question, and the second pair the why underlying it, the next two should state how to find his answer. That answer would be the last stone.

You are correct, Huginn confirmed. **Surprising.**

Tilda turned the fifth stone, but Ted missed its name and significance in the shrillness of the ravens cackling at Huginn's joke.

"Your answers will not be found here," the Norn added.

Hit the Road, Jack.

The sixth stone was an arrow pointing upwards, or in this case, as it rested on the silken rune cloth, towards Ted.

"*Tiwaz*. The rune of justice, self-sacrifice, faith and loyalty. It is another, older name for the god Tyr."

"The one who lost his hand to Fenrir?"

"The same," Tilda said, nodding. "He thought he would save the world of the gods. All he did was delay the inevitable."

Ted tried to catch a glimpse beyond Tilda's veil. "Self-sacrifice."

"Yes."

"I'm going to die."

"Runes can have more than one meaning. *Tiwaz* is also the rune of—"

"The dwarves turned me into their goddamned Dirty Dozen—"

Tilda broke in firmly. "If death is the fate you seek, I'm sure Hel will oblige you. But I don't see your death. Sacrifice, yes, but not death. The two are not the same. You must find a way to reconcile the divine and the human, the natural and the supernatural. You will be placed in a crucible to resolve your past. You will earn your own answer. *Tiwaz* is also protection through power; you know the old football saying: the best defence is a good offence?"

"Yeah," Ted muttered. "But defence wins championships."

Tilda smiled. "Fortunate then, that you are so armoured as well."

"Last one," Ted said quickly and looking back to the runes. "What's my answer?"

She corrected him again. "This is not your answer, only a representation."

The final rune was a vertical line bisected by a diagonal, making the symbol look like a slightly squashed "x."

"What is it?" Ted asked.

"Me." She sounded like she didn't believe it.

"What?"

"This rune, *Naudhiz*, it's my rune, in the same way that

Hagalaz is Amma's. It's the fire that burns in the darkness of the future. The last rune is need."

"So you're saying I'll get what I need? If I take this journey and get Mimir's Head, my powers will be the sacrifice and I'll have my life back?"

Tilda didn't answer as she removed her veil. Plucking up the stone, she rolled it over and over in her fingers, her face a mix of wonderment and uncertainty.

9. Scary Monsters
(And Super Creeps)

A tangle of masts rose up from the harbour to greet them. Ted was surprised how many actual sailing boats were moored here. He half-expected to see a longship hidden in the cluster of docks and boats, its complement of fierce, bearded warriors scowling down at him and banging their swords against wooden shields.

Tilda had changed into a pair of denim cut-offs; underneath a loose-fitting shirt, she wore a deep blue bikini top. She led him and Loki along the docks, passing aluminum boats and covered old fishing crafts that reminded Ted of something out of *The Beachcombers*. A dead fish floated in a pocket of scummy water, belly up, its open mouth just above the surface. Ted wrinkled his nose at the smell.

Tilda stopped at a new-looking aluminum craft with a large outboard motor. It had a dock all to itself.

"Back in Amma's day, we had a bad reputation," Tilda said by way of explanation.

"Nice lady like your Amma?" Loki harrumphed. "Hard to believe."

"Not liking you, trickster, is by no means a character flaw."

She stepped into the boat and hurled a damp, smelly lifejacket at Loki. "Just in case. It's not a comment on my piloting."

Tilda guided the boat dubbed *The Grey Lady* out of the harbour past—to Ted's surprise—a Canadian Coast Guard ship, and headed north. Across the lake Ted could just make out the far eastern bank and the trees that grew upon it. Staring straight ahead, they may as well have been upon the ocean: water stretched out ahead of the small craft, seemingly forever, blue in patches, green where the sunlight brushed it as it peered through the clouds. There were a few other vessels out, the occupants either fishing or skiing, but as Tilda angled the boat towards the centre of the lake, it wasn't long before they were alone on the water.

They skipped over the shallow rises and troughs, sending mist and spray over the bow to splash the faces of the boat's occupants. Ted glanced over at Tilda. She seemed happy to have shucked herself out of the grey woollen shroud her family had wrapped her in.

"Oh, Ted," Loki hollered with a false, saccharine sweetness. "Do try to control your temper out here, would you? This isn't the place, or craft, we want to face another thunderhead in."

"That was you?" Tilda yelled over the wind and howling engine.

"Yeah," Ted nodded.

She punched his shoulder. "Asshole. You left me with a hell of a mess to clean up."

"Sorry," he yelled against the wind.

"I'm in enough shit with Amma over your reading, try not to swamp our boat too."

"If it's worth consideration," Loki said, laying a hand on Tilda's thigh as he leaned over to speak into her ear. "I had angered young Theodore."

"You're good at that," Tilda said.

"You have no idea," Ted muttered.

"Adventure." Loki grinned and clapped him on the shoulder. "It's just like the good old days."

As the boat revved forward, Ted yelled at Loki, "So how are we going to find your boy?" The shore had disappeared behind them, and Ted felt insignificant and ill at ease. His chest itched as if ants were crawling over him, and clouds were rolling in from the north and gathering over the lake.

"Calm yourself," Loki said, eyeing the sky.

"I'm trying."

"Might I suggest you try harder?"

Ted gripped the aluminum bench he was sitting upon. He closed his eyes and breathed, slowly and deeply, through his nose.

The boat slowed and Tilda killed the motor.

"Drop the anchor," she said. "This should do."

"Did you bring the ox head?" Loki asked.

"What?" Ted answered.

"I told you, we'd need an ox head to go fishing. Jorry always had a taste for oxen." Loki sighed. "Do I have to do everything?

You'll have to talk fast when we find my boy now. If you don't want to be eaten that is."

"Fuck," Ted muttered.

"Focus, Ted," Tilda said warningly. The sky was growing darker above them.

The boat rocked gently as it rode the water. Shadows from advancing thunderheads slid over the lake, pushing a wall of chill wind before them. Behind them clouds had swallowed the sun, though those didn't hold the same malice.

Ted squinted out over the water. "Are those islands?"

"No," Tilda said, shaking her head. Gooseflesh puckered her exposed skin. "They aren't."

Three small shapes jutted from beneath the surface of the lake. It was difficult to track their motion as they grew closer. The shapes were the green of clear water, kissed by sunlight, and blended neatly into the lake.

Ted had a feeling that—as with icebergs—what dwelt beneath was far larger.

And far more dangerous.

Every second another shape pierced the surface, some barely breaking the water, while others arched over the lapping waves as the preceding coils slipped back into the depths of the lake. The undulating barrier formed a wide circle around the boat.

"We seem to be surrounded," Loki said.

"No shit," Tilda answered. She pulled a leather pouch from the bag at her feet; Ted recognized it as the one that held her rune stones, but couldn't imagine how a reading would help them right now.

The boat rocked dangerously, nearly capsizing, as something lanced up from the depths of the lake. Water sprayed over them, soaking them to the skin.

What rose before them defied belief. And that was saying something, given Ted's current week.

A serpent, a car-length in diameter, shook violently. More waves slapped against the boat, pushing it backwards. Capping the scaly body was a head that came close to resembling an alligator's—excepting the many frills and spined ridges that jutted from it. It opened its maw and bellowed.

The teeth were conical, and slightly curved, each looking about the length of Ted's arm. Ted hoped fear was causing him to exaggerate. The head lowered slowly to rest upon the surface of the water. And the creature grinned.

Nope, no exaggeration there.

Every breath the serpent took sent a spray of misted lake water into the air. Loki stood and spread his arms wide. The action rocked the boat precipitously, and Ted clenched the small comfort of his aluminum seat, feeling it crumple in his hands .

"Loki," he said through ground teeth. "Sit the fuck down."

The trickster ignored him, instead smiling widely at his monstrous son.

"Jorry!"

"Loki," the serpent replied flatly. Its breath was rank with rotting fish, chlorine, and worse. A lipless smile revealed a shape that may have been a human arm further back among the rows of teeth.

"My boy," Loki said, clucking his tongue. "Is that all you have to say to your dear old dad?"

"Those days are long over." Jormungandur said coldly. Resting on the surface of the water the head of the serpent stared eye to eye with Loki. Jormungandur's voice was wet. Wheezing. The serpent spoke like someone with pneumonia. And yet, it didn't sound weak at all. Even Jormungandur's voice held a vastness that beggared description. "This is the new world. And you shouldn't be in it."

Splashes from all around them drew Ted's attention, and he watched the coiled lengths of the serpent's ever-moving body as they kept the giant maw above the surface.

"Nor should you, my boy, nor should you."

"I have repaid you for that, with interest. Where's my tribute?"

The trickster glanced at Ted, who felt a sudden stab of fear and worry that he was about to be sold out.

Loki looked as relaxed as if he was lounging in a corner booth at a bar.

"I don't have it *with* me," he said, drawing out the "with."

"Then you've brought me nothing. And that makes two you owe me." The serpent snorted a green cloud from its nostrils. "And here there are two on your craft. Two who stink of the Nine Worlds, sitting helpless in my domain."

Ted rose unsteadily to his feet, and rolled back his sleeves and held up his hammer hand.

"We're not as helpless as you think."

Membranes slid horizontally over the serpent's eyes, and a long slender tongue slid from its maw to taste the air. The thing shuddered, as if barely containing some torrent of emotion, and the shudder sped through the length of the beast. Small waves slapped against the hull of *The Grey Lady*. Ted wondered if he had doomed them.

The serpent chuckled a wet, derisive laugh. "This is the instrument?"

Ted didn't like being ignored, and knew his temper was about to get the better of him.

"Why does everyone keep calling me that, I'm not a fucking guitar," Ted said in the low voice he saved for when drunken mayhem was about to be unleashed.

"And yet you are being played." The serpent cocked its head back and laughed. At least Ted assumed it was a laugh. If a human even could have made that sound, it would have sounded more like choking. "You seek to fight me? To try your "hammer" against me? I am Jormungandur! I am the monster. I have killed gods. What are you to me?"

Ted said, "More like Nessie's white-trash cousin."

Jormungandur hissed. A puff of green mist clouded around Ted's face. The serpent's every breath was poison, according to the ravens. Loki's eyes went wide and he almost capsized them in his rush to get himself to the back of the boat.

"*Algiz*," Tilda said, holding up a rune stone. A gust of wind, blowing against the clouds dispersed the mist. The after-image of the rune remained in the air. Ted took a breath; the air stank, but didn't affect him otherwise. No watering eyes, no coughing or burning.

"Nessie," he taunted again.

"Stop it," the serpent howled. "I can kill you."

"Can you? You need tribute brought to you. You can't affect

the world anymore. You're a legend at best, and a laughingstock to most. Ogopogo, Manipogo. More people know those names now, than the Midgard Serpent. You're not so terrible. You're just a mouldering old story."

"Oh, I can kill you. You've been touched by the Nine Worlds. I have no restrictions about acting against you." Jormungandr snaked its eye line across the entire boat. "Against any of you. And it won't be so long before the fence Odin built around Midgard is gone entirely. A dead god's wishes cannot hold forever."

Ted lowered his right arm, and slid his shirtsleeve over most of the image of Mjölnir. It was comforting, though, to have the hammerhead peering out from the fabric.

The dvergar gave you more than the hammer, Huginn hissed.

"Do you think Mjölnir's my only weapon?" Ted opened his other hand, and the light of day poured out of it. Ted pushed his shirt up to reveal the horn that curled about his left arm.

The Gjallarhorn, Muninn prompted.

Summon the honoured dead, Huginn added. And they will come to fight for you. Dwarves give their gifts in threes. Three dvergar gifted you, Theodore. Three times three. You are the Nine Worlds. If he sinks this vessel you will stride upon the waters like Njord the Sea Lord. You will send him cowering and hiding back to the depths.

"No man, no god, between Asgard and Hel's cold hall has ever spoken to me thus," Jormungandur hissed.

"He talks to me like that all the time," Loki muttered.

Ted hadn't realized he'd been speaking the ravens' words. That scared him, that Thought and Memory could be so insidious.

"The last time that hammer fell upon me, my breath—what should have been my dying breath—poison to man and god, sent the Thunderer to his Doom. But I woke. And now it seems he has too."

"I'm not him," Ted said.

"We died linked together, as we were when we lived, as we are now, after the end of days. Mere stories. We are legends told to children. And you are a child now, newly born into the Nine Worlds. Mewling and shitting, wailing and pissing. It should be so easy to kill you now."

"But you won't."

"Why do you protect them still?"

"I'm one of them," Ted answered.

"No, you're not. No longer a man, not quite a god. You will have a shadow of life, a reflection of existence." Jormungandur sighed, and closed its maw. Here and there teeth jutted from beneath the serpent's scaled jaw. It was as close to a smile as Ted expected to see. "Valhalla is shattered. There will be no feast hall waiting for you after your death. Only Hel's grey mists. My sister waits for all now, especially you." Ted hoped the serpent meant Loki and not him.

"This world is soiled. Soiled with the filth those pitiful humans you fought so hard to protect spew into my realm. More with every passing day. I drink them in—the poisons man dumps into my home. They feed me as mother's milk from my father's breast.

"Your cities. Your stinking cities. Once I could have swept them from the face of Midgard with a swipe of my tail, leaving them to swim or drown in my ocean. I could have coiled round and squeezed, crushing them as I did the ships of so many who dared cross my seas."

"Those days are gone," Ted said. "I'm not."

"It's a new world," the serpent sighed, and breathed out another cloud of stinking green gas. "And I resent my place in it."

The poison pressed up against the rune, the shield buckled, but did not break. Tilda was sweating, veins bulging on her furrowed brow. A shaking hand kept the protective rune stone aloft.

"Then do something about it," Ted offered. The serpent stared, unmoved. "Help us. Why does the hero always have to slay the dragon?"

"Ted—" Loki warned.

"How would you have me help you?" Jormungandur rumbled.

"I need the Head of Mimir."

Many of the coils surrounding the boat slid under the water until only Jormungandr's head remained above the surface.

"And why do you seek that stuffed old wizard?"

"It is the price the Norns demand."

"And you trust them?" The serpent levelled its head at Tilda. "Are you trustworthy?"

"I am." Tilda said. "We are."

"We shall see." Jormungandur grinned wide, showing many, many teeth. "Go north, you may find Mimir in Ross Lake."

Ted squinted and scowled.

"Flin Flon," Tilda said behind him.

North. Flin Flon. *The dwarves.* Ted clasped his hammer hand and cracked his knuckles. *Better and better.*

He must have muttered it aloud; the Midgard Serpent bobbed his head. "Yes, the dwarves will be there." The serpent's response would have been comical if Ted wasn't worried about being eaten. "But you should know that they and the Norns are not the only ones who seek Mimir's counsel."

"Who else?" Ted asked.

The Serpent laughed. "Who haunts your nightmares, mortal man?"

"Surtur," Ted said, his voice barely a whisper.

"Shit," Loki muttered. "That'll complicate things."

They couldn't let Surtur get the Head. If Mimir was as wise as the Norns made him out to be Ted didn't want to think about what Surtur could use him for.

"Enjoy the hospitality of the Grey Ladies," Jormungandur said suddenly. "Loki, consider us even."

"Does that mean—?"

Ted felt himself and the boat get lifted from the water and thrown. He saw Loki and Tilda pin-wheeling through the air. Lake spray and wind rushed past his face. The trickster's words came back to him—*he's not a dragon, he's a serpent*—and as the waters of Lake Winnipeg waited to welcome him, he couldn't shake a childhood of Sunday school lectures about the evil, twisted nature of snakes.

10. Walk on the Water

For a time when he'd been a boy, Ted had wanted to be an astronaut. Now, in a way, he'd been given his wish.

He could feel a brief moment of weightless suspension as he stopped rising into the air and just before he began to plummet towards the churning waters. For a second, the motorboat hung in the air beside him, caught in a thick, jade coil. The aluminum squealed as Jormungandur tightened its grip, crushing the small vessel.

"Fuck!" Ted yelled.

He pinwheeled his arms and legs, trying learn to fly in a few seconds. Ted had lost sight of the others. Annoyingly, Huginn and Muninn chose this moment to remain silent. A whiff of gasoline tickled his nose as he fell. With his luck the wreck would catch fire.

One of Ted's shoes had been knocked off in the impact, taking his sock with it. He twisted around, trying to straighten himself out so that he would knife into the water feet-first. Was this the deepest part of the lake? The World Serpent was able to hide here. How much of that was nature, and how much was magic?

Ted's feet hit the water and his fall stopped dead. The foot that still bore its sneaker sank a few inches into the lake, throwing him off balance. Spinning his arms in an effort to remain upright, Ted put all his weight on his bare right foot.

"Fucking magic," Ted muttered. Hopping atop the waves, he slipped his other shoe and sock off, letting them slide under the water. Ted set his left foot down gingerly. It didn't sink either.

Sleipnir, Huginn said.

Did one of you just sneeze?

The first of Loki's children, Muninn corrected sharply. **Odin's eight-legged horse.**

Odin rode Loki's son? Ted shook his head; he didn't want to know.

Sleipnir ran as easily over air and water as solid ground, bringing the High One into battle, Huginn lectured. Ted let the raven drone on. He was more concerned with finding Tilda. **And he was as lusty as his father. Odin's valkyries all rode one of Sleipnir's brood.**

You have horse legs tattooed upon your own. Like Ted might have fucking forgotten. **And horseshoes on the bottoms of your feet. Four shoes per foot. Sleipnir.**

Wreckage was strewn over the water, but there was no sign of Tilda. No Loki either. Ted tossed pieces of the boat aside, scanning the water. *There!* Ted rushed to Tilda.

He wondered what his old Sunday school teacher would have said about him walking on water to rescue a Norse seeress. Mrs. Weins had always said he'd come to a bad end. Too many questions. Not enough belief. The belief wasn't going to be a problem anymore. What he believed in, perhaps, but not faith itself. Amazing what the endless coils of a mythological sea serpent will do to hammer home that you're living a saga. Of course he felt more like Elmer Fudd than Leif Eiriksson.

Tilda was floating face up. Her eyes were closed, and a line of blood ran from her scalp. Ted knelt down and pulled Tilda out of the water, cradling her gently in his arms. Her chest rose and fell with a shallow breath. Ted let out a relieved sigh.

She's alive.

"Tilda?" Her rune stone bag dangled from her wrist; her fist was clenched shut. When she didn't answer, Ted pried her hand open, revealing a rune stone. He tucked the stone into a pocket. *She'd hate to lose this.*

Looking around, there were no other boats visible on the water. There was nothing but water. A fish poked its head up from below the lake. Large eyes stared at Ted strangely while its jaw moved.

What the hell?

The fish's stare intensified and a voice came from its mouth, sounding wet and small.

"Took you long enough. I'm not built to be life-support you know."

Ted shook his head. Now a fish was talking to him.

Fucking magic.

Loki has used a salmon's shape before, Muninn muttered. **Trying to escape the Aesir's wrath.**

At the moment Ted didn't care about what the trickster had done, or had been said to have done, or if there was a difference. Despite everything, Loki had saved Tilda.

"Thanks," Ted said sincerely.

Sliding its gills below the surface of the lake, the fish asked, "For what?"

"Keeping Tilda above water," Ted said.

"Yeah, well about that," Fish-Loki said. "I don't think you'll thank me when the other Norns come after you."

"They won't. They need me."

"Maybe, but think about it, Ted: they want Mimir to end magic on Midgard. You're magic now. Urd won't trust you to give up power. They won't let you go. Or live."

"I want my old life back," Ted said automatically.

"Do you?"

Do I? He'd been saying it so often, the desire had lost its meaning.

"Urd has seen what happens when mortals are given gifts from the gods."

"But Tilda—"

"Is one of them."

"So why'd you save her?"

If a fish could look embarrassed, Loki did. "Your foolishness and bullheaded nature must be rubbing off on me."

Ted smirked down at the talking fish.

"Given your history, that can only be a good thing." Ted looked around again. "Now what?"

"Now, we run for the shore," Loki said. His jaw rested upon Ted's foot. The fish scales felt cool and slimy. Loki had raised the head again to the point where the gills had left the water, and his mouth worked feverishly as if gulping for air.

And then a foot-long rat stared up from Ted's foot.

"Christ!" he yelled, shaking his leg. The rat clung tightly to Ted's jeans.

"Ted! It's me!" Loki squeaked.

Clambering up Ted's leg and around his waist, Rat-Loki seemed to know how his every motion made Ted's skin crawl. When the rat came to rest on his right shoulder Ted fought the urge to reach out and grab the rodent. To crush it and hurl it away. With one last shudder, he let Loki be instead of using the trickster's rat body as a skip rock.

"Okay, start running," Loki said, pointing with his little rat paw. "That way."

Ted shook his head, exasperated.

"You can't even swim for yourself?"

"It's far, and you're so much bigger than me," the rat pleaded from Ted's shoulder, rubbing its hands, and twitching its whiskers and acting like some orphan from a Dickens story.

It was as if his bare feet weren't touching the waves. They didn't even feel wet, as if he was moving over the surface tension of the water. It had been a long time since he'd run and Ted doubted he could still pull off a four-five in the forty. Coach Dean would be pissed. Ted started running at a long distance pace.

"You should have dragged her on a piece of the boat," Loki offered. "It would have been faster. Or you could drop her, and drag her by her hair."

"Or… I could… drop you," Ted replied through steady deep breaths.

"Keep running," Rat-Loki squeaked. "You're doing great. Almost there."

"I… don't need… a fucking… coach."

"If you're breathing so hard, maybe you should quit smoking?"

Ted ignored the rat. But he did wonder. The dwarves had made him strong. Tough. They couldn't have helped him out with the fucking cardio?

The shoreline was coming into sight, and as it grew closer, Ted could see the rich-looking cabins, that at intervals lined the lake.

"Shit," Ted muttered, slowing down. "I can't be seen running on water."

"Fog," Loki said. "Summon up some fog."

"The weather's not right for fog, won't that be suspicious?"

"Ted," Loki said, crossing his rat arms. "You are walking on water, carrying an unconscious woman and a rat. You think fog will look suspicious?"

"Point taken."

Summon some fog. Change the weather. It had happened often enough on its own. The last time he'd tried to affect the skies consciously he'd been struck by lightning. If he lost control again, he'd survive.

Tilda wouldn't.

Electricity still arced around the hammer tattoo on Ted's arm and hand. He didn't want to summon another storm. But the thunder came so easily. It wanted to be called. It needed to be called.

But not now. Reaching inward, Ted grasped the trapped power of the storm. His chest tingled. He felt the clouds thicken, growing upwards and outwards. Filling the sky. But Ted tapped the smallest portion he could hold.

Interesting, Huginn noted clinically, **the thunderhead tattoo is changing to match the weather you have summoned.**

Ted ignored the raven, and let the power trickle free. The clouds dropped to the water. They were thick and heavy with moisture.

That way, Muninn said. **We came from that way.**

What good to know where we came from? Huginn asked, nudging Ted in a different direction. **It is too far to return. The closest point ashore is that way.**

Loki pointed in the same direction Huginn had suggested. "Shore is that way, Ted."

You'd agree with Loki? Muninn accused Huginn.

He agreed with me.

Hardly an endorsement, Muninn muttered.

Tilda moaned softly in Ted's arms. She was still out, but she no longer hung limp in Ted's grasp. While he ran, she had twined her arms around his torso. Occasionally, it felt as if she were trying to burrow her head into his chest.

"Tilda?" Ted whispered.

The young woman looked up at him blinking. "Don' go… not safe for you… sorry Ted. So… sorry."

Ted shushed her. "It's not your fault." He wasn't sure she'd heard him; she was already unconscious again.

"She's right, though," Loki said. "It's not safe. Not if Surtur's involved. We can't go back to Gimli. We need to get the Head before him."

"But—"

"No. You're going to have to leave The Goat there."

"Fuck," said Ted.

"We can pick it up later. If we survive until later."

"Can't you magic it here? Like you did with the beer?"

The rat on his shoulder stared at him like he was insane.

"A car is a little bigger than a couple of beers, Ted."

"Fuck."

Ted's next step brought the sound of shale crunching beneath his foot. They'd made landfall. Through the soup-thick fog he'd conjured, Ted could just make out the cabin jutting from the trees.

Loki hopped off Ted's shoulder and changed into his familiar skinny man's shape. He started walking bare-assed towards the cabin.

"C'mon Ted," he said over his shoulder. "We'll get some dry clothes, boost their van, and get the fuck out of here."

"What if someone's home?" Ted asked.

Loki rolled his eyes. "I think we can take some cottagers. They have a dock, but there's no boat moored here. They're out on the lake or in town."

Ted felt a twinge of guilt, stranding a family in magical fog. Of course the cottage belonged to a family. Who else would drive a minivan by choice?

"And what about Tilda? Are we taking her to Flin Flon?"

"Damn it, man," Loki said, shaking his head and turning around. Ted looked away from the bony, naked little man. "We should leave her here. I'm sure the noble citizens who will shortly be donating to our cause will take excellent care of her."

"You can't know that."

"When have I been wrong?"

"Let's see," Ted said sourly. "How about: Let's go see my son, Jorry?"

Loki flipped him the bird. "If we hadn't gone to Jorry we wouldn't know where the Head was at all, Mister I'm-Shit-at-Asking-Questions." Ted tried to interrupt but Loki kept talking over top of him. "Or that Surtur was trying to find the Head too. If you'd listened to me and we'd come here first, without the stink of the Norns on us, it might've gone better. They want to end *his* existence too, you know."

Ted shook his head but remained silent.

"Definitely would've gone better if you'd brought the ox head," Loki muttered.

He had reached the door to the cabin, and bent over to examine the lock on the door.

"*Ahh!*" Ted looked away to avoid the view. "Do you mind?"

"For gods' sakes," Loki muttered. He changed again, and Ted found himself looking at his ex-wife's body. When Loki leaned forward to work the locked door, she—*no, he, always remember Loki is he*—arched Susanna's back and thrust her butt towards Ted. "Happy now?"

Ted felt a very different concern. And wasn't sure he would call it happiness.

"Not funny, Loki."

"Don't be such a prude, Ted. C'mon. Once more around the block. You know you want to. You know it'll be good." Loki turned around, revealing Susanna's all-too-familiar body. He arched an eyebrow coyly. "I've had a lot more time to practise than her."

There was a click, then Loki pushed the door open with a flourish, and sighed. "So nice to do things the old-fashioned way." Ted was uncertain if he was referring to sex, or picking locks, and quite frankly didn't want the point clarified. "Nothing beats practice."

"Just get some fucking clothes on."

Ted pushed past Loki, with Tilda still in his arms. Loki took a half-step forward, brushing against Ted, who did his best to ignore the contact with Susanna's body.

Old and new were at war inside the cabin. The timbers were exposed, the banister on the staircase was lacquered but otherwise looked roughly cut. As they stepped from the porch into the kitchen they moved over gleaming modern dark and light tile. The fireplace was wood-burning, not gas; every appliance was stainless steel. A large island in the centre of the kitchen was covered in a variety of clutter: keys, papers, hats, and what looked like a portable game console.

Ted carried Tilda through the open kitchen and to the living room where an antique rocking chair faced a chocolate leather couch and chair set. He set her down carefully on the couch.

Pacing the floor, he asked the trickster, "Are you going to find some clothes?"

"Eventually," came a husky voice from behind the open fridge door—now he was talking like her too. Ted wasn't sure what was worse about Loki in that body—using her voice or his own. Ted sighed as Loki held up an apple and some sandwich meat. "Hungry?"

Loki closed the refrigerator and sauntered into the living room, plopping Susanna's body down on the chair and putting a dirty foot up on an ottoman. He took a loud, slurping bite of the apple.

"Do you have to walk around looking like her?"

"Hey, buddy," Loki said, pointing a finger and giving him a wink and a wiggle, "you're the one who married her. I figured you'd be more comfortable looking at this body than mine."

"Right now, neither option is much of a prize."

Ted traced a finger around the cut on Tilda's head. She winced slightly, but didn't open her eyes.

"C'mon, Ted, get it out of your system."

"What?"

"You forget," Loki said. "I know what your last several months together were like. I figured I'd give you another chance to storm the back gate."

Ted ground his teeth. He was getting tired of this.

Loki affected a soap-opera pout. "I'm a woman, Ted. I have needs."

"Yeah," Ted muttered. "The need to fuck with me."

"Part right," Loki agreed.

Ted shook his head, and turned back to Tilda. He watched her chest rise and fall in slow, steady breaths. As much as he wanted to pretend Loki's posturing and games didn't bother him, they did. Of course they did. He had spent too many nights wondering if either he or Susanna had just reached out, started talking again, would they still be together. Maybe.

Probably not.

But reality had no sway with desire. It had been a while—*too fucking long*—since he'd had sex. A no-questions-asked, breakup fuck with Susanna was not something Ted would have turned down. A reminder of the happier times. Fucking Loki in Susanna's body would be no such thing. Ted wanted better. Hell, Susanna deserved better too.

Ted felt for Tilda's pulse. It was there, and steady. The action was also a good excuse to ignore Loki. The Norn's skin seemed almost a talisman against the trickster's taunts.

"I know what your problem is," Loki said from behind him. It was Loki's voice. Ted hoped for a moment that Loki had stopped using Susanna's form. He glanced back.

Nope.

"You're afraid you'll like it."

Ted grimaced. "I should have left your fucking mouth sewn shut in Gimli."

Bare feet padded over the area rug that covered the hardwoods in this part of the house and Loki stood behind Tilda, leaning on the couch.

"What are we going to do with her?"

"Take her home."

Loki shook his head. Susanna's long blonde hair swayed with the motion, "No time." He looked down, admiring the body he was wearing. "You know, a brass bra and some strappy sandals, and she would have been a hell of a valkyrie. We can't go back to Gimli, Ted. And we can't take her with us."

"Why not?" Ted asked.

"Her offer of hospitality ended when Jorry wrecked the *Grey Lady*. We can't trust her not to betray us."

"The God of Lies is telling me not to trust someone," Ted snorted. "That is fucking rich."

"Believe it, Ted. The Norns want us both dead. Okay, they want me dead and you neutered. Bring them Mimir's Head, and you're handing them your balls." Susanna-Loki twined his hand in Tilda's hair. "And she won't be able to help herself. She'll have to do us in. Whether she wants to or not. Whether she wants you or not."

The trickster tightened his grip on Tilda's hair, and jerked her head back. Tilda gasped and her eyes opened.

She jumped to her feet, clawing at the bag of rune stones around her wrist. "Who're you?"

"I'm Ted's wife," Loki screamed back. Fuck if he hadn't managed to nail Susanna's angry voice perfectly. "Who the Hel are you?"

Tilda started for a moment, blinking in confusion. She rubbed at her forehead and winced.

"Nah, I'm just kidding," Loki said in his own voice.

"Where is it?

"Til—"

"My stone. What did you do with it?"

Loki smiled. "Why would you think I took it?"

"Why would I think you didn't?"

The trickster shrugged. "Don't have it."

Tilda looked to Ted. "He doesn't."

Burying her face in her hands before Ted could say more, Tilda started to cry. "Amma's gonna kill me."

Loki nodded. "Welcome to the club."

"I've got it," Ted said, digging in his pocket. "Here."

The Norn took the stone from Ted, almost gingerly, and then pulled him into a crushing hug.

"Thank you," she whispered, giving him a peck on the cheek.

She felt good pressed up against him—damn good.

Ted tucked a strand of Tilda's uneven black hair behind an ear. "That was quite a knock you took."

"Is he… is that really your wife?"

Ted looked back. Loki was still wearing Susanna's body, and still naked. "Yeah."

Loki cupped Susanna's breasts. "Jealous? You're jealous. If you're worried, you could use some of Urd's gold to trade up a size."

"Sure you're okay?" Ted asked. "You have a headache? Nausea?"

She shot a glare at Loki. "Only from him."

"The Norns will soon know what she knows," Loki accused. "Leave her."

Ted turned to Tilda. "Is he right?"

"I don't want to." She buried her face in her hands. "I can't say no to Mom and Amma. I... I just can't. This is who we are."

"You extended hospitality to us when you didn't need to, Tilda," Ted said, kneeling down, and gently nudging her head out of her hands. "I'm sure they weren't happy about that. You volunteered your boat to look for Jormungandur. You've helped us."

"It won't last," Loki said.

"Can they really see us now?" Ted asked.

"I don't know. Maybe Amma could read where we've been. Mom's control is better than mine, but she still needs a vision or the runes to watch us in the now."

Loki asked Ted, "Want to test your luck?"

A door creaked open and they all turned.

A boy, maybe thirteen, with sandy blond hair and freckles walked out scratching his head. He wore an X-Men T-shirt and pyjama bottoms. "Mom, have you seen my—" His eyes went wide as he saw the three strangers who had broken into his home. "Who are you?"

Loki walked Susanna's body front and centre, and the boy's eyes went even wider with the naked woman blocking his view of Ted. The trickster looked back and winked.

"Sleep, Seamus," Loki said, and the boy collapsed. He picked the boy up, set him in the rocking chair, and leaned in close to the boy's ear. "And dream well."

"Great," Ted said. "That kid is going to be jerking off to the thought of my ex-wife for the rest of his life."

"He could do worse." Loki cracked his neck back and forth,

and leaned over to reach behind the couch. "Let's get out of here."

Loki straightened up with a set of men's clothes in his hands. As he slid the pants up his legs, his body changed back to his normal appearance.

"Beer's in the fridge and keys are on the table," he said.

Ted pulled Tilda to her feet.

"Run upstairs and look for some dry clothes."

"Yeah, Ted. No," Loki said, shrugging on a too-large suit jacket.

"Go, on," he said to her. "We're not leaving without you."

"I'm going to get you killed," she said, her voice near breaking.

Ted smiled. "No. If anyone is going to get me killed—" he jerked a finger back at Loki— "It's that asshole."

Loki busied himself filling a cooler full of beer and food while Ted looked through the shoes piled near the entrance for something that fit him.

"So, you're bringing her with us, then?"

"Yeah."

"I can't change your mind?" Loki asked.

"Nope."

"All right," Loki shrugged and hefted the cooler, groaning. "Could you carry this out for me, then?"

"Too heavy? You're a fucking god."

"Yeah, but you're bigger than me."

"Oh, for fuck's sake," Ted grumbled and stuck his feet into a pair of neon flip-flops, the only shoes in his size. He grabbed the cooler, hoisting it over his shoulder.

Peeking around the stairwell, as if she was surprised to see him, was Tilda.

Holy shit. Ted's breath caught. He felt a jolt in his chest and he knew the storm was moving beneath his skin. Thunder rumbled outside the cabin. As she came padding down the stairs barefoot, dressed in a simple sundress, Ted couldn't help but gawk at Tilda. Every bullshit stunt Loki had pulled hadn't stirred more than anger in him. But seeing Tilda now… Ted let out a long breath.

She smiled. Pleased he hadn't left, or amused at the look on his face, Ted wasn't sure.

Loki grabbed a set of keys off the island.

"Let's roll," he said with a grin. "I'm driving."

11. Born to Run

The drive was torture.

Absolute torture.

Loki had the stolen van headed north on Manitoba Highway 6. They'd just passed through the town of Ashern. There were probably a couple hours before they'd reach the junction where they'd turn northwest on No. 60 to get to Flin Flon through The Pas. Twilight had fallen. The moon was full, or near enough to appear so, and light reflected off a growing number of rocks in the ditch.

The highway was shit. The only CDs in the van were a while-you-drive Spanish primer, an impressive assortment of harp music and the Avril Lavigne CD that Loki had already sung along with. Twice.

"I love her," he said, nodding in time with the music and turning up the air conditioning. "She's more real than the other pop stars."

Loki skipped the disc back to "Skater Boy." Again.

"Whatever," Ted mumbled.

"Plus, have you seen her?" Loki took his hands off the wheel to cup imaginary breasts. The van drifted into the oncoming lane, which was fortunately empty. There had been remarkably little traffic so far.

"You have an unhealthy obsession with women who are too young for you," Ted said.

"And you don't, buddy?" Loki gestured towards where Tilda sat. The Norn stared out the windows and into the dark depths hidden by stands of spruce trees.

"Are you sure you can't just reach behind the seat and grab my iPod out of The Goat?"

"Ted," Loki said with exaggerated graveness. "I'm driving."

He started to sing again.

Tilda was silent on the bench seat behind them. Ted figured that she was trying to block both the CD and Loki from her mind. *If she can, she's luckier than I am.*

Ted tensed as he saw lights of an RCMP vehicle crest a dip in the road. It passed them and he exhaled only as the cruiser's white ghost disappeared in the rear view mirror. Still, Ted kept a nervous eye on the reflection, waiting for the car to swing around and begin pursuit. No doubt by now, the van had been reported stolen. The car disappeared from sight. No cherries flashed. No siren wailed. No one was on their tail.

"Relax, Ted," Loki said. "I swapped the plates before we left."

"Great, so they see a vehicle matching the make and model that's been reported stolen, run the plates and find they belong to a truck not a van."

"Please," Loki rolled his eyes. "You should know me better than that. I swapped the plates with a van of this make and model. I'm not an idiot."

"If you say so," Ted said, easing his seat back.

"Besides, do you have any idea how many cars get stolen in

Winnipeg? The cops don't care. They can't care. They don't have the time, or the money, to do anything about it. Unless you're driving like a dickhead, or you're dumb enough to steal a Hummer, they have no reason to pull you over. Now, pass me another beer."

Ted shook his head, thought about reminding Loki that they hadn't taken the van from Winnipeg. *What's the point?* With a sigh he reached back into the cooler to grope for another drink. He handed it to Loki, and then reached for one himself.

The cabin had been stocked with beers like Stella Artois, Heineken, and Newcastle Brown. To be honest, Ted would have been happier with a case of Bud or Pilsner, but he'd never claimed to be a connoisseur of beers. He didn't recognize the taste of the beer he was sipping, and checked the label in the dash lights—Fort Garry Pale. He'd never heard of it.

In the rear-view mirror Ted caught a glimpse of Tilda. Her lips were moving slowly, as if to form words, but no sound escaped from them. Clasped in her hands, the pouch of runes shook slightly.

"Til?" he asked.

She shook her head and covered her ears. Her brow furrowed as she clenched her eyes tightly shut. The speed of her silent recitation increased.

Worried, Ted asked, "What's happening?"

Tilda stopped chanting. "I think I blocked them."

"Who?"

"The Norns," Loki said matter-of-factly. "Her mother is trying to use Tilda to find us."

"She can really do that?"

"She's the Witch of the Present, Ted. A mother sees nothing but the present—the now—she can see us, hear us, smell us through her daughter if she so chooses." Loki reached around the seat and snapped Tilda in the forehead sharply with his middle finger. She hunched up, shielding her face partially with her forearms. "That's for making me do dishes."

"Hey!" Ted said.

"It didn't feel like Mom, or Amma." Tilda leaned forward to swat at the trickster. He shifted neatly aside so that she only hit the side of his seat.

"I told you not to bring her." Loki looked at him; there was no mischief on the trickster's face. No hint of a smile, no twinkle in the eyes. The scars dotting his upper and lower lips were pale, almost white, where Loki's sparse fringe beard had once hidden them. He licked his thin lips. "She puts us in terrible danger."

"So do you," Ted noted.

"But when I do it, it's funny."

"For you."

Now Loki smiled. "That, my friend, is the point."

"Touch her again, and I'll punch you through the fucking door."

"I love it when you talk butch."

"You think I won't?"

"Of course you won't. You're not an idiot. You'd survive the crash, but would the Norns' sugar-tittied little spy? She's not as resilient as we are. I wonder if her *jötunn* and *álfur* blood would keep her alive?"

"What makes you think there'd be a crash?"

"Ted, buddy, if a calamity can happen, I can will it to happen." Loki smiled. "Remember that the next time you decide to jerk off with that hammer hand of yours."

"I don't—"

Loki cocked his head and smirked. "So what were you doing all those nights you slept on the couch?"

"Just keep your fucking hands off her," Ted said, scowling and crossing his arms.

"You too, Teddy. You too."

They'd driven on in silence. Loki made no attempt to start the Avril CD again, and for that at least, Ted was grateful. The steady thrum of the tires over asphalt and vibrations the uneven surface sent through the vehicle were starting to pull at him, lulling him towards sleep. He fought the urge.

Ted had never been comfortable sleeping in cars, a result of being a driver. He was a terrible passenger and knew it. Unless he trusted whoever was in control of the vehicle, Ted was as twitchy as Joe Cocker. He could tick off his trusted drivers on the fingers of one hand, and Loki was not among them.

Even if he could ignore the fact Loki was a mythological figure, a god of lies and trickery—and Ted couldn't—the man's temperament would never have garnered trust or even much slack from the former oilman. In fact, if Loki hadn't raised such a stink about getting to drive, Ted probably would have wrestled the keys to the van away from him. Of course, he didn't like imagining the many annoying and petty ways in which Loki would have had his revenge during the long drive. Loki also would have been freer to torment Tilda.

Sleep beckoned. Despite his worry and misgivings, powers or no, Ted had been using his body hard since the dwarves' gift. *Gift.* He shook his head trying to knock the weariness from it. He couldn't wait to meet the *dvergar*, and thank them personally for their "gifts." As his mind drifted from worry about Loki's driving to far more pleasant thoughts of revenge, sleep finally took him.

He still thought of them as zz Top, *which was a little unsettling, as he liked the Texas bluesmen, but his clouded memory mixed the musicians liberally with his twisted makers. Lightning flashed as he scattered them like toys with his hammer hand. He stood above them. He was standing a foot above the ground, the soles of his bare feet resting on air. The only thing spared from his wrath was the red '30s coupe the dwarves had been driving around in.*

As he hovered above them, victorious, with his hammer hand clutching lightning, Avril Lavigne was cradled in his other arm, and she screamed with Loki's voice:

"FUCK!"

Ted opened his eyes in time to see the horizon pivot, and feel the lurch in his stomach as the nose of the van dipped down. A moment after the scream of metal and fibreglass crumpling in on itself, Ted felt the punch of the airbag across his face and chest, and the lurching snap of the seatbelt fighting his momentum to keep him in his seat. He pushed the airbag out of his vision.

They'd driven off the road and into a tree.

"Tilda?" Ted asked over his shoulder. "Are you all right?"

"I'm fine," Loki answered. "Thanks for asking."

Ted scowled at Loki and tore the seatbelt from its moorings. He slid over the console and into the seat next to Tilda. She was rubbing her shoulder. She seemed more startled than injured.

"It called them—the illusion—I could feel it call them."

"What?" Ted asked. His hand was tightening over her arm. He forced a deep breath, and loosened his grip. "Who'd it call?"

"The *jötnar*."

"Damn it," Loki muttered. He tried to open his door, but the crash had seized up some mechanism in it, and it stayed shut tight. "Ted, you need to get us the Hel out of here."

"In a minute."

"We may not have a minute," said Loki, his voice getting higher pitched and more desperate with each word. He slammed his shoulder into the jammed door.

Ted didn't check to see if the van's sliding side door would open. He lashed out with his fist. Metal squealed. The fasteners broke, and the deformed door flew free to tumble down into the trench. Ted stepped out and reached out to Tilda. She waved it away, hopping out after him.

Loki followed quickly on their heels, sniffing at the air. He spat on the loose earth.

"Damn AC. Must have masked their scent. That's what I get for wanting a taste of the cold winds of home."

Ted ignored him, but Loki kept talking.

"It was illusion. I can smell it in the air now." Loki spat again. "I can't believe I fell for one of their crude tricks."

"The *jötnar* have pulled more than a bit of wool over your eyes," Tilda said.

Loki's glare went from Tilda to Ted's raven tattoos. "Don't believe everything a bird tells you, Ted." He scrambled up the side of the ditch to the highway. "The Aesir just never listened to me."

"I can't imagine why not," Ted muttered. "Maybe they're working alone? The giants, that is."

Loki shook his head. "They were waiting for us."

"Maybe," Ted said, skeptical. "But they had to expect the Norns would send someone to get the Head." Ted turned to Tilda. "We're not the first who've been sent for Mimir, are we?"

Tilda shook her head. "No, you're not."

"You see, Loki." Ted said. "They expected us, doesn't mean the Norns set us up. They want us to succeed, not get killed."

"If you say so." Loki did not sound convinced.

Ted and Tilda joined the trickster on the shoulder of the highway.

She smoothed her stolen sundress over her hips and shivered slightly in the chill air. Ted admired her toughness. She hadn't complained, despite everything she'd been through. She was fun. She knew music, cared about it like he did. Didn't take shit from Loki. Hell, she didn't even hate football.

He dropped his eyes. Loki had been right about one thing: Ted was starting to take an interest in a woman too young for him.

Black spruce surrounded the road, jabbing up at the sky like spear tips, swaying slightly in the breeze. For a moment Ted wished Tilda had only been a sweet hitchhiker. Not a mythic seer. Not some harbinger of his doom, *wyrd*, fate, or whatever the fuck the vikings had called destiny. Maybe he wouldn't be in this mess. But then, maybe he would have never seen her again.

"Where are we?" Ted asked.

Loki scowled at Tilda before he answered. "We just passed through The Pas, not long ago. Hundred klicks to Flin Flon."

"Bit of a walk ahead of us."

"For you."

Loki's rumpled suit fell to the dirt. A large hawk hopped free of the suit jacket and keened sharply as it took to the air. The bird circled them in a wide arc before landing on Ted's shoulder, digging its talons through the fabric of his shirt. Ted felt the bird's weight, but no pain from its grip. "No giants yet," Loki squawked. "I'm going to find us another car."

"Fantastic," Ted said. "Just remember to come back for us when you find one."

"Teddy, baby, I just can't quit you." Membranes flickered over the hawk's piercing eyes, and Loki launched himself northward.

Ted nudged the clothes with his foot, grimacing. "You know, I think he changes his shape just so he can show up places naked."

A light laugh from Tilda made Ted smile.

"No sense in waiting around," Ted said. He took Tilda's hand in his, and started walking on the narrow gravel shoulder of the highway. They both kept an eye on the trees.

"Do you think he'll come back?" Tilda asked. She was walking stiffly, wincing a bit with every step. Ted made a conscious effort to slow his long stride, so she could keep up.

"Of course he's coming back," Ted said wryly. "Loki knows how much he irritates me. He lives for stirring up shit. Especially mine. Trust me, any peace and quiet will be short fucking lived."

Tilda's cheek dimpled as she fought to keep a smile from her face.

"I was taught to hate him, you know. For all he did before and after Ragnarök," Tilda said. "But now... he certainly has a way about him, doesn't he? I can almost see why the Aesir put up with him."

"That makes one of us," Ted tried to joke, but his heart wasn't in it. The truth was the annoying little man had grown on him. "What's keeping the fucking giants?" He looked at his watch; it had broken in the crash, its time frozen at the moment the van hit the ditch. "Are they afraid of me?" he asked, not really believing it.

"Maybe they're afraid of me."

Tilda ran her fingers over Ted's tattoos. She traced the outline of Thought and Memory. Ted stopped her. "It's not your fault."

"It is," she said. "If I hadn't done your reading, the *dvergar* never would have picked you out. Or Loki. I did this to you as surely as if I'd held the needle myself."

"Bullshit."

"Ted—"

"Did you blow up the patch? No. Did you carve me up? No. Did you pretend to be my dog while I slept with my wife?"

"What?"

"Forget it."

"You must hate me."

"I... I'm not sure what I feel for you, Til, but none of it's hate. I. Don't. Blame. You."

"I do."

"Stop. Doesn't do us any fucking good. I saw Surtur before I ever met you. That must be what drew you to me. And what drew Loki, and the dwarves." He looked at Tilda. "Right now, though, it sure doesn't seem so bad."

Tilda smiled.

"Do you think the giants will catch us before or after Loki gets back?"

"Before." It was more than a guess. She sounded certain. Knowing a seer was going to take some getting used to.

"Figures," Ted muttered. He shrugged. God or no, he had his doubts about how useful Loki would be in a fight. But at least he could have kept an eye on Tilda. Ted was feeling pretty confident about his own usefulness. The bouncers. The crash. Hell, he'd taken a lightning strike unscathed. Giants, how big could they really be, anyway?

The world was created from the bones of Ymir, the first jötunn.

Muninn superimposed visions over the road and trees. Shaggy men, dressed in rough furs and hides. They carried shattered trees as clubs, broken branches jutting out all over the length of them. They were huge, ranging in height between eight and twelve feet. And then, a second rank appeared behind the first. These wore coats of mail, and carried swords, axes, or spears. They dwarfed their fellows of the first ring, their helmets bobbing above the treetops. Then, pushing through the second rank came one too large to believe.

He would have shared a height with Surtur himself. Skin the blue of a frozen mountain lake, icicles dangled precariously from its long, hooked nose. Hoarfrost crusted a heavy beard and moustache. The giant grinned—a gap-toothed smile—through teeth like broken boulders.

Standing in the giant's long shadow was like being caught in an Alberta Clipper. Ted shuddered. Even looking at the apparition was making his fingers numb.

That's how big they can be, Huginn said smugly.

Ymir, Muninn prodded. The primordial Frost Giant. Surtur's opposite.

Ted's power had made him confident—cocky even. Seeing Ymir, he decided that rethinking that attitude might be a fantastic way to stay alive. How could someone fight something that big?

Huginn and Muninn took his stray concern as a request, and their voices, loud and penetrating in his ears, drowned out all the sounds of nature. Images of ancient battle were dredged into Ted's mind.

Things shaped like men have the same vulnerabilities as men. The same joints, soft spots, nerve centres, Huginn said.

In his vision a hammer crushed oversized feet and ankles. Ted clenched and released his fist. Lightning still danced in his palm. He knew the hammer he saw was Mjölnir, wielded by Thor's hand. It shattered hips, flew repeatedly into heavy fore-heads. Blood flowed as rivers from those wounds.

Giants bleed out quick, Huginn added. **Their oversized hearts and vessels like—**

"Hydraulics," Ted said.

Very good. You see, Muninn, he can think.

Fucking mouthy birds.

Tilda shivered. That little sundress she'd taken from the cabin would be of little warmth. Ted peeled off his shirt and pressed it into her hand. "Here," he said. "You need this more than I do."

"Won't you get cold?" she asked as she pulled the shirt over her head.

"I'll be fine."

Ted sat down next to the road and picked a stone from one of his flip-flops. It was annoying rather than painful, but the awareness of it between his foot and the shoe was distracting. Tilda sat next to him and rubbed at her own feet. There was a broad gravel clearing across the ditch and past some railway tracks. Hundreds of rail ties had been stacked there. Nearby, in the reflected light of the moon, a yellow sign exhorted readers to REPORT AND PREVENT FOREST FIRES.

In the moonlight, her eyes were taking in the electric blue of his tattoos. The markings were glowing faintly, almost phosphorescently in the gathering darkness.

"Your back," Tilda said. "Yggdrasill, the World Ash."

"So I've been told," Ted said, taking a seat beside her. "The tattoo is made up of the Elder Runes, but I haven't tried to touch that power yet."

He felt her fingers on his skin, and shivered. From her touch, rather than the cold.

"I thought you said you didn't need your shirt," Tilda said.

"I'm not cold, babe, just—"

"Horny?"

"I was trying to think of a nicer way to say it, but yeah." Ted laughed.

"Been a while?"

"Hell, yeah."

"For me too."

"I find that hard to believe."

"What does that mean?" Tilda demanded.

Fuck. That came out wrong. "You're beautiful," he stammered. "Who wouldn't want to be with you? That's all I meant."

"Sweet talker," Tilda teased. But Ted could make out her smile. "With my nature, I'd get pregnant. Once you get me pregnant, I take on Mom's role, and Mom takes Amma's."

"What makes you think you'll get pregnant?"

"That's my doom, Ted," she sighed. "I've always known it to be so. The women in our family are made to have a child. One child. And as quickly as possible. I've been dodging it for so long—"

"There's always condoms."

She snorted. "You holding? Anyway, tried that. A condom will break. It did before. I swore off sex after that." There wasn't anything magical to Ted about a rubber breaking. He'd torn a few here and there, and had some scares. It was like Urd was giving Tilda the opposite of the old you-can't-get pregnant-your-first-time myth. Her smile returned. "Well, mostly."

"So what happened?" Ted asked finally. "With the one that broke. If it's none of my business, just tell me to fuck off."

"Nah, I don't mind. He was just a boy at school. I liked him. We—condom broke, of course. I freaked, got one of those morning-after pills. Amma was so pissed with me. Delaying her retirement, she said."

"How old were you?"

"Thirteen."

"That is fucked up."

"It was for the best. He probably would've given me a son, then Amma would've been really pissed." She laughed a short, bitter laugh. "I stuck out Gimli and her nagging for a couple more years, then I hit the road. Only a matter of time before I'm stuck back there. That's my fate."

"Doesn't have to be. My offer still stands."

"You gonna take me away on your noble steed?"

Feigning hurt, Ted asked, "You don't like the GTO?"

Tilda smiled. "I love the GTO."

"Well, we won't be driving off into the sunset tonight," Ted said. He poked a finger lightly between her eyes. They crossed slightly trying to focus on the digit. "I doubt I could get it up knowing your whole family is riding around in there."

She brushed his finger aside. *This is a bad idea,* he tried to tell himself. There were so many fucking ways kissing her was a bad idea. He didn't care. Ted moved in to kiss her lips. She turned her head at the last second and his kiss landed on her neck instead.

"Ah, fuck," she said suddenly. "They're coming now."

There was a loud crashing from the east. The sound of heavy footsteps, and branches cracking. Silhouetted against the dark sky, above stacks of rail ties, Ted could see the tops of the black spruce swaying wildly, caroming into each other. He stood up and put himself between Tilda and the trees.

"Motherfuckers could've picked a better time," he observed.

The tattoo of Mjölnir was glowing brightly on his hand. Ready to unleash hell.

12. Your Lucky Day in Hell

There it was.

A giant.

An honest-to-God, real fucking giant.

Ted should have been scared shitless. He should have been running as fast as he could in the other direction. What he should not have been doing was rushing forward—barehanded, no less—to fight the thing. He wasn't sure what was crazier: giants existing, or believing he had a chance in hell of beating one.

But what choice did he have?

From high on a hill, the giant, a hairy thing just shy of ten foot, cocked its arm back to throw a rock at Ted. Rock. That was a bit of an understatement. It was the size of Ted's torso. Ted clenched his fist as the rock hurtled towards him. Mjölnir hummed with the power of a storm. Thunderclouds of black ink rolled over Ted's forearm. Arcs of electricity danced on the surface of his skin.

Hurtling granite met flesh and bone. The rock burst apart in a cloud of dust and debris. Instinct forced Ted to look away, unsure if his eyes shared the rest of his body's fortitude.

He held his clenched fist up above his head, the tattoo of the hammer glowing brightly.

"Mjölnir!" the giant yelled through blocky, yellowed teeth. "*Mjölnir!*"

"Fuck, yeah!" Ted yelled back.

The giant screamed again, its anger too great to form words.

Ted smiled. He'd been spoiling for a fight. Loki, the dwarves, the night in prison, Surtur. He welcomed the surge of adrenaline—and a fight where he didn't have to hold back.

The giant charged Ted, hurling itself down the hill in a long, loping gait. As it gathered speed, it brushed aside the trees like grass. Then it hunched over, bounding down the steep grade on all fours, more like a bear than a man. Great clumps of earth and grass kicked up in the giant's wake.

Ted stamped his feet down hard against the dry earth, preparing to meet the charge. Little clouds of dust rose and then settled. He kept his arm up, keeping the giant's focus on the glowing hammer. The giant roared, closing ground. Ted wrinkled his nose. The stink coming off the thing was like a landfill at midsummer.

The giant wrapped one meaty fist in the other and swung, two-handed, at Ted's side. Ted stood his ground. A car crash hadn't hurt him, he doubted he'd feel this impact either.

He felt it.

Not pain. Not really, but the force of the strike was unreal. As it turned out, his invulnerability was still subject to the laws of physics. Which hardly seemed fucking fair. Especially if the giants could flaunt their size so freely. Ted was lifted from the ground and into the air. He sailed over Tilda to crash into the railway ties. A crack filled his ears. Ted thought he would be all right, until a slow creak tingled up his spine.

"Ted! Look out!" Tilda yelled.

The pile was falling over. First one rail tie and then another struck Ted. He couldn't hear Tilda's response as the pile toppled, burying him.

Struggling beneath the weight, Ted felt the wind pick up. It howled through the pile, filling his mouth with dirt and grit. He groaned, and heaved a rail tie aside. The pile shifted and Ted stood up, scattering the heavy lengths of wood around the clearing.

Before he could get his bearings, the giant landed another two-handed blow, spit flying from its mouth as its doubled fist rebounded from Ted's chest.

The impact pushed Ted back to the earth. It should have killed him. Without the tattoos, it certainly would have. Of course, without the tattoos, there would be no reason for Ted to be here, in the middle of butt-fuck nowhere getting his ass kicked. By a giant.

"Ted!" Tilda screamed.

She was alive. A relief, but Ted wished she hadn't drawn attention to herself.

"Woman?" the giant said, getting a strange look on its face. It leaned forward and ran its tongue over a furred lip. "Your woman? Mine now."

The giant's rancid breath washed over Ted. Pushing against him, the giant levered itself back to its feet. There was a conspicuous and disturbing strain against a dirty mess of hockey jerseys that had been roughly stitched together to form its kilt.

"Woman!" it bellowed.

"Oh, fuck me," Tilda said, ducking behind a tree.

"Yes!"

"That wasn't an invitation," Tilda yelled, interposing her fist between her and the giant. "*Thurisaz!*"

A rune appeared, hanging in the air. The symbol was a straight line with a triangle jutting from its middle towards the right. The giant stopped dead in its tracks. It circled, its heavy feet slapping repeatedly against the earth as it tried to corner the Norn.

Tilda's body shook with strain. Her eyes were closed. If the rune failed, Ted knew she was done for. He dug his fingers into the ground and hauled himself out of the dirt. He hardly felt his feet touching grass as he hurled himself forward.

The giant turned to face Ted, slapping him aside. He couldn't get inside the damn thing's reach. It knelt over top of him now. Laughing.

"Weak," it taunted.

Let it mock. Ted was close enough now. When Mjölnir struck home, the squeal that passed the giant's lips was remarkably high-pitched. It doubled over, clutching at itself, moaning and rolling in the dirt. Judging by the way its kilt was now lying flat, Ted had knocked the wind out of its sails.

As Ted cocked his fist back, the giant kicked out at him. Mjölnir caught the giant's right knee. The giant cried out again as its kneecap was split, flailing at him, but Ted brushed the weak strikes aside. He struck again, this time at the giant's jaw, hoping to knock the thing out. There was another loud crack as the jaw shattered. Thick as the giant's bones were, to Mjölnir they were like glass.

The giant wailed and rocked back and forth. Tears, snot and spit mingled in the air as it beat at the earth. Ted wasn't sure what to do next. No doubt Loki would have told him to kill the thing. But Ted didn't have the heart for it.

He stood, dusted himself off and walked towards Tilda. "You okay?" he asked.

She nodded. "Yeah," she said, looking past him. "Yeah."

"What's wrong?"

"You have to kill him, Ted."

"Jesus, you too?"

Confused, Tilda asked, "What?"

"Well, I figured Loki would tell me to kill it, but you?"

"Him, Ted, him."

"What?" Now Ted was confused.

"He's not an it, as was painfully obvious by how he came at me. He's a dumb brute, but he can think."

"Giants are people too, now?" Ted shook his head.

"You won't live long in this world if you view everything touched by the Nine Worlds as a monster. My ancestors were *jötnar*. *Álfur*. Am I really just a myth with tits?"

"I…." Ted stopped, ashamed now to have his own words thrown back at him. Tilda confused the shit out of him. "No, of course not."

"Finish him. He's as good as dead anyway. He can't walk, can't hunt, can't even eat. His tribe won't take care of him. They'll feed him to their young."

"Christ." Ted shuddered. "They're cannibals?"

"They are what they are. The battle dead are honoured,

everyone else is… just food." Tilda's frown softened and she took Ted's hand in hers. "You're not doing him any favours. If you kill him now, he won't be awake when they start eating."

"Fuck."

The giant continued to wail behind them. Ted turned and watched it struggle. It—he—had churned the ground wherever his long arms could reach. Gravel and rock were pulled and tossed in large clumps, and deep furrows scarred the dry earth beneath.

Ted traced the outline of Mjölnir on his forearm. The lightning trapped within danced just beneath his flesh, waiting, craving the opportunity to strike. Call the thunder. Release the lightning. Strike him down.

There had to be another way.

He took a deep breath and exhaled slowly. He heard Huginn and Muninn but he wondered: could he speak to them? Would they answer? They'd listened when he'd told them to shut up. He shook his head, talking to ravens, talking to his tattoos. He must be losing his mind.

Can I help him instead?

Ted directed the thought towards the ravens. They didn't respond at first, and for a brief moment, Ted wondered if he had imagined all of their previous—and unwanted—advice and knowledge.

Why would you want to? Huginn asked. Muninn flooded Ted's mind with some of the atrocities committed by the giants in different times. Villages burned, people rent and eaten. Finally, the raven showed Ted exactly where this particular giant had won the many hockey jerseys it used to clothe himself. Children screamed as rocks pushed their bus from the road and into the ditch. Ted wondered how the giants had been able to attack the bus. Which of the children had been touched by the Nine Worlds? The answer didn't matter. They were all gone now. All dead.

I can't kill every thing that looks at me cross-eyed, Ted thought.

Yes, Huginn spat back, **you can.**

I won't.

Then you'll die.

Ted shrugged.

We won't let you. If you die, we go back into the black. Maybe we never come out again. This new world of yours is too interesting to give up.

To Ted it had become a little too interesting recently.

When I get Mimir's Head, I'll ask it how to get rid of you.

An empty threat, Huginn said. **We already know this is your goal.**

I'll ask him how to be rid of only *you. Strength and walking on water I can live with. Having Heckle and Jeckle stuck in my head is getting old fucking fast.*

How could he—? Muninn squawked, concerned. **He can't be serious.**

He is, Huginn said sadly. **He would do this thing just to spite us.**

Like Loki.

Huginn sighed. **Yes, unfortunate the trickster found him so quickly.**

"Tell me," Ted said, aloud this time.

"Who are you talking to?" Tilda asked.

The sun, Huginn said finally. Use the sun.

Ignoring the ravens' sulking withdrawal from the forefront of his consciousness, Ted looked at his left palm and the stylized sun the *dvergar* tattooed upon it. The tattoo felt warm to the touch. Walking to the giant's side, Ted knelt by its knee. The giant whimpered as Ted grew closer, baring his throat. Ted didn't know what the giant saw, looking at him. Was he old enough to remember the end of his world? Was this giant only a youth, raised on bedtime stories about the hammer of Thor? Was Mjölnir used to frighten him into being a good little *jötunn*?

Slowly, deliberately, Ted closed his hand over the shattered kneecap and took a deep breath. As heat spread and light flared from under Ted's grip the wounded joint began to knit itself back together. Cartilage reformed. Muscle and tendons reattached. The giant made a confused grunt, and looked at Ted, eyes wide and unbelieving. Ted held his left hand towards the giant, palm out, golden light reflecting off the creature's wet face and moved it slowly down to the shattered ankle.

Ted pointed at the giant's jaw. He nodded slowly, tensing his body and flexing the newly healed knee. And Ted rebuilt the giant's shattered face. By the time he released his grip, he was sweating like he'd run a marathon. The light that had surrounded his hand died. The golden ink outlining the sun's image slowly turned black. Ted blinked at the darkness now enveloping him.

And then the giant slammed into Ted, bowling him over.

Branches cracked as they were snapped from trees, and the crash of heavy footfalls receded into the night.

"You're fucking welcome," Ted yelled after him.

He could feel Tilda's uncomprehending stare. "Why'd you heal him?" she asked. "He'll tell the rest of them where we are."

Hesitating, Ted grasped for an answer. *Why had he done it?*

Tilda offered her hand to help him to his feet and Ted took it, more to feel her touch than out of need.

"They probably already know." Ted sighed. "I'm not ready yet."

"To kill?"

"It's not… I mean, I've gone hunting, shot geese, deer, whatever. I don't know. Am I fooling myself? Is it all right for me to kill giants because that's what I was made to do?"

"I can't answer that."

Ted smiled. "Some fortune teller you are."

She swatted his arm. "Watch it, mister."

"Who do you think tipped off the giants?"

"I don't know," Tilda said, exasperated. "I didn't see this coming. The *dvergar*? Pushing for a confrontation?"

"You think?"

"The *jötnar* hate the *dvergar* almost as much as they do the Aesir."

"Mimir's Head for Mjölnir?"

Tilda thought about it, and then nodded. "It's possible. The *jötnar* might deal for a crack at you."

"Then the dwarves went through a lot of fucking effort to make me into this just to trade me in. What would they want Mimir's Head for? Or—"

"Loki could be playing a larger game."

Ted nodded, exhausted. "The thought had crossed my mind."

Huginn cackled with mirth, but Ted didn't rise to the bird's bait. He patted himself down to find his cigarette pack, and grimaced when he pulled the crushed cardboard from his pocket. Tobacco spilled freely from the gaps in the folds. Opening the pack, Ted salvaged what he could. Taking two cigarettes broken close to their filters, Ted tapped the butt end to knock out the loose tobacco. And then he twisted the long end back into the paper. It held. The smoke had a sad, crooked look.

"Ladies first," he said offering the repaired cigarette to Tilda. She took it with a smile, and cupped her hands around the lighter flame as Ted lit the smoke for her. He smiled back and went to work fixing one for himself.

The first intake of smoke was like heaven. Ted exhaled slowly through his nostrils and took another deep drag. Sated, he put an arm around Tilda, noting absently how neatly her body fit against his. He could feel her shivering, even wearing his shirt.

"Let's get off the road a ways and build a fire," he said, jerking a thumb at the trees.

"But Loki's looking for us on the road."

Ted levelled a look at her, and grinned.

"All the more reason to leave the road. He'll find us. My life is too quiet at the moment for him not to find us."

Tilda slipped her hand in Ted's back pocket and gave him a squeeze.

"Quiet is something I can fix even better. C'mon."

She hadn't led Ted too far into the trees before they found a my ass" variety. Thoughts of his ex flickered across his mind. He didn't mean to compare them, but it was impossible not to. Every experience was built on what had come before. Sex was no different. Ted groaned against Tilda's neck. A touch, a breath was enough to dredge once-monumental acts out of the sands to peer at the present. Things had been like this once with Susanna. Hadn't they? Before the distance had grown between them. Why couldn't he remember it? Why was he trying?

A hissing intake of breath. Tilda's. It had been so long since he'd felt this way that it was almost as distant a memory as when radio was meaningful. Given what he and Tilda were about to walk into, the likelihood of another opportunity like this seemed remote. The past was no friend to him. The future held mortal danger, but the present....

Ted wanted to taste her. To discover her. She stood and pulled dress and shirt over her head, letting the clothes fall in a tangle outside the sketched circle. The delicate hair on her arms was like a halo in the firelight. Following Tilda's lead, Ted kicked off his sandals and peeled his jeans and underwear off all together, leaving them in one jumbled pile beside her dress.

Naked now, the Norn's eyes reflected strangely, either from the fire or the moonlight or some combination of the two. Pale like a wolf's, her eyes never left him as she lowered her body onto his.

They moved slowly against each other at first. The crackle of the fire, their breathing the only sounds. All thoughts of future and past were gone. There was only now.

Between kisses Tilda whispered the names of the runes.

another. And another. Something was coming towards him—a red shape, gliding effortlessly along the path. Surtur. At first the shape seemed so far away, a trick of the light—or magic. But it closed rapidly, an arrow aimed at Ted's heart. Ted steeled himself, clenching his fists. His clawed fingers bit into the flesh of his palms. Blood spattered the road, each drop a thunderclap, sending out ripples towards the oncoming shape. Ted's blood drifted forward—black and inky—as if driven by a current, stretching thin, rope-like, towards whatever approached.

It wasn't Surtur that emerged from the flames, but a swan. Unfurling wings exploded from the swan's sides, snapping like a whip crack. Held in relief against Surtur's fires, the flames shone through them, glaring like a setting sun. Ted squinted, averting his eyes. When he looked back, it was Tilda standing before him, her bare toes hovering inches above the path.

Ted sighed, relieved. A familiar face. He was no longer alone.

The swan wings settled upon her shoulders, a cloak now, draped to cover most, but not all, of her nakedness. Runes wrapped around her body like strings of pearls. She looked different. Older, but not. Harder. Fiercer. From beneath the cloak a spear lanced, its tip rested at Ted's throat. A familiar face, but not a friendly one. Not here. She had the same look of loathing as at their reunion in Gimli. A piercing cry made him squint and he knew somehow that this spear could mean his death. That he could die "here" more easily than… elsewhere.

"Are you man, or beast?"

Seeing her, he could feel the touch of her skin upon his, somewhere. In that place, there was no more fear, no more uncertainty. There was purpose and the pleasure that came with it. But here, Tilda didn't recognize him. Regarding his claws, he wondered, what was he? Monster? Weapon? Man?

She spat a word, a name, and it slammed him like a hammer. Lightning crackled along the seams of his scales.

"No."

The energy begged to be released. A rush of pain and fire.

"I'm… me."

She canted her head to the side, curious now.

"Ted?"

And when she said his name, it was as if she'd made it so. Claws were gone. Scales still peppered his body, but they were tattoos once more. Lightning raced over where Thor's hammer had been tattooed on his right forearm and hand. He'd hoped for a minute that the tattoos would be gone also, that he would be as he was when they'd met, but no, he was changed by knowing her world. Changed by knowing her.

Tilda lowered her spear, casting it aside into the darkness beside the path. Her cloak fell to her feet, disappearing as if the path were water.

"Seethe," she said, trembling. The runes wrapped about her body, stretched for Ted, as if she'd cast him a lifeline.

The fire had caught them, enveloping the path. He was hot. With fear. With desire.

"There will be a cost." Tilda cupped Ted's jaw in her hands. "There is always a cost."

"A child," he whispered. "Our child."

Tilda smiled. "Yes. No. All that means and more. We will

never be rid of each other if we do this. Even if magic ends. Even if Surtur burns the world. Choose."

A breath. Hers. Hot past his ear. It had travelled from their bodies to here.

Pulling her close, he made his choice.

The runes bound them together, tighter than the dwarves' golden chain ever held him. As they had in the clearing, the runes circled their joined bodies. Tilda named each flaring symbol. With each whispered word, Ted felt a tug, like the runes were rising from his flesh, from his tattoo of Yggdrasill. Swirling around them, the runes were proof against the flames. One by one they settled on Ted's back, each pricking him like a hornet's sting. Tilda's fingers touched his skin and a storm grew in the sky, blacking out the fire's glow. Ink thunderclouds raced over Ted's chest in the wake of the Norn's touch. Thunder rumbled; an aftershock shook the path.

They could only see one another in the flashes of lightning. Mirrored in the reflective path, Ted saw their physical act play out. A different binding, but no less powerful. Long ago he'd made peace with the idea that he'd never have this kind of moment again. He'd been married, there weren't supposed to be any more discoveries. No tentative touches under starlight. No more surprises. He couldn't have been more wrong.

He turned back to Tilda, her eyes lit up by lightning.

"Now," Tilda said. "Now."

They wrapped one another in a fierce embrace. Only one road ahead of them, a path leading to battle. To fire and blood.

To Surtur. They would walk that road. But not in this moment. Ted stepped off the path and they fell into the unknown.

Wind licked at their bodies as leaves rustled. Clouds covered the moon, and within their bellies, thunder rumbled as sheets of lightning flashed.

Tilda's cry was dangerously loud, carrying across the still wilderness air like a falcon's keen. They both shuddered in release, sweating, panting.

Her hands ran over his chest, and along his arm, until they cupped Mjölnir. Lightning arced behind her fingers. Glowing, her body seemed to steal colour from the flames.

"Was... was that real?" Ted gasped.

"More than real."

Tilda trailed a finger back to Ted's chest. The thunderstorm tattooed there followed her movements. In wonderment, Ted watched the clouds above shoot across the sky even as the wind died in the clearing.

Behind them a slow clap started up, and Loki's mocking laugh filled the clearing. He ran a hand through his hair and whistled. "I don't know about you two, but I could use a cigarette."

13. When Worlds Collide

'm all out," Loki said, tossing an empty cigarette pack on the fire. "Can one of you front me?"

Ted felt the blood rushing to his face. There was no good way to confront the trickster, and Ted was getting a little tired of mythological figures ambushing him while his pants were down—or off entirely. Tilda unlocked her legs and slid off of Ted, standing gingerly. He pawed for an article of clothing to cover himself, but the only item in reach was Tilda's sundress. Ted sighed and held the dress in between them to at least block Loki's view of her.

"Ted, brother, if I'd had my cellphone you two would have been Internet sensations."

"Say another word," Ted practically growled as he pulled on his pants and underwear in one motion, "and the next time your mouth is sewn shut, your dick'll be inside. I. Guarantee. It."

"That's cold buddy, real cold." Loki shook his head and then grinned. "I'd just grow a new one, you know."

"Then I'll do it again. And again. Until you fucking learn. I've got the time. You?"

Loki frowned. "Dirty pool."

"Says the God of Lies."

"Trickery," Loki said, his voice lilting to a school marm's correcting tone.

"Whatever."

Loki's eyes were looking past Ted, and the trickster murmured, squinting and pursing his lips, "*Mmm, mmm, mmm.*"

Turning, Ted caught Tilda smoothing her dress, and brushing the dirt and twigs from her knees and shins.

"Did you find a car?" she asked, clearly unbothered, and tossed Ted's shirt back to him.

"In a manner of speaking," Loki answered. "It's a beater, and not nearly as roomy as the van Ted ruined, but it runs."

"I ruined?" Ted said incredulous. "You were driving."

"You were shotgun. The navigator," Loki said. "And you fell asleep. You really dropped the ball, Ted. Now, about that cigarette?"

"We're out," Ted said, with no little satisfaction. "They got crushed in a giant attack."

Loki shrugged, and pulled a package from inside his jacket and put a cigarette between his lips.

"Pity," the trickster said with a smile. He turned and walked back towards the road.

Ted pulled the centre stone from the fire and the flames died. He kicked dirt over the embers to be safe, finished dressing and followed Loki. Tilda fell in beside him, twining her fingers in his. She looked more content than he'd seen her since their first meeting. She'd acknowledged her doom then. Now she had finally accepted it.

Loki was sitting in the passenger seat when Ted and Tilda arrived at the truck. It was a battered and rust-pocked three-quarter-ton pickup. Years of dirt and grime had been caked on so heavily that the original paint job lay somewhere in between distant memory and complete mystery. There was a winch mounted on the front grille that looked like it might even work, and an oversized, padlocked toolbox in the box of the truck. The trickster had his elbow jutting out of the open passenger window.

"Since you don't trust my driving, I figured I'd let you do the honours."

Ted eyed him suspiciously. "Really?"

"And I'm tired from flying."

Ted held the door open for Tilda as she shimmied into the truck. He hopped in after her and slammed the door shut behind him, shaking the old vehicle a little with the impact. Turning the ignition, Ted let out the clutch and pulled from the shoulder onto the highway. As he shifted into second, the motion brought the floor-mounted gearshift and Ted's hand against Tilda's thigh. He glanced over at her, she was smiling. Ted caught his reflection in the rear-view mirror as he fought to put his eyes back on the road. *Grinning like a fucking idiot.* He gave his head a little shake; he hadn't smiled like that since the first time he'd got laid.

"Glad I left my window down," Loki said, wrinkling his nose and flicking his cigarette away. "It smells like Freyja's linen closet in here."

Under the scent of woodsmoke that permeated the cab, there was a strong hint of sex and sweat.

"Sorry, you showed up before we could find the shower," Tilda said.

"Look who's all mouthy now that she's fulfilled her destiny," Loki said.

"Watch it," Ted warned.

"It's okay, Ted," Tilda said. "I don't need you to defend me against him."

Loki sighed. "Even schoolgirls are getting the better of me… dark days, Ted. Dark days."

Ted was about to protest that Tilda was no schoolgirl, but didn't want to get dragged into their arguing any more than he wanted to listen to them bicker for the rest of the drive. When he reached to turn on the stereo, he saw the ravaged magnetic tape of a cassette spooling from the deck like a carcass on *Wild Kingdom. Radio it is.*

Ted eased the old truck up to highway speed. The truck shuddered every time he shifted gears and the vehicle's suspension was as hidden as the factory paint. They shook and bounced along the rough asphalt. The radio was on some damned talk station, and the host sounded like some sort of little dog barking at his betters. Ted reached to change the station.

"I wouldn't," Loki said.

"Why the fuck not?" Ted asked. "Don't tell me you're able to stand this guy?"

"Not really, but it took me most of the drive here to get any reception on that thing, and this was the only station that came in clear."

"Yeah, you found a real prize," Ted muttered.

"Well, they're sure to get 'round to the news soon," Loki said with a smile. "There's something you'll need to hear."

"What?"

"Not telling."

"What are you, five?"

"Sure, insult me, that'll make me talk."

"Sorry." Ted made an exaggerated apology. "It's not like it ever made you shut up in the past."

Loki held up a hand like a puppet and played at it speaking, matching his movements to Ted's words.

"I'm gonna get a beer," the trickster said eventually. "Anybody want one?"

"I'll take one," Ted said.

"No, thanks," Tilda answered.

Loki smiled, but his eyes were hard. "I suppose you've swallowed enough tonight."

"And who did you bend over for to get this piece of shit?" Tilda shot back.

He ignored her, reached behind the seat, and pulled out a can of beer. Loki flicked the tab open, and suds foamed out of the small opening and over his hand. He took a deep gulp, burped, and turned to sigh in Tilda's face with an exaggerated "*Ahhhhhh.*"

"You used to have more class than that," Tilda said, waving at the smell lingering between them. "You're acting like you were born to Odin's house."

"Bitch," Loki muttered.

Ted looked over at the two. "What the fuck's that about?"

Tilda answered first. "For some reason, Odin made the little shit his blood brother. Welcomed him into his hall. Practically made him family. Told all that he'd never taste a drink not offered to Loki. Or did you lie about *that* too?"

"You don't know what you're talking about," Loki growled, draining his beer and tossing the can out the window.

"He can toss the barbs, but can't take them," Tilda leaned in to whisper into Ted's ear. "He never could."

"I can hear you," Loki said.

Tilda turned to face him. "And I don't give a shit if you do."

"See how cruel she is?" Loki whined at Ted. "You should have killed her."

"I'm not going to kill her," Ted said through his teeth.

"Pity," Loki said suddenly chipper. "Since you're so fucking in love, I guess there's no point in trying to make her appear cunt of the week."

"If we're talking this week," Ted shot back, "then you're definitely the frontrunner."

"You're probably right," Loki nodded sagely. "You're probably right. But I do play to win."

"Are you going to give me that fucking beer?" Ted asked.

Loki rolled his eyes as if he was being horribly put upon and reached behind the seat, this time pulling out a bottle and passing it to Tilda.

"Fine, but you have to open it for him."

"Fine by me," Tilda said. She grimaced as she tried to twist the cap off, and then looked at the label. "Bastard."

It wasn't a twist-off.

A slow grin spread over Loki's face. Ted couldn't help himself. He started laughing, and eventually Tilda joined in.

She held the beer against the dash, looking for a proper edge. With a sharp slap she knocked her palm against the cap, popping it free and sloshing some beer over her hand. Tilda held the bottle up to Loki as if in toast.

"Cheers, asshole."

He pulled another bottle of beer from behind the seat and clinked it in toast with her.

"Cheers, harlot of fortune."

She and Loki stared at each other for a moment, each giving a curt nod. Perhaps an acknowledgement of a fresh start. She passed Ted his beer.

"And now the news," the annoying man on the radio intoned.

Loki had gone strangely quiet, but Ted could see the anticipation in the trickster's face. The smaller man really wanted him to hear this. Ted reached for the volume knob; the radio crackled with static as he eased it louder. Tilda had fallen into a fitful slumber against Ted's shoulder. She shifted slightly as the radio volume increased, but didn't wake.

"In our top story, police have issued a warrant for Theodore Benjamin Callan, who's wanted for questioning in the deaths of Lester Braun and Ernest Friesen."

The announcer's voice cut out and a bad audio clip of a police spokesman went out over the air.

"Callan was released from police custody just this morning,

after an altercation with the two men, both employees at the local hotel. Shortly afterwards the two men were found dead in their hospital rooms, each killed by a single puncture wound to the throat. Callan is to be considered armed and dangerous, described as six-foot-four, early to mid-forties, muscular, and heavily tattooed."

"God-fucking-dammit!" Tilda stirred and Ted hissed out a long, angry breath. Wanted for murder. Again. And this time there were bodies. After what the cops had seen at the hotel, they'd make the evidence fit Ted. Unless the Norns vouched for him, he'd look very good for the crime.

"Callan has also been implicated in the disappearance of twenty-three-year-old Tilda Eilifsdottir of Gimli."

Fuck.

Ted lost track of what the cop was saying. He realized it was the first time he'd heard Tilda's last name. It embarrassed him that he'd never asked. Loki reached across Tilda to give him a poke. "He's believed to be heading north with an unknown accomplice. Photos are available on our website. If you see this man do not approach him."

Loki turned to Ted. "You're famous."

"This is what you wanted me to hear?"

"Yeah," Loki said. "Can you believe the fucking gall of her family?"

"Accusing me of kidnapping?"

"No." Loki rolled his eyes. "Calling me an unknown accomplice? For gods' sake. I'm known! Bitches."

"How do you know it was them?" Ted asked. "They want us

to find the Head. Can't do that from prison. Maybe the dwarves are trying to keep me from shoving my boot up their asses."

"You're not wearing boots," Loki said, considering Ted's neon flip-flops. He pursed his lips in thought, tapping them with his index finger. "But, point taken. I do wonder what the cops *aren't* saying about this. I mean, obviously you didn't do it. You were with me most of that time. Unless you can teleport or something. Can you? 'Cause that would be pretty handy."

Ted took a deep breath and tried to calm himself. He didn't want to wake Tilda. "I'm wanted for murder, Loki. Do you think this is the time to crack wise?"

"Correction," Loki said. "You're wanted for questioning, in connection with a murder. That's different."

"I'm sure my family will be thrilled by the distinction."

"To Hel with them," Loki said. "If they were so great, you'd have stayed in Alberta."

"Shit, those bouncers were assholes, but they didn't deserve to die. I wonder what really happened."

"You."

"What?"

"They met you, Ted. You used the *dvergar*'s gifts to fight them, didn't you? You opened the swinging gate of Odin's fence and they came in contact with the Nine Worlds. After that the safety they once enjoyed was taken away."

"So you're saying if I'd just beat the shit out of them without using my powers they'd be alive?"

Tilda shook herself awake.

"Maybe," Loki said. "Maybe not. Like it or not, you're a

creature of the Nine Worlds now too. Not using your power…
hard to say. They encountered you. That might be enough for
others to sense them."

"So you mean—"

"All fair game."

"Fuck. Jenny," Ted muttered, suddenly worried.

Her voice tight, Tilda asked, "Who's Jenny?"

"A friend. She was going to put me up in Winnipeg while I
get settled."

"Oh." She turned her head away from Ted.

"I sure as shit won't be staying with her now. This has got to
stop. People need to know what's happening."

"What do you want to do?" Loki asked. "Tell them the truth?"

"What's the alternative? Let them die? People need to know
what kind of world they live in."

"People need no such damn thing. They already think they
know what kind of world they live in. Your kind doesn't appreciate its illusions being shattered. Best-case scenario, you end up
in the loony bin. Where, by the way, you'll sentence a bunch of
innocent, and unlikely to be missed, spastics to death. Just let
it go."

"Fuck you," Ted said. "I've gotta warn Jenny."

"No, you don't," Loki said. "Trust me. If something from
the Nine Worlds wanted her, she'd be dead already, like those
bouncers. Hot little number like her?" Loki looked to Tilda with
a wolfish grin, and she frowned. "Her death would've made the
news. So she's safe. If she's safe, then remember, the cops are
looking for you. And Winnipeg isn't that big."

"But—"

"It's better this way," Loki cut him off. "You don't have to like it, but I'm telling the truth. She's safer without you than with you. She can't be touched. Not if she doesn't know."

Ted clenched the wheel. "I didn't know," he said tightly.

Tilda squeezed his leg. "Ted…."

He brushed the hand aside. Her soothing tone only made him angrier. "I didn't fucking know, and that didn't stop a mythological fire demon from exploding out of my workplace."

"Accidents happen. Eggs, omelettes, and all that," Loki said, looking away. "It was a fluke, nothing more."

"How many more of these flukes are there going to be?"

"No one can say," Tilda said. She was trying to calm him, but Ted could sense her worry. "But accidents like yours have been happening more and more. That's why Amma—"

"Oh, horseshit," Loki spat.

"You'd know," Tilda shot back. "Horsefucker."

Accident. Fluke. The explosion at the patch was one of the worst things Ted had ever seen. Before Surtur had walked from the flames, at least. Neither Loki's jokes, nor Tilda's acceptance, sat well with him.

"How many died when Surtur was freed?"

"A lot," Loki said.

Ted ground his teeth. "How. Many."

"Five hundred," he answered, but Ted was hardly listening, until the trickster added: "and counting."

"What?"

"There were other survivors, Ted. They're like you, like those two asshole bouncers, they've been touched. Fair game." Loki looked Ted up and down. "Okay, not quite like you. They lack your advantages, obviously."

"That is all the more reason—"

"All the more reason," Loki yelled over him. Tilda flinched. "To let them go about their meaningless, short, safe little lives. Leave monsters, gods, and heroes to the shadows and stories. That's where they shunted us to long ago."

"I'd want to know," Ted said.

"Right."

"Even knowing what I do now," Ted said. "Seeing what I've seen, doing… whatever the fuck it is that I'm doing. I'd want to know. And… I'm glad it's me, and not someone else having to deal with this."

Loki flashed a crooked smile. "What a crock of shit."

"You don't understand. At my old job, they told me to delegate more. I never did. I ran my ass ragged, but I knew—I just knew—that if I did the work, it was getting done right. And right now I don't trust anyone else to do this."

"It's your life. How you deal with it is up to you, I can only offer advice. Ignore me as you see fit. But I wouldn't."

Ted sighed. "So, Surtur has been killing off everyone who survived his escape?"

"Possibly," Loki said, pausing before he spoke again. "Or he's buying their allegiance. So he can send them to bring more and more people to him. He'll want to extend his influence and power. The fires are still burning, Ted. Fort McMurray is gone. They had time to evacuate, but the city's been wiped from the face of the earth. Some of the rig victims may live on having been changed by Surtur's power. But most… they were his Big Macs. Would you tell Susanna? Knowing that knowledge could kill her?"

"I could protect her. I could get her out of there."

"What if she didn't want to leave? She doesn't want you anymore, Ted."

"I know that," Ted said testily.

"What if her new guy answered the door and picked a fight? Would you show him what a big man you are? Get him killed too? What—"

"What if you shut the fuck up, and let me drive?"

Loki turned and smiled at Tilda, who was silent next to Ted. She was staring intently at the gearshift, avoiding Loki's eyes— and Ted's. Her face had grown hard at the mention of Susanna; Ted reached out to give her arm a squeeze, but she shook it off. Inching away from him, she settled in the centre of the bench seat.

"About Susanna—"

"I'm not mad about that." Which Ted didn't believe for a fucking second. "You have a right to worry about her. You loved her once."

There was a hitch in Tilda's voice, it caught just as she said once. Ted recognized the fragility of the tone. The hope that once, wasn't still.

"Yeah, yeah. I did."

"Do… do you—"

For all her worldliness and outward confidence, it was easy to forget that Tilda was so young. Given what Ted knew of her—and there was little enough of that—she didn't exactly have a winning record with relationships. Ted knew what she wanted to hear, he just wasn't sure what his answer really was.

"Do I still love her?"

Tilda opened her mouth but no words came. She nodded instead.

"I guess," Ted said half-heartedly.

"You guess? You guess?" Tilda sounded hurt and angry.

"Yes... maybe... no... all three. How I feel doesn't really matter. She won't take me back. And I don't want to go back."

"But you still want—"

For the briefest moment, Ted had forgotten Loki was in the truck. "She wants to know if you still want to rack 'em up one last time," he said.

"Thanks," Tilda said dryly.

"Happy to help."

"Tilda," Ted said gently, trying to ignore the trickster. "I know it's probably hard for someone your age to understand—"

"Don't," she said, anger staining her face. "Don't you goddamn patronize me."

"Fuck... just listen to me. She was someone that I thought I was going to spend the rest of my life with. That depth of feeling never just goes away. It can be changed to resentment, to hate. But it never goes away. Not entirely. Just because I don't want to see her involved in this..." —Ted stopped himself from saying "shit"— "...in the Nine Worlds, doesn't mean I want her back.

So I hope she's safe and happy? It doesn't mean I want her back in my bed." Ted nudged Tilda's chin up. "I don't even own a bed."

A smiled turned up the corners of her mouth as she fought to keep the frown on her face.

"We'll have to do something about that." She rubbed her knees. "Not all of us are invulnerable, you know."

"May I suggest—" Loki started.

Ted and Tilda both cut him off before he could finish. "No."

"Fine, be that way," he said. "Nothing I haven't seen before, and I have a very good memory. Don't mind me, I'm just going to sit back and reminisce. *Mmmm*. Don't stop. *Mmmm*. I want it to be you."

Tilda stuck her tongue out at the trickster and Ted flipped him off, noting it really was a wonder Loki had lived this long.

So do something about him, Huginn prodded. Kill him.

A harsh sentence for a peeping Tom, but Muninn cawed in agreement. The raven flashed an image of Loki shearing the head of a beautiful blonde woman—Sif, Thor's wife.

Sif looked a lot like Susanna. Ted didn't appreciate the heavy-handed ploy.

Loki will not be returning with gifts as recompense for his crimes, not this time. There will be no gold, no weapons.

Only betrayal, Huginn added. It is all he knows.

We need him, Ted thought.

Muninn did not agree. Odin often said that very same mollifying phrase.

And now it's we? Huginn added, cackling a laugh. Tied

yourself to the Nornling so quickly. Too quickly. You've let her get her claws in us too deep, they'll never let go.

Good, I don't want her to.

The Norns want to end magic forever, Muninn reminded him. That means us. And you.

Peace and quiet, Ted shot back.

That shut the raven up. Ted could almost feel the feathers shaking loose as Huginn and Muninn retreated to the depths of his consciousness.

He drove on in silence. The northern lights were draped over the night sky, shimmering and dancing, brighter and fiercer than Ted had ever seen them.

"Pretty, aren't they?" Loki said sadly.

"Sure are," Ted agreed.

"Amma says they're the remnants of Bifrost. I wish I could have seen the Rainbow Bridge."

"It was beautiful." Loki's voice broke. "At least before the weight of our arrogance and pride shattered it."

There was a moment, just a moment, when the lights seemed to shift, mimicking the shape of a great, grinning skull with its jaws gaping wide.

Loki kept his head turned towards the passenger-side window and Tilda remained pressed against Ted. He turned the radio down, but not off. Who knows? Maybe there would be more important updates. The sounds of the road, the hum of bald tires over rough asphalt, wind seeping past time-eroded window seals to whistle through the cab, and the creaks and groans of the rickety old pickup mostly drowned out the talk-radio station.

After they'd driven through the town of Cranberry-Portage, they finally saw the Canadian Shield. Huge outcroppings of slatey rock jutted out of the ground along the roadside. In places trees had rooted into the rock face. Mostly, though, the road was lined with sheer, jagged edges. The headlights caught graffiti on damn near every flat surface. So-and-so loves so-and-so, in loving memory of, Grad 2000.

Before long the rocks loomed up on either side of them, like a canyon had been carved to build the road. Maybe it had. There was an orange glow against the sky in the distance, the lights of Flin Flon. Headlights crested a rise, and Ted winced. He'd always had a good gut instinct for spotting a cop car. This could be one. They'd had luck avoiding the RCMP so far, but after the announcement by the Winnipeg police, the Mounties would be on the lookout.

"Look lively," Ted whispered to Tilda and Loki, as if the words would carry out of the cab and into the police cruiser. "I think we have cops up ahead."

As the truck's dim headlights illuminated the passing car, Ted was proven right. It had been a police cruiser. He also noticed he was holding his breath. Scenarios ran through his mind. How careful had Loki been when he'd "acquired" this truck? Had its theft gone reported? What if they'd found the wrecked van?

Ted cast a nervous glance in the rear-view mirror. He knew the cops wouldn't be able to hurt him. That no force they could bring to bear would be able to contain him if he didn't want to be apprehended. And Loki was… well, Loki, after all. He'd find a way out. And likely a cleaner one than Ted could manage.

He didn't want a fight with the cops. What purpose would that serve? All he'd do would be to open up another victim to the Nine Worlds. How long before the constable was sniffed out by some rogue giant or dwarf? There was enough blood on Ted's hands already.

The tail lights were finally swallowed by the darkness, and Ted eased out a sigh of relief. A feeling that was short-lived.

Headlights lit up the road behind them, and were gaining fast. Ted felt his body tense. This was it. Any second the cherries would light up and the siren would sound. The car blew past them, rounding a corner and ignoring the solid double line with barely enough room to spare.

It wasn't the Mounties.

If Ted had been hanging his elbow out the window they would have clipped him. Then Ted saw the lights go up behind him followed by the wail of the patrol siren. He waited until he saw the headlights of the Caprice behind him and started to slow down.

"What are you doing?" Loki asked. "He doesn't want us!"

"No, but I'm getting out of his way—like a good citizen. If I hit the shoulder at highway speed in this rust-bucket, we'll probably blow a tire. You willing to change it?"

"Oh," Loki said. "I'd just steal a new ride. Less fuss, more fun."

Ted eased the truck on to the gravel. The RCMP cruiser wailed past them like a banshee, and Ted watched until its tail lights vanished again into the night.

Ted drove on and made the turn off the highway and into Flin Flon. A great dark smokestack stabbed up into the sky.

Three warning lights blinked on and off in unison. The stack was backlit by the moon. Smoke drifted lazily out of its top and hung like clouds over the far end of the city. An arch lit up to his right. It shifted colours between red, green, and white, seemingly dancing in unison with the aurora borealis.

Hunching behind the arch, peering through some trees, was a giant.

14. Dirty Old Town

Ted hit the brakes.

The pickup's bald tires squealed against the paved road. Tools in the locked box slammed into the wall of the cab. Ted held an arm out to keep Tilda's forehead from cracking the dash. She gave a grunt as her chest compressed against Ted's arm. There was a crack, the sound of glass breaking.

"What the fuck?" Loki said, rubbing his head. A teardrop of blood trickled down his forehead where his impact with the windshield had broken the skin.

"Giant," Ted said, unbuckling his seatbelt and opening the driver's-side door.

He stepped out. Bugs swarmed him immediately. Tiny little flies that flew up his nose, into his ears and mouth. Ted waved them away, spitting out the ones he'd nearly swallowed.

The giant hadn't moved. Ted eased away from the truck. His hammer hand was cocked back, ready to strike. The storm within it crackled over his flesh; the readiness to fight almost tickled. He tried to ignore the feeling. The giant still hadn't moved.

How could it have missed them?

Ted took a few steps closer, and realized why it hadn't moved. It wasn't a giant.

He would have preferred that, actually.

Instead, he was looking at a statue of a funny-looking prospector in a green coat and round, red glasses.

The statue was sculpted to appear to be walking jauntily atop a cairn of fieldstones. It was illuminated by a series of small floodlights.

Ted buried his head in his hand. Loki would never let him hear the end of this.

Loki howled a mocking laugh. "Thanks for protecting us from that 'giant.' I'm really thankful you kept it from... I don't know, cracking me on the head."

He could take some satisfaction that the sarcasm caused the trickster to wince, and cup his forehead again.

As his tensed muscles relaxed, Ted's senses opened up to the city. It smelled... he wasn't sure what it smelled like. It was foreign and familiar all at once.

"Dwarves," Loki said, wrinkling his nose.

"What?" Ted asked.

"It smells like *dvergar*. I'd know their forge stink anywhere. I hovered over them long enough when they first crafted Mjölnir."

"Can you find them?" Ted asked, looming over the smaller man.

Loki slipped backwards and adjusted his jacket.

"Probably," he said. "But I wouldn't advise that. They don't like me."

"Who does?" Tilda asked from inside the truck.

"You say that now; wait until you get to know me."

"Oh, I know you," Tilda said. "As well as I ever intend to."

"I can't believe you're still sore that I watched you getting pounded." Loki nudged Ted with an elbow and winked. "Or are you just sore?"

Ted nudged Loki back. The smaller man toppled over into the ditch.

"Watch your fucking mouth," Ted warned. Loki scowled, but flinched as Ted stepped in front of him. The larger man offered his hand, and the trickster took it. Ted pulled him to his feet, not entirely gently. Loki wrinkled his nose again, and brushed some dirt and dust from his jacket.

"The dwarves, Loki. Where can I find the dwarves?"

"They don't have the Head."

"What?"

"The Head of Mimir. You know, why you're here in the first place?"

"I don't care about that. Those twisted fucks who did this to me are here. They gave me nine gifts, and I have a few for them too."

"You'd better start caring. If Surtur—or her Amma—" Loki said, jerking a thumb at Tilda. "Gets to Mimir first… you and I are done for. Besides, I thought you were starting to enjoy what you can do," Loki said.

He was right, damn him. But it wasn't so much the abilities he'd gained that bothered him… but the tattoos and how the dwarves had seen fit to grant their gifts. There were some things Ted would never forget: the terror choking him when the *dvergar* had bound him, or the shame and confusion that followed. He was part of a vast, new world he hadn't known before the dwarves had assaulted him. His life mattered—more than it had before.

But he still wanted revenge.

"You weren't in that room. You don't know what they did to me."

"No, but I have my own long and bitter history with them. Let it go."

"When have *you* let anything go?"

"We don't have a lot of time," Tilda said. "Not if we want to get to the Head before all hell breaks loose."

Ted stewed, but didn't speak.

Tilda shook her head. "You're wanted for murder and kidnapping. The giants know where we are, so it's safe to say the dwarves do too. It won't be long until either they or someone else corrals us. Together, we're like a beacon for bored monsters looking to play."

"She's right." Loki gave Ted's shoulder a familiar squeeze, but Ted shrugged him off. "Listen to me. There are worse things than giants this far north."

"You?" Ted asked with a sigh.

Loki grinned and chuckled.

"Well, obviously. But not what I meant." He struck a pose aping the statue of fictional explorer Josiah Flintabbatey Flonatin and affected a faux British accent when he spoke again. "Come along, old tops, time to explore for a hotel room."

"Explore? There's one right across the street." Ted shook his head and climbed back into the truck. "I'm never going to live this down, am I?"

"Not in a million years," Loki said with a grin. He knuckled a fake tear from his eye as he rounded the passenger side of the pickup. "Ah, if only Valhalla wasn't broken. This would be a jest for the feast hall."

He helped to break Valhalla, Muninn reminded Ted, flashing images of Loki's many betrayals of the Aesir.

And he's helping to make up for it, Ted noted.

Is he? Huginn cackled. **Or is he helping only himself? His nature runs deeper than you think.**

Thought and Memory flitted off again to the depths of his mind. Ted truly wished he could control the ravens better. Or that they could do him some good.

The hotel was a three-storey affair built on a slight rise. There was a parking lot both in front of and behind it. Ted pulled around the back, where the lot was surprisingly full. "I don't have the cash and we can't show them ID or credit cards without giving ourselves up for the cops."

"Speak for yourselves," Loki said.

"What?" Ted asked.

"This is where the unidentified accomplice comes into his own. I'm more than comic relief, you know. I'll get us a room."

"Good."

"With a king-sized bed."

"No chance," Ted said.

Loki laughed. "You'll take what I give you."

242

Loki palmed the card key and pushed open the door to their room. Ted followed him. It was a hotel room, like any other in the country. The bathroom door was open on their right. Loki hung his coat in the closet, muttering to himself as he walked into the room proper to flop on one of the beds. Ted reached a hand into Loki's jacket pocket while the trickster's back was turned and swiped a pack of cigarettes.

"All they had was a room with two doubles," Loki said with a put-upon sigh. "And if you wanted a smoke, you only had to ask."

"Mother, may I?" Ted said, tossing the pack towards the nightstand.

"If you two promise to be good."

The two beds featured thin, scratchy blankets and ridiculously high pillows that would ensure Ted didn't have a good night's sleep. Although, between sharing the room with Loki and Tilda, Ted doubted he'd drift peacefully into the never-never, regardless where he laid his head. There was an old CRT television, next to which was a much newer-looking DVD player, on a dresser. There was a mini-fridge, the requisite small round table in a corner, and a nightstand between the beds with a gift waiting from the Gideons.

Ted plucked the remote from the nightstand, hit the power button, and started scanning the channels.

Loki asked, "Anything decent on?"

"I'm trying to see if there's any more news on us."

"Boring," Loki said, linking his hands behind his head. "We

know what happened. Look for *Family Guy* instead, I love that little kid."

Ted ignored him.

"Fine, be that way," Loki said.

He walked over to the fridge, opened it, and started passing around little bottles of alcohol. Ted doubted they came with the room. Looking at the Jim Beam in his hand, he didn't care. Tilda waved away a bottle of Crown Royal, and Loki closed the door after sampling his gin.

"Adequate," he judged. "We need some ice, and some clean clothes. Especially you two."

"Clothes'll have to wait until tomorrow," Tilda said.

Loki looked at her and smiled. "Not the way I shop."

Ted remembered the ease with which Loki had procured clothing for him in the past. He smiled at the thought of what the trickster would bring back this time. Loki winked as he stepped into the bathroom.

Ted sighed. "Alone at last."

Tilda leaned forward and kissed him, lightly, almost hesitant. He tasted the stale hint of her last cigarette. Just like honey.

Ted handed her another smoke. She accepted it with a nod, lit it, and exhaled as she spoke. "You know he'll come back at the most awkward time. He always does."

"Yeah, I figured so. I swear, the only reason he leaves is so he can interrupt something he shouldn't."

Tilda wrapped her arms around Ted, and hugged him tightly. She nestled her head against his shoulder.

"Thanks for sticking up for me earlier."

"No worries," Ted said, playing idly with her hair.

"I can take care of myself, you know that, right?"

"Absolutely," Ted said, and meant it. "But sometimes… sometimes I just want to hit that skinny little fucker until there's nothing left."

Tilda laughed and kissed Ted on the forehead. She wrinkled her nose. "You need a shower, Mr. Callan." She gave him a light little shove and peeled off his shirt. "Go on. Get cleaned up."

Ted caught a whiff of his underarms as the shirt left his body. *Definitely time for a shower.*

The door to the small bathroom wasn't locked. Loki had left the light on when he'd disappeared. Ted wondered why that didn't bother him more. Maybe, when gods and monsters were running around waging a secret war, some filched liquor and clothes were hard to get riled up about. He peered behind the shower curtain.

Tilda asked, "Worried he's waiting to surprise you?"

Ted rolled his eyes and stepped out of his pants and underwear. "Too easy." He patted Tilda's face, giving her jaw and nose light squeezes. "You are you, aren't you? Not Loki? This isn't just some trick to fuck me, is it?"

Tilda slapped his ass. "Start the shower."

"Don't think I didn't notice you're avoiding an answer."

"Loki's not gay."

"He's sure as shit not straight, either."

Tilda laughed. "You've got that right. He's just… he is what he is. He's a shapeshifter. His morality and biology can't be held to our views."

"Sounds like you're starting to admire him."

She shrugged. "I just hate him for who he is."

Ted leaned over the tub to start the water. He liked a hot shower—practically scalding—but doubted somehow Tilda would feel the same. If she planned on joining him. She was leaning against the sink, showing no sign of getting undressed.

"Get in there, stinky man."

Ted laughed and popped the button to start the shower spray. He stepped in and tried to squeeze his frame under the stream. He let the water beat upon his neck; to his surprise, the hotel had decent water pressure. As his fingers ran over his scalp, Ted could feel the hint of stubble. Maybe his hair would come back enough to hide some of the dwarves' handiwork. He let the rinse take the edge off his stink, turning around and scouring at his armpits with his hands.

Mesh at eye level of the shower curtain allowed Ted to see Tilda clearly. He could also make out his own silhouette in the hotel mirror. He shook his head. Even through the curtain he could still see the tattoos. Couldn't see his own face, but he could see them.

"I know that night is still raw, Ted," Tilda said softly. "I know what they did still hurts you."

He wondered how she knew what he was thinking, if her sight peered into his thoughts as well.

"But regardless of what you think of the *dvergar*, they gave you a great gift. I can see that. I hope someday you will, too."

"You can see the future." Ted felt the unintended edge to his voice. "Of course you'd take the long view."

"Ted...."

He could sense the beginnings of an apology, and headed her off. "No," he said, "I'm sorry. We have enough worries without me jumping down your throat. Don't worry, babe," Ted gave his chest a punch. "I'm pretty thick-skinned."

Tilda smiled. She pushed herself off the sink and shimmied out of her clothes, dropping them on Ted's pants, and joined him in the shower. Tilda went up on her tiptoes and gave him a wet kiss.

"I have some doubts about our chances of getting clean if we're both naked," Ted said smiling.

"Oh, no, you don't," Tilda said. "That wise-assed little shit was right about one thing. I am sore. Too sore for what I'd like to do."

"Damn."

She gave him a playful flick. "Give me a break, I'm a little out of practice with the equipment."

Ted stepped aside and let her under the water stream. Tilda tilted her head back into the spray of water, soaking her hair first and then letting the flow run down her face. Not needing to worry about shampoo, Ted ripped the paper off the bar of soap and began to scrub his body. He started with his pits, groin, and feet—the stinkables—and then moved on to coat the rest of his body in the weak suds.

As the water ran clear behind Tilda, she opened her eyes.

"Awww, I wanted to soap you up."

Ted pressed the bar into her hand and slid past her, leaving a trail of foamy white bubbles over her torso.

"Next time," Ted said with a smile.

"I'll hold you to that," she said.

"You won't have to."

Ted wrapped his arms around her. She tried to slide free, and almost succeeded, but he was determined. He hauled her bodily under the water to rinse off.

"Look, now you've got me all soapy," Ted said, depositing a ball of suds on the tip of Tilda's nose.

A crooked smile chipped its way past her anger, and she pulled him back against her body, letting the shower beat down on them. Tilda nestled her head in the crook between Ted's jaw and shoulder. She leaned against his back. He could feel the light prickle of her pressed against him. Ted was glad that whatever the dwarves had done to give him his invulnerability, he hadn't lost his sense of touch. What a torture that would have been, to be with this amazing woman and never to feel her. They swayed under the water, as if dancing, murmuring nothing in particular.

After they were dry, Tilda and Ted wrapped their bodies in the hotel's plain white towels. Ted knotted one of them around his waist, and Tilda did the same. He certainly wasn't complaining, but was surprised she hadn't tied the towel higher.

His look must've been clear. "I don't care what Loki sees."

"I care," he said, choosing honesty.

"That's sweet." Tilda gave him a quick peck on the cheek. "Especially considering what the dirty bastard's already seen."

Ted smiled. "Why wear the towel at all then?"

"Have to make the little weasel work for it, don't I?" Tilda gave Ted a shove and he let himself be tumbled on top of the bed. "I hope he at least remembers to get me some new panties."

Tilda rummaged in the fridge. She crawled back on the bed, and handed Ted a small bottle. Ted had to admit, it was nice of Loki to stock the bar before he left.

"I meant to ask you...."

He wondered what she might be afraid to say. Was it about Susanna? Jenny? "Ask away."

"What's with the damn football tattoo on your back?"

Ted smiled, he couldn't help it. Football had been one of the best times of his life. Memories of the glory days flooded back. Coach Dean's red-faced yelling. An undefeated season. His first real girlfriend wearing nothing but his practice jersey. It was pleasant for a change, to have a memory that was his own. One not accompanied by the shrill cries of a raven.

"You don't know, little miss fortune?"

"I see the future, not the past, old man."

He smiled.

"My high school football team—"

She shook her head. "I can't believe I slept with a jock."

"Not all jocks are assholes," Ted said defensively.

He had to admit he looked back at high school through the somewhat rosy lenses of someone who was popular, gifted and—in certain circles—loved. Being on a championship team opened a lot of doors in small towns. He couldn't remember torturing underclassmen, or riding the weird kids. He couldn't remember being an asshole. But he probably had been.

"You're in luck, I've grown up since then."

"Why'd you play football?"

Ted shrugged. "I liked it. I was good at it."

"You'd be better, now."

"Hardly fair." Ted laughed. "But I bet Loki would make some wagers if I tried a comeback."

"I imagine he would. Little cheater."

He nodded slowly, and squeezed her hand. "I've been known to make exceptions to rules. I don't normally pick up hitchhikers, either."

"I'm glad you did."

"Me too. Despite everything. But what those bearded fucks did to me, Til, I can't let it stand. They have a lot to answer for."

Ted finished his drink in silence. Television slowly overpowered their desire to speak. Ted didn't think it was such a bad thing, to be able to just sit together in silence.

"You see the future," Ted said finally.

"For now," Tilda answered.

"When did you know?"

"Know what?" she said playfully. "I know lots of things."

"That we'd be together?"

"A long time ago."

"How long?"

"It was one of my first visions that I remember. I must've been five? Six, maybe."

Ted's stomach lurched. "What… what did you see?"

Tilda read the queasy look on his face and blushed. "I didn't see... tonight. I didn't recognize you on the road. In all of my visions you were already... who you are now."

"Surprise," Ted said.

"I assumed it would be a long time until we met, since you're so much older than me." Ted winced a bit at that. "It's why I never listened to Amma. I thought I had all the time in the world. When I see things about myself, they are always through my own eyes, so unless I am near a mirror or calendar, when the vision is happening is... hard to judge."

"So, do you remember everything that you see?"

"I remember what's important, to me at least. Everything else, it gets written down by Mom and Amma, to be used or ignored later. It'll drive 'em nuts, that I picked you. Amma would've preferred a nice Gimli boy whose family goes right back to the New Iceland settlers."

"Sorry, German-Irish by way of Edmonton."

She smiled. "But they'll still be glad to hear I'm pregnant."

"I just don't get that."

"Oracles need to be young, Ted. When you're young, all life is possibilities. You're less likely to read your own wants and desires into what you see."

"So when do you lose the sight?"

Tilda rubbed at her belly idly; she wasn't a gym girl obsessed with a stomach you could bounce quarters off of, but she was the perfect mix of soft and firm.

"Don't know."

"Well, they say a woman can tell the moment conception happens."

Tilda punched Ted hard in the chest.

"Ow," she said, shaking her hand.

"Invulnerable, remember?"

"You're one vision I'm glad came true," she said, leaning back into him.

As Ted kissed Tilda on the lips, the bathroom door was thrust open, slamming loudly into the doorstop.

Loki's eyes sparkled at the sight of Ted and Tilda on the bed. "So, did I miss anything good?"

15. Castles
Made of Sand

Tilda held up a small garment with her thumb and forefinger, staring at it and Loki quizzically.

"And just what the fuck am I supposed to do with this? Floss?"

"Could you?"

The thong was a tiny triangular swatch of fabric with "Sinner" emblazoned upon it, which (admittedly) Ted really wanted to watch Tilda try on—just not with company. She still had the towel tied around her hips, but had fastened a bra the trickster had brought for her.

"Do I want to know how you knew my cup size?" she asked.

"Well, I've been seeing enough of them on this trip," Loki said, smirking. "It wasn't that hard." Where the skinny man had just been, Ted was now looking at another Tilda. Loki examined his borrowed form. "A girl just knows."

Even standing side by side in different clothes, the two Tildas were difficult to tell apart, at least to Ted. If it hadn't been for the clothes it would've been impossible.

Ted and one of the Tildas spoke together. "Never do that again."

"Ted." Loki turned away from the Norn. "Talk sense. Think of the options."

"No," they repeated together.

"I wonder, if I stay in this form long enough, will I get your visions too?"

"Change!" Tilda yelled.

"Don't be sore," the trickster said, smirking.

The Norn grabbed the bag that contained her new clothes and stomped to the bathroom. She slammed the door closed with enough force to make Ted wince.

"Well, that went about as well as could be expected. What got up her ass?" Loki returned to his familiar shape and tossed another bag at Ted. "You? Tell me it was you. Shit! I missed it."

Ted flipped the trickster the bird and dumped the contents of the bag, fearing the worst.

A pair of dark wash jeans and a grey T-shirt tumbled out. It read FLIN FLON BOMBERS and the mascot was an over-muscled miner with a pickaxe standing in front of a smokestack. Athletic socks—also grey—and a pair of black boxer briefs followed. There was even a pair of well-worn, steel-toed work boots. Ted sighed with relief. No more ugly sandals.

Loki took a seat on the opposite bed. "What were you expecting?" he asked.

"Knowing you, a Hawaiian shirt and a kilt. So I could blend in."

"That would've been great." Loki nodded. "But I had to work with what was here already."

The trickster leaned forward and dropped his voice to a

whisper. "We don't have long," he said. "I brought her a bunch of outfits. But she doesn't strike me as the type to be choosy."

"What are you talking about?" Ted asked sharply.

Loki rolled his eyes. "I did some scouting, and we can't stay here, Ted."

"Why not?"

"The dwarves haven't made any effort to hide themselves. I bet the whole town knows about the Nine Worlds. I can feel it. Maybe the *dvergar* protect them from the *jötnar*. Maybe they're all in league. The dwarves have always been able to sense their own handiwork. They'll find us soon. And the giants living out here? Meaner'n Old Flinty."

"Fuck you," Ted said. "So why can't Tilda know this?"

"In case the Norns are watching us right now. As much as I like the idea of their only sight being a close-up view of your cock, even you don't have the stamina to keep it up until we get Mimir."

"Well, I hope the dwarves are with the giants. When I find those ZZ Top fuckers," Ted said, massaging his fist, running fingers over the tattoo of Mjölnir. "I intend to do some re-gifting."

"So leave her here and come with me." Loki pointed a finger towards the bathroom. "If the Norns get their hands on Mimir, we're all gone. You, me, everything touched by the Nine."

Ted snorted. "So you keep saying. Would that be so bad?"

"For me it damn well would be!" Loki smoothed at his beard—he'd grown it back in the time he was away—it was too short to need any grooming, but the action seemed to calm him. "Mimir's Head has the knowledge to stop Surtur."

"And if the Norns use that knowledge, won't he disappear too? World saved."

Loki shook his head; he looked serious. "I was supposed to die at Ragnarök, he wasn't. He set fire to the Old World. When magic's gone—when we're gone—there will be nothing to stop him. Who are they to decide that for the world, Ted? Who the hell are they to make that call?"

"I'm surprised you care."

"Of course I care. I *like* living. I like smoking and drinking and stealing. I like pussy, I like cock. Magic makes all of that more fun. I can't do any of it if I'm dead."

"Very noble."

"Are you willing to throw the world into a crucible so you can have your old life back?" Loki grabbed Ted and shook him. "News flash, buddy. It don't want you back."

Ted scowled. "I didn't ask for any of this, you know."

"But you'll have to settle for what you got. Later, we'll go kill some goddamn dwarves. It'll be fun, I'll make cocktails. But first we get Mimir."

"Why do *you* want him?" Ted asked. "Everybody's looking for him for some high or dark reason. What's yours?"

Loki shrugged. "Someone from before. Someone to talk to. We were friends, he and I."

"Bullshit," Ted said.

"Look, let's duck out, run north and get the Head. Leave the Norn here. It'll be just like the old days."

"I'm not Th—"

"Don't say his name. He'll hear you."

"He's dead."

"So am I, so the story goes. I wouldn't bet that hearing his name wouldn't wake him up."

Good point. "Fine, I'm not your fucking sidekick, either."

"And I don't trust her family, or her. She'll distract you, maybe she'll get you killed," Loki said. "You'll try to protect her."

"Damn right. If you think I'll leave her alone with a city full of dwarves and giants—"

"It's not that full," Loki interrupted.

Ted ignored him. "No way. What'll they do to her if I'm not here?"

"She's been all over the news, Ted. They'll leave her be."

Ted shook his head. "Not if they can pin what they do to her on me. And they will."

Loki considered that. "Shit," he said. "You're probably right. Damned if you do…."

The bathroom door creaked, and Tilda stepped out. She still had the towel around her hips, but had pulled a T-shirt over her head.

"Damned if you do what?" she asked.

"Loki was telling me to leave you."

Her stare could've melted steel, and even the mythical trickster squirmed under its intensity.

"Was he?" Tilda said, dripping venom.

Loki held up his palms. "He exaggerates. I was only suggesting he leave you behind while we go for the Head. For safety's sake, of course. Nothing personal."

"I'm sure."

Tilda climbed under the covers and pulled the towel off, letting it drop to the floor. "Next time, try to steal me something I can wear."

"Those clothes all fit," Loki protested.

"I have hips, you jackass, I can't get away with a skinny jean. You'd think with all the times you've pretended to be a woman you would've learned to dress like one."

"You could have worn the skirt."

"Yeah, that's practical. Wear a skirt for crawling through the bush and fighting giants."

"Like you'll be doing the fighting," Loki said. "That's why we keep him around."

"Thanks," Ted said. He took his new briefs and walked to the bathroom, closing the door behind him. The clothes that Loki had stolen for Tilda were strewn about the floor. As restrained as he'd been with Ted's wardrobe, Loki had pulled out all the stops for her. Amid pairs of jeans and rumpled shirts were a black-and-white polka-dot dress that looked straight off a Hutterite colony, a tiny pink belly shirt that read JUICY, denim overall shorts. None of them seemed to suit her, even if they might've been the right size. Ted let the towel drop to the floor and pulled up the underwear. He leaned against the top of the vanity and looked into the mirror; he hardly recognized himself.

Ted supposed that he didn't really look any different from the last time he'd studied his reflection. He hadn't shaved since... since the dwarves had shaved him. Red and grey stubble broke the skin on his scalp and chin, and Ted figured he had a slightly less haunted look on his face. He took a deep breath and started to run some cold water into the sink.

Ted grabbed a washcloth from the rack behind him and dropped it under the water until it was saturated. He rung out the cloth and pressed it against his face.

You can't protect them both, Huginn said softly. **Whom will you choose?**

The tattooed beak of the raven moved beneath Ted's skin as it "spoke" to him.

Even though he knew the ravens understood his thoughts, Ted ground his teeth and whispered aloud, "Why don't you two actually help me, instead of criticizing every fucking thing that I do?"

The heads of both Huginn and Muninn seemed to perk up at that; their beaks slipped away from Ted's ears onto his cheeks. One eye on each tattoo shone golden as the birds watched him in the mirror. They spoke in unison.

What would you have us do?

"Seriously?"

Yes.

"About fucking time," Ted muttered. "What can you do?"

When we were clothed in flesh we flew over the known world each day, and whispered our findings to the All-Father come dark, Muninn said.

"That's great, but you're not birds anymore. You're tattoos."

We were never mere birds. Huginn almost sounded offended. **We were spirits wrapped in flesh. Now we are spirits clothed in ink. You have but to command us, and we will find flesh to wear again.**

"Really?"

Yes.

"Do it."

The tattoos spread their wings, and seeped from Ted's skin in deep blue mist. He grunted, wincing at the sensation. It felt like he'd pressed his face against a belt sander. Solidifying upon the vanity, the mist split into the shape of two iridescent blue ravens. They hopped from clawed foot to clawed foot, and stretched out their wings slowly, before they took to the air and disappeared into the mirror.

"I wish I'd known you could do this sooner."

You never asked, the ravens shot back, and then were gone from Ted's awareness as well as his vision.

Taking a deep breath, Ted stepped out of the washroom and slid into bed next to Tilda. He gave her knee a squeeze and she wormed her body closer against him. On the other bed, Loki was snoring atop the covers, still fully dressed.

"You all right?" Tilda whispered. "I thought I heard you talking in there."

"Yeah, I just had to sort some stuff out in my head," Ted answered quietly.

"Aren't you missing a couple of tattoos?"

"I sent them out to scout the town—and to give me some peace and quiet."

"Sort out stuff about us?" she asked, trailing a finger over the void the raven tattoos had left behind.

"About everything."

"Come to any conclusions I should know about?"

Ted ran his hand over Tilda's bare hip.

"Don't worry, you're the best damn thing that's happened to me since… well, ever."

"Better than football?" she asked.

Ted smiled. "Hell, yeah."

"It took you a long time to figure that out."

"I'm too old to process things quickly."

"You're not too old," she whispered in his ear and gave it a little nibble.

"You say that now."

"I have a feeling that when I'm forty you'll be holding up better than me."

"Doubtful."

Walking his fingers over Tilda's bare skin, Ted whispered, "I think he's sleeping," glancing briefly at the other bed.

"He's faking," she said, moving Ted's hand up to her thigh.

"Yeah," he said, disappointed. "Probably."

Loki continued to snore softly.

"So…" Ted said settling his palm against Tilda's belly. "Any regrets?"

"Of course not," Tilda answered firmly. Her voice sounded less sure when she added: "What about you?"

"What's to regret?"

"I knew I was going to be a mother. For as long as I've been able to reason, I knew this was going to happen."

"I wanted kids," Ted said slowly. He and Susanna had tried. It had been one of the last things they'd agreed upon. Their attempt hadn't worked out. The failure one of many nails in the coffin of a dead marriage. The one Ted least liked to think about.

"Yeah… with your wife. Not some hitchhiker you've known for a few days."

"I wasn't always married," Ted said. "And I wasn't always careful. Hell, I could have a kid out there somewhere."

"If you do," Tilda said cryptically, "you'll never meet him."

"You sure?"

She gave him a flat stare.

"Right, fortune teller."

Ted reached over, pulled a cigarette out of Loki's pack on the nightstand, and lit it.

"Guess I'm gonna have to give this shit up," Tilda said, looking wistfully at Ted's cigarette.

"Shit." Ted moved to butt out the smoke.

Tilda waved him off. "How many women smoke and drink until they realize they're late? Our daughter will be born healthy, Ted. I've seen it. Nothing I do until then matters."

Ted butted out anyway.

Tilda smiled. "You gonna quit with me?"

"If I have to."

"You will if you have to. What a bunch of bullshit."

"Wait… you said we're having a daughter?"

Ted imagined the slack look on his face.

"Of course we're having a daughter. I'm a Norn, what else will the baby be?"

"I'm outside of fate and shit, maybe I'll gum up the works."

"I know you jocks always want sons, but would a little girl be so bad?"

"No," said Ted. "It wouldn't, not at all. At least, not until she gets to be a teenager. If she takes after either of us, then I'll likely have a stroke."

Tilda snorted a short laugh before covering her mouth.

"Well, I guess I have nine months to get it together." Ted sighed. "You know, you really should have paid attention to the fact your prince is a pauper. I don't have shit to my name but a warrant. How are we going to afford this kid?"

Tilda patted his head. "You don't have to worry about anything. Things will work out just fine."

"Think, or know?"

"We'll be okay." She smiled a small, arcane smile. "I'd hate to ruin it for you."

"If you two aren't going to fuck," Loki said irritably, "I'm going to go get something to eat."

Daylight stabbed through the blinds, which they'd forgotten to close, and at the ungodly hour of eight o'clock, no less. Ted tried to blink the sleep from his eyes. Tilda had turned her back to him at some point in the night and burrowed her head under her pillow, as if anticipating the morning's rude awakening.

Loki's bed was made, if a little rumpled. Of the trickster himself, there was no sign. In the mirror beside the bureau, Ted could see Huginn and Muninn had returned to their perch over his ears.

About time you woke up, Huginn chided. **The jötnar have Loki.**

"Shit."

It gets worse.

"How could it get worse?"

They have one of the Norns with them.

"Prisoner?"

Uncertain.

Resting on the round table on the far side of the room and next to Loki's bed was a rectangular stone tablet. Angular writing was chiselled into the stone's surface.

"Where did this come from?"

It's dwarvish script, Munin said.

Ted shuddered. Had the dwarves snuck into his room again? Why had they only left a tablet? What was their fucking game? Ted picked up the stone, regarding the script. The words were just at the cusp of Ted's consciousness, but he couldn't quite make them out.

Would you like me to translate? Huginn asked.

The ravens seem far more agreeable since he had given them wing. Or maybe they were happy to see Loki gone.

"Yes," Ted said. "I would."

For what was made...

A debt unpaid...

By twisted mocking words...

But time has turned...

And what was earned...

Will ne'er again be heard.

"What does it mean?" Ted asked.

Loki promised his head to the dwarves in exchange for certain gifts they crafted for the gods. He tricked his way out of paying them, Muninn said.

"So?"

Someone wants you to think the dwarves have him, Huginn said. And that they've taken his head.

16. I Fought the Law

Throwing on his clothes in a rush, Ted shouted, "Wake up!"

Tilda stretched her arms above her head and yawned, rubbing the sleep from her eyes.

Squinting at the morning light, she asked, "What's the hurry?"

"The giants," Ted barked. He didn't want to tell her one of the Norns was with them. Not yet. "They've taken Loki. I'm going to get him back."

"What about Mimir's Head?"

"I can't leave him."

"How do we know he's even still alive?"

Ted stood up; he had one boot tied, the other he'd slipped on, its tongue hanging out like a dog's.

"Would he help you?"

"He's helped me," Ted said.

Tilda tilted her head, surprised. "Sure he has. What has he done for you other than steal beer and smokes?"

"He…." Ted struggled to think of something, but couldn't. He leaned over, defeated, and tied his other boot. "Maybe, but it still doesn't mean he deserves to die."

"He was supposed to die," Tilda said, standing up from the

bed. Her hair stood out at all angles, giving her a wild, almost feral, look. Her bare bottom certainly added to the picture. "He rolled the dice with fate at every turn, he fought it, cheated it, fucked it, he finally thought he'd beaten it. He 'owes' those dwarves his head. Loki never should have lived long enough for anyone but Heimdall to collect. There's nothing you can do."

"There has to be," Ted said, straightening his shirt. He had a brief moment of anxiety, wondering if Loki had taken his shape to check the fit. And what other mischief he would've gotten into.

"You don't know where they've taken him."

"Yes," Ted said, tapping a raven tattoo. "I do. But there's more." If Loki had been here, he'd have told Ted to leave this out. But if he had to choose to trust anyone, it would be Tilda. "They have one of the Norns too."

Tilda's face fell. When she spoke, it was barely a whisper. "Is… is it Mom?"

"They didn't say."

"What she doing up here?" the Norn asked, mostly to herself. "Okay, you're already on the run, even a city of six thousand will have cops, and it's not like you can blend. How do we get to them?"

"The cops won't do shit to stop me."

"What makes you so sure?"

"They're on the dwarves' payroll, according to Loki."

"Assuming he's right, how does that help us?"

"Us?"

"You think I'm not going with you?"

"The fuck you are," Ted said, putting his hand on Tilda's shoulder. "It's too dangerous."

She slapped his hand away. "What makes you think I need protecting?"

"I have no idea what I'm getting my ass into; I can't ask you to come along."

"You didn't ask. I'm insisting. You're right; you don't know what you're getting into, but my family is there. And you'll need me, dumbass."

"But—"

"I'll be fine," Tilda insisted.

"Have you seen something, or is that just wishful thinking?"

"I told you our daughter would be born healthy right? Has that happened?"

Ted didn't answer. There was no arguing with her. *No point arguing with any women, they all think they know the future.* He still wasn't used to the idea of being with one who actually did.

He pulled her into a rough embrace, and buried his face in her hair. Feeling her pressed against his body, Ted couldn't think of anything better.

"I'll be fine," she said.

"You better be."

"Don't get all weak-sister on me, Ted, you're supposed to be the tough guy." A crooked smile played across her lips, but there were tears in her eyes. "Man up and act like it."

"Hey," Ted said. "Who needs to act?"

He nodded towards her lack of pants. "Are you going out like that? If so, I don't think we need to worry about the cops recognizing me."

Tilda's face flushed bright red. Ted had never seen her look embarrassed. So far she had always been the one catching him off-guard.

Revenge was sweet.

Tilda picked the underwear out of her butt for at least the fifth time. After the third attempt, she'd given up even trying to be surreptitious about it. "Why are we walking?"

"I don't know where Loki found that shitty pickup, but I don't want to chance being recognized with us in it." They'd drawn some looks, but Ted figured the puzzled glances were due to him and Tilda being strangers in town, or his tattoos, as most of the folks had said hello, instead of screaming and running. "But for some reason the dwarves gave me these gifts. I'm not sure I believe Loki that they did it to spite him. Someone wants me in jail and out of the fight. You said your family wouldn't be too happy about me being with you."

"Maybe," Tilda agreed half-heartedly. "But they wanted you to get them Mimir's Head. You can't do that from prison."

"I doubt they ever believed I'd get it for them. Maybe they think Loki and I are holding you hostage as a bargaining chip for later. Did you ever tell them about—"

"I didn't tell them who the father would be, but they probably know now."

An older man, walking past at just that moment, heard the one titillating part of their conversation, and *tsked* in dismay. For the first time in ages, Ted didn't feel old.

"So," Tilda began cautiously. "You know where he is?"

"Yeah. Sorta."

"Where?"

"Underground," Ted said.

"Could you be more specific? Canada has a lot of ground."

Ted smiled. "Heckle and Jeckle know the way."

By daylight, the town was quite picturesque, once they got a little further in from the highway and the hotel. Flin Flon was hilly, with great rock faces everywhere. The slabs of stone, like those on the highway, were thick with graffiti. They kept walking in silence following Huginn and Muninn's prodding.

After several minutes, Tilda said, "I'm starting to think Amma lied to me about the whole pregnancy thing."

"Why would she do that?"

"I don't know." Tilda paused and thought about his question. "It's like she wanted me to think I'd lose my powers as soon as I conceived."

"Maybe you're not pregnant yet," Ted said. "I guess we'll have to try again soon."

"Smooth talker."

"I'd say I was well-trained, but if that had been the case, we wouldn't be having this conversation."

Tilda smiled. "You think I couldn't have stolen you away?"

Ted held a hand over his chest. "Hey. I have my principles."

"Yeah," Tilda said, pulling him closer and resting her head on his shoulder. "You do."

Ted gave her shoulder a squeeze, and they walked in lockstep. After a few moments of banging ankles and knees, however, they gave each other a little distance.

As they passed a car dealership, a reflected glimpse of Muninn made him stop in his tracks.

"How's your memory?" he asked suddenly.

"What?"

"Your memory? How good is it?"

"Pretty good, I guess. Even after a bender I usually remember what happened. Mom and Amma made me play all these stupid memory games growing up so that I'd remember my visions long enough to write them down. Why?"

Understanding crept over Tilda's face. "Oh, shit," she said.

Ted nodded. "What good is seeing the future if you don't remember it?"

"Mom and Amma have all their own visions, and anything they'd have forgotten would still be recorded in detail. Mom always told me to write my visions down, that they may be important later."

"They still have all those journals, and they know a lot more than us," Ted said. "They know everything your family has ever seen. That's what brought them up here."

Tilda stopped, deep in thought. "Maybe."

"The Norns are trying to change the future. They came for the Head themselves."

"You can't change it," Tilda said. "You can't control it. It just is."

"They told you that, too?"

"Shit," Tilda said through her teeth.

"Maybe you aren't as safe as you think, babe."

The strong scent of water brought back the memory of his brief stay in Gimli. While Ross Lake was no Lake Winnipeg, it was a pretty significant body of water to be enclosed within city limits. There was something else that tickled at his nose, and it wasn't the flies. A hint of rot, of stagnant water and dead vegetation, wafted just underneath. It was subtle. He was surprised he'd noticed it at all. Tilda had her nose to the wind too.

"You smell it too?" he asked.

She nodded. "Yeah, I do."

"Jormungandur claimed I might find Mimir's Head by Ross Lake." Ted pointed past another statue of the fictional explorer Flonatin, riding atop a fish-shaped submarine. "That's it."

They walked a little closer. A sign swung in the breeze proclaiming FLINTY'S BOARDWALK. It was a trail of crushed grey rock that made up a path that seemed to go entirely around the northern arm of the lake.

"You think that we'll find the *jötnar* hiding off a public boardwalk? A tourist attraction, no less?"

Ted shrugged. "Why not? Giants are skilled with illusion,

right? Good enough to fool Loki. Good enough to hide from people who wouldn't believe in them."

"Maybe," said Tilda. "So you're just gonna walk up to their door and knock?"

"I have to find them first." He held up his tattoo of Mjölnir. "But I do carry around this big skeleton key."

"Try not to get yourself killed over him."

"Who, Mimir?" Ted asked.

"No, you goof." Tilda dropped her eyes. "Loki. He doesn't deserve your friendship."

"You'd be singing a different tune if you'd known me in Alberta."

They crossed a set of railway tracks and walked down a slope towards the lake. The boardwalk was split both east and west; the western path curled back towards the highway. Ted turned east. He wondered if they'd used rock to line the path because of the waste left by the mine's tunnelling. Here and there among the uniformity of grey stone were specks of white, calcite, and quartz that caught the sunlight. The edges of the path had a great deal of black and brown stone. Mine slag, maybe. It looked metallic and Ted couldn't place the stuff. It had been a long time since he'd had to use any real geology. Even longer since he'd had to memorize the minerals and their properties. This city would be a rockhound's dream, though.

He shook his head. That was his old life. The only rocks he'd see now would probably be hurled at him.

A rickety fence separated someone's property and vegetable garden from the boardwalk. Weathered grey wood had rusted barbed wire fastened to it. Slats that had once criss-crossed between the posts lay broken on the earth and the barbed wire drooped as if something large had levered itself over the top of the fence.

Maybe something had.

Farther along the boardwalk, underneath a wooden foot-bridge, a creek babbled over green-stained stones and into Ross Lake. Its current cut a swath through the reeds and algae. The boardwalk forked up ahead, near a large boulder that had a plaque next to it. One path headed over some rail tracks back towards the residential part of Flin Flon, the other continued around the lake. The boulder looked like a glacier deposit—an erratic, abandoned at the end of the last ice age—not native to the rocks Ted had so far seen around the city.

"I still can't believe they reported me missing," Tilda said.

"We'll be fine." Ted rubbed his scalp. "We're running free, aren't we?"

"And if they find us, fighting the cops is our last-ditch option."

Ted nodded. "I'd like to be able to see you without a visitor's permit clipped to your shirt. The bogus charges can be explained away. It'll just take time."

"Time we don't have," Tilda said. "If you want to save the trickster."

She was right. "All of it is just a delay. The kidnapping charges, wanting us to think the dwarves have Loki." Ted thought of how long the night had felt when he'd been in the holding cell at Winnipeg Remand and how quick he was to run off to the trickster's rescue. "But it'd take long enough to clear me if we were caught, or we'd be running in the wrong direction and by the time we figured it out—"

"The Norns get the Head and magic is toast. Or Surtur has it and we're toast."

"Fuck," Ted muttered. "Huginn, I need a favour."

Tilda looked at him oddly. "You actually talk to them?"

"Yeah," Ted said. He didn't want to tell Tilda he found it easier to speak to them than to admit they were roaming around in his thoughts.

You've but to command.

"Shit!" She traced a finger over Huginn's image. "Your tattoos are moving."

"Take a message to Loki."

And what should I tell him?

"Tell him… tell him I'm coming, but we've hit a snag. He'll need to stall."

As you wish.

Ted's skin burned as the tattoo slid free, though not as badly as the first time.

But I would recommend you just let him die. He's been stalling long enough.

Tilda shook her head in wonderment. "Thought loose upon Midgard," she muttered. "I never thought I'd see the day."

When its misty form had solidified into flesh, Huginn took wing, leaving Ted and Tilda behind.

Muninn asked hopefully, **Have you any tasks for me?**

"Not right now," Ted answered.

Then I shall remind you that the authorities are still pursuing you.

"I'm aware of that, thanks."

Indeed.

"Freeze!" a voice yelled from behind Ted. "Police!"

Ted turned slowly and raised his hands, cursing the snotty bird.

Distracted by the barrel of a gun, Ted couldn't make out enough of the cop's uniform under the bulky tac vest to decide if he was local or federal. *Did Flin Flon even have their own police?* Many rural towns just relied on the Mounties. The cop was big, at least Ted's height, probably an inch or two taller.

"Easy," Ted said, trying to keep eye contact with the cop. He was young, maybe just out of college. Ted figured him for a Fed. The gun remained level at Ted's torso. That was good. He couldn't know that Ted was invulnerable. At least, Ted hoped he was. No one had shot him yet. "Don't shoot."

The cop took one hand off his gun to work the radio clipped to his shoulder.

"Dispatch, this is Fontaine. I've apprehended the fugitive... yes, Callan. The girl's with him. Requesting backup... up at the boardwalk by Manitoba Avenue... yeah, the path just over the tracks."

"There was no kidnapping," Tilda said, peeking out from behind Ted. "I wanted to leave with him."

"Please move out where I can see you," the cop said. "And keep your hands where I can see them."

"But—"

He cut her off with a raised hand.

"There was no kidnapping, you ass," Tilda repeated angrily. "We're together."

"Then I'm sure you'll be happy to be tried together for the murders of Leslie Braun and Ernest Friesen."

"We were in Gimli when that happened," Tilda insisted. She looked up at Ted but he kept quiet. The cop had made up his mind about them. They were hooped. And unless Ted wanted to risk Tilda being caught in the gunfire, they were going to stay that way. Ted hoped Loki was as good at stalling as he was at pissing people off.

"Any witnesses willing to swear to that?" the cop asked. "Because the WPS have several saying you were there."

Ted opened his mouth to say something then snapped it shut; the only people who could testify on their behalf had likely been the ones to drop the tip to the cops. They could ask the Midgard Serpent to testify. Having the entire court swallowed whole would be grounds for a mistrial, but Ted doubted would help their case in the long run.

"I didn't think so." The cop didn't say it smugly, as Ted would have expected.

"Look, we're eloping," Ted lied. "I only just heard about the murders. I left my car at her parents'. We took the bus. I think I still have my ticket in my wallet. Call it in, and you'll find a GTO registered to me in front of The Grey Ladies Tea House in Gimli."

"Fine," the cop said, sliding to the side to have a different angle on Ted. "Pull out your wallet—slowly. Left-handed, please. Set it on the ground."

"I don't want to cause any trouble," Ted said, doing as he was told. "But they're just mad at us. I know they think I'm too old for Til, but I didn't think they'd take their grudge this far."

"Step back from the wallet."

Ted did so, bumping into Tilda. She followed him back several steps as the officer advanced. The cop stood over the wallet, but made no attempt to pick it up. Instead, he kept his gun trained on them.

"Aren't you going to check it out?" Ted asked.

"I'll leave that to the inspectors, thank you."

"I'm not going to jump you."

"No," the cop said. "You're not."

"So," Ted asked, "where's that backup?"

"On its way." The officer stiffened, and brought his off hand back up to steady his weapon. "What's your hurry?"

"I want this cleared up and sorted out, so we can press charges against whoever set me up."

"That'll make Thanksgivings interesting," the cop said.

Ted found the small joke refreshing. He knew it was an act, that the cop was trying to keep them casual, to dull the threat of violence until his backup arrived.

"Obstruction of justice can be a serious charge," the cop said.

"Not as serious as kidnapping and murder," Ted answered. "She's old, trying to protect her precious grandchild. Judge'll likely let her off with time served and some community service."

"Maybe, maybe not. She could do a couple years."

"Fuck that," Ted said. "Kiddy fiddlers barely do that anymore. She'd never see the inside of a real cell."

"You okay with that, Miss Eilifsdottir? Letting him press charges on your family?"

Tilda nodded curtly. "Right now, she better hope he gets to press those charges. It'll keep me from making the rest of her bitter, old life a living hell."

The cop radioed again asking for backup. He was considerably less polite this time. In the distance there was a car alarm that no one was attending to, but no sirens.

"Fuck," the cop muttered. He grabbed a set of handcuffs and tossed them at Tilda. "Cuff yourself." He looked at Ted. "You," he said. "Step back." Ted did so. "Now, move."

The cop gestured with his pistol for them to head up the path that led away from the lake. Ted complied. His boots crunched over the rocks as he climbed towards the RCMP cruiser. Across the road there was a set of wooden steps built onto the rocky hill. The car was parked opposite the stairs. Ted could hear an engine working hard. Rubber squealed on asphalt as a vehicle rounded a corner too sharply, skidding to a stop.

Fontaine looked worried. "What the fuck?"

That, Ted decided wasn't a good sign. He half-turned to see what was happening.

"Don't move," the cop ordered. The angle of his weapon had shifted, no longer centred on Ted's torso, but up and over his shoulder.

There was a big, white Econoline van blocking the road. A gold nugget logo above a sign on it read SVARTA MINING AND SMELTING. The side door of the van flew open and there were two loud bangs, so close together Ted almost lost the second one in the echo of the first. He dove into Tilda, knocking her to the ground beneath him. She grunted as his weight settled on her.

Rusty shocks squeaked as the van rocked. Ted heard two heavy footfalls behind him and turned to look. Something almost as large as the van was trying to squeeze its way past the open side door. The creature was as big as the giant that Ted had fought by the highway, but was made of rocks instead of meat.

Rock troll, Muninn cawed.

The thing's colouring shifted as it took a step closer to Ted, turning grey to match the asphalt. Veins of mortar stood out from its neck as it roared, a sound like falling down a scree of loose shale.

Two more rounds popped from the cop's gun. Bullets chimed against the troll's rocky skin, chipping small holes away before ricocheting into the ground and the trees lining the road.

Ted heard the guttural language of the dwarves. He pushed himself to his feet, and smiled.

"Well, it's about fucking time you assholes showed up."

17. The Payback

The dwarves waited for the cop to empty his clip at their pet monster before hopping out of the van. There were two of them, neither of whom Ted recognized. But they were dwarves. They'd do.

"Get down!" the cop yelled at Ted as he snapped another clip of bullets into place. "You're blocking my shot."

The dwarves slipped out from behind the creature; each had a fibreglass compound bow in his left hand and a broad head-hunting arrow in his right. They drew their bows and loosed the arrows in one smooth motion. At this distance aiming was hardly necessary. Both bolts zipped past Ted close enough that he could hear them cutting through the air. The arrows thunked solidly into something soft behind him.

Tilda!

Ted chanced a glance behind him. She was fine, ducking low and fishing in the leather pouch which held her runes as she made for shelter. But Fontaine had slumped to the ground with two aluminum shafts deeply imbedded in his body. He groaned, fired another shot wildly, and fell over.

"Get out of here!" Ted yelled at Tilda.

"No! You—"

"You can't help me with this."

Ted turned back in time to see the troll's huge fist rushing towards him. Something with that much momentum would send him flying. Ted slid his feet, turning out of the way of the punch. The troll's roundhouse missed, throwing it off-balance. It leaned forward to steady itself.

Ted cocked his fist back and Mjölnir crackled with power. He slammed his hand into the thing. There was a loud crack as one of the rocks broke apart. Red mortar seeped around the broken stone and the troll roared.

It raised its arm as if it was driving fence posts and Ted was the stake. He swung up at the socket where the rocky arm rotated. The impact pulverized the joint. The troll's arm fell to the cement, cracking further, and the thing bellowed.

The rock troll cradled the empty socket. Roaring, it lunged for Ted. Liquid, thick and dark, seeped from both the wound and the broken appendage. Blood. Shouts from the dwarves were being translated by Muninn.

They are upset that you've maimed their pet.

"Shut up!" Ted yelled.

Don't you want to know what they are saying?

"I'm a little busy right now."

A back-handed swat slammed Ted across the road and into the hillside. He heard a rock crack behind him. The troll closed the distance quicker than Lawrence Taylor in his linebacker prime, and its oversized hand pressed Ted against the wall of rock lining the street, its palm covering his torso. Stone fingers dug into his shoulders. Ted's skin couldn't be pierced, but under that vice-like pressure he couldn't breathe. The troll's grip kept

Ted from raising his own arms. It tightened its hand around him. What little air Ted had left, escaped his lungs in a rush.

He was in trouble.

"*Ófriður*," the dwarves said.

The word is Icelandic, Muninn told him. **It means war, but the dwarves are using it more like a title, or proper name.**

"Get in the van or we pierce your woman," said one dwarf in heavily accented English.

The other laughed. "And then we put an arrow in her."

"Go. Fuck. Yourself," Ted coughed out.

"*Tiwaz!*" Tilda yelled. A glowing rune, like a spear point, lanced from her hand.

There was an explosion to Ted's right, and then the smile was wiped from the dwarf's face, along with most of the front of his head. Tilda held the stone in a shaking hand, sunlight glinting off the handcuffs around her wrists. The coppery scent of blood filled Ted's nostrils. For a moment the dwarf stood rigid on his heavy, broad feet and then he exhaled a last breath, his knees buckled, and his body fell to the ground.

Dropping Ted, the troll went down to one knee next to the dead dwarf. It roared again and lunged towards Tilda.

Ted had no time to catch his breath. The troll was too fast. He gulped a mouthful of air—it hurt to do so—and hurled himself at the thing. In the open field with only ten yards to run, a linebacker can hit with thousands of pounds of force. Ted didn't have ten yards to build up a head of steam, but thanks to the dwarves he'd hit a lot harder—and he sure as shit wasn't worried about crippling the troll.

Had the rock troll been human-sized, Ted's shoulder would have caught it in the ribs, a painful, but clean, hit. Instead, Ted rammed his shoulder into the joint of the creature's knee.

Some delicate mechanism of worked stone that allowed the thing to ape human movement went off-track. The troll roared and fell to the side as its leg gave out, unable to support its weight. Another howl echoed off the rocks as the creature landed on the broken knee.

An engine revved behind him and the van peeled out and away from them. The dwarf had left his pet monster behind. The rock troll seemed to sense its abandonment.

Pain-filled howls became piteous cries. It stopped trying to claw its way towards Tilda and stopped over the body of the fallen dwarf. The same oversized hand that had tried to crush Ted plucked the corpse from the ground gently. Giving its hand a little shake, the troll made the dwarf's limbs spasm wildly. The troll made a hopeful little trill at the movement, too stupid to realize it had caused the motion, and waited. When the dwarf didn't move, the troll started to shake harder. Blood and gore sprayed out from the broken skull, painting the road.

Ted inched past the creature, not wanting to draw any more of its ire, even though it was seemingly crippled. He felt strangely guilty. It was just a pet, albeit a deadly one. Smart enough to realize it had been left alone, dumb enough to miss its masters.

Tilda was standing still, her hands shaking a little, but she had lowered her hand to her side. She turned and started to retch. Ted hoped she would be okay, but right now, someone was dying.

By the time he reached the cop's side, the troll seemed to have resigned itself to the fact its master wasn't getting back up. It had cocked its smallish, lumpy head back and started a series of racking, braying yells. Ted knelt by the officer. He was still breathing, though shallowly. Shock glazed his eyes—from his wounds or what he'd seen, Ted didn't know. Maybe both.

One of the arrows had entered just below the cop's collar-bone. That one probably wasn't too serious, though it would hurt like hell. The other, Ted winced just to look at the wound. The arrow was sticking out of the cop's gut, just below his belly button. Only the fletching had kept it from passing entirely through the man's body. Modern body armour wasn't designed to fend off arrows and the Kevlar may as well have been cotton. So far the cop wasn't screaming.

That was probably a bad thing.

Ted had seen a man take a length of rebar through the gut during a fall on a worksite. He'd never thought a human voice could make sounds like that. After the screams stopped and the man passed out, he never woke up again. His punctured guts had leaked waste into his body and he'd died of sepsis.

"Wake up!" Ted yelled at the cop. He had to yell to be heard over the rock troll, and there was no time to be gentle.

The cop blinked and tears trickled from his glazed eyes. Ted had to get him awake and talking. Shock can kill as easily as the wound that caused it.

"Stay with me." Ted looked down the man's vest, he'd forgotten how the cop had identified himself. His name was stencilled on it. Fontaine.

"*Nnnn,*" was the best answer Fontaine was able to make.

"What's your first name?" Ted asked.

"D… D… Dennis." The cop shook his head and winced from the effort. "You're… you're still under arrest."

"Fine, but we need to get you to a hospital."

It would mean jail, but he wasn't about to leave the cop here with the grieving rock troll. He also didn't expect the wounded cop to survive any treatment he would receive if they left him and just called it in.

"Tilda, can you help me?"

Ted knew he could have easily hoisted up Fontaine by himself. But the man was seriously wounded, and Ted worried he'd only make the wounds worse. There was no answer from the Norn.

"Til!"

"I… I…."

She was in shock as much as the cop. Her gaze was locked on the ruined face of the dwarf she'd killed.

The troll and the giant were far enough from human that Ted imagined he would not have deeply mourned their deaths. Ted had grown up hunting with his father and brother; death was not as much of a stranger to him as it was to many. But having taken lives, and witnessed death, Ted also had a greater appreciation for life. Staring at what remained of the dwarf's head, he knew that killing a dwarf would be no different than killing a man. Ted knew that he, too, would stand in shock at his actions. The satisfaction of vengeance crumbled to guilt.

"I… I didn't mean to kill him," Tilda said, shaking.

"I know you didn't," Ted said softly. "But we can still save someone."

Ted picked up Fontaine's gun, thumbed the safety on and tucked it into the back of his jeans. He didn't want the wrong person to find it.

"Ready?" he asked as much of Fontaine as Tilda. "We need to keep him as straight as possible. We don't want the arrow shaft twisting inside him."

Both nodded and Ted hoisted the cop up by his armpits while Tilda lifted the wounded man's feet from the ground.

Fontaine screamed. Ted winced and glanced back over his shoulder. The rock troll hadn't moved. Its squatting form blocked a lane of the road. Fortunately, there hadn't been any traffic yet.

They set the cop down next to the cruiser. He hoped they hadn't aggravated his wounds.

"Do you know first aid?" he asked Tilda.

She shook her head.

Ted opened the driver's side door and popped the trunk; there was an emergency kit inside. He grabbed that and the shotgun strapped to the hatch. There was a box of rubber slugs and a box of buckshot. Ted figured one dead dwarf was enough killing for one day, and took the rubber slugs in case they were accosted by human authorities. He loaded the shotgun and handed it to Tilda.

Ted started to unbuckle the armour but his hands were slick with the cop's blood, and he couldn't work the clasps to free the vest.

"I need a knife," Ted said. "Do you have one?"

Fontaine's coppery skin was becoming ashen.

"What for?" he asked.

"I'll need to cut you free."

"Console," Fontaine said.

Tilda passed the knife to him. It was in a plain deerhide sheath. Ted pulled the knife free. It was a beautiful weapon. Old, too. The handle was antler—maybe caribou—and intricately carved to resemble a running wolf. Decades of sweat and blood had stained the worked bone a reddish-brown. The blade itself was a little better than six inches long; both edges had been sharpened, but from its balance and heft, Ted knew it was weighted for throwing.

"Nice," he said, trying to keep Fontaine talking. "Where'd you get it?"

"My... my grandfather. Gave it to me on... deathbed." Fontaine coughed, and there was bloody froth on his lips. Once he started coughing, it took a long time for him to stop. The motion jerked at the arrows through his body, forcing him to scream. Screams brought more coughs. He finally forced a semblance of control over his body. Ted was impressed. Fontaine was one tough fucker.

"Tell me about that day."

"Mishoom said the knife was from a time before... before the Europeans. Before the Hudson's Bay Company, at least. Said that the metal blade was taken from some red-haired demons that came here riding... riding... dragons." Fontaine tried to chuckle, but winced and coughed again. "Always... always thought his story was bullshit. Mishoom loved to tell stories. But it's a great knife."

Ted nodded and sliced away the shoulder straps of the armoured vest, easing it away from Fontaine's chest. Even that small motion tugged at the shafts and the officer's screams made Ted stop.

There was a hell of a lot of blood. Ted's mind flashed back to his first morning in Winnipeg, waking up at the motor hotel, drenched in the stuff. He ground his teeth and formed two doughnut bandages around the arrows to slow the seepage.

"Fuck!" Fontaine yelled.

He'd healed that wounded giant. He could do the same for Fontaine, couldn't he? The giant was a creature of the Nine Worlds, would that make a difference?

No, it would not. Huginn said. And in any case, he has witnessed the Nine.

And if what Loki had told Ted was true, then Dennis Fontaine was bound to it, for the rest of his life, *however long that would be.*

"Where's the nearest hospital?" Tilda asked from the driver's seat. Ted noticed she'd put Dennis's cap on. It would keep casual suspicion at bay once they hit the road. People see the cruiser, the hat, and that's all they notice.

"Third and Church," Fontaine said.

"We're not from here," Ted told him. "We don't know where that is."

"Fuck!" Fontaine yelled again, and forced out some directions.

Ted didn't think the officer was going to survive being moved into the car, let alone to the hospital. The selfish part of him worried about the reception he and Tilda would see when they rolled in with a mortally-wounded Mountie. Would Fontaine even be safe there? Ted still didn't know. And he'd be damned if he'd get himself arrested, and only end up delivering the cop to his death.

The sun tattoo on Ted's left hand was still clearly visible through the blood. In fact the image was so clean it seemed the cop's blood wouldn't even coat the ink.

"Dennis?" Ted held the tattoo up Fontaine's eyes. The soft glow of sunlight brought some colour back to the wounded man's face. Even Ted could feel the warmth coming from the icon. "I'm going to take the arrows out."

"No!" the cop said, wincing. "I'll bleed out."

"No, you won't. Trust me."

Fontaine barked a short laugh, and winced from the effort.

"Sure… why not? Trust… an accused murderer and kidnapper to perform surgery in the back seat of my cruiser."

Ted forced a smile. "The key word there is accused."

"Can… still charge her with impersonating an officer—"

"Let's hope you live long enough to change your mind."

"Practising surgery without… licence."

Ted laughed at that one. "That's the spirit," he said, putting the knife sheath in Fontaine's mouth. "Bite down, this is gonna hurt like fuck."

Fontaine nodded, and ground his jaw into the hide.

It was a good thing the arrows were aluminum. Wood had more of a tendency to splinter and leave bits behind to fester and get infected. It was also easier to remove the broad head points than it would have been with a traditional arrow.

The arrow point sliced into his fingers.

What the fuck?

He shook the surprise away. There was no time for it. The dwarves had made him what he was—no surprise then, they'd have something that could hurt him. This weakness might make things difficult later, but Ted was almost glad of the reminder. He was getting a little too convinced of his own invulnerability. With a little more care than he had previously shown, Ted finished unscrewing the arrowheads and tossed them to the floor.

"Ready?"

Fontaine nodded and crushed his eyelids closed.

Ted closed his hand over the arrow in the cop's shoulder. With a jerk, he wrenched the shaft free. His elbow hit the cage that separated the front seat from the back, denting it. Blood gushed up in an arcing trail, following Ted's arm. Fontaine convulsed briefly from the pain, and Ted used his weight, rather than his strength, to hold the man against the car.

"One down," Ted said. *The easy one.* "One to go."

He waited for the cop to settle himself. Fontaine gave Ted a feeble nod.

Ted grunted and grabbed the second shaft. His hand was slippery with the cop's blood and it slipped up the length of the arrow. Ted squeezed harder, feeling the metal deform in his grip, and pulled the second shaft free.

Blood spattered his face, bubbled up out of the cop's guts and started to soak the car. Fontaine spat the hide sheath from his mouth.

"Fuuuuuuuuuuck!" he hollered. If Ted hadn't already been holding the larger man down, he figured Fontaine would've punched him.

The cop was forcing ragged breaths through his teeth. "If… you're gonna do something," he said. "Now's the time."

Ted pressed the hot palm of his left hand against the man's wounded belly. Fontaine gasped. Blood dried and flaked away from the hole. The cop's eyes were wide as the wound sealed itself. Ted reached up to heal the second puncture, but the warmth and light had already dimmed from the tattoo, the golden ink had faded to black. It was just an image now, its magic spent.

He is brave, Muninn observed, meaning Fontaine. **This one would have been welcomed in Valhalla.**

"Valhalla's broken," Ted muttered. "And he's not one of yours."

One of yours, actually. And he is now.

"Dammit," Ted cursed.

Fontaine sat on the seat in the back of the cruiser. He opened his ruined shirt to look at the smooth, unmarked skin. "Hey, not to sound ungrateful…." He ran tentative fingers over his stomach, as if fearing any but the lightest touch would reopen the wound. "Whatever you did worked, but you missed a spot."

"That's all I got, it seems."

Strange, he'd healed more than one wound the first time he'd used the sun tattoo.

None of its wounds were mortal, Muninn reminded him. As the sun rises but once a day, it appears you may save but one life.

The cop winced as he tried to rotate his shoulder. "I'll live." He waited just a moment before adding: "Thanks."

"Don't mention it."

Ted grabbed the alcohol from the kit and poured it into the wound. Fontaine hissed but held steady as the liquid foamed.

"We'll take you to the hospital. Better safe than sorry," Ted said. "Who knows the last time those dirty fuckers washed their hands."

The cop nodded, and held still while Ted slapped bandages over the entrance and exit wounds.

"I've lived up here my whole life," Fontaine said. "And I've seen some crazy shit. But nothing like this."

"Count yourself lucky, then; you'll be seeing a lot more of it."

If he survived what was coming, Ted promised himself that he'd at least warn Fontaine about the Nine Worlds.

Tilda turned where the cop directed, and drove around the hospital grounds to get to the Emergency entrance. She pulled up the ramp that led to the sliding doors by Admitting.

"Get out," Ted said, opening the rear door of the cruiser.

"No."

Ted handed the cop his service weapon. "You might need this. We can't take you with us. And you can't fucking stop me. Get out, or I swear to God I'll knock you out."

Fontaine seethed. His nostrils flared as the cop forced out short, staccato breaths. "This isn't over."

Ted answered, hoping his words were truth. "For you, it is."

As they headed out of town, Tilda's driving became erratic. Drifting into the oncoming lane, speeding up and slowing down. Finally, she hit the gravel shoulder and skidded to a stop across from the smokestack that dominated the Flin Flon skyline.

"Til?"

Sick gurgles were her only answer. Her eyes were glazed over and watering. Convulsing, she threw her head against the driver's side window. The glass cracked.

Ted wasn't sure if this was normal for her or not. She hadn't reacted this way when he'd first met her, and she'd done his reading in The Goat. He couldn't take the strangled choking sounds she was making. He eased his index and forefingers into Tilda's mouth and flattened her tongue back down against her jaw. Her teeth ground against the skin of his fingers, but Ted didn't feel it. He waited until she came out of the fit.

Her eyes cleared and she blinked away the gathered tears

and mumbled around the obstruction in her mouth. "What happened?"

"You went blank there for a minute," Ted said. "I wasn't sure if it was a seizure or a vision."

"I… I think someone was trying to reach me. It was like before, in the van. But more insistent. I couldn't grab my runes."

"Do you remember anything?"

Tilda shook her head, her eyes going wide. "Nothing. They're gone. They're gone!"

"What's gone?" Ted asked, putting a hand on her shoulder, hoping to calm her. She felt frailer, diminished.

"My… my visions." She took a deep breath, trying to compose herself. She held a rune stone to her breast, pressed hard against her skin. "*Naudhiz! Naudhiz!*"

She stared at the rune stone, uncomprehending. Ted recognized the symbol from his reading in Gimli. The need stone. "Her" stone.

"I can't see anything. Even the memory of them is gone. My magic… I don't know… I don't know what's going to happen."

"Neither do I, but it'll be okay."

She shook her head weakly. "I've always known."

Ted nudged her chin up. "So we find out together."

Tilda sniffed and rubbed at her running nose with her shoulder. "All right."

"Maybe I should drive."

She nodded. Her legs dangled out of the car and she rested her head between her knees. "Yeah," she said without raising her head.

Ted offered a hand to help her up from her seat. She brushed it aside at first, but when her first attempt to rise failed and she slumped back into the car, she let him draw her to her feet. Tilda climbed into the backseat and lay down.

My brother returns, Muninn said.

A large raven dropped like a stone before spreading its wings to land lightly on the roof of the cruiser. Huginn cawed loudly, seemingly in pain. Feathers had been torn from its body, and small spatters of blood dropped to run down the side of the car.

Huginn hopped twice before its borrowed flesh melted in on itself, leaving a shell of black feathers and red blood upon the car. Mist rose from the body, coalescing upon Ted's neck as Huginn reclaimed his post and started to speak.

Loki is still alive.

"That's good," Ted said, nodding.

But not for long, I fear. The giants are using him hard and the dvergar are sniffing around.

"Why would the dwarves want the Head?"

And Urd is seeking to make a trade.

"Why? She sent us here to get the damned thing."

Perhaps she does not trust you to follow through. After all, they seek—

"To put an end to the Nine Worlds on Midgard. I know. Can you make yourself audible?" Ted asked Thought and Memory.

If you wish it, they both intoned.

"I do," Ted said.

Perhaps because he had witnessed it earlier or because the ravens were now talking aloud, Ted could feel them moving just beneath his skin, the ink that formed them sliding over muscle and bone. It was a very disconcerting feeling. Ted got into the driver's seat and set the shotgun down next to him.

"Urd's here," Ted said.

The raven tattoos nodded on either side of Ted's face.

Yes, Huginn said.

Tilda asked, "Amma?"

"Seems like," Ted said. "She's with Loki and the giants."

"But the *jötnar* hate us." Tilda sounded confused.

She plans on making a trade for the Head of Mimir.

"But they hate Loki even more," Tilda said. "I still can't believe the giants would do such a trade. Not for Loki. And what else could Amma be offering them?" Tilda shook her head.

The trickster played as many games with the jötnar as he did with the Aesir, Muninn said. Though Loki took their side at the end of days, even during Ragnarök they bore him no love.

And though he is greatly diminished, Huginn said. He is still a god. And able to act amongst the mortals. Something even the lowest jötunn cannot do.

"Where will the meeting take place?" Ted asked.

The jötnar will not leave their den, Huginn said. They have the Head. They will make the Norns and dvergar come to them.

"Ted?" Tilda asked with a bit of a quaver in her voice.

"Yeah?"

"Whatever else happens… that's my Amma…." She let the words hang in the air between them.

Ted nodded. "I don't want to hurt her," he said, wiping sweat from his brow. "I'm fucking pissed at her and her goddamn meddling. But I wasn't raised to hit old ladies, and all she did was drive us together. I'll try to keep her safe."

She smiled weakly.

You mean to keep that oath? the ravens asked. Ted watched Tilda's face but she didn't seem to notice the words. They were speaking in his mind again.

If I can. Ted thought back.

Do not try too hard, Huginn said. **If you die, so do we.**

Thanks for your concern.

Do not mention it, the ravens answered.

"Are you okay to shoot the gun?" Ted asked. Tilda nodded from the back seat. "Aim for the dwarves. Leave the giants to me."

"Sure thing," she said grimly. "The *dvergar* are probably behind as many missing persons up here as the giants."

"Why would they do that?" Ted asked over his shoulder.

"Their makings all require blood."

Muninn stirred something in Ted's mind. First the blood the dwarves had bathed him in after their carving work was done, then the blood that had mortared the rock troll. He remembered Les and Ernie, the two bouncers he'd put in the hospital. Two men that had been exposed to power from the Nine Worlds. Ted's power.

The men you were accused of murdering, Muninn confirmed, **were found drained dry.**

Rock rose up on either side of the highway, another stretch where a canyon had been carved into the rock to make a road. The cruiser passed over a red patch on the highway, the last bloody remnants of a deer or moose collision and then through a wisp of cloud, or fog.

Be cautious! Huginn yelled shrilly.

Before they could say any more a van appeared in the cruiser's lane. Mere yards away.

"Motherfuck!" Ted yelled, cranking the wheel to the right and hitting the shoulder. The passenger side of the car squealed as it kissed the rock face. Ted didn't slow the cruiser down. He hit the gas, powering them through the needle of open space between the graffiti-covered rock and the oncoming van. Behind them, the large van skidded to a stop and Ted saw the gold nugget logo of Svarta Mining and Smelting.

Ted jerked the jake brake and spun them around so fast the car continued rolling backwards. Rubber smoked over asphalt as Ted directed the cruiser forward, straight at the van. He had to admit, that was a sweet move.

The van was still in the middle of a three-point turn to get back to facing them head on, and Ted was closing fast.

"Buckle up back there," he said, as he belted himself in.

Tilda just managed to fasten her harness as the front end of the cruiser smashed the angled back end of the van. The van's front tires were just onto the steep edge of the road and the impact caused it to spin lightly. The top-heavy vehicle tipped over, sliding on its side over rocks and small spruce into the bottom of the ditch. Ted hit the brakes, and threw the car into reverse, the engine *thunking* in protest.

Just in time for a second van to slam into the passenger side of the cruiser.

18. Where Evil Grows

Ted was trapped.

The impact of the van against the cruiser had buckled the frame of the car around him. He strained against the crumpled dash. His legs were pinned against the radio and traffic computer and there was no leverage for him to do anything. A spatter of blood stained the cracked windshield. The rearview mirror had been twisted out of place by the impact, and despite how he strained, Ted couldn't see the back seat.

He couldn't see Tilda.

"Tilda?" he hollered. There was no answer.

Dwarves were gathering around the crippled cruiser, inspecting the damage and laughing—at each other or Ted, he wasn't sure.

"Tilda?" He tried again. "Come on, let me know you're okay. Til?"

She was just knocked out. She had to be. Loki had said she had *jötunn* blood. *Álfur* blood. She must be tougher than a normal woman; she'd shrugged off one car crash already, but she had her magic then.

Cracks had spiderwebbed the entire surface of the window on Ted's side of the cruiser. Thankfully, the safety glass kept it from shattering all over the car. A vague shape drew closer, and a thick-fingered hand pushed at the broken window, shoving it free and onto Ted's lap. The face that leaned in was a familiar one.

"You have been bringing us no end of sport," Moustache said, grinning. Ted noticed for the first time how each of his teeth seemed to be twice as broad and thick as a human's. "And messes to clean up. Our city—"

"Your city?"

Moustache shrugged. "As much ours as anyone else's. We can act more openly here than we can in the south. Far too many rules. Far too little sport. But you will change that for us, Ófriður. You are changing it. It has already begun."

Ted ignored the dwarf. He wanted to spit in Moustache's face. Swear. Take the shotgun and blow the smug grin off the fucker. Instead, he strained to get a glimpse of Tilda.

"You worry for your Norn whore?" Moustache said. He reached in, adjusting the rear-view mirror. Ted could see Tilda now. She was slumped forward, held in position by her seatbelt. Her chest rose and fell in slow, shallow breaths.

"She's not—"

The dwarf waved away his protest. "She lives," he said. "For now."

"What the fuck does that mean?"

"Well, Weapon. Like Mjölnir in the past, I fear we forged you too well. Not even a rock troll was able to stop you." Moustache nodded. The dwarf seemed proud—proud!—of what they'd done to Ted. "We will use the Norn to ensure your cooperation. Step out of line, and we will make our sport with her. You would like that less than she, I think."

Ted could see Beards One and Two walking around the car. Each tried a different passenger side door, grunting and wrenching at the handles. Neither opened.

"I guess we need to wait for the Jaws of Life," Ted said, smirking.

"Oh, you needn't worry," Moustache said. Beards One and Two started to chant in the dwarf tongue and pressed their palms against the metal of the cruiser. The frame squealed as it bent itself back into shape and the two dwarves pulled open the doors. "We have our own."

Beard One snatched the pouch bearing Tilda's rune stones. He bounced it happily on his palm before cutting her seatbelt. Pulling her unconscious body from the vehicle roughly by the hair, he dropped her to the asphalt. Beard Two grabbed the shotgun from the dash and turned the weapon on Ted. He mock fired the gun and laughed as Ted flinched.

"Still worried?" Moustache laughed. "Don't be, we forged you better than that."

When the dwarves had used their magic on the car frame to force it open, in their haste, they had given Ted some more space. Enough to move an arm. He lunged at Moustache's throat. But the dwarf was quicker and Ted's fingers slipped from his skin to grasp the dwarf's collar instead.

"Perhaps I was not clear," Moustache said. He nodded at Beard Two.

The dwarf flipped the shotgun to point it at Tilda.

"No!" Ted yelled, releasing his grip on Moustache to strain futilely towards the armed dwarf.

Somehow over his shout, Ted was able to hear the soft click of the trigger, before his world was swallowed by the eruption from the shotgun's barrel. The fired slug kicked up a spray of dirt and grass, but no blood.

Ted strained at the twisted metal enveloping him. He panted and seethed; there was no sating his anger. The sky darkened. Wind kicked up, catching the dwarf's elaborate moustache. Electricity crackled over Ted's chest. This time, he would give in to the storm's fury. This time when he called the lightning, it wouldn't be striking Ted.

He tried to calm himself. *I'll need some control. Don't want to hit Tilda.* He'd loaded the shotgun with rubber slugs. If the dwarves did shoot her, it shouldn't be fatal. She was still okay. But how close was safe with those slugs? There was no way the dwarves would have known the weapon wasn't deadly. They hadn't shot her. They were fucking with him. They had to be fucking with him. Her life was the only thing keeping him from killing them all.

"Stop!" Ted yelled.

Beard One nudged Tilda over to lie on her back. The dwarf tore the fabric of her shirt. Pale skin, but no abrasions. No blood.

"No wound. Yet."

Grunting peevishly, the dwarf took a step back and fired again. Dirt sprayed over the Norn. If Tilda cried out, it was lost in the echo of the report. Thunder rumbled an answer.

"Stop," Ted pleaded now. He was trapped. Helpless. Hopeless.

Beard One barked a laugh and tried to pull the gun from Beard Two. "Stop playing. Shoot her."

The dwarf with the gun shook off his fellow and aimed at the prone Norn again, looking expectantly back at Moustache.

"You're fucking dead," Ted said tightly.

Moustache brushed Ted's hand free. The dwarf affected a mock pout. "And you are in no position to threaten us."

Beard Two pulled Tilda from the ground; his rough fingers pressing tightly into her jaw. Ted remembered the feeling, but could do nothing but grind his teeth as he watched. A metal bit, so very like the one they'd used on Ted—perhaps the same one—was forced into the Norn's mouth. She gagged and suddenly flailed in the dwarf's strong grip.

Ted struggled against the frame of the car that imprisoned him. Moustache laid a hand on the wreck and whispered in the guttural dwarf tongue. The car bent and twisted further, forcing Ted to look the dwarf in the eye. Preventing him from watching Tilda.

"Since the Norn's misfortune," he chuckled at that, "disturbs you so much, I suggest you look elsewhere. We have much to discuss."

The Beards laughed and Ted's back bristled. The same mocking laugh as when they'd tortured him in the motel. It went on far too long but he couldn't see what they found so funny.

"You're not inspiring me to want to sit and listen, you sick fuck."

Moustache shrugged. "She comes from giant stock. She will live. She will live no matter what we do to her."

Ted didn't like the implication behind that threat. They didn't know what had happened. Their sick joking might kill her.

"Here you are," Moustache said. The car frame bent, twisting and pitching Ted slightly forward. "On your knees before your creator, isn't this how you people love to spend so much of your time? Begging for answers that won't come? I have answers for you. And unlike some, more selfish creators, I am willing to share them with you."

"I don't give a shit what you have to say."

Moustache laughed. "No? You don't sound certain to me."

Now Ted did spit at the dwarf, a small gesture, but it was the only defiance he could offer.

The dwarf let the spittle run down his hatchet nose, finally catching it on his finger before it dripped from his chin. Moustache whispered a word and Ted felt the wreck tighten around him like he was being crushed in a fist. Increasing pressure slowly squeezed the air from his lungs. He tried to breathe in, but felt only pins in his chest.

"I am only so patient," Moustache said, sounding bored. "And you can only hold your breath for so long. Will you hear me out?"

Claws of metal peeled free of the cruiser's roof to grip Ted's scalp. The wreck groaned again, and Ted felt his head being moved up and down, nodding.

"Just leave her be."

"Excellent," the dwarf said, and the pressure eased. He leaned in with a fat, bloody thumb and wiped the digit over Ted's cheeks. "As you wish." Moustache turned to the Beards and jerked his chin towards Tilda. "Leave the Norn. For now."

The dwarves have done something to lock me within your flesh, Huginn said. I cannot leave.

She still lives, if that was your worry.

It was.

You will soon have more. It seems the trickster wasn't what the giants demanded from the Norns for Mimir's Head.

What do they want?

You.

Me? Ted asked. *Why me?*

Huginn cawed a barking laugh and Muninn joined in. It is as simple as the symbol on your right hand, Huginn explained. Mjölnir. That hammer has ever been their bane. And oh, how they have always coveted it. And here it is. Free from its original wielder, but wrapped in the meat of a human who can be toyed with, but not hurt. You are to give them years of sport and revenge, I am afraid.

We do not look forward to the experience, Muninn said sadly.

And Tilda? Ted asked.

If Urd has her way, Skuld will likely be returned unharmed, Huginn answered.

But not necessarily, Muninn added. The dvergar and jötnar have ever been tricksome barterers.

It all depends on who gets the Head, Huginn said. If Surtur arrives, we will likely all die.

The hell with that, Ted thought.

You are not currently in a position to argue, Huginn reminded him.

That, Ted thought with grim satisfaction, *is about to change.*

He sucked in a mouthful of air, released it in staccato exhalations, and then breathed deeply. His chest tingled again. Not the pins and needles of breathlessness, but the sensation that told him the weather was changing, that he was changing it. Ted fought to keep the anger from his face. No sense in warning the dwarves any sooner than necessary.

Lightning, trapped within Mjölnir, danced, hidden, in anticipation. He practically quivered in the wreck. A feeling like on the day, not so long ago, when Ted had pulled the tarp off The Goat for the first time in years. As if he were taking back something that was his. Ted could feel the hammer calling out to the sky. Static electricity raised Moustache's long namesake into the air.

"What?" the dwarf muttered, surprised.

Ted laughed and closed his eyes.

His vision went white even behind clenched lids. Ozone filled his nostrils. Thunder boomed, so close it shook the car.

Like a clenched fist again the wreck tightened around Ted, crushing him. Moustache convulsed, sliding down the car's side, until except for his broad, burned hand that seemed melted to the cruiser, he had fallen out of sight.

With the dwarf's control of the metal cut off, Ted had enough room to tear his hammer hand free. He shoved at the door. Metal squealed and buckled. There was a snap as the hinges broke, and the door flew free of the car.

He had no time to gain his bearings. Tilda had to be freed before the Beards recovered from their surprise and used her as a hostage. Ted slammed his hand into the pavement for leverage and tore his body from the crumpled mess of Fontaine's cruiser. Jagged metal edges ripped at his clothes as he slid free.

Moustache moaned and stirred as Ted stood up. He wanted to kick the dwarf in the face to silence him, but the Beards were already dusting themselves off. Tilda was motionless at their feet.

Ted hopped up on the hood of the cruiser. Moustache's hand compressed under his foot as he leapt over the wreck and rushed the two dwarves. He spread his arms wide to envelope the first dwarf. Ted kept his feet moving forward and he shoved one dwarf into another and landed on them.

They struggled on the ground as Ted tried to free himself from the tangle of arms and legs. He felt something crunch under his elbow and felt the wet spatter of blood that followed. They were trying to keep him on his belly, but he was through crawling. It was past time the dwarves saw what happened when they fucked with the wrong man.

His hammer hand slammed into a rib. He heard the crack. One of the dwarves cried out in pain and loosened his grip. Ted grabbed a mitt full of hair and slammed the Beard's face into the pavement. He kicked the second dwarf free as he stood. Tilda's pouch of rune stones fell from a limp hand. Ted knelt to pick them up and backed up to where Tilda was lying.

"We… we didn't want… to… to fight you," Moustache's ragged voice said from behind him.

"I wouldn't, either," Ted shot back. He called out, louder, to the others: "The next beard that stands up is gonna ride the lightning, I swear to God."

Moustache coughed out a hoarse laugh. "Still you call upon him. You are more of a god than he."

Ignoring the dwarf, Ted knelt next to Tilda.

She choked back coughs, one hand holding her torn shirt closed. Ted knew only time would get the taste of that bit out of her mouth. Tears glistened in the corners of her eyes and trickled down her face. Ted reached slowly to her, to return her stones. Tilda's hand shot up to intercept him. He could feel her muscles straining to wrench one of his fingers, but after a moment her skin remembered his touch and she opened her eyes, blinking the tears away.

Wind splayed her hair across her face. Gently, Ted brushed it away and tucked it behind her ear. It was a futile gesture. Once-blue skies had gone slate grey; thunder rumbled as lightning leapt from cloud to cloud. Wind caught Tilda's hair again, dragging it free in strands. She smiled weakly. Ted returned the grin, but it felt forced.

He stood and faced the dwarves. "You're gonna pay for this," he said.

"Everything has a price," Moustache said simply. "Especially Mimir's Head."

"I don't know what you're talking about," Ted said.

"Don't pretend ignorance. Why else would they send you? That long-dead wizard is the only reason they would ever sully themselves to consort again with Nine Worlds. The what… the what is easy. The where, well, we know that as well. But the why? Ask yourself that, Callan. Why do they want to put an end to magic? Why do you?"

"I just want my old life back," Ted said.

"Do you?" Moustache grinned at Tilda. "Do you really?"

Ted looked down at her, body bruised and clothing torn. What was left for him? An ex-wife. A job he'd hated. Now he had power. Excitement. Tilda. Some of the defiance went out of his posture as he reached out a hand to help her to her feet. She winced as he drew her up and leaned heavily against him.

He turned to the dwarf. "No, I guess not. Doesn't make us friends."

"No, it does not. I will not apologize for our actions. We did what was needed. The Norns would have made us all extinct."

"Really?" Ted looked at Tilda.

She shrugged. "News to me."

"You believe that they could pull the magic from you and leave you alive?" Moustache asked. He put a finger to his hatchet nose, pressed the nostril down and blew out bloody snot, then repeated the act with the other side. "You *are* the magic now. You'd be gone as well. No, there was no time for politeness, no time for the false niceties of your society. You had something we needed and we took it."

"What could I have had?"

"The touch of the Nine," said Beard One.

"It was thick on you," Beard Two finished.

Moustache nodded. "You were... suitable, and there was no time to be picky. We saw Loki anger you in the bar—"

"Bullshit," Ted said. "That's no reason. What did you really want?"

The dwarf thought about his answer for a moment, then sighed. "We wanted the Head as well."

"Why?"

"To keep it from *her* kind." Moustache jabbed a finger at Tilda. "To protect ourselves."

Ted was skeptical. "Really? That's it?"

"And to find treasures long thought lost to us."

"Such as?"

"That is *our* business." The dwarf shook his head. Ted waited for him to elaborate. He didn't.

"Not anymore. What were you looking for?"

"I swear, our business does not concern you, Ófriður," Moustache said. "Not in the least. We could sense the touch of the Nine upon you. If it had not been us, *something* would have found you. You were no friend of the trickster—already a point in your favour—so we assumed it was he who had first marked you, but that was not so, was it?"

"No," Ted said.

"We know that now. It made choosing you all the better for us. Our working was taken deeper into your flesh because of your previous exposure to the Nine. Surtur, Loki. Your Norn slut—"

Ted shoved Moustache hard in the chest. "Watch your fucking mouth, or you won't have one."

Beards One and Two reached for the knives at their belts. The sky rumbled.

"Go ahead, draw," Ted said. A sheet of lightning flashed in the clouds. "You draw and so do I."

"Such spirit." Moustache grinned, and waved the others away. "So ready to fight. To kill. Hang on to that anger. It will keep you alive. Perhaps you were given too much power. But not enough to coax this answer from me. Once, I told a man, young and full of himself, as you are, about this thing that we seek. It ended… poorly."

"Like I give a shit."

Moustache shrugged. "Never have our dealings gone as expected when Loki pokes his nose in. This I think will end better than most—it must, or it will be the end everything."

Black spruce zipped by. Ted couldn't believe he'd got into the Econoline with the dwarves—or agreed to their plan. If you could call pretending to trade Ted to giants in order to enter their hall any kind of fucking plan. Tilda had insisted it was the only way. But Ted hadn't forgotten how they'd treated her—or him. The books were far from balanced.

It is not as though you had any better ideas, Huginn chided.

"Can I have your names, at least?" Ted asked. "I've been calling you Moustache and the Beards."

The dwarves laughed.

"Of course you cannot," Moustache said. "Names have power. Words have power. Haven't we given you enough?"

"Power I didn't ask for."

"No, you did not," the dwarf said. "But that is not what you are unhappy about, is it? Not the power. You have come to enjoy that. It is the how, not the what, of our actions that has set you against us."

"No shit. Let's see how close we are after I tie you down and shave your fucking balls."

Moustache snorted. Beards One and Two whispered something to each other in their own tongue. "Have you learned nothing of how our world works?"

"Some," Ted said. "Not enough. Too much. Take your fucking pick."

"Everything has a price that must be paid. That much power, even in one thrice touched, there had to be a cost in blood and flesh, Ófriður."

"So why didn't you just kill me, then? Like you killed those bouncers I put in the hospital?"

Moustache turned his head slightly to look back at the Beards. They shook their heads.

"That wasn't us," he said.

"Right," Ted said, looking away from the dwarf. "So, what was it? The tooth fairy? Something slit their throats and took their blood. You use blood in your magic." He didn't wait for the dwarves to admit or deny the accusation. They'd coated him in blood after tattooing him. Rock trolls seemed mortared with the stuff.

"I swear to you that was not us."

"Whatever."

"No," Moustache said. "Not whatever, this is what is. We

did no such thing. You think after all I have done, I would balk at admitting to murder? Of course I've killed." He gestured back at the Beards. "So have they. I'll kill again. So will they. So will *she*. In many ways we murdered your old life when we gave you our gifts. But we had nothing to do with the deaths of those two men. There are others whose workings use blood. We haven't needed to kill to fuel our magic since long before you were born."

"So where do you get your 'fuel' from, then?"

"Blood drives at the mine," Moustache said, smiling. "We can sense those who have felt the touch of the Nine. That blood makes its way to us. The rest… accidents do happen, and we ensure the hospital is well stocked."

"Do you know who killed the bouncers?"

The dwarf shook his head. "And I do not care. You may, if it makes you feel more human. If you do not help us get Mimir, we will all be dead. Because of her, and her family."

Tilda had remained silent so far. It may have been her idea to play along, but that didn't make her any happier at the situation. Small spots of rust flaked from her heavy iron manacles.

Ted had argued that they wouldn't be necessary, but the dwarves would have none of it. The only way they would take him to the giants' lair was with Tilda in chains. He was afraid to say she'd lost her powers. They laughed themselves silly at the idea that he could find the giants without them. She was in between the Beards. Behind them was a pile of bloodstained basalt that, presumably, could be formed into another rock troll. Ted sat shotgun, next to Moustache. Between them, coiled neatly on the floor of the van was a golden chain. The same golden chain they had bound him with in the hotel. Just looking at it gave him chills.

Gleipnir, Muninn said reverently.

Ted wasn't sure he could do this. He wasn't sure he could let them bind him again. The chain was unbreakable.

It was broken once before, Muninn reminded Ted, **when Loki's son Fenrir had shaken loose to fight the Aesir at Ragnarök.**

There had to be a way for Ted to free himself if the dwarves double-crossed him.

Ted directed his question at Muninn, *How did Fenrir break the chain?* He wasn't about to take the dwarves at their word that they'd release him when the time came to fight.

It was his destiny to do so. Gleipnir was to hold until Ragnarök. Now it is nothing but slender braided gold. You could break it in a heartbeat.

I wasn't able to before, he said.

You were but a man. Huginn spoke now. **Gold is soft, but still it is made of harder stuff than flesh. If they concentrate, the dwarves may speak to the chain, as they speak to all metal, convincing Gleipnir that the end has yet to come, and that whomever they bind is indeed the Wolf of Ragnarök.**

Shit.

They call you Ófriður, Huginn said. **Remember what they have named you. Names have power.**

So the dwarves said.

They did not lie. And Urd may know who you were, not who you are.

He had expected the dwarves to drive deep into the forest primeval to meet the giants at their lair. Somewhere far from prying eyes, where the monsters of legend could hunt without fear of being seen. Instead, after passing under a pipeline bridge, Moustache swung the van onto gravel. Ted hadn't even noticed the road there.

Steep, and more rock than road, the route barely deserved the name. The van hopped and jostled as it trundled up the grade. They were heading back towards Flin Flon. That was a surprise. But then Ted remembered Jormungandur's words.

Go north, you may find Mimir in Ross Lake.

The lake appeared larger than it truly was, as it mirrored the grey sky above, but certainly nothing compared to the vastness of Lake Winnipeg. But the lake had been right there, in sight. If Fontaine hadn't found them, he and Tilda might've had Mimir's Head and been on the road south and back to Gimli.

Jötnar are masters of illusion; at least, the greatest of them were, Muninn said.

You would not have found Mimir if they did not wish it, Huginn added.

But I didn't even look. Loki's been taken, and now we're about to walk into the jötnar's *hands too.*

You let your feelings for the Norn distract you, Muninn said.

Huginn chuckled. **Understandable.**

Now they were all going to pay for his stupidity.

Do not despair, Theodore, Huginn said. You have done well enough. This is a new world to you. Loki has never taken anything seriously.

Except his vengeance, Muninn said. Though he is in no position to see to it.

Isn't he? Huginn asked.

What do you mean? Ted wondered.

You are as much Loki's instrument as the dvergar's. He set events in motion. Perhaps he knew what the dvergar would make of you. Perhaps he only hoped. I assure you, he still holds a grudge for the humiliation he received at their hands over his previous wager. Perhaps you are to be Loki's revenge. Perhaps he hoped you'd kill them for him.

Ted started to disagree, but stopped himself. What had he wanted to do to the dwarves? They'd marked him. They'd killed innocents. They'd hurt Tilda. Suddenly Huginn's words didn't seem so far-fetched. Loki was shifty enough to engineer Ted's transformation, and then he just needed to direct Ted into a position to fulfill his vengeance.

Out the van's grimy back window, the trees and rock shifted, closing in tightly, obscuring the road from the highway. Black spruce loomed on either side of the road, taller than any Ted had ever seen. Huge boulders were unevenly spaced before the trees. Runes were etched over every inch of the stones's surfaces.

Illusion? Or some other weird magical shit?

Huginn answered, The jötnar have tied this place to

a remnant of Jötunheim, trees such as these would never take root upon Midgard without aid.

Howls chased the van down the trail. The cries didn't sound like any dog Ted had ever heard. He caught a glimpse of grey or brown fur half-hidden by stands of stone. With every yap, bark, or howl, Moustache tightened his knuckles on the steering wheel. Beards One and Two exchanged glances.

Fenrir's get, Muninn said. They sense the chain. After so long, even their very blood remembers and hates it. This pack is descended from Loki's son. Some may speak the human tongue, or take human shape, depending on the strength of their blood.

One of the origins of your werewolf legends, Huginn added. An origin based on truth rather than fear or ignorance, like most.

Will they help us? Ted asked.

Impossible to say, said Huginn. Some are large enough that they hunt the jötnar who travel or live alone. Others, the whelps, often serve in exchange for scraps and shelter.

Shit.

Many forces are coming together in this place, Huginn said. The jötnar, the dvergar, the Norns, Fenris's get; and, in you, the Aesir. So many remnants of the Nine Worlds have not gathered together since Ragnarök.

Why not?

Trust, hate, fear. It will be a storm worthy of the Thunderer himself when you finally meet. One simple spark may ignite a war the likes of which this world has never seen. You must be careful.

Ted thought of the fires burning where Fort McMurray had once stood. Fires that burned closer to his old home every day. Fires that had a living will directing them. Surtur, who wished an end to this world as well.

We are already at war. Maybe it's time the rest of the world knows it, Ted said.

Loki cautioned you against that path, Muninn reminded. One of his few words of advice that I would heed, were I you.

The van broke through the trees and the ground dropped away before them, as if a great hand had scooped handfuls of the rock face away to form a valley. A steep, rough road led to the floor of the depression and a great hall, larger than an airplane hangar. Wooden stakes—whole trees, really—made up the fifty-foot tall fence that surrounded the giant hall.

Ted remembered how giants came larger than the one he had fought—much larger. The mass of tangled hair that he could see bobbing just over the pointed tips of the barricade was not encouraging.

Ross Lake stretched out in front of the structure and he could see the town across the grey water shimmering like a heat mirage; they were in plain view and yet invisible to the citizens of Flin Flon.

A hand that could have plucked the dwarves' van from the road and bounced the vehicle upon its palm wrapped itself over the top of the fence and pulled back, lifting the wooden gate just high enough for the van to pass underneath.

The van rolled to a stop and Beard Two slid the side door open, filling the van with the smell of rank unwashed flesh, rotting meat, and shit. He pulled Tilda free. She stood, but slightly doubled over; a limp was obvious even from the few steps she had taken. That account still wasn't settled, Ted noted. The dwarves were going to pay for every hurt they'd visited on her.

"Are you ready?" Moustache asked.

Ted took a deep breath, exhaling slowly. "As I'll ever be."

Moustache nodded. He wrapped the golden chain around Ted and pulled him out of the van.

Ted shook. The fear was back. Like he had never left the hotel room in Winnipeg. He couldn't go through with this. Couldn't be bound again. But he had to.

He didn't try to calm himself. His fear would help sell the ploy.

"We have it!" the dwarf yelled.

Rusting vehicles of different eras littered the compound. Their roofs had all been peeled back like sardine cans to get at whomever had been within. What would have come next was not a pleasant thought. The upholstery and tires of many had long since succumbed to the elements and vermin. Too-large wolves peered out from the rent side door of another Econoline van, growling as the prisoners came into view.

Only one vehicle appeared untouched—The Goat. Ted ground his teeth. *Urd.*

The bitch had come here in Ted's own goddamn car.

The giant who had opened the gate sniffed at the air, though what he could scent in this pigsty was a mystery to Ted. He dropped down to his knees and leaned forward, squinting at Beards One and Two, and their prisoner.

He barked a short laugh and the stink of his breath washed over them. A couple drops of spit hit Ted and slid slowly down his face. Even if he had been able to move, he wouldn't have given the giant the satisfaction of reacting.

"Mjölnir?" He spoke almost in a whisper. The giant sniffed again. "Mjölnir!" he repeated excitedly and much louder.

The giant reached out towards Ted; a grisly charm bracelet of four freshly severed, bearded heads—dwarves—shook upon his wrist. Moustache pulled a heavy blade, wider than Ted's hand, but only about two feet long and jabbed it at the giant, sinking the weapon's tip into an outstretched finger.

"Not yet," the dwarf said. "And not for you."

The giant laughed and put the wounded digit in his mouth.

Moustache growled something in the dwarven tongue that Huginn and Muninn didn't bother to translate. The giant answered in a different, yet similarly brutal language.

He wants to play, Huginn translated.

I gathered, Ted answered.

Wolves hopped from the rusted husks of cars and trucks. They knew the sound of a challenge, and they wanted to answer it. The giant stood tall and laughed again. Moustache glanced at Ted strangely, but kept speaking to the giant.

"Afraid?" Ted hoped his mocking tone would translate. "I've

fought bigger than you, you know. You don't scare me. Bring it."
Ted spat on the dirt and paused, letting the challenge sink in.

The giant's nostrils flared in and out as he breathed. His
teeth clenched and his brow furrowed. He took a booming step
forward. Dust billowed up. Ted tried not to wince. The sound,
though different, reminded him of Surtur's arrival at the patch.

Moustache brandished his sword and yelled first at the giant
and then at Beard One.

"You gonna listen to him?" Ted yelled over the dwarf. "You
afraid of him? He's smaller than I am. C'mon, pussy. Let's fight.
They can't shut me up, and they can't hold me forever."

Tilda grunted in pain behind him and Ted turned. Her leg
gave out as she limped along behind him. Moustache offered
a hand to help her to her feet, but the Norn shrugged him off.
She took two quick limping steps that brought her behind Beard
Two and slammed her manacled hands down on the dwarf's
head. The heavy iron split Beard Two's scalp, and thick, bright
blood ran freely down the dwarf's back. He slumped and she hit
him again. The giant laughed, Ted's challenge forgotten for now.

"You don't touch me again, you twisted freak," she yelled as
Moustache moved to grip her arms tightly and pull her back.
"You don't fuck with the Norns."

"No," said a familiar voice. Ted and Tilda both whipped their
heads towards the speaker.

"Amma?" Tilda said weakly.

19. Grandmother Waits For You

Well, *dvergar*?" Urd asked. "Are you ready to trade?"

The dwarves nodded. "We are," Moustache said.

"The hammer for the ring, a fair trade." The Norn smiled.

"It is no such thing," the dwarf said. "Not when you will use Mimir against us as soon as we turn Callan over."

Urd snorted. "At least you will have finally held the ring in your hand once more. Cross me, and I won't even give you that much."

Moustache's eyes fell and his shoulders drooped as he stood before the Norn.

"I would feel better if I held on to this." Urd took the braided strand of Gleipnir from Moustache and whispered a word to the chain. It constricted tightly around Ted, pushing the breath from his lungs. "You are not the only one who knows that spell, little maggot."

The dwarves shrugged apologetically, but made no move to free him. Urd tugged at his leash, and he was led into the giant's hall. Like the walls that surrounded it, it was made of solid timber. It was immense and the floor had been dug a giant's height into the mound. A ramp of mortared stone and packed earth wound along the edges of the hall, leading gradually to the bottom.

Most of the floor was taken up by an immense wooden table with logs piled as benches on either side. Shields that could be used to roof a house and swords and axes large enough to rend a house asunder leaned against the timber walls, and in places, were mounted upon them.

Four giants, each north of twenty feet tall, stood with hands folded over knotted clubs. When they looked upon Ted, all four tensed. He flashed a cocky grin he didn't feel and their grips tightened on their weapons. Urd dragged Ted forward. For all the Norn's bold talk, the chain, while it bound him, did not hold the same menace as when the dwarves had first used it on him. Not with Mjölnir's power to call upon.

Tilda had fallen in step behind her grandmother. She may as well have been sleepwalking for how little she regarded her surroundings. Urd had pried apart the dwarves' iron manacles, freeing her, and reclaimed the rune stones at the same time.

"Til?" Ted asked, trying to draw her out of herself.

Urd turned and stabbed an accusing stare at Ted. "You have done enough," she said. "Involving her in this mess. She was never supposed to be here. She should have been home. She should have been safe."

"I didn't—" Ted let the protest drop. Urd had already turned her back to him. The Norns walked briskly down the ramp, dragging Ted by his lead.

With every step downward, the rank scent of the giants'

home seemed to grow stronger. Sweat, must, blood, and shit. A rattling breath came from behind the giant guards, and each took a step to the side and turned to face each other. Behind them was the most immense thing Ted had ever seen, like someone had poured a whale into clothes. This giant—and giant hardly seemed enough to describe him—was no warrior. Flabby flesh sagged from his body as he lay on his side. A preserved human head was tied through a hole in his ear like a grisly hoop earring.

Rungnir! Muninn said, sounding surprised. He shouldn't be here. No jötunn could survive a strike from Mjölnir.

Loki was supposed to be dead, too, Huginn said.

So much for certainty.

Rungnir had a concave depression on one side of his forehead; a vicious scar ran down that valley's centre. The giant's eyelid below drooped slightly, weeping fluid. His jaw also hung slackly on his wounded side and his tongue lapped at a sore crusting his top lip.

"*Mjölnir!*" the giant yelled, struggling to sit upright. Once-legendary might had long ago gone to seed. "I'll never forget the cursed hammer's touch. It is here! Give it to me!"

"In time, great Rungnir," Urd said.

The giant sighed again, but the sound was lost amid a wet-sounding release of gas. And Ted had thought there had been a strong smell of shit before. Rungnir grinned with the glee of a child as the dwarves and humans both fought to control their faces against his stink.

"The king's shat himself," a quiet voice said.

Ted looked around for the speaker, but couldn't see anyone else.

"Send for the maid," the voice spoke again. Ted saw now that the head at Rungnir's ear was the speaker. And that made it—

Mimir, Huginn finished the thought.

Looks like we found him.

From behind the cushions that Rungnir was propped up on came a wild-eyed Loki carrying a bucket and rag. Filth crusted his clothes and skin, and the trickster clenched his jaw tightly against his task.

Ted waited for Loki to make some sort of joke, or to greet them warmly as if he'd been expecting them, but he said nothing. Then Ted caught the glint of gold on Loki's lips in the torchlight illuminating the giant's hall, a glint twinned by the chain wrapped around Ted's arms and torso—another fragment of Gleipnir. Loki's mouth had been sewn shut again.

The trickster went to work, cleaning Rungnir, who smiled dumbly.

Never before has the Lord of Lies been so humbled, Muninn said.

No shit, Ted answered.

An amusing, if ironic choice of words. He fought against Asgard during Ragnarök after the Aesir had dared punish him. What will he do after this? His pride is strong, and they seek to break him.

Even a day ago, this sight, a humbled Loki, would have been laugh-out-loud funny. But events had a way of changing perspective.

"You're all gonna fucking pay," Ted said tightly.

Urd laughed. "Men are so amusing. Like children. You think you will be able to do something? You are bound; it took the end of the world for the wolf to shake that chain, and you are but a pup next to Fenrir."

Thunder rumbled above and Ted smiled grimly.

"Storm's comin'," he said. "You ready for it?"

"I've seen how this ends. I've known how you were going to die since before you were even born. Before your father spilled his first seed, I laughed at your end."

"Get over yourself, bitch." Ted felt tightness and tingling in his chest. It wasn't hard to keep his anger up. Here in this large chamber was everyone and everything responsible for the train wreck the Nine Worlds had made of his new life. "Speaking of seed, where's Vera anyway?"

Urd tightened her jaw. "I'm going to enjoy what you have coming to you."

"Right back at ya."

"Amma," Tilda spoke—finally—to the matriarch of the Norns. "Don't do this, please."

"Skuld, this once you will listen to me."

"That's not my name," Tilda said. It cheered Ted to see that spark of life, of resistance, in her.

"What would you have me call you? Mathilda? That foolish human name you chose to protect you in their world? That is not who you are. You are Skuld, you are That Which Needs To Be. And if you had done what was necessary, none of us would be here."

"You want the Nine to end, magic to bleed dry; so why do you insist on calling me that? When the visions are gone, so is Skuld. So is Urd, so is Verdandi. I know who I am. Who will you be? What will you do to Mom?"

"Your mother is no longer troubled by her visions, nor will you be."

"What did you do to her?" Anger brought a flush to Tilda's face. "She's dead, isn't she?"

Now it was Urd's turn to be shocked. Shock turned to anger quickly, and she slapped Tilda hard across the face. Tilda staggered. Urd looked ready to give her granddaughter another. Instead, seeing a trickle of blood run from a split lip, she took a deep breath and tightened the elastic that bound her grey hair.

"What is wrong with you? How could you think that? Your time with him," she said as she jerked Gleipnir and dragged Ted forward a step, "and the trickster have obviously poisoned you against your family. How could you think I would do that to my own blood?"

"It gets easier every second," Ted muttered. Urd heard him however.

"Verdandi is fine," she said tightly. "She sleeps unburdened by That Which Is. I did what I did to save you both. Without your visions, you both would have survived what is coming. With your new 'connection'… With the bastard he put in you…." Urd touched Tilda's belly, and shook her head. "I'm sorry, child. I can't say for sure."

Tilda looked as if she were about to be sick. "What about you?"

"I have lived long enough. I do not long survive today, I know that much. You, too, Theodore, are shortly coming to the end of your saga."

Rungnir's guards laughed, amused at their guests' bickering, and were soon followed by their slack-jawed master.

Urd stood before Rungnir with Tilda just behind her.

"Kneel," she commanded Ted.

"No," he shot back.

"Kneel," said Urd.

"Fuck you."

The old Norn whispered a word to the golden chain, and Ted was forced to his knees. The chain's constrictions didn't stop until Ted's nose touched the earth.

"Great king," Urd said. "We come before you with a gift. Behold, Mjölnir!"

"I see no hammer," the grotesque giant said, slowly forcing the words around his thick tongue. "Only a man. A pretty, painted man. But just a man." He furrowed his brow, and winced slightly, as if the wound Thor had dealt so long ago still pained him.

"Show him," said Urd.

Ted smiled. "I'm a little tied up at the moment."

"Show him the hammer!" the Norn screamed.

"Oh, I intend to."

Ted flexed against the chain. Gleipnir strained, and its woven braids of gold began to fray. Urd quickly repeated her spell, repairing the chain. Ted groaned. It was a fine line to walk, stoking his anger to build the storm outside, but not working himself up to the point that he actually broke the chain.

Moustache stomped forward and bent Ted's arm up against the bonds. Ted didn't resist, but still the dwarf had a hard time moving him, as if he was fighting against the efforts of the Norn to keep her prisoner bound. The dwarf's thick fingers pressed hard against Ted's flesh, turning his forearm so that Rungnir might see the tattoo of Mjölnir.

"Open your palm," Moustache said, prodding Ted's arm.

"Can't," Ted said smugly.

Moustache grumbled, but pried open Ted's fingers to show the hammerhead imprinted upon the palm.

Rungnir shrugged, loosing a sagging breast from his ill-fitting tunic. "I don't care for pretty pictures. I care for things. We were promised Mjölnir. I can smell its stink in the air. You will give us the hammer of the Thunderer, or you will not be guests before my table, but a meal upon it."

"I do sense the power of the Aesir within your domain, Rungnir," Mimir said in the king's ear. The preserved head turned; its dead eyes met Ted's.

"Of course you do," said Rungnir. "We have Loki. The Norns are playing a trick, and I am growing hungry."

A small speck of filth hit the giant's face above his mouth. Loki readied another handful, but one of the guards reached out and plucked the trickster from his feet. The giant hurled Loki to the earth and stepped on his body, pressing it into the dirt.

"Come on, Amma," Ted said. "They want to see the hammer. Let me show them."

"Shut up!"

"Tell the dwarves to release me, Rungy, and I'll give you the hammer."

"Truly?" Rungnir asked, inching his bulk forward on his cushions. "Release him!"

"Rungnir…" Mimir said. "That is unwise."

The giant wasn't listening. "Release him! I would look again upon the hammer that dared topple great Rungnir."

"You heard the king," Ted said, looking back at Moustache. "Better do what he says. I'm pretty sure they'll break their teeth on me, but you lot will be a tasty—if hairy—snack."

The dwarf was a good actor. He looked like he'd swallowed a handful from Loki's bucket, but he nodded at Beards One and Two. "Do it."

"Wait," Urd interrupted. "There is one in your home who can speak of the power held in this pretty picture. You have a son do you not?"

Rungnir nodded slowly. "Fool that he is."

She pointed at Ted. "He witnessed Mjölnir's power only yesterday."

The giant lolled his head towards one of his guards. "Bring me my son. If you are lying, Norn, I choose your doom."

Urd continued to chant over the chain, keeping Ted supplicant on his knees. Running her hand over his scalp, she bent closer and whispered into his ear, "A nice try. You almost made them release you. But the times of the Nine running around free are over. You and Loki will remain here, living out your days at the pleasure of the *jötnar*; Mimir and I will cut this place loose from Midgard and put an end to Surtur, and an end to all the dark things that stalk Midgard's night."

"That'll end yours too," Ted said.

"I welcome it. Mimir does, as well. An end to the visions. Endlessly replaying the mistakes of youth. No more broken trusts with our gods. After seeing how the world will end if I do not act, I see little choice."

"What about Vera?" Ted asked. "What about Tilda?"

She sighed. For a moment, it seemed as if the Norn's stony façade would crumble. "Skuld is doomed now. You've seen to that. You've tied her to the Nine Worlds for the rest of her life."

"Strange," Ted said, "how she saw things differently."

Urd chanced a look back at the young Norn. Tilda was clutching at her arms and had turned her back to her grandmother; Ted couldn't see her face.

"She would. She waited too long. If only she had kept that first child. She never would have met you. You would have bled out in that alley as your doom truly intended. The world of Midgard has coloured her visions. As if you two would make some perfect suburban couple doting over a stroller. Skuld saw what she wished to. That is why I took her sight from her. Your old world will not take you back, and there is no place for you in mine."

Ted was saved from having to come up with a clever and insulting retort by the arrival of the giant king's son. The same giant Ted had fought, and healed, along the roadside. Rungnir the younger, *Youngnir, or whatever the fuck his name might be,* limped awkwardly into the sight of his father. Beaten savagely, he looked worse than he had when he'd run from Ted and Tilda by the roadside. He whimpered and tried to cover himself as one of the guards pushed him before Rungnir.

The king shook his jowled head, jostling Mimir roughly. "You disgust me. A shameful price I paid for being serviced by a human."

Rungnir's son had his eyes closed, but his nose twitched as if the giant were trying to recognize a scent. His eyes shot open and he scrambled backwards, tripping on Loki's prone form and crashing into his father's divan.

"Mjölnir!" he yelled, pointing at Ted. "Mjölnir! Mjölnir!"

Well, Ted thought. *I guess that's that.*

Rungnir grinned. "So you have spoken true, Urd. You have given me the weapon of my enemy. You will ever be welcome at my table. And the dwarves who have made this wondrous thing, I will welcome them as well. Upon it."

The dwarves' leader held up a heavy-bladed dagger and pressed it against Ted's throat. "We can deny you your pleasure. This weapon was tempered in the blood of the dragon Fáfnir. The same blood that sealed the power of the Aesir within this mortal's flesh."

Mimir spoke a word and Rungnir's eyes glazed over. Those of his guards followed. A glowing rune hung in the air between the giants and the humans and dwarves.

"I do not think you will do that," Mimir said. "That is not why you forged this weapon. He was not to be bartered, or sacrificed. He was to ring in the old days, when from far and wide men and gods came to the dwarves for trade and favours. You will not unmake him now. Your forge is naught but bellows air, words, *dvergar*. I do not fear words."

Moustache asked, "So you will try your instruments against ours?"

"I believe I will," Mimir said.

The dwarf looked at Ted and then smiled. "Ófriður...."

Ted strained against the chain, and despite Urd's now frantic chants, he could feel it loosening. He wasn't about to wait. He closed his hammer hand about the remnants of Gleipnir and tore it from his body.

Urd flinched as he hurled the gold at her feet. "How?"

"Stupid crone," Moustache smiled. "We made Gleipnir. We made him."

The dwarves hurriedly slipped away from Ted. Dazed giants blocked them from the exit ramp.

Thunder boomed; the timbers of the hall shook, dust fell like rain.

"Why?" Ted asked.

"Bloody Odin," Mimir said. "Cast his spells to preserve me, knowing—goddamned well knowing—he would die in Ragnarök. But he was so full of himself he still couldn't fathom that fate happening. When he couldn't leave me to my peace, I whispered the secret of life to Loki and left the All-Father short-sighted. He could have ended my torment! I have hungered and thirsted for eternity. I was a man once. I want a good rut. A whore's lips wrapped around what I no longer have. But this will never happen. Surtur couldn't have found us quickly enough."

"Boo-fucking-hoo," Ted said, pointing at himself. "You think this was the new life that I wanted? You want to end your life? I'll fucking end it, but you're not taking the world with you."

Mimir ignored him. "In the end, Odin asked my counsel, begged for a way to win the last battle, to stop the end of the Aesir. But I held my tongue. 'It is your doom,' I said, and let him ride out to die. They could have won, had they listened to me. Had I chosen to speak. I thought the end of days would be the end of me, my torment. But Odin's magic was too potent. But this time all will end, and finally Mimir will sleep."

"And Surtur will go back into the black beyond worlds," Urd added. "And Midgard will again just be Earth."

"No," Mimir said. "Midgard must perish too. I orchestrated all of this to end my own existence, not out of any desire to preserve the world from Surtur."

"What?" the Norn screamed.

Mimir smiled. The head was smug as it regarded them, dangling from the ear of the giant king. "Foolish woman, for someone with the Sight, you were easily blinded. You never saw this coming. The Norns will perish. Everyone with a touch of the Nine Worlds will perish. Surtur's death-throes will consume the world as quickly as his victory would have. I care not, for it will be the end of me. Finally, an end."

Urd snatched the dragon-tempered dagger from Moustache. With surprising speed she hurled it towards the living head. Mimir spoke another rune and a halo of light surrounded the weapon. It changed direction and sped straight for Ted's heart.

Ted dove to the side but the dagger shifted to match him.

This was it. It was the end, all right. But he hadn't expected to go out like this. His eyes closed and he winced, expecting the pain of death. There was a quiet thud, but Ted felt nothing. He opened his eyes as Tilda slumped against him. The weapon was sunk to the hilt in her back, its tip just peeking out from the belly of her dirty sundress. A drop of blood hit his hand. Such a small thing, but to Ted it felt like a cannonball.

"No!" Ted and Urd yelled together. Urd screamed as Tilda dropped, crimson welling up from her belly. She'd done this for him. This had happened because of him.

No.

Because of them.

"This… this… is what you saw, Amma." Tilda turned to face her grandmother. "It wasn't Ted. It was never Ted."

"It was me," the elder Norn barely whispered.

Tilda pressed her hands to her belly and winced when they came away bloody. Ted took them in his own, and tried to ignore their slickness.

"That blade would have killed you," she said.

"Now it will kill you."

She tapped her head and smiled weakly, before a painful grimace returned. "Believe."

"I'm sorry."

She was crying. So was he.

"It appears you won't be a father after all," Mimir laughed.

"She saw it, it'll come true."

Tilda smiled. Her face took on the faraway look of someone slipping into shock. "I'd like that," she whispered.

"Me too," Ted said, and knew he meant it.

Mimir smiled from his perch on Rungnir's ear as Urd fell to her knees. Ted lowered Tilda to the floor. The rune still glowed in the air, and the giants in the hall stood as if hypnotized.

If only he hadn't used his healing touch on Fontaine earlier. He could save Tilda. A terrible thought; Fontaine was alive and Tilda wasn't the type who would lightly trade another's life for her own. For all his strength, in that moment Ted had never felt so powerless.

He turned to Urd. "Get her the fuck out of here." He pressed the keys to The Goat into the Norn's hand.

Urd looked at her wounded granddaughter and nodded. "You can't beat them alone."

"*Take her,*" said Ted.

She went. Urd carried Tilda towards the ramp, watching the motionless giants warily. Tilda didn't seem like much weight in the old woman's arms, but Ted could see the strain on her face.

She'd manage. She had to.

Mimir released the rune and the giants snapped to attention.

"Kill them!" Rungnir yelled.

"Yes, kill them," Mimir's Head echoed, smiling.

The giants closed in a rough circle surrounding Ted and the dwarves, looming hungrily. Rungnir leered from his cushions, clapping with glee.

"Clear me a path," Urd yelled. Fear stained her voice.

Ted ground his teeth into a grim smile and cracked his knuckles as his hands tightened into fists.

"You got it."

20. If You Want Blood (You've Got It)

ed wasn't sure what was louder: the thunder booming outside or the impact of Mjölnir on the giant's club. The club shattered, spraying Ted with kindling. The giant shook his meaty fist from the sting. Rungnir's hall was enormous to Ted, but given most of his opponents were on the high side of twenty foot, it was filling up quick.

He chanced a look over his shoulder. Urd was struggling up the ramp behind him. Rain was pouring into the structure and creating a river flowing down the packed dirt. The timbers of the giant's hall creaked as the ripping winds battered the wood.

The sounds of the storm veiled the whistle of another club. It connected solidly with Ted's ribs. Ted was lifted from his feet and felt the vertigo of weightlessness. Air rushed past him before he slammed into the far wall. Timbers cracked from the impact and Ted tumbled to the earthen floor. If not for the dwarves' work he'd have been dead.

One of the giant guards was making for the exit and lunging for Urd and Tilda. Ted felt as if he were running before he'd even found his feet. He vaulted from the piled log seats to the oak tabletop and ran for the giant, dodging clubs and fists like opposing linebackers. At the end of the table Ted launched himself back into the air. Catching his left hand in the tangled mass of the giant's hair, Ted looped the greasy strands around his forearm to secure his grip. There was a satisfying crunch as he slammed his hammer hand into the base of the giant's skull. The giant bellowed like a steer on the killing floor before he dropped, dead.

It was an animal. A dumb animal.

He had to tell himself that. Tilda's earlier cautions aside, if Ted thought of the giants as people, he was done for. And yet, he didn't want to start enjoying this either. But for the first time he was allowed to truly release the storm and fury that had grown within him since the dwarves had "welcomed" him into the Nine Worlds. They'd hurt Tilda. They, Loki, and Surtur all wanted to turn a clueless world into a mythological battlefield.

Ted rode the dead giant to the ground. It had tumbled halfway over the ramp and would at least serve to slow any others who might chase the Norns.

Beards One and Two crawled on their hands and knees amid the chaos, trying to stay out from under giant feet. Moustache held something in his hand and chanted over the object in the strange dwarven tongue. Ted went back to the relative high ground of the tabletop. He needed to be able to swing at more than the giants' ankles. Clubs thudded behind him as he ran on top of the oak. His odds still weren't great. Even with his gifts, they had the numbers. Ted knew his strength would mean little against their size. He needed leverage of his own.

Mimir.

Ted darted forward. A club descended for him; the giant wielding it was going headhunting. Ted ducked, wondering if enough force would be able to tear his head free from his shoulders.

Huginn asked, **Do you truly desire such an answer?**

"Not now," Ted said aloud.

As you wish.

The giants were used to hunting smaller, faster prey. As Ted ducked the first swing, a second came from behind. A club crashed into his legs and tipped him ass-over-teakettle to slam flat on his back onto the table. A third giant slammed his palm down flat on Ted's chest, pinning him. Another giant, in its haste to subdue Ted, reversed its club, slamming it down atop the trapping hand.

Through the giant's flesh and bones, Ted felt the immense impact. His hardened skin sloughed it off and down into the oak, but even the stout table could only take so much. It cracked from the force. The giant howled in pain but didn't move his hand and shoved Ted down through the splintered wood to hit the floor below.

Ted could see only through a small fork between two huge fingers. Tons of weight pressed him against the earth. There was no room to swing a fist, or kick a leg. He considered biting the fucking thing. So he did. The giant pinning him squatted down and leaned forward, putting even more of his weight into trapping Ted. Laughing, it ground Ted beneath the heel of its palm. He sank deeper into the ground. Rough, calloused fingers hit his face like rolling logs.

I am well and truly fucked.

"Your instrument is not playing so fine a tune, Master Smith," Mimir called to the dwarves.

Rungnir clapped and laughed.

"Give him to me. I will swallow him, and Mjölnir's power will run in my veins, strengthening me. Once again, Rungnir will be great!"

"My king," said Mimir. "Perhaps we should first put the dwarves' blade to the test?"

"No! I will not be denied again. I will not allow a drop of his power or life to nourish the barren earth. Once Rungnir was counted mighty by god and *jötunn*. It will be so again."

Ted couldn't hear Mimir's response over the pounding of blood in his temples. He fought to stay conscious as the giant crushed him.

With a jerk it pulled him from the earth. Dirt sifted out from the giant's grip like sand in an hourglass. Ted couldn't help but think his time would soon be up, too.

His chest was tingling. The grim clouds etched across it, vibrating in sympathy to their storm-fat brethren in the sky. Electricity ran through the length of Ted's body, gathering in his hammer hand. He just had the room to clench his fist, trapped as he was within the giant's hand. Ted released the power Mjöl-nir had gathered.

He closed his eyes. The giant's hand spasmed. Ted gasped for breath as the giant's grip tightened. Screaming filled his ears, the giant's bellows mixing with the cries of timbers strained beyond what they could bear. The howl of the wind rushed to fill the hall before he felt its wet, rain-drenched slap across his face.

Thunder pealed and Ted opened his eyes. Where the sky wasn't shot through with sheets of lightning, it was blacker than a dwarf's heart. There was a circular mark of char on the giant's chest; small flames, fuelled by wind, fought against the rain, growing and trying to consume the thing. The lightning strike had boiled the eyes from its head, and judging from the stillness, stopped the giant's heart. Prying himself free from dead fingers, Ted felt a momentary pang of pity.

A familiar bellow sounded from the entrance to the hall—a rock troll. The troll hit one of the giants like an avalanche. They tumbled down the ramp, a deadly mixture of flesh and stone. Urd dove to the ground with Tilda just as a flailing limb passed over them. Giants fell in the wake of the falling combatants. The way out was clear but it wouldn't remain so for long. Ted called to the lightning, raining it upon the giants.

"Go!" he yelled to the Norn. The giants who hadn't been blinded by the lightning strikes watched the sky warily for more.

Loki ran towards him, pointing at the golden thread stitched through his lips and shook his head.

It would seem that small scrap of Gleipnir keeps Loki from changing his shape or using his magic, Huginn said.

Serves him right, Muninn added.

"We need him."

Pull the toy's cord and it will talk, Huginn said.

Ted looped a finger under the braided golden chain. "This is gonna hurt," he said.

343

The trickster winced and nodded. Ted pulled as hard as he could. Whatever magic the dwarves had sealed in the chain may have prevented Loki from freeing himself. But it didn't hold up to Ted's force. Savaging Loki's lips into a roughly carved jack-o'-lantern mouth, the chain tore free. Blood and spit frothed out and streamed down the god's chin.

"Motherfucker!" said Loki.

For a moment, Ted thought Loki would just turn into a bird and fly away, leaving him to fight alone. But the God of Trickery had a few tricks left in him. There was a flash of the fire that must have burned within Loki when he fought against his family at Ragnarök, and he was spoiling for a fight. He swelled in size to match the giants. His face changed, growing fairer of skin and hair. Burn-scars marred the skin of his face and chest. Long claws sprouted from Loki's fingers and toes, and Ted realized he was getting a glimpse of Loki as he truly was, naked in the form of his birth. The hatred in his stare was more terrifying than his size.

"Loki," Ted said. "The gate is shut. There's no way for Tilda to get out of here."

He didn't move at first and Ted was worried Loki would stay to exact his revenge instead of helping Tilda escape. Then Loki nodded. Ted called lightning to strike the giants on the ramp. He followed in Loki's wake, running overtop of fallen giants.

The storm raged outside. It was damn near impossible to see. Day had turned to night and the only constant illumination was the tail lights of The Goat, punctuated by sporadic flashes of lightning. Ted ran towards the twin red glows. Pounding rain had turned the giant's compound into a quagmire, but with the tattoos of Sleipnir, the muck may as well have been cement.

Lightning flashed. Golden eyes reflected the light within the rusting hulks of old abandoned cars. The wolves howled in time with the rolling thunder. Ted needed to get that gate open. He had to give Urd a chance to get Tilda away from here.

Loki wrestled with a group of giants that had gathered round the entrance to the hall. They threw him to the sodden ground in a spray of mud, laughing as they kicked at him.

Even if Ted had been strong enough to open the gate he doubted he would have the weight and leverage to shift it from the muck. But he didn't care about keeping the gate intact. He cocked his fist back and slammed it into the wooden timbers. The impact sent the gate swinging upward so hard the hinge shattered and Ted had to duck away as the bound timbers fell to the earth.

Urd was revving The Goat's engine before the wood landed. Mud sprayed as the GTO's wheels sought purchase, fishtailing in the muck. Then the rear wheels caught the timbers of the fallen gate, and the GTO roared out of the giants' compound, up the rocky road towards the highway and the relative safety of Flin Flon. Two wolves tore after the vehicle, and Ted called lightning to strike the beasts. He heard their yelping cries over the rain as they fell in the road. Two more bolts for good measure. They didn't rise. Ted turned back to Rungnir's hall. Giants and wolves blocked his path back to Mimir.

He needed an army.

You have one, Huginn said. **Blow the Gjallarhorn. Summon the Einherjar. Summon the Honoured Dead.**

"How?" Ted asked.

Touch the horn and think of them.

The suggestion felt ridiculous, but Ted did as Huginn said. Starting at the bell of the horn, he ran his fingers over the golden ink of the Horn of Valhalla. Valhalla was broken, the ravens had said. Odin's legions of hand-picked warriors were gone.

Believe and its call will be answered, Huginn and Muninn said together.

He heard Tilda's earlier plea.

Believe.

As his fingers moved up his arm, Ted could feel the note building. He touched the mouthpiece tattooed upon his shoulder and a sound was released. The note was so deep, it rumbled like a volcano. Impossibly, it was also sharp. So sharp it pierced the noise of the storm like shattering glass.

The note was beautiful and painful all at once. Revelry and mourning intertwined seamlessly. He wished there were someone to record the sound.

A foggy mist spread, swallowing the wind. Stillness ate the storm. Shadows moved within the growing cloud and a booted foot stepped from it, then others.

He knew them, he realized. Somehow, though he'd never met them. There were only five of them. They wore the uniforms of the Canadian Expeditionary Forces, circa 1914. Their forms were transparent, and glowed with a cold fire.

A giant loomed over Ted now, its club raised to strike. The

einherjar jerked their spectral Enfields to their shoulders and fired. Reports echoed with history, travelling through the years, from the time of their deaths into the now. Ted swore he could smell the cordite drifting in the air. Bullets flew over his head, slapping into the giant's flesh with wet impacts. Blood, hot and slick, splashed over Ted as the giant slumped forward.

A surprised grunt trailed into a low moan as it dropped to its knees. The dead giant collapsed on one of the rusted and gutted vans, crumpling it under his weight. Blood and brains leaked from a tight circle of holes in the thing's forehead.

Gunfire sounded as the *einherjar* advanced on the giants and wolves blocking the entrance to the hall. They didn't wait for Ted's orders. He didn't have any to give; they knew more about fighting than he ever wanted to learn. They concentrated their fire, dropping the wolves first, one at a time. The giants retaliated, throwing whatever was nearby at their spectral tormentors: rocks, engine blocks, Loki.

Every projectile passed through the implacable advance of the dead. The *einherjar* killed one giant. Then another. As one, the giants turned from the hall and Rungnir within. They ran.

There was a break in the storm, and the *einherjar* stood at attention, glowing softly and facing Ted. It was then he realized how he knew them.

They were his family.

Had the dwarves twisted their afterlife in the same way they'd bent Ted's life? His grandfather and his great-uncle, they and three cousins had all left family and friends to fight against the Kaiser in the Great War. They stood at attention, wide-brimmed helmets tied under their chins, Enfield rifles resting against their shoulders. Ted knew them only from old, grainy black-and-white photographs.

But he knew them.

Only one of them had made it home from the mud, blood, and death of the hill at Vimy Ridge. Ted's grandfather. He had been the youngest. Too young to have been there—as if war accounted for such things—but he'd gone. He had been young enough to re-enlist when Canada fought the Nazis. The Great War had changed him, and when he went overseas the second time he'd left wife and child behind, determined to join his brother and cousins. He did. Grandfather hadn't made it out of that war, dying not far from the ridge that claimed his family.

Here they were, reunited. Brothers. Warriors. Family. They'd come to fight for Ted, as they'd fought and died for him before he'd ever been born.

Your family's honoured dead, Muninn said.

There were so few of them.

Not all who die may enter Valhalla, Huginn said. And if too many had died, you would not have been.

"How did they…."

They did not, not truly, Huginn answered. But there must be a tie. In your family, whether you know it or not, these are the names spoken in awe. With reverence. It is these five who are remembered as being more than just the dead. Their life was war; war was their death. They will come when you fight, should you call them from their rest.

But there will be a price, Muninn cautioned.

"What kind of price?"

There is no stopping death. Hel is jealous and strong. She will not be pleased that for even this moment, her subjects have been taken from her to step freely. With Valhalla broken, there is nothing but the grey mists of Niflheim. Nowhere for the dead to go but to Hel.

"I don't suppose knowing Loki will help me?"

No, Huginn said. **She hates her father most of all, for escaping his doom.**

"I'll just have to blow up that bridge when I see it in front of me."

Ted re-entered Rungnir's home with thunder at his back.

Two of the king's four guards remained alive, and were closing in on the dwarves. Other giants had found their way into the fray. Ted heard the Moustache's guttural shouts. He snapped his head around and saw that the three dwarves were making for the ramp, behind the swinging fists of a rock troll.

Pointing Mjölnir at the king, Ted shot lightning from outstretched fingers. "We're not done, fat boy."

"Break him!" Rungnir yelled from his divan. "Break him and feed him to Rungnir!"

The giants took large strides forward, but their eyes were on the sky more than on Ted and Loki. While Ted had been outside the hall they'd discarded their clubs and grabbed shields and swords from the walls.

Loki rushed them. Ted followed hot on the trickster's heels. So far, the god hadn't been particularly effective in confronting the giants. But there were some things that could only be answered with physical force. If they'd put Ted through that kind of humiliation, putting boot to ass would be option one.

Conservation of mass evidently went out the window with gods and magic. Loki took the form of a bird again and shot through the reach of the first of Rungnir's guards, flapping his wings against the giant's broad, ugly face.

The giant's bellow of anger turned to shrill shrieks as Loki pulled away with blood and meat trailing from his talons. A sword thudded to the earthen floor as the giant put a hand over its savaged eye.

There was no time to feel sorry for the giant. It was still a threat. Ted circled to its blind side and slammed his fist into the side of its knee. The giant howled again and tumbled, unbalanced, to the floor. Ted pulled himself on to the giant's back hand-over-hand, gripping the rough hides it wore for clothing. When he felt its spine shift beneath his bare feet, Ted punched straight down. The impact was lost in the booming thunder. If the giant survived, it would be crippled. Either way, remembering their cannibalistic nature, Ted supposed he'd killed it.

Loki harassed another giant, but it knew he was striking to blind. His raven form got close once, but instead of plucking the giant's eye free, Loki changed. A black and white shape opened a deep gash in the giant's brow, sliding down its face, opening shallow furrows. Ted caught a whiff of a familiar, pungent stink as Loki sprayed musk over the giant's face. A fine distraction, but the giant was still able to defend itself.

It grabbed Loki, crushed him in a fist and hurled the savaged remains at the timbered walls. But it was not a skunk that left the giant's hand, but a snake. Loki turned back into a bird as soon as he tasted air. Ted picked up the crippled giant's sword. The blade was at least half again as long as Ted was tall. Even with two hands it would be awkward to wield. Fortunately Ted had no intention of fencing. He spun in a circle like an Olympic hurler and released the sword towards a clutch of giants. The weapon pinwheeled from his hands to slam flat into the back of one giant's legs, tripping it.

Loki had disappeared into the darkness of the storm, only occasionally backlit against a flash of lightning. He saw his opportunity though, and took it, diving down out of the clouds to land on the giant's face in a flutter of feathers and shrill bird cries. A familiar scream cut through the wind and Ted knew the trickster had completed his grisly business. Loki cawed in triumph as his wings spread to return him to the air. His feathers must have been heavy with rain, and he didn't gain altitude quickly enough. A giant bashed Loki's retreating form against the wall with its shield and leaned its weight against it.

"Fly now, pretty bird," it said. "Try and take my eye, god of shit."

The giant pulled the shield away from the wall. Loki had returned to his more familiar human form and fell, unconscious or dead, to the mud below. The giant raised both weapon and shield above its head, bellowing at the storm.

Ted answered.

Lightning fell on the giant. Bolts rained from the sky as if it it were the end days, as if Thor himself now spent his anger on his ancient foes. The giant fell, smoking, to the churned earth floor. Rain struggled to put out the fires started by Ted's lightning.

Rifle reports sounded behind Ted. Five spectral guns fired in unison, again and again. When they were finally silent, Rungnir and his son were the only giants left alive within the hall.

The storm without was nearly spent, and with it, much of Ted's fury. Grey mist was seeping into the hall. The *einherjar* stepped backwards into the fog. Ted's grandfather gave a sharp salute and then he too was gone, back to Hel, and the mist with him. Ted wished he could have spoken with him—with all of them. He'd never known the man. His grandmother had remarried after the war, to the man Ted had called Grandfather, the children of their union becoming his aunts and uncles. But the fight was over.

Moustache stood over the bodies of Beards One and Two. In the melee they had fallen to Rungnir's guards. Satisfaction burned like bile in Ted's throat. The rock troll had been smashed, lying in a tumble of bloody rocks and crumbling mortar.

Ted walked silently to where Loki lay, afraid of what he would find. He searched, but there was no body. Ted smiled. He had a feeling that he'd be seeing the god again—probably when it was least convenient. It felt strange to welcome that feeling, but he did. Maybe he really was becoming a part of the Nine Worlds.

Moustache knelt between his dead brethren. Ted surprised himself again by offering a hand to the grieving dwarf. With a nod of thanks, Moustache pulled himself to his feet. Ted returned the nod curtly and made his way before Rungnir.

The fat king cowered upon his cushions, still smelling of shit and stale sweat. Tears flowed into snot and drool as the once-great foe of the gods—a giant who had challenged Thor—wailed upon his padded throne. Killing the crippled giant would be a kindness. When his subjects returned—eventually they would have to—they would be none too pleased with how their master's tricks had played out. Taking in the fullness of the giant's bulk, the *jötnar* would eat well—like kings. Ted climbed onto the divan and pressed his fist against Rungnir's scar, where Mjölnir had felled the king in another time and place.

"I'll make this quick," he told the giant.

A large hand turned him around roughly. Ted stood face-to-face with the king's child. It seemed Youngnir had gained some measure of courage.

"No," the child giant said, tongue thick with emotion or unfamiliar words. "Not father."

Ted nodded. That giant had felt the sting of Thor's hammer too. That he was willing to chance another blow to protect the last of his kin said much.

"He doesn't deserve you," Ted said. "But I'll leave him to your care."

"No!" the king yelled, almost hysterical. "Kill me! Mjölnir must finish me." When his commands didn't work, he wailed, "Please, please."

Ted ignored him. He stood beside the unsteady mountain of flesh that was Rungnir, King of the Giants and reached for the Head of Mimir.

"You need me, Theodore Callan," Mimir said. "He's coming. The Lord of the Flame is coming. Without me, Midgard will burn."

Ted fumbled with the knot binding Mimir's hair to Rungnir's ear.

Moustache climbed up on the divan joining Ted. "Allow me." He slid his sword over the hair, leaving a lock still tied through the king's ear. He stuck the blade between his belt and his jeans and held the Head of Mimir up to meet Ted's eye.

"The world's burning with you," Ted said, taking the head from the dwarf. He shifted his grip so that his hands were on either side of the head. "You wanted peace? You wanted the grave? Time to go home, old boy." Then he pushed.

"No!" Moustache yelled.

Mimir named rune after rune. Hanging in the air surrounding Ted, they lit up the giants' lodge. Yggdrasill, inked upon Ted's back, pulled at the runes. He could almost sense a feeling of rough bark beneath his hands. As if Ted himself was climbing the World Tree.

"Stop him!" Mimir screamed.

The runes slid around Ted. Odin had hanged himself from the Tree to learn the runes, and it seemed the Tree was still their master. One by one, the symbols disappeared. He grunted and pressed his hands together harder.

"Protect me!" Mimir begged.

More symbols appeared, now orbiting Mimir. These were no more effective. A sharp crack broke the silence. Ted forced the imposed life from what remained of Odin's counsellor. Magically preserved flesh turned to the dust Mimir had earned so long ago, and trickled through Ted's fingers. Like a crown, the runes hung in the air. Hesitant, Ted reached out to touch them. They disappeared entirely.

"Are you mad?" the dwarf yelled.

Ted turned to face him. Moustache's face was ashen. Tears ran freely down his ugly face, mingling with rain. The dwarf slumped to the wet earth like a broken doll.

"He knew how to end the world," Ted said.

Moustache didn't answer at first. "And how to save it."

"We'll have to find our own way."

A crash shook the hall, and Ted knew that it wasn't thunder.

21. Fire and Brimstone

mpact tremors shook the hall of Rungnir. They came in regular intervals, travelling through the ground and up into Ted's body. A sense of familiarity gripped him like a vice around his guts. It couldn't be.

Then the booming laugh.

Lock, lock, lock.

Ted closed his eyes and dropped his chin to his chest. There was no mistaking it.

Surtur was here.

The scent of burning conifer needles cut through the thick stink of Rungnir's hall.

Ted stood stock-still. Thunder was replaced by the crackle of flames as wood popped and was consumed. It was still cool in the hall, with so much of it buried beneath the earth. But that coolness wouldn't last. The fires that had been his ticket into the Nine Worlds of the Aesir were now here. They were here and controlled by a living will that Ted had set himself against. Surtur would not turn a blind eye to that.

Even with the gifts of the dwarves, even with all his power, Ted doubted he'd be a bother to the great giant. Surtur was the end of the cycle, the consumer of worlds. Stopping him would be like trying to stop the comet that killed the dinosaurs. Surtur was here, and humanity was extinct.

Dimly, Ted could hear his name being called over the din outside. He hoped Urd had managed to get Tilda to the hospital in time, but he slumped to the earth and shook his head.

In time for what?

"Ted!"

The voice came from his left. He turned in time to catch Loki's fist on his nose. The punch didn't hurt, and he heard something crack in the trickster's hand. But the surprise was enough to draw him at least partially out of his stupor.

"Motherfucker!" cried Loki, shaking his wounded fist before cracking the bones back into place.

Moustache stood in front of Ted with his thick arms crossed over a barrel chest.

"You said you would find another way to save the world, Ófriður. Now would be a good time."

Ted looked up at the dwarf. "And just what the fuck do you think I can do?"

"Something. Anything. Self-pity does not suit you, and it is not why we made you."

"Yeah," said Loki. "Besides, self-pity's more my thing. I'm the one who's been hard done by here, remember?"

Ted snorted a short laugh. It felt good.

Loki held out his hand and Ted took it, hauling himself to his feet.

"So how'd he find us?"

"You called him," Huginn said, speaking aloud.

"How?" Ted asked.

"The lightning strikes," Muninn said. "They have started a forest fire."

"A fire born of the powers of the Nine Worlds," Huginn said. "This land has deep ties to the Nine, from the dvergar and jötnar."

"And it was the Lord of Muspelheim who revealed the hidden Worlds of the Nine to you," Muninn said. "He would sense the working of one he had marked."

"So he thinks I want him here?"

"Possibly," said Huginn.

"Maybe we can use that—"

"It's hard to trick a force of nature, Ted," Loki said.

"I'm sure you've pulled it off before."

Loki smiled. "Well, I hate to brag, but—"

"Care to try again?" Ted asked.

"I've grown pretty fond of living. You invited the pyro, you tell him to leave."

"Thanks."

The first time he'd called lightning, and it had struck him, Ted hadn't been burned. His clothes had caught, been singed and ruined, but the fire hadn't touched his skin, thanks to the gifts of the dwarves. Dragon-scale tattoos for armour, sealed to his skin in dragon's blood. If he couldn't be burned, maybe he could fight the thing.

"I wouldn't recommend that." Huginn's voice echoed in his thoughts.

"It didn't do Freyr any good," Muninn added. Riding

on the raven's words were images of a tall, handsome man, so fair he was almost golden. He was trying to hold back Surtur's advance with nothing but a sharpened set of antlers. "But then he traded his magic sword for the love of a giant. With the sword he might have won. Unlikely, but he would have bought the other Aesir some more time."

And none of the other gods thought to loan him a fucking weapon? Ted wondered.

"Freyr was too proud to accept their offerings after trading his sword for a bride," Muninn said. "And too proud to ask for its return."

Ted clenched and unclenched his hammer hand.

"Good thing I have more than a pair of antlers," he muttered.

"Your power won't do you any good," Loki said. "Only one weapon was forged that could harm Surtur."

"And you conveniently saw it stripped from its bearer?"

Loki shrugged. "That wasn't me. We've been through this before. The past is past. I had my vengeance, hollow though it was. Asgard fell. I don't want to see it happen to Earth too. Plus, you have a better sense of humour than the Aesir ever did."

"I wouldn't be so sure."

"If you didn't, you'd have never freed me from the Norn's spell."

"Don't make me wish I hadn't. Do you know what happened to Freyr's sword after Ragnarök?"

Loki shook his head.

"I don't know if it even survived long enough to see the final battle. If I had been Surtur, I would have seen that the blade was melted into slag rather than leaving it lying about."

"Shit," said Ted. "It would be too easy to have you magic up a sword to kill the giant."

"I would if I could, *kemosabe*. You need to find your own silver bullet."

Rungnir's hall shook again, as another set of regular, booming steps drew closer. Ted had to stop him. Flin Flon named itself The City Built on Rock; if Surtur was allowed to have his way, it would be consumed in the blink of an eye. Scoured down to that very same rock.

"The concentration of jötnar and dvergar, and other powers of the Nine Worlds, will mean it happens even faster here than the destruction in Alberta," Huginn said.

"There has to be a way to send him back."

"Put out the flames," Huginn prompted. **"Surtur still needs them to feed his hunger. And his existence."**

Ted shook his head. The fires in Fort Mac would not let themselves be put out. Water bombers, and what had seemed like every damned firefighter in Alberta and then North America had come to kill the blaze. Their efforts hadn't even slowed Surtur's advance. And Ted was no firefighter.

But Surtur did need the flames. He—and his followers—had fled back into the fires at the first site explosion. Ted's lightning had started this fire, and drawn the fire giant's attention. If Ted summoned the rains, would it make any difference?

Huginn and Muninn didn't answer. Perhaps they didn't know. Perhaps their silence was agreement. Or, maybe, they figured it was about fucking time Ted made a decision on his own.

Ted touched the storm clouds of ink that moved beneath the skin of his chest. He felt how they matched the weather outside.

There was too much wind. It was driving the flames, feeding them into a frenzy of consumption. Kill the wind. That was the first step. Even with the sky fat with rain, the wind would keep fanning the fire hotter. What they needed was a steady downpour. Ted imagined Surtur's white-hot metallic grin. He'd need enough rain to make Noah take notice and stop talking about how things were worse back in his day.

Black clouds swept across Ted's bare chest, seeping onto his hand. Lightning arced from the tattoo of Mjölnir. Ted ground his teeth as he tried to ignore the sounds of flame and fear, the smells within the giants' den, and the blaze without. He thought of five hundred dead from the initial explosion. Too many lost friends. He thought of Susanna, back in Edmonton, and how he could never warn her. Ted thought of Tilda, maybe dying, maybe dead.

Reaching out to the one thing that had kept him sane when he was pulling fourteen-hour days for three weeks at a time, Ted grasped for music. He thought of every song he could, of every singer who'd dreamed of rain.

"*Happy When It Rains.*" "*When the Levee Breaks.*" "*Flood.*" "*Rain Must Fall.*" "*Drown.*" "*Nine Million Rainy Days.*"

His voice grew from whisper to shout. Loki and Moustache looked at him as if he had gone mad. But Huginn and Muninn drew song after song from him, each playing overtop the next, yet somehow distinct and clear.

"Rain!"

He still smelled the fire, but there was something else, straining to be noticed, at the absolute limit of his senses.

Ted smelled rain on the wind.

He started up the ramp that led outside, his steps perhaps more deliberate than he would have liked. He should be running. But to fight, or flee? As Ted climbed nearer to the broken door of Rungnir's hall, he could feel pulses of heat slapping into him like breaking waves. When he stepped outside, what he saw was an ocean.

An ocean of fire.

Smoke choked out what stars should have been visible. Over Ross Lake Ted heard the piercing wail of sirens. Two more footsteps shook the burning spruce.

Doom. Doom.

Surtur was growing closer.

And he wasn't alone.

Familiar screeches filled the relative silence in between Surtur's steps. Sounds, like the giant's laugh, that had haunted Ted's nightmares since the rig fire. He was bringing the help.

Ted reached out to the gathering clouds, thickening them, pulling all available moisture into them. The heat of the fire vapourized what little moisture had been left in the dry forest. What was locked within the trees, the flames were consuming. He grabbed the vapour as it rose on the heated air currents and locked it within the cloud cover. Even the natural evaporation coming off of Ross Lake added to the density of the clouds.

Ted didn't know if it would be enough.

He turned to Loki. "Can you get airborne and spot Surtur for me? I'm going to have to concentrate the rain on him if this will have any chance of working."

Loki whistled. "That smoke goes up thousands of feet. I won't be able to see a damned thing. And if I get too close… Surtur'll just knock me out of the sky."

"We will lead you to him," the ravens said together. **"If the trickster is too frightened."**

"Do it," Ted said.

Ted felt the curious sensation as Huginn and Muninn pulled themselves from his skin. They hung in the air like paintings. Flesh and feathers gathered, they took to the sky.

"So you're really going to do this?" Loki asked. "Follow them?"

"I have to," Ted said. "If I don't come back, I just want to say…" he paused, unsure of how to continue, so he shrugged. "Fuck you."

Loki nodded. "You too, buddy."

Ted turned and stepped towards the flames, looking up and trying to spot Huginn and Muninn in the night sky.

Sleipnir, Odin's horse, had been able to run as fast over air and water as it could over land. Water had already proved as hard as concrete to Ted. Air…. He didn't know if his idea would work, but he had to try. His nerve would break in the flames long before Surtur had a chance to kill him.

He kept his eyes closed as he took the first few steps, imagining he was ascending a flight of stairs. His feet met with resistance.

"Go, man, go!" Loki yelled.

Ted was about six feet in the air. His bare feet rested solidly on wisps of smoke. He grinned wide. He couldn't help it. He could fly.

He could fucking fly.

Ted gained more altitude. He could see a break after the front of the fire, as if the flames had jumped a few kilometres. Maybe they had. The wind could have carried embers from the ignition point, carried them from Surtur.

Burning humanoid forms stepped from the larger fire, into the break. Ted could see the small fires their footsteps were starting. He debated tossing lightning down on them, but that was what had gotten him into this jam in the first place. All he'd accomplish would be to worsen the flames.

And strengthen Surtur's power.

The fire giant's minions were looking up now. They had stopped their movement and were pointing upwards. Ted imagined their screeching. Nothing could really be heard over the din of the wildfire. Nothing but Surtur's footsteps growing ever closer.

Doom. Doom.

They stepped back into the fire and Ted lost them in the smoke and flames. Off to warn their master, no doubt.

Nearing the epicentre of the fire, Ted sensed the ozone in the air from where an undirected lightning strike had landed in the dry, black spruce. He should have been more careful, the weather wasn't a toy, and he'd known it was a tinderbox out here. Anger and fear had gotten the best of him. But without that anger and fear, he'd have been dead, and Tilda and Loki with him.

The flames had to be put out before they took the town. They were too close for an evacuation to be feasible. Ted hoped no one had been caught in the forest when the fire had started.

Huginn and Muninn circled Ted briefly in an elliptical orbit before settling in at his side.

"He draws near," the ravens said.

Ted scanned the fire; a circle, only ten feet in diameter, stood out white against the orange and yellow flames.

There.

The clouds groaned in protest. He was here. It was time to open the floodgates and say *fuck you* to the destroyer of worlds.

Ted heard a great crack, like the booming of thunder. But he hadn't called the thunder. A huge ring of trees collapsed around the small epicentre of the fire, and the whiteness spread to encompass this new ring. It was large enough now, that Surtur would be able to step through it.

That belly laugh rumbled through the crackling of fire.

Lock, lock, lock.

He was here.

Ted stabbed the clouds with his will and felt the rain come.

It fell as a trickle at first. Sizzling and popping, hissing into vapour as it hit the flames. The rain ran over Ted, washing the soot, mud, and smoke from his body. As if through a growing rend, the rain came faster, falling thickly in heavy drops. Steam rose from the fire as the elements met and mingled.

And Surtur laughed.

Fingertips thick as tree trunks dug themselves into the scorched earth below Ted. The acetylene blue of Surtur's eyes burned from within the circle of white heat.

Ted felt as if he were trapped in a light bulb, as the heat from Surtur's portal baked into him. He poured more of his will into the rain. Surtur was vapourizing the water before it even touched the flames, let alone had a chance to reach the earth or the giant.

Vaguely, Ted felt the sensation of Huginn and Muninn slipping back under his skin.

His power is too great. He will consume us.

In the steam, he could see human forms coalescing. They rose on currents of superheated air. He didn't know what the giant was sending after him now, didn't want to know. Instead he pushed harder at the clouds. Squeezing at them as if he were wringing out a dishtowel. The rain intensified, but the vapour ghosts twisted their forms, slipping between the raindrops, and growing closer.

Ted felt the searing pain as one of the apparitions grabbed his ankle. He looked down and recognized the face the vapour had formed. Terry Whitehorse, a pipefitter who'd been working the rig on the day it exploded. They'd spoken off and on over the years, over cigarettes and whiskey, though Ted wouldn't claim to really have known him. But whatever Terry had become, he recognized Ted.

"We missed you, brother," he said with a breathy, sibilant voice. "Welcome home."

Ted screamed as the thing clawed up his body. He swung

his hammer hand at Terry's head. His fist passed through the vapour. Ted winced as his flesh burned at the touch.

"Can't kill us, brother," the thing that had been Terry said. "We're already dead. Don't worry, you'll soon be with us. It only hurts forever."

More of the vapour ghosts were growing closer. How many did Surtur have? How many had died in the explosion? Hundreds. One was enough to finish him. How did he think he was up to this?

"Gods' balls, Ted." Loki's voice cut through the fire and pain like a splash of cold water. "Can't I trust you to do anything without me?"

The trickster floated in the sky beside Ted, wearing the *jötunn* form of his birth. His skin was a pale blue and his smile like ice. For the briefest of moments, Ted felt himself enveloped by a cold breeze.

"No!" the thing that had been Terry Whitehorse screamed. Its fellows joined in as a north wind, flowing somehow out of the south—out of Loki—and enveloped them, turning their vapour to snow.

They melted over Ted, the cool water washing away the burns of their touch. He opened his mouth to thank Loki, but the trickster cut him off.

"You call this a rainstorm? My dead old poppa pisses harder than this."

"Maybe you should've had the dwarves tattoo his ass then," Ted said bitterly.

"I just spent the last of the colds of Jötunheim I'd kept within me." Loki smiled and pointed at Surtur. "Send him home."

The trickster's grin was short-lived.

Surtur's arm shot from the wildfire. It stretched to an impossible length as the cracked, black fingers of the Lord of Muspelheim closed over Loki.

The fire giant had his entire torso outside of the white hot circle. Surtur leaned on his right forearm as he reeled Loki down towards him—and the flames.

Loki screamed.

Ted could feel the hate on Surtur's face rather than see it. The heat that radiated from the giant and his fires distorted his image. Flames burst from the cracks in the giant's skin as glowing liquid seeped from beneath the fires like lava.

But Surtur had made a mistake. At the limit of his reach, his great fist imprisoned Loki. And Surtur had reached too far. Rain still hissed as it hit the giant's black craggy skin, but now the water wasn't evaporating, and Surtur wasn't laughing.

Ted thought of that night, only days ago, when he met Tilda standing in the road under the pounding rain, and poured his will into the clouds.

Believe.

Now Surtur screamed. It was what Krakatoa must have sounded like as it ceased to be.

Ted could feel the storm within him trying to grow beyond the boundaries he had set for it. The lightning wanted to be called. It wanted to ride free on the winds, to strike Surtur, Loki, to pay back every hurt Ted had received since the fire giant had first opened the Nine Worlds to him.

Instead, Ted clenched his eyes shut and concentrated on the steady feel of the rain. It ran over him, washing the giants' blood and muck from his body, taking some of the hate and rage with it.

Surtur's scream continued, growing in intensity until it was almost a physical thing. Ted felt himself being buffeted in the air but he did not relent.

And then the cry was gone. All of a sudden, Ted could hear the whine of a prop engine plane growing closer. Water bombers must have been scrambled by now. No one else would be brave—or foolhardy—enough to fly into this inferno. Ted doubted he'd see them; they'd hit the edges of the fire first, trying to keep it from spreading to the town, or at least trying to buy time for an evacuation. They weren't there to put the fire out.

That was his job.

The fireman of the Nine Worlds.

Ted hadn't asked for the position, but it was more important than any job he'd ever applied for. Maybe he couldn't use these powers to help the world sort out its mundane problems, but he'd be damned if he'd let giants, trolls, and witches take that world away from anyone else.

He opened his eyes; it felt as if they had been closed for so long.

Surtur collapsed back into the slowly diminishing circle of white heat. The steady rain was wearing down the flames. Steam still shot up from the blackened trees, but Ted knew he was having an effect now.

The giant's arm, which had stretched up into the sky to entrap Loki, was still there. It looked more like hardened mud than rock now and the rain was beginning to dissolve the force that had made the arm solid. Loki sluiced free from the bottom of Surtur's fist and plummeted, tumbling towards the flames.

Ted ran for him, leaping from wisps of smoke as if he were taking stairs two at a time, never once thinking the resourceful trickster would be able to find his own way out of danger. Loki's fall was anything but controlled, and Ted doubted the god had the wherewithal to change shape. While Loki might survive the impact and the flames, Ted didn't want to take the chance.

The burning canopy of black spruce was drawing near. Ted lost Loki more than once as he chased the trickster's falling body through the smoke and the rain. He felt something soft, grabbed it, and stopped short. There was a loud crack that might have been a tree knot exploding in the flames, or Loki's shoulder dislocating. Ted didn't care. He had him. The trickster had dodged his final day for at least a little while longer.

The heat from the fire was intense. Ted hoisted Loki over his shoulder and walked up and out of the smoke. He saw the white circle shrink to a pinprick, and then disappear entirely, drawing with it all traces of the forest fire.

He'd driven Surtur off, but the giant wasn't gone. Not really. His fires were still growing in Alberta. Ted knew it was only a matter of time before their paths crossed for a third and—somehow, Ted knew—final time. He wasn't sure whether he feared that meeting more, or less, now that he knew what he had to deal with. But there was no one else.

"I can't help but think," Loki's weak voice said through coughs and grunts of air, "that your little Norn would've been cradled in your arms and not bouncing over your fucking shoulder."

"I can always put you back where I found you."

"If only I could say the same thing." Loki sighed. "You're going to be more trouble than you're worth."

"Look who's talking."

They were nearing Rungnir's hall. Ted felt the clammy mud of the yard squeeze between his toes as he settled back to the earth and set Loki down.

The trickster wobbled, for a moment unsteady. Ted reached out but his hand was brushed aside. Loki gave his ruined clothing a sharp tug and straightened himself.

He looked different. His coppery tone and dark hair, which had initially made Ted think the trickster was Native, were both gone. They'd been replaced with white blond hair and milk-white skin. Burns and scars still marred Loki's face, but Ted felt he was close to seeing how the god had appeared to the Aesir when he'd faced them at Ragnarök.

"Thanks," Loki said finally.

There was no hint of sarcasm or malice in the trickster's voice. Ted wondered how hard it had been for him to deliver sincere gratitude, it almost left him speechless.

"You're welcome."

"Raven is going to be pissed when he finds out."

"When who finds out what?" Ted asked.

"Raven," Loki said. "He's the one I tricked into loaning me his power."

"What can he do if you've spent the power?" Ted asked. "Isn't it gone?"

"He'll grow back what I took from him eventually. Raven invented death—at least on this continent he did. Nothing is really beyond him. I on the other hand—"

"You beat him once."

Loki smiled. "I'm glad you think highly of me Ted, but—"

Loki was cut off by a loud ring tone. It was the Who's "Who Are You?" A funny coincidence, Ted had used that same song for anyone who wasn't in his list of contacts. But his phone was on the bottom of Lake Winnipeg. Loki pulled Ted's phone from seemingly out of nowhere.

The trickster looked at the display and offered it to Ted. "It's for you."

Ted wondered how many long-distance calls Loki had made since he had lost the phone, and what his roaming charges might be. "Hello?"

"Ted Callan?"

"Yeah?"

"It's Robin."

Ted racked his brain, but he couldn't place the name.

"The tattoo artist."

"Oh. Uh, right." The man had said he would call back. "What's up?"

"There's been some seriously weird shit going on since you walked out these doors," Robin said.

Ted didn't doubt it, but he supposed he had to be happy that

Robin was still alive. And the shop was still standing. At least, Ted assumed it was still standing.

"I'll bet," he said. "That why you called?"

"Yeah," Robin said. "I did some digging on your tats, and now I might need a favour, if you're game."

Ted looked around at the scorched trees and the giant's destroyed compound. "Yeah," Ted said. "I guess I am."

Epilogue
Don't Look Back in Anger

Ted couldn't say he was too sorry that Beards One and Two had been killed in the battle, but he helped Moustache load their bodies into the van and cover them with a tarp all the same. He and the dwarf circled each other like children on a playground, neither ready to make the first move, either to fight or forgive.

Moustache cracked first. "I am proud of you, Ófriður."

"Proud of me, or proud of what you made of me?"

"Both."

"So how's it going to be from now on? I don't want to be looking over my shoulder every day."

"That, unfortunately, will be a necessity. Word of this will spread, you may count on that. You've beaten Urd, and Rungnir. You've killed immortal Mimir, beaten back Surtur. You are of the Nine Worlds now." Moustache smiled grimly. "We do not do peace well. You will find yourself tested in battle again, but you do not need to fear the *dvergar*. We want you out in the world, doing great things. Before long, things will be as they once were, and mortals will be knocking upon our doors to barter gold and more for our creations."

A lascivious twinkle lit up the dwarf's sunken eyes. "Pussy," he laughed. "No having to pay for it anymore. I have not forgotten the tumble that Freyja gave us for her necklace." Moustache licked his lips at the thought. "If only she had made it out the ass-end of Ragnarök instead of Loki."

"Who knows, she may turn up." Ted shrugged. "I'm sure she was more clever than her taste in lovers would have you believe."

"Ha!" Moustache laughed. "If you see her, you let her know I waited for her."

"I'm sure your sensitivity will touch her heart."

"That is not what I want to touch. You want a ride back into town? Less obvious than running across the lake, yeah? Though you should maybe clean up first? They won't let you in the hospital like you are."

Ted knew he was filthy but he was too exhausted to care.

"Sure."

They piled into the Econoline. "I'm sorry about your friends," Ted said, hitching a thumb back at the bodies of Beards One and Two.

Moustache stared ahead. "There is no need to lie," he said quietly. "You would have killed them, and me, given the right opportunity."

"Yeah, I guess. I'm glad I didn't have to."

Moustache had insisted on taking some of the giant's stolen wealth. By some, he'd meant everything he could find. Evidently he'd been loading the van the whole time Ted had fought Surtur. When Ted had finally pulled him from Rungnir's hall, the dwarf's nose was twitching like a bloodhound and his fat fingers clutched a single golden ring he'd pulled from the earth.

The dwarf bounced the ring in his palm as he drove, bit into the gold, and sighed. Satisfied, he tucked it into a shirt pocket. He pulled out something else gold and pressed that into Ted's palm.

"Take it," Moustache said.

Ted flipped his palm over. It was a credit card. With his name on it.

"I don't want your money. I'm not on your payroll, so I don't need the company card. You don't have anything I want."

"No?"

"Not unless you have a bootleg of Bon Scott singing 'Back in Black.'"

"Take it," the dwarf insisted. "I don't want to see you rotting in a jail cell. The mortal police are a little too close to you."

"About that," Ted said. "Officer Fontaine?"

"The Native?"

"Yeah, he isn't to be touched. He goes missing, I don't care if it's your fault or not, I'm coming back here and it's your ass. I don't think the *dvergar* want that."

Moustache nodded. "I will do all that I can to ensure his safety, if that is what you wish."

"You'd better."

"It will be difficult. The Nine Worlds have touched him deeply. Perhaps too deeply."

"Just because something is difficult, doesn't mean it isn't worth doing," Ted said. "He's a good man."

"If you say so."

"I do."

Moustache nodded. "I will give you my word, Ófriður, and unlike some, I intend to keep it. What will you do about the elder Norn?"

"She's Tilda's grandmother," Ted said, defeated. What could he do? For good or ill, Tilda would still love the miserable old bird. "I don't know."

"Urd will never thank you for your kindness."

"Maybe she won't, but never is a long time, and I have a feeling her granddaughter will."

The dwarf barked a laugh. "I bet I know how, too."

The illusion that hid the giant's road from the highway was starting to peel back. A large black wolf loped onto the trail and stopped dead to regard the van's occupants. Moustache brought the van to a sliding stop. Casually, the wolf licked its balls, then turned its face back to the van. Mouth open and tongue lolling out, Loki was somehow still recognizable to Ted. Even in the shape of a wolf, the same grin he'd flashed Ted in the basement bar was splayed over the trickster's face.

"I'll meet you later," the wolf said in Loki's voice. "I have something to take care of."

Ted nodded. Kicking up mud, the god disappeared into the trees.

"I doubt you will see him again," Moustache said. "His use for you is over."

"Somehow," Ted said, "I doubt that."

"Remember, fire can be tool and devil both, friend and foe. It can light up the night or, unfettered, plunge us back into darkness. So has it ever been with Loki. Watch yourself. If the wind shifts, so will he, and then… then you'll find yourself burned."

"I control the winds now," Ted reminded the dwarf.

"As you say," Moustache said, but he sounded unconvinced.

Ted was nervous for the entire drive, the weather matched his mood, and unpredictable patches of rain and wind still hammered at Flin Flon. Moustache waited in the van while Ted went into the hotel, showered quickly, and changed into clothes not torn or covered in mud or blood.

When they arrived at the hospital, he did finally get the dwarf's name. Moustache had seemed hesitant to give up even that small piece of himself, but finally relented. Ted supposed the act was a huge show of trust for the dwarf.

"Andvari," he'd called himself. The revelation seemed to excite Huginn and Muninn, but Ted decided he'd listen to the ravens later. For now, his only worry was Tilda. The Goat was in the parking lot. Ted spotted it immediately. They'd made it here at least, and he was thankful for that. Andvari let him out in front of the building and drove off.

"Beware the brood," he said cryptically, then peeled out of the lot in the Econoline.

Fontaine was waiting for him inside. The cop rose from a

chair set against the brick wall of the admitting room and shook Ted's hand.

Ted asked, "So am I under arrest now?"

"No," the cop shook his head. "I didn't even have to lie for you. It seems some big muckety-muck lawyer for the Company got involved. I was sorry to hear that girl of yours was injured in a small accident at the mine. Bad luck it happening during your job interview tour. I had no idea you were looking into taking work up here."

"Neither did I," Ted said.

Fontaine laughed.

"Svarta Smelting is covering your expenses and your ass. They're even covering the cost of my cruiser, which I've been told was totalled in a hit and run after you dropped me here. Officially you're a free man. I'll still want to get a statement from you."

Ted nodded. "How is she?"

"She'll be fine. It was touch and go for a while. She has a very rare blood type. The doc thought they'd have to fly her to Winnipeg for surgery, but her grandmother was a donor match and she pulled through. That's one tough girl you have there."

"I know."

"Her grandmother isn't doing so well, though."

"Yeah." Ted nodded and followed the cop into the elevator. It took them to the fifth floor, and Tilda's room. A doctor was just stepping out.

"Is she okay?" Ted asked.

The doctor was young, with a thin, harried face and dark

tightly trimmed hair. He was not so young as to make Ted worry, though. His pin said his name was Dr. W. Brown.

"And you are—"

"Fiancé," Ted lied.

The doctor scanned Ted with a furrowed brow, clearly skeptical. If he were going to lie, he probably should have said uncle or father. More believable, potentially more awkward later.

"She'll live. She's resting now. She and her grandmother."

Ted breathed a sigh of relief. "What about the baby?"

"She was pregnant?" the doctor asked.

"We had reason to think so."

"How far along would she have been? She's not showing, it couldn't be far."

Ted rubbed his forehead. "Only a day or so."

The corners of the doctor's mouth twitched slightly and he coughed into his sleeve. "That recently, there is a good chance conception has yet to occur. I wouldn't worry, if I were you. If the two of you are trying to get pregnant, just… take things easy until Miss Eilifsdottir has healed up a bit."

Doctor Brown walked away and Ted entered the Norn's room. Fontaine followed.

If Urd had looked old when he'd first met her, she was ancient now. There was no confusion about which side of the sixty or six hundred scale the Norn fell on. Next to the Norn's bed was a second empty and unmade bed, but no Tilda.

Urd raised her head unsteadily as Ted entered the room and patted the sheets of her bed. Ted walked in and took a seat.

"You lived," the Norn said.

"Yeah."

"I felt him come. Surtur. I felt his arrival."

Ted nodded. "I pushed him back."

"For now."

Ted said nothing.

"It is all upon you now. Were you at least able to wring anything from Mimir? I felt his destruction."

"There was no time."

Urd's hand shot out to grasp Ted's. Her fingers wrapped tightly around the tattoo of Mjölnir. Her grip was surprisingly powerful.

"You must find a way. You must."

He patted her wrinkled skin awkwardly. "I know."

"I won't be around much longer. Tilda…." Ted was surprised. He'd never heard Urd use that name for her grandddaughter. "She wasn't going to survive. I gave her back what I had taken. It wasn't enough. I gave her the gifts that belonged to her mother. Still she was dying. I gave her what was mine. What I've guarded so jealously for millennia. She has everything now. All we have ever known, or will know. May she be strong enough, may you be strong enough to use that power. I doubt I will live to see her child—and yours—born. Name her well."

A door opened and Tilda stood in the entrance to the washroom. Ted blinked; her hair was iron-grey now, her eyes a deeper blue. She walked towards him and there wasn't the faintest hint of pain in her steps.

Ted didn't know what to say. The silence was thick in the

room until Fontaine finally spoke. "Don't take this the wrong way, but I hope I never see either of you again."

"I wouldn't count on it."

Appendix

Loki's Guide to the Petty Gods and Monsters, and Fantastical Locales and Artifacts of Norse Mythology

Loki: Do you mind if I introduce myself first? I am father and mother to gods and monsters. Some call me a trickster. Some a liar. What I am is the most misunderstood god or giant (I swing both ways) in Norse legend. I've done almost as much good as harm. I'll always give you the truth, so long as it serves me.

Fenrir: The Wolf of Ragnarök. Maimer of Tyr and Gobbler of Odin. Killed for his efforts and then killed again before I found my way back to Midgard.

Hel: The apple of my eye, my sweet baby girl, and goddess of the dead. She's never quite forgiven me for not dying and joining her at last.

Jormungandur: My boy, the Midgard Serpent. Jorry will always hold a special place in my heart for ridding all Nine Worlds of that windbag of a Thunder God, Thor.

Sleipnir: My firstborn. The fastest thing on two, four, or eight legs, and so naturally he became Odin's beast of burden.

Odin: Murderer, adulterer, liar, and thief—and those are the lord of Asgard's good qualities—All-Father, but not *my* father, my blood brother never forgave me for my part in his fated fall at Ragnarök.

Frigga: Odin's long-suffering wife. She was fond of me once, before the "incident." She might have forgiven me for taking her favourite son Baldur from her, if only I'd allowed him to return.

Huginn: A meddlesome raven, once provider of Odin's thoughts, now he pecks away at a thicker, but kinder, skull.

Muninn: A quarrelsome raven, and the holder of Odin's grudges.

Mimir: The wise counsellor responsible for much of the legend of Odin's wisdom. A shame he spent most of his time on the job as a severed head on a mantel.

Thor: Don't believe what you see in the movies or read in the comics, the God of Thunder was a brute and a murderer like all of Odin's sons.

Mjölnir: The hammer of Thor. I wonder, is it less potent now that it is locked in the flesh of a mortal or more so, because this mortal has a brain (more or less)?

Sif: Wife of Thor. She was well pleased with the gifts I gave her. Her husband, not so much.

Tyr: If Thor was Odin's right-hand son, Tyr the War God was the left. At least until Fenrir ate Tyr's sword hand. He never quite forgave me for that.

Heimdall: Watcher of the rainbow bridge to Asgard, sounder of the horn of Valhalla, son of Odin, and Holmes to my Moriarty.

Freyr: Son of Njord and brother to Freyja. A fool and his sword are soon parted. One of the few things Odin couldn't blame me for.

Freyja: Practitioner of sex magic, and very popular at parties.

Njord: Father to Freyr and Freyja. The sea god should've been the Lord of Imagination.

Baldur: Oddly enough, despite my being responsible for his death, *he* forgave me.

Dvergar: Dwarves, forgers of weapons of legend.

Gleipnir: A golden chain created from various impossible things by the dwarves to hold fast my equally impossibly strong son, Fenrir.

Ófriður: Some new weapon the dwarves cobbled together, hoping to bring back their glory days.

Einherjar: The bravest souls of warring mortals. They died in battle only to earn the privilege of doing so eternally in their gods' service.

Fáfnir: A dragon whose blood has been used to create more than one invulnerable weapon.

Jötnar: Giants, most commonly of the fire or frost variety. Mostly brutish and violent, though some (if I do say so myself) are beings of exemplary taste.

Norns: Back in the day, any witch, elf, or giant with a touch of the sight would call themselves a norn. But there are only three left, the only three who matter (or so they see it): Urd, Skuld, and Verdandi, mistresses of past, future, and present.

Urd: The eldest of the Norns, Urd may have had her fill of looking at the past, but she's privy to almost as many secrets as I am. She still hates me for my role in the Greenland Affair.

Skuld: The youngest of the three Norns, and the one upon whom Midgard's future will turn.

Verdandi: The Norn of the present. Mother to Skuld. She doesn't much like me, though with her it's not anything personal, just Urd's stories.

Ymir: The first giant. The first being. The real All-Father. It is his bones that make up Midgard, so show him some respect.

Surtur: Skychoker, and earthburner. Surtur is meant to be the end of all things, so well done Midgard for waking him up.

Midgard: Earth—or as I like to refer to it, where the fun happens.

The Nine Realms: Asgard, Vanaheim, Alfheim, Jötunheim, Midgard, Svartalfheim, Muspelheim, Niflheim, Hel. Nine worlds, home to gods and giants, dwarves and elves, and of course, to humanity. Nine Worlds, and not a one of them safe.

Ginnungagap: The space between the Nine Worlds, where dark things wait for gods to fall.

Valhalla: Land of feasting and fighting, two of the three big "F's" for the vikings. There wasn't nearly enough of that all-important third "F" to be found for my liking.

Acknowledgements

I'd like to acknowledge the support and aid of the Manitoba Arts Council, who helped get me to Flin Flon and to make the city and my ending feel as real as possible (what with the giants and dwarves and such). Thank you to Turnstone Press for spreading the wings of Ravenstone Books and welcoming fantasy into the nest. Wayne Tefs, my editor who lent a sure hand and occasionally a red pen to *Thunder Road*. David Jón Fuller for his attention to detail (and many, many umlauts), knowledge of Icelandic, and his devotion to the Norse myths and sagas—any mistakes are mine, or if you're feeling charitable, Loki's. Robert J. Sawyer, I was a fan before I was a friend, so thank you for your generous words and your critique of chapter one while you were writer-in-residence at Canadian Light Source in Saskatoon. Thank you to the home team at McNally Robinson for all your support over the years. To Kelly Hughes and Aqua Books, thank you for making me Emerging Writer-in-Residence and hosting the first public reading of my work. Brad, thank you for the crazy stories of life on the patch, Ted wouldn't be the same without them. Steven Benstead, Shen Braun, Karen Dudley, Mike Friesen, Bev Geddes, and Chris Smith who were there at Ted's beginning. To my parents, Sunday and Charles, thank you for well… everything. Thank you to friends and family too numerous to mention here, and of course, thanks to you, the reader

Originally from Morden, Manitoba, and an active member of the Canadian SpecFic community, Chadwick Ginther's writing has appeared in numerous publications including *On Spec, Quill & Quire, the Winnipeg Review, Prairie Books NOW,* and has been featured as guest blogs for *Manitoba Scene.* He was Aqua Books' Emerging Writer-in-Residence in 2011. Chadwick lives and writes in Winnipeg. *Thunder Road* is his first novel.